The Business of Playing

THE BUSINESS
OF PLAYING

The Beginnings of the
Adult Professional Theater
in Elizabethan London

WILLIAM INGRAM

Cornell University Press

ITHACA AND LONDON

First published 1992 by Cornell University Press.

The opening epigraph is from Richard Flecknoe, *A Short Discourse of the English Stage*, appended to the 1664 edition of his *Love's Kingdom, A Pastoral Trage-Comedy . . . With a short Treatise of the English Stage &c*, 1664.

International Standard Book Number 0-8014-2671-5
Library of Congress Catalog Card Number 92–52760
Printed in the United States of America
*Librarians: Library of Congress cataloging information
appears on the last page of the book.*

⊗ The paper in this book meets the minimum requirements
of the American National Standard for Information Sciences—
Permanence of Paper for Printed Library Materials, ANSI Z39.48-1984.

PN
2596
.L6
I54
1992

For Betty and Claire

Μούσαις ἐμαῖς

. . . those who call him a Player do him wrong, no man being less idle then he, whose whole life is nothing else but action; with only this difference from other mens, that as what is but a Play to them, is his Business; so their business is but a play to him.

—Richard Flecknoe, writing about Burbage

Contents

Figures

Acknowledgments

One finds new documents bearing on the early history of players, playing companies, and playhouses by levying strongly upon the resources of archives and archivists. One assesses the significance of such finds by recourse to contemporary theorists and practitioners. One turns the results of such a search into acceptable arguments and passable prose by taxing the patience of colleagues and friends. In all these areas I have accumulated numerous debts.

Parts of this book have already been made public in one way or another. I am principally grateful to the continuing members of the Theatre History Seminar of the Shakespeare Association of America for providing a challenging and congenial forum in which, over several years, almost all the major ideas in the book were first tested. My thanks go also to the Tenth Waterloo Conference on Elizabethan Theatre for giving me an opportunity to present some ideas about the Red Lion playhouse and for subsequently publishing the remarks that, in substantially revised form, now appear as Chapter 4; and to John Astington and the AMS Press for first publishing (in *The Development of Shakespeare's Theater*, 1992) the essay that, considerably expanded, now forms the basis of Chapter 3. I also owe thanks to Diana Greenway of the Institute for Historical Research for unraveling a piece of crabbed and knotty secretary-hand Latin for me, and to Paul Hoftijzer of the Sir Thomas Browne Institute of the University of Leiden for transcribing and translating for me a manuscript passage written in sixteenth-century Dutch which I was quite unable to decipher. I am also indebted to Mary Pedley and David Bosse of the William L. Clements Library at the University of Michigan for constructing the illustrative maps for the book.

    I am grateful as well to the National Endowment for the Humanities for the year-long fellowship that allowed me to break much of the ground for this book, and also to my own university for continued help from its various research funds. Such support is enabling in the best sense; but I could not have completed this book, indeed could not have begun it, without access to the collections of documents whose contents form the basis of my argument. My debt to the institutions that house the documents and to the librarians and archivists of those institutions is large, and I do not discharge it here by the mere listing of names; nevertheless I record my thanks to the following. In London: the Public Record Office (especially David Lea), the Greater London Record Office (especially Harriet Kenealy), the Guildhall Library and its Manuscripts Division, the Corporation of London Records Office, Dulwich College, the Newington Library, the Southwark Local Studies Library, the Minet Library, the Tower Hamlets Local History Library, the Archives Section of the Westminster City Library, the Corporation of Wardens of the Parish of St. Saviour's, the worshipful companies of Carpenters, Clothworkers, Drapers, Dyers, Goldsmiths, Grocers, Ironmongers, Mercers, Merchant Taylors, Pewterers, and Skinners, the British Library, the Institute of Historical Research, and the Society of Genealogists. Elsewhere in England: the Cathedral Archives and Record Office in Canterbury (and especially the archivist, Anne Oakley, for allowing me access to her collections even though the Record Office was officially closed for renovations at the time of my visit), the Department of Manuscripts of the Cambridge University Library, and the Record Offices of Cambridgeshire, Kent, Northamptonshire, Surrey, and Worcester. Outside of England: the Folger Shakespeare Library, the Huntington Library, and the University of Michigan Library, which, though named last, has been perhaps the most heavily used resource of all those mentioned. Finally, I am grateful to the staff of Cornell University Press for thoughtful and supportive guidance at the end of these labors.

    The encouragement of colleagues and friends, in Ann Arbor and elsewhere, has been an essential factor in this undertaking. Time and energy that might have been devoted to their own work was spent instead in worrying about mine. They have educated me in endless ways and spared me innumerable faults. I name no names here, out of deference to their own expressed wishes; but they know who they are, and they know also how much I am in their debt. Finally, the index was not prepared by my wife, who has always had better things to do with her time. The role played in the furtherance of this project by my two dedicatees has been quite intangible from the outset and may well be beyond rational description, but it was, and continues to be, both central and vital.

WILLIAM INGRAM

Ann Arbor, Michigan

Documentation

The following abbreviations have been used.

APC	*Acts of the Privy Council*
BL	British Library
ms. Add.	Additional manuscript
ms. Eg.	Egerton manuscript
ms. Harl.	Harleian manuscript
ms. Lansd.	Lansdowne manuscript
CLRO	Corporation of London Record Office
Jor.	Journal (minute book) of the Common Council
Rep.	Repertory (minute book) of the Court of Aldermen
CSPD	*Calendar of State Papers, Domestic*
Diary	*Henslowe's Diary*, ed. Foakes & Rickert, Cambridge, 1961
ES	E. K. Chambers, *The Elizabethan Stage*, 4 vols., Oxford, 1923
GHL	Guildhall Library
GLRO	Greater London Record Office
Greg	*Henslowe's Diary*, ed. W. W. Greg, 2 vols., London, 1904–1908.
HuSocP	Huguenot Society Publications
L&P	*Letters and Papers of Henry VIII*, 21 vols., London: Longmans, 1862–1910
MS	E. K. Chambers, *The Medieval Stage*, 2 vols., Oxford, 1903
MSC	A volume in the Malone Society *Collections* series
PRO	Public Record Office
A.O.	Audit Office
C.	Court of Chancery
E.	Court of Exchequer
K.B.	Court of King's Bench
P.C.	Privy Council

P.C.C.	Prerogative Court of Canterbury
Prob.	Probate
Req.	Court of Requests
S.P.	State Papers
Stac.	Court of Star Chamber
REED	A volume in the Records of Early English Drama series
STC	*Short-Title Catalogue*, 2d ed., 3 vols., London, 1976–1991

All citations from manuscript documents are in their original spelling, though in the interest of readability I have (with minor exceptions) expanded scribal contractions in italics. Transcriptions of documents at the Public Record Office appear by permission of the Controller of Her Majesty's Stationery Office. Sixteenth- and seventeenth-century books referred to in the text and notes were published in London unless otherwise noted. I take the year as beginning on 1 January.

PART ONE

NARRATIVE CONCERNS

PROLOGUE

That it would not be possible to discover a passage like the one I
have just quoted [from *The Crying of Lot 49*] in a genuine historical
work is an indication that we mostly go about our business as if the
contrary of what we profess to believe were the truth; somehow,
from somewhere, a privilege, an authority, descends upon our
researches; and as long as we do things as they have generally been
done—as long, that is, as the institution which guarantees our
studies upholds the fictions that give them value—we shall continue to write historical narrative as if it were an altogether different
matter from making fictions or, *a fortiori*, from telling lies.

—Frank Kermode

It may be true, to restate an old canard about scientists, that
most of the theater historians who have ever lived are now alive. In
the mid-nineteenth century, theater historians were not yet a
distinct species; theater history was then an avocation, not a
discipline. There was no methodology to speak of, and communication occurred primarily when selected individuals assembled in
small learned societies to announce their privately reached conclusions to one another. The newness and singularity of the field in that
distant time did not go unremarked, even by the early practitioners
themselves: J. O. Halliwell, commenting in 1853 on some of John
Payne Collier's forgeries, professed not to understand what purpose
they served, noting that only in very recent times had "the slightest

The epigraph is from Frank Kermode, *The Genesis of Secrecy: On the Interpretation of
Narrative* (Cambridge: Harvard University Press, 1979), pp. 108–9.

literary interest . . . been taken in the history of our early theatres, or even in the biography of Shakespeare";[1] and F. J. Furnivall, in founding the New Shakspere Society two decades later, remarked on the absence of any organized or coherent notion of what people ought to be doing by way of scholarship, or even of who was interested in what.[2]

Such matters are presumably less random today, though in fact the forms of interchange are not much different; and although one can find periodic indications of consensus, at times even of cohesion, in the modern discipline, these are mostly signs of collegiality among its practitioners rather than signals from a coherent field of theory and practice. An energetic and often healthy pluralism now predominates, differing from the wide-ranging inquiries of the early Victorians perhaps only in that today's scholars concur more frequently about strategies the discipline should eschew than about those it should embrace. While those of us who work in the Renaissance agree that we no longer take Shakespeare's greatness to be the primary justification for an interest in the early stage, we have not replaced that Victorian formulation with anything remotely approaching the persuasiveness it exercised in its heyday. Our own work, taken as a whole, is characterized either by a broad range of usefully divergent premises and practices, if one is a sanguine observer, or by a hodge-podge of unexamined assumptions and approaches, if one is a melancholic.

Whichever of these choices one prefers, the lack of ongoing discussion about purpose or methodology will seem as striking as it did in Furnivall's day. This situation is in marked contrast to that in the more traditional fields of history. A contemporary historian has observed that the "increase in the number of books on historiography and historical methodology is proportionally far greater than the increase in the number of historians."[3] No corresponding claim could be made in the field of theater history, in part because of its relative newness as a discipline and of a consequent paucity of competing ideologies, but only in part. For most present-day theater

---

[1] James Orchard Halliwell, *Observations on the Shaksperian Forgeries at Bridgewater House* (London, 1853), p. 4.

[2] F. J. Furnivall, *The New Shakspere Society's Transactions* (London, 1874), p. 7.

[3] Joseph Strayer, Foreword to Marc Bloch, *The Historian's Craft*, trans. Peter Putnam (Manchester: Manchester University Press, 1954), p. iii. Against this view should be set the remark of Keith Thomas ("An Anthropology of Religion and Magic, II," *Journal of Interdisciplinary History* 6 [1975], 91) that "most working historians tend to be impatient of anything which looks like methodological discussion."

historians, methodology is simply not a pressing issue. We justify our work, as Mark Cousins observes, "by privileging the craft of investigation,"[4] trusting thereby that the point of what we are doing will be self-evident and that whatever theoretical premises seem called for will appear both reasonable and manifest in our practice. Our collegial aim is to "do" theater history better than it was done before, honoring a notion of objectivity and presuming an attitude of rigor toward our resources.

But the relative lack of interest in methodology is a recurrent phenomenon rather than a continuous feature of the discipline. In the first two decades of this century, questions of method and procedure in the practice of theater history formed a regular part of the agenda of the newly organized Malone Society, whose founders saw as their task not only the recovery and dissemination of evidence from the past, but, more importantly, the determination of an appropriate attitude toward that evidence. In raising and confronting these issues they showed both an awareness of contemporary historical debate and a collegially argued position within that debate. The early volumes of the society's *Publications* bear witness to that interest, though the most impressive monument to their ideology remains the four volumes of *The Elizabethan Stage*, by the society's first president, E. K. Chambers.

The methodological stance adopted by these scholars was a latter-day recapitulation of the nineteenth-century reassessment of historiographic thinking in Europe, itself a part of the Romantic realignment of our sensibilities. Earlier modes of historical discourse, nourished and sanctioned by the Enlightenment, had run their course by the early nineteenth century; even as Macaulay and Carlyle were setting their pens to paper, the proponents of new ideologies were seizing the initiative, rejecting the notion of historical studies as a branch of literature and redefining it in terms that carried more suasive force. At one end of this spectrum stood the empiricists, for whom facts and evidence were both necessary and sufficient building blocks for any historical inquiry, and for whom history was not a philosophical or literary activity but rather a scientific undertaking whose particularities could be mastered only by a methodical and inductive study of historical documents. Such work was carried out at the newly founded École des Chartes in

---

[4] Mark Cousins, "The Practice of Historical Investigation," in *Post-Structuralism and the Question of History*, ed. Derek Attridge, Geoff Bennington, and Robert Young (Cambridge: Cambridge University Press, 1987), p. 131.

Paris and at Leopold von Ranke's innovative *Quellenkritik* seminars at the University of Berlin. At the other end stood the positivists, who took the generalities of human experience to be more historically meaningful than the details of individual encounters; for them, the evidential bias of the empiricists was merely the first step in discovering—on the analogy of the natural or "positive" sciences— the general principles that underlay the growth and development of political and social institutions. Adherents of both schools equally invoked the adjective "scientific" to characterize what they were doing; the word connoted objectivity to the empiricists, universality to the positivists.

Positivism exercised the stronger hold on the minds of early theater historians. One of them, J. Thomas Looney, having concluded that the earl of Oxford wrote the plays ascribed to Shakespeare, constructed on positivist principles a set of general rules which would make possible the identification of the author of the plays.[5] F. G. Fleay, an equally committed positivist though not an Oxfordian, felt strongly that the sciences marked out the only proper path for approaching the plays of Shakespeare. Fleay, like the French historian Georges Lefebvre in our own century, believed in the virtue of counting up; his route to the heart of Shakespeare's mystery was by way of metrical tests, feminine-ending tests, and statistics about rhyme. In advocating such tests, he argued that the great need for any critic attempting to use them was to have had "a thorough training in the Natural Sciences," for "the methods of all these sciences are applicable to this kind of criticism, which, indeed, can scarcely be understood without them."[6]

Fleay was the man Furnivall chose to speak on this very subject at the inaugural meeting of the New Shakspere Society in 1874. Furnivall was himself sympathetic to such views; in his Prospectus for the formation of the society he wrote that at that particular moment, "when our geniuses of Science are so wresting her secrets from Nature as to make our days memorable for ever, the faithful student of SHAKSPERE need not fear that he will be unable to pierce through the crowds of forms that exhibit SHAKSPERE's mind, to the mind itself, the man himself, and see him as he was."[7]

---

[5] S. Schoenbaum, *Shakespeare's Lives* (Oxford: Clarendon Press, 1970), pp. 598, 602.

[6] Frederick Gard Fleay, *A Shakespeare Manual* (London, 1876), p. 108. Lefebvre's maxim, *il faut compter*, has become one of the catch phrases of modern French historical study.

[7] In *The New Shakspere Society's Transactions* (London, 1874), p. 7.

"And see him as he was"—an oddly empiricist sentiment in an otherwise positivist manifesto, the words echoing (perhaps unconsciously) Ranke's earlier claim that the task of the historian was not to produce universal truths but simply to show how things actually were.[8] For a later generation of scholars—among them Chambers, W. W. Greg, A. F. Pollard, and the other founders of the Malone Society, for whom the premises of positivism were in any case uncongenial—Furnivall's mixed bag of notions and Fleay's erratic enthusiasms exemplified the limitations of an uncritical dilettantism. In their view, the purpose and procedures of theater history could only suffer from such eclecticism. A proper intellectual stand had to be made, and for these scholars the only banner to march under was that of *Quellenkritik*.

Their timing, it seems, was right. No better monument to Rankean historical methodology can be found in the field of theater history than *The Elizabethan Stage*, which rode the crest of the new empiricism to a position of unquestioned eminence in the field and which is still commonly viewed as one of the central enabling texts in the discipline. Chambers aimed to collect within the covers of his four volumes all the known evidence, facts, and responsible opinion available to him about the Elizabethan theater, though the first two of these categories were to have preeminence over the third. Twenty years earlier, in his preface to *The Medieval Stage*, he had remarked on the oddity of finding his predecessors "but little curious about the social and economic facts upon which the medieval drama rested. Yet from a study of such facts, I am sure, any literary history, which does not confine itself solely to the analysis of genius, must make a stand."[9]

These were the ascendant notions of the age, empiricist and pragmatic, established by the turn of the century in teaching academies on both sides of the Atlantic. Two successive Regius professors of history at Cambridge, Lord Acton (founding editor of the *Cambridge Modern History*) and J. B. Bury, were firmly in this camp; so, in varying degrees, were Friedrich Meinecke in Germany, Henri Pirenne in Belgium, Carl Becker in the United States, Georges Lefebvre in France. Scholars who preferred a positivist approach found a more congenial reception in such allied fields as sociology and economics. The empirical "method" was soon codified for a

---

[8] "Er will blos zeigen wie es eigentlich gewesen" (Leopold von Ranke, *Geschichten der romanischen und germanischen Völker von 1494 bis 1514* [Leipzig, 1824], p. vii).

[9] E. K. Chambers, *The Medieval Stage*, 2 vols. (Oxford: Clarendon Press, 1903), 1:v.

new generation of historical researchers in a variety of summary handbooks which began to proliferate in this period. The most popular of the handbooks, that by Charles-Victor Langlois and Charles Seignobos of the Sorbonne, encapsulated the essence of late-nineteenth-century empiricist thought. Taking minimal notice of those who, following Auguste Comte, claimed to have raised history to the rank of a positive science, Langlois and Seignobos adopted as their clarion call the dictum "no documents, no history" (*pas de documents, pas d'histoire*).[10] This primary aspect of Rankean ideology was firmly installed at the center of the new scholarship.

Another of Ranke's ambitions, however—to show how things actually were—was on shakier ground by century's end. In its heyday this goal had seemed to inform, or at least to explain, the approach taken by many of Chambers's predecessors, and its fall from status by Chambers's own time is made clear in the dismissive terms of Langlois and Seignobos: "Under the influence of the romantic movement historians sought for more vivid methods of exposition than those employed by their predecessors, methods better adapted to strike the imagination and rouse the emotions of the public, by filling the mind with poetical images of vanished realities" (300–301, English ed.).

So much for *wie es eigentlich gewesen*, a notion that had come to be regarded by many historians by the end of the nineteenth century as suspect, as characteristically imbued with the spirit of German Romanticism despite its pose as a dispassionate and objective path to those same vanished realities.[11] The theater historians' task, thus defined as our present century dawned, was no longer to be "the analysis of genius" (itself a perfectly legitimate Romantic aim), or the "recovery of the past," or the breathing of life into the subject matter; rather, it was to ground their work firmly on documents and concurrently to eschew the false dream of re-creating a former age. Chambers aimed to succeed in both categories, though with typical self-effacement he remarked in the Preface to *The Medieval Stage*, "The remorseless ideal of the historian's duties laid down in the *Introduction aux Études Historiques* of MM Langlois and Seignobos

---

[10] Charles-Victor Langlois and Charles Seignobos, *Introduction aux études historiques* (Paris, 1898), p. 29. Also published as *Introduction to the Study of History* (London, 1898); quotations on p. 17.

[11] In a memorial address given in 1936, Meinecke observed that Ranke took "a delight in being able to summon up gay and lively pictures fresh from the living source." See his *Entstehung des Historismus*, published in English as *Historism: The Rise of a New Historical Outlook* (London: Routledge & Kegan Paul, 1972), p. 497.

floats before me like an accusing spirit. I know how very far I am from having reached that austere standard of scientific completeness" (1: vii).

Chambers's modest disclaimer carried with it an implicit indictment of such earlier practitioners as Furnivall and Fleay, whose distance from "that austere standard" must have struck him as immeasurable. The work of these Victorians was riddled with faults, to be sure; but they did no more nor less than what Chambers did a half century later, that is, they followed the prevailing standards of their own time, taking as their proper province the imaginative and persuasive reconstruction of the past, the creation of a rhetorical *locus amoenus* that the mind could inhabit, a perspective from which we might see "how it actually was." Langlois and Seignobos pointed out at century's end that these notions were no longer in favor, and a generation later *The Elizabethan Stage* drove home the idea that a fundamental shift had taken place in the nature of the theater historians' approach to their materials. It thus became incumbent on the followers of Chambers to eschew "more vivid methods of exposition" and "poetical images of vanished realities." Chambers himself had taken this message to heart; with his dispassionate, leaden prose, he moved the writing of theater history forcefully into a new and different rhetorical register. Gone were the hallmarks of the Victorian essayist, the well crafted phrases, the urbane speculations, the Ciceronian diction, the antiquarian musings, the intimations of omniscience. In their place stood an alternative mode of discourse, a deft approximation of objective analytical inquiry, which won over its readers with surprising quickness.[12]

Behind that new discursive model, however, lay premises whose modality was not so very different from the ones being discarded. One might expect, for example, that a theater historian who claimed that his subject would "be studied in that truest spirit of criticism which deals with facts in preference to conjecture and sentiment,"

---

[12] Hayden White, considering a passage by the historian A. J. P. Taylor, suggests some reasons for the power of such prose: "One could hardly praise the passage for the vividness of its language. Indeed, most of the metaphors contained in it are dead ones, but the appeal of dead metaphors to particular groups of readers should not be underestimated. They can, in fact, be comforting, having the effect of reinforcing views already held and serving to familiarize phenomena that otherwise would remain exotic or alien. It is seldom noted how the effect of 'objectivity' can be attained by the use of nonpoetic language, that is to say, by language in which dead metaphors rather than vivid ones provide the substance of the discourse" (*Tropics of Discourse: Essays in Cultural Criticism* [Baltimore: Johns Hopkins University Press, 1978], p. 114).

or one who said that his work had been purged of "an element which I desired it to be free from as far as possible,—the subjective element," would be an adherent of the new empiricism; but any follower of Ranke might have written these sentences. They are in fact the words of Halliwell and Fleay, respectively. An easy response will of course be that professions of intention are one thing, performance another, and with this observation I will not quarrel; my aim is not to justify or rehabilitate the old patriarchs, or Chambers either, for that matter, but merely to contemplate what they thought they were doing, in their own terms.

I find it useful to know, for example, that Fleay was capable of such a statement as this one: "I should also state that in many instances I may seem to assert too positively: the fact is that there are so many points on which nothing more than strong probability is attainable, that the constant iteration of possibly, probably, it seems to me, I venture to think, and the like, becomes so tiresome, both to writer and reader, that I have preferred to risk the accusation of over-confidence in my own reasoning, to that of producing lassitude by perpetual repetitions of my inability to give positive statements where it is palpable that nothing more than great likelihood can be obtained."[13] Chambers, more laconic in addressing the same issue, says merely that "one cannot always be giving expression to the minuter shades of probability" (*MS* i:vii). Fleay's sentiment reflects a perfectly creditable if verbose concern about the relation of an author's prose to his evidence and would not be out of place in many a modern work. Fleay and Chambers equally understood the rhetorical nature of the problem that confronted them. Chambers dealt with it by resolving to omit speculation from his work, though modern scholars are agreed that his resolve went beyond his achievement. Fleay preferred to wrestle with the problem, not erase it; his chosen remedy was one of the casualties of the new empiricist approach, but his readiness to discuss it should remind us that we are unjustified in presuming, as we often do of our Victorian predecessors, that they were oblivious of these issues.

Indeed, consciousness of the rhetorical dimension was central in an earlier age. Langlois and Seignobos noted that the works of their own predecessors, that is, of earlier nineteenth century writers of handbooks for historical study, "are nearly all of them mere treatises on rhetoric" (p. 6, English ed.). And no wonder—history itself

---

[13] Fleay, pp. xxii–xxiii.

occupied that ground (even as, according to modern historians such as G. M. Trevelyan, it still should); and in an age in which professional historians often defined their problems in rhetorical terms, the concerns and preferred strategies of a Fleay do not seem out of place.

Yet by the 1920s and 30s, even as *The Elizabethan Stage* was making its appearance, still another shift in historical thinking was underway. The widespread scepticism and disillusionment with old absolutes which marked the years after the First World War, given voice by Wittgenstein and coupled with popular simplifications of Einsteinian physics, finally led to a growing conviction among historians that the very certitudes of their profession—the dispassionate nature of their inquiry, the objectivity of their methodologies, the truth of their facts—were themselves subjective notions, even (though not all historians would go so far) cultural constructs. Ranke himself had remarked upon the contingent nature of historical facts,[14] but in the early nineteenth century his comment, sorting ill with Romantic notions of particularity and value, had fallen on barren ground. It would have fared better a century later, in Chambers's own day, when the premises of empiricism were coming under attack. The Elizabethan historian J. B. Black wrote in 1926 that "direct observation of historical events is out of the question: they must always be seen indirectly, reflected so to speak, in the mirror of the present."[15] Other historians, led by the American Carl Becker, felt even more strongly that the relentless pursuit of "hard facts" had gotten out of hand and that the notion of *historical facts*, and indeed of empiricism itself, had to be set in a proper cultural context.

As theater historians, we seem less aware of (or perhaps only less interested in) this more recent shift in historical thinking than we are of the earlier one emblematized for us by Chambers, perhaps simply because there is no equivalent monumental text to embody it for us. But its implications are vast. Culturally we seem to be on the verge of abandoning the notion that historical inquiry can be free of subjective bias, and giving up this belief may put us right back with Fleay and Furnivall and Collier. Black felt that nineteenth-century scientific objectivity existed only in theory, not in practice, and that

---

[14] "Strenge Darstellung der Tatsache, wie bedingt und unschön sie auch sei, ist ohne Zweifel das oberste Gesetz" ("A strict presentation of fact, however contingent and unlovely it may be, is without doubt the primary rule"); (Ranke, p. vii).

[15] J. B. Black, *The Art of History* (London: Methuen, 1926), p. 8.

any writer of history was inevitably present in his work; he endorsed the view of the German historian Heinrich von Treitschke, who had written in 1913, "The impressive power of a historical work always lies in the vigorous personality of the historian."[16] Voicing on his own behalf a sentiment Fleay might have supported, Black claimed that "the 'subjectivity' of history is, in the nature of things, not only ineradicable, but also, if properly controlled, advantageous" (p. 8). To the intellectual and stylistic heirs of Chambers, these must have seemed like retrograde notions.

One finds little evidence in the writings of modern theater historians that this current view of the nature of historical inquiry bulks large in their thinking.[17] What is missing in such writing is not advocacy or espousal—a matter of personal choice in any event— but mere acknowledgment. On this ground, one might be tempted to argue that the patriarchs were better in touch with the prevailing historical attitudes of their own time than we are with ours. In such a construct it is we, not they, who are lost to the tradition. Their premises, romantic and rhetorical though they might have been, were appropriate to their intellectual milieu, perhaps more so than are our own. Unlike Chambers, they would have rejected Comte's notion of a distinction between "literary and rhetorical talent" on the one hand and "real intellectual power" on the other;[18] so would we, I suspect, despite the legacy of Chambers, and for reasons that may not be fully clear to us. Our Victorian predecessors had no wish to make their language transparent; they made pronouncements, not statements, in the full consciousness of what they were doing. They were fashioning a new area of study, a new craft, and they knew that their readers had less need of accurate citations from documents than of an authoritative assurance of being in reliable hands. Their prose fashioned that assurance. (Unhappily some, like Collier, even fashioned the documents.) These are the very features we now find dissonant, even as the premises of our own craft are being called into question, overtaken by an advancing tide of textual understand-

---

[16] Cited by Black, p. 11.

[17] In recent years the work of the so-called new historicists has encouraged some theater historians to take a renewed interest in methodology, though their principal motivation for doing so seems to be their dissatisfaction with the unargued premises of much new historicist scholarship. See, for example, Leeds Barroll, "A New History for Shakespeare and His Time," *Shakespeare Quarterly* 39 (1988), 441–64.

[18] Cited by Hayden White, "Rhetoric and History," in *Theories of History: Papers Read at a Clark Library Seminar, March 6, 1976*, intro. Peter Hanns Reill (Los Angeles: UCLA, 1978), p. 11.

ing in which all utterance is seen as contingent, and even such previously unassailable notions as gender and human nature itself are said to be socially constructed.[19]

We resist these insights only at some cost to our own work, even though they inevitably undercut whatever empirical assumptions we find ourselves holding onto about the histories we write for one another. As makers of historical narratives we face new demands not only on our awareness but on our actual practice; the new premises require not only rumination but testing as well. In the remainder of this section I try to assess the implications of this claim. In the first chapter I look at some materials both familiar and unfamiliar and consider the kinds of narrative responses they invite. In the second chapter I summarize some existing evidence and present some new data, implying thereby a refiguration of assumptions. In both cases I have tried to explicate the concerns that have guided me in the remainder of the book.

[19] For more on this last point see D. W. Robertson, "Some Observations on Method in Literary Studies," reprinted in *New Directions in Literary History*, ed. Ralph Cohen (Baltimore: Johns Hopkins University Press, 1974).

CHAPTER ONE

Evidence and Narrative

I

All that the historian means, when he describes certain historical facts as his data, is that for the purposes of a particular piece of work there are certain historical problems relevant to that work which for the present he proposes to treat as settled; though, if they are settled, it is only because historical thinking has settled them in the past, and they remain settled only until he or some one else decides to reopen them.

—R. G. Collingwood

There is an old story about two professors, one of literature and one of economics, discussing the widespread practice of allowing students to keep their examination questions. "We don't mind if our questions become public knowledge," says the literature professor, "because we make up new questions every year." "We don't mind either," replies the economics professor, "but unlike you, we use the same questions over and over. With us, every year the answers are different." I used to find this story amusing, in what I took to be its pleasant contrast between settled and unsettled disciplines, positivist and relativist mind sets, belief and doubt; I used to know unhesitatingly which professor represented my own point of view. But as these kinds of polarities become increasingly empty of significance in our culture, under the pressure of new ideas about reality testing and social construction, the point of the story—if such an easy contrast is its point—fades with them. Yet the story itself, chameleon-like, does not fade; it stays on and fits itself to our newer predilec-

The epigraph is from R. G. Collingwood, *The Idea of History* (Oxford: Clarendon Press, 1946), pp. 243–44.

tions. I continue to enjoy it, even though I now read it differently than I used to; I take it currently to be—and am even prepared to imagine that this is what it was all along—an anecdote about differing notions of the relation between questions and answers, or even about the different values that can be assigned to the question-answer paradigm as a mode of discourse.

A similar shift has taken place in my attitude toward the story I address in this book. I had brought the remains of a settled certitude with me when I began exploring the issues that underlie it; I knew pretty well what the questions were and also what the best answers ought to be. What remained of this assurance disappeared under the pressure of writing, however, not only because the available data were inadequate to support some of the more attractive assertions but because the nature of the assertions themselves had become problematic. What I had earlier taken to be a convincing set of arguments, merely needing fuller support, soon showed discontinuities that, rather than simply being flaws in my construction of events, seemed integral to any construction. My earlier remedy for such an impasse, more digging about in the records, now no longer seemed sufficient. The new material I was assembling kept reconfiguring both questions and answers—in itself a good development—but brought with it an increasing uncertainty about the context in which the questioning and answering was taking place. The very resistance of the subject matter was one of the issues requiring attention, as well as the kind of evidence on which it was to be grounded, the kind of rhetorical presentation that was to eventuate from it, indeed even the nature of historical argument in general.

My principal theme is the early development of the adult professional theater in Tudor London, though this is not nearly so straightforward and clear-cut a topic as it might seem from my simple statement. Glynne Wickham understands "professional" in this context to mean "actors who reckoned to earn a living from presenting plays regularly to a public that paid cash to gain admission to see them," and this is probably the least problematic of the terms I use.[1] I say "adult" because I mean to exclude consideration of companies of children, though the line of demarcation between companies of adults and companies of children is stronger in some cases than in others; we know that some of the "children" in some

---

[1] Glynne Wickham, *Early English Stages* (London: Routledge and Kegan Paul, 1966), 2, pt. 1:158.

commercial children's companies were adults, and one might be hard pressed to say what the difference was between, say, the children's company at Whitefriars in 1608 and the adult company at the Rose in 1597.[2] Nonetheless, because most of the early development I discuss was well on track by the time children's companies first regularly appeared publicly in London, and because the adult players of the time (as we learn from *Hamlet*) found it easy to make some sort of distinction, I do so here as well. Similarly, because my focus is on London, I do not discuss players and playing companies based primarily in the provinces, even though for the period under discussion we have no general criteria for determining that a company is nonprovincial. During the Tudor period all companies played in the provinces; indeed, at present the study of provincial playing is probably the fastest-growing branch of Elizabethan theater history. Many of these same companies also played in London, some of them with regularity, and I try to say a few things about the most prominent of them; but the term "London-based" is a shifting one, potentially misleading.

The weakening of these older distinctions under the pressure of new scholarship is a welcome development, though the relativist thrust of modern research has inevitably left us without an equivalent set of new categories to accommodate our current insights. We will probably have to learn to do without them; a theatrical equivalent of the Unified Field Theory, which would give us a clear understanding of the parameters of these activities and their relationship to one another, is far less achievable for us than its prototype is for physicists, and would be far too positivist in any event. Theater historians stand now at a Kuhnian juncture where neither old nor new paradigms command general assent; I see this as a condition to be taken into account rather than as a difficulty to be overcome. My aim is to explore the circumstances in which theatrical enterprises grew in London in the sixteenth century. From quasi-amateur part-time activities in the early 1500s, they had become by the end of the century sources of regular income and often the sole means of livelihood for grown men with families, for those who pursued the craft of stage playing as well as for those who organized or managed companies of players and those who leased playing space or

---

[2] See my essay "The Playhouse as an Investment, 1607–1614: Thomas Woodford and Whitefriars," *Medieval and Renaissance Drama in England* (New York: AMS Press, 1985), 2: 209–30.

eventually built playhouses. This list of differentiated activities is of course arbitrary, proposing modern distinctions where none may be needed: in the early Elizabethan period, finding a place to play and finding someone to take care of company business would have seemed natural extensions of the business of stage playing, without necessarily implying any new division of labor or of personnel. Even at the end of the century a handful of people, Edward Alleyn and Richard Burbage among them, were still active across the whole spectrum of playing, managing, and financing, and such men as Christopher Beeston and Andrew Cane continued the tradition well into the seventeenth century. The same is true of the ancillary activities of making fair copies of play texts and actors' parts, or playing musical instruments, or supplying costumes. One can point to private individuals who contracted to do such things for others, but increasingly as well to companies of players who served their own needs in those capacities. It is an old cliché that the drama is the most social of literary forms, but the society referred to in the cliché is the audience, gathered communally in an act of witnessing. The other community—the network of social, and hence economic, interdependencies that formed among the men who provided these early Elizabethan entertainments—has only recently come into focus as a subject worthy of study on its own terms. Thus we cannot say with any surety what effect the forces within that community may have had on the kinds of texts or improvisations that came to be performed, or ultimately on the way "the Elizabethan drama," that iconic entity, grew out of this early activity.

Any comprehensive view of these men and their endeavors would have to locate them not only in the context of the drama that is now our chief grounds for remembering them but also in the context of their times, a period of foreign wars and political intrigue, of spiraling inflation and civic unrest, of entrepreneurship and piety. All these categories have modern significance, and a desire for "relevance" may tempt us to postulate parallels with our own age. Even if we resist that snare, there is some danger of distortion perhaps in our very choice of topics to attend to. All too easily one can find oneself constructing a hypothetical Tudor *zeitgeist* to explain or affirm or even to invent a contextual significance for one's own interests. Ideally one would avoid all such traps, but actual practice is another matter. For my own part, I am motivated by what Siegfried Kracauer characterized as "a compassionate interest—an antiquarian interest, as it were—in certain moments of the past," and I try wherever possible to take those moments on their own terms and in the context of their own values.[3]

I approach the materials of this book not through the eyes of the literary historian—that is, as the record of an activity whose primary achievement was the production of texts for critical study—but rather from the point of view of the participants themselves, the people active across the whole range of stage playing, managing, and financing, or as many of them as we may be able to learn about at our four hundred years' remove. Everyone involved in the enterprise in this period, including the vast majority of writers for the stage, would have seen his activity (I believe) indifferently as an art, a craft, and a means of producing wealth. Certainly a principal charge laid against stage players by their opponents was that they grew rich: in 1591 a Londoner named Samuel Cox lamented the "infinite numbers of poore people" who "goo a begging about the streates," while stage players "wax rytche by iuggling & iestinge."[4]

This theme, even with its attendant overstatement, was common to the age. Shakespeare himself, who clearly did grow rich, cannot be insulated from the charge of being interested in such matters, though it has long been thought unseemly to suggest as much, even as it was thought indecorous a century ago to draw attention to his having been a stage player—unfortunate that he had been, surely, but then he mustn't have been very good at it, for it was no more than a base mechanical trade from which the earl of Southampton ought to have purchased his release. We have learned, in our own day, to see Shakespeare's competence as a player more clearly and to reject the claims that he was fit only for small parts like old Adam in *As You Like It* or the Ghost in *Hamlet*. Similarly we must understand, not merely acknowledge dismissively, that stage playing was the primary source of income for him and his fellows and that a proper concern about this way of making money was part of the texture of their lives. Tawney reminds us that "if we forget the economic motive altogether and overlook the material conditions on which the production of wealth depends"—or, one might interpolate,

---

[3] Siegfried Kracauer, *History: The Last Things before the Last* (New York: Oxford University Press, 1969), p. 6. Alternatively, M. M. Postan argues that "antiquarians collect facts" while "historians study problems" and that to a historian "facts are of little value unless they are causes . . . of the phenomena which he studies" (*Fact and Relevance: Essays on Historical Method* [Cambridge: Cambridge University Press, 1971], p. 25).

[4] BL, ms. Add. 15,891, fo. 184[v].

if we presume that the production of wealth was not an important consideration—"we become mere sentimentalists and dreamers."[5]

In his important book *Drama and Society in the Age of Jonson*, L. C. Knights set out in 1937 to describe the major economic movements of the late sixteenth and early seventeenth centuries in England and to explore the reflection of those movements, and the popular responses to them, in the dramatic texts of the age. Like Knights, I am interested in the economic conditions of the period, to the extent that they may be known; but where Knights's aim was to show those conditions, or the popular perception of them, as reflected in subsequent dramatic literature, mine is to discover how the more particularized economic circumstances in London, a generation or two earlier, might have affected the makers and performers of that dramatic literature and thus influenced the development of the professional playing company and the commercial playhouse.

My field of exploration is thus in one sense narrower than that of Knights's study, for while the dramatist may take the whole range of human affairs as grist for his writing, only a small subset of those same affairs will directly affect his own life or the lives of his colleagues in the playhouse. The enclosure of common fields was certainly a frequent theme in the sixteenth century, while the increasing pressure of population upon the means of subsistence, which affected a London stage player's daily life much more directly, was not; resentment of the increasing numbers of foreign artisans in the City of London was a common theme, while the monetary roots of inflation and unemployment were not. Indeed, the popular understanding of social and economic issues in the latter half of the sixteenth century is itself a potentially fruitful subject of study. For one anonymous writer in 1550, a major source of difficulty was that "there be to many clothes made to carye over Sees, to many clothemakers, to many marchauntes aventurre[r]s."[6] Modern economic historians will of course prefer their own constructs to such imaginative explanations as these, the fictions of an earlier age; nor do I presume to offer anything more than my own correlative set of assumptions, perhaps equally fictitious, in the pages that follow. I share the view of many of my contemporaries that, in the words of a modern noneconomic historian, "man is not

---

[5] *History and Society: Essays by R. H. Tawney*, ed. J. M. Winter (London: Routledge & Kegan Paul, 1978), p. 4.
[6] BL, ms. Eg. 2623, item 7, fo. 9, a single sheet of paper listing contemporary abuses, by an unknown writer, dated October 1550.

entirely rational, and society is held together as much by beliefs and customs as by economic interests."[7] Throughout the present book I have tried to do justice to both the irrational beliefs and the economic interests of the men involved in the development of the Elizabethan theater. I have tried to focus not only on what seem to me the kinds of issues that might arise under these headings but also on the acceptable ranges of response to them. Accordingly, I have allowed myself certain liberties of conjecture and speculation, not only where evidence is lacking but often where it is present, for I think that a coherent narrative is desirable as long as it is neither fraudulently achieved nor misrepresented as truth. Throughout the book I have tried to be scrupulous in identifying all my speculations, lest they be inadvertently taken for certainties.

II

> I'll marry this lady
> Today, and I'll marry
> The other
> Tomorrow.
> —W. S. Gilbert, *Trial by Jury*

The stance I have chosen has its dangers, of course. The hardening of conjectures into certainties, a common feature in the history of any discipline, is often consequent upon the valorizing of narrative coherence as the preferred mode of accounting for events. If a suitably constructed story line gives sufficient satisfaction to its clientele, the certainties on which it is based may cease to be questioned or examined, their truths taken for granted rather than demonstrated. Proponents of any narrative so produced and endorsed may come to see its premises as self-evident, as "nuggets of reality embedded in the evidence," in M. M. Postan's telling phrase,[8] rather than as factual devisings of their own.

I say "factual" deliberately, for such facts, and the accounts that grow from them, arise from an activity not unlike Jack Horner's in

---

[7] Joseph Strayer, Foreword to Marc Bloch's *Historian's Craft* (Manchester: Manchester University Press, 1954), p. v.

[8] M. M. Postan, "Fact and Relevance in Historical Study," in *Fact and Relevance*, p. 54.

producing his plums, often accompanied by the same kind of evaluative *non sequitur*. Facts of this sort must be confused neither with the past events of which they purport to be a reflection or interpretation nor with the data that survive as a partial and perhaps not even accurate record of those events. Indeed, the very etymology of "fact" should teach us that it is a construct, not a given or *datum*; it has no *a priori* claim to our attention. In pragmatic terms the datum, the historical record itself, is all we have. "That is the case of the historian," observed Carl Becker over half a century ago. "The only external world he has to deal with is the records. He can indeed look at the records as often as he likes, and he can get dozens of others to look at them: and some things, some 'facts,' can in this way be established and agreed upon."[9]

But the hazard in even this seemingly dispassionate approach is that consensus about facts is itself a contingent affair, relying on shared paradigms of understanding and assent among the observers. This is not an exclusively modern view: Wilhelm von Humboldt, one of Ranke's mentors, wrote in 1821 that "the facts of history are in their several connecting circumstances little more than the results of tradition and scholarship which one has agreed to accept as true."[10]

Perhaps the best way for a student of Elizabethan theater history to witness this process at work is to consider the set of circumstances surrounding Shakespeare's marriage. This celebrated crux provides an almost paradigmatic model of the way we devise facts in order to construct narratives. The bits of evidence from which the process has taken shape in this particular instance are to be found in the English midlands:

1. The Diocesan Record Office at Worcester is an episcopal archive, a repository for various documents generated by, or received by, the bishop's secretariat over a span of several centuries. Many documents in the archive date from the sixteenth century. Some of these earlier records are loose parchment sheets, while others are bound into register volumes. Any

---

[9] Carl Becker, "What Are Historical Facts?" in *Detachment and the Writing of History: Essays and Letters of Carl L. Becker*, ed. Phil Snyder (Ithaca: Cornell University Press, 1958), p. 57.

[10] Wilhelm von Humboldt, "On the Historian's Task" (1821), reprinted in *The Theory and Practice of History: Leopold von Ranke*, ed. Georg G. Iggers and Konrad von Moltke (New York: Bobbs-Merrill, 1973), p. 58.

one of us could go to Worcester and determine for ourselves that these remarks are correct. This is evidence.

2. Both the loose sheets and the registers from the sixteenth century contain entries made presumably by diocesan clerks, and normally in a fair secretary hand. Some of the entries appear to be copies or transcripts of documents whose originals subsequently went elsewhere; some of them are notations of actions taken or alleged to have been taken; some of them are mere memoranda. This too is evidence.

3. One of the items in the archive, a loose parchment sheet, is evidently the registry copy of a bond, dated 28 November 1582, a Wednesday. The text of the bond affirms the readiness of Fulk Sandells and John Richardson, two men identified as farmers or husbandmen from Warwickshire, to stand surety for the wedding of one "William Shagspere . . . and Anne Hathwey of Stratford in the Dioces of Worcester maiden." Forty pounds of Sandells and Richardson's own money backs up their assurance that there is no let or hindrance to the marriage; in return, the bishop's clerk agrees to issue the couple a special license that will allow them to proceed with the marriage after only one reading of the banns. The document records these matters; that it does so is evidence.[11]

Of the several claims, explicit and implicit, made in this document, we may say only that they have been made; the document offers no means for testing their accuracy or inaccuracy. But it is conventional, in the absence of suspicions or of contrary evidence, to allow the benefit of the doubt. So with this document; it appears genuine, and nothing prevents us from taking all its statements at face value, as assertions pertaining to a disappeared event. One reading of the banns, while unusual, is not beyond precedent. From other kinds of documents we can discover that, during this period of English history, marriages seem to have been prohibited during Advent and that in 1582, the year of this bond, Advent began on Sunday 2 December, that is, four days after the date of the bond. On that imminent Sunday, presumably, the first and only banns would be read for the William Shagspere and Anne Hathwey named in this document, and then the marriage performed.

---

[11] This and related documents are discussed in E. K. Chambers, *William Shakespeare* (Oxford, 1930), 2:41–52.

From the assertions in the document we may easily devise a set of facts, that is, propositions that seem to be called forth by the evidence of the document, but which are nowhere explicitly recorded in the document. These facts will form a superset of assertions which we, as hermeneutic readers, will create in the process of interpreting or "deciphering" the document; or, in more familiar reader-response terms, they are meanings which we bring to the document to contextualize it. Here are some of those facts: (a) a William Shagspere and an Anne Hathwey wished to marry, or at least their associates Sandells and Richardson claimed that they wished to marry, as of 28 November 1582; (b) they were not yet married as of that date; (c) they were presumably free to marry, else they would not be going to all this trouble; (c) it was important that they be married within four days; (d) in exchange for the execution of this bond, the clerk would issue them the requisite license, and they could then be married on Sunday 2 December.

To confirm these facts to our full satisfaction we need only find a record of the marriage license itself. Unfortunately, there is no record of such a license ever having been issued. What we find, instead, is more matter for confusion.

> 4. Register number 32 of the series of episcopal registers in the Record Office at Worcester contains an entry on folio 43^v dated 27 November 1582, a Tuesday, just one day before the date of the bond mentioned above. The entry is a clerical notation that a marriage license had been issued on this date to one William Shaxpere and one Anne Whateley of Temple Grafton.[12]

The document appears equally genuine, and its statements equally valid as assertions. We have here another set of data, different from the former set. We can repeat the exercise above, and see what facts our reading of this document will invite us to devise. They might look like this: (a) a William Shaxpere and an Anne Whateley wished to marry, each presumably having claimed as much before the clerk *in propria persona*, as of 27 November 1582; (b) they were not yet married as of that date; (c) they were presumably free to marry, else they would not be going to all this trouble; (d) they were also free,

---

[12] This document, like the earlier one, is reproduced in facsimile in J. W. Gray, *Shakespeare's Marriage* (London: Chapman & Hall, 1905), and in transcription in Chambers, *William Shakespeare*.

once having secured their license, to set the process in motion, most likely by having banns read; (e) given the imminent arrival of Advent, they were not likely married before January; (f) they did, however, have a license to marry.

The parish of Temple Grafton lies only some four miles from Stratford and was also a part of the diocese of Worcester; this license is thus legitimate. Indeed, the data implicit in this latter document are as valid as the earlier data about the woman named Hathwey, but they have failed to command equal assent in the scholarly community. Or, to put it perhaps more precisely, modern scholars, gazing collectively at this latter document, have generally declined to create the facts I have proposed. When pressed about this omission—when asked why the former document is valorized while the latter one is not—they will usually respond by explaining that the bishop's clerk must have "erred" in writing Whateley for Hathwey, and in writing Temple Grafton for Stratford.

The rationale of the erring clerk was so widespread, even by the end of the nineteenth century, that Sir Sidney Lee, writing his *Life of Shakespeare* in 1898, felt obliged to combat the notion. "It is unsafe," he argued,

> to assume that the bishop's clerk, when making a note of the grant of the license in his register, erred so extensively as to write "Anne Whateley of Temple Grafton" for "Anne Hathaway of Shottery." The husband of Anne Whateley cannot reasonably be identified with the poet. He was doubtless another of the numerous William Shakespeares who abounded in the diocese of Worcester. Had a license for the poet's marriage been secured on November 27, it is unlikely that the Shottery husbandmen would have entered next day into a bond "against impediments," the execution of which might well have been demanded as a preliminary to the grant of a license but was wholly supererogatory after the grant was made.[13]

Lee's distrust of the "errors" explanation, and his claim that the bond must precede the license, are commendable. As the dates written into the records show the license issued before the bond, it was self-evident to Lee that the license and the bond were for two different marriages; and as there were two different brides named, Lee's sensibility required that there be two grooms. In support of this claim he found himself required to assert that the diocese of

---

[13] Sir Sidney Lee, *A Life of William Shakespeare* (1st ed.; London: Smith, Elder, 1898), pp. 23–24.

Worcester "abounded" with "numerous William Shakespeares," a statement easier to make rhetorically than to document.[14] The names "Whateley" and "Temple Grafton" are not so easily finessed; despite Lee's efforts, we are left where we began.

However, if we do not want our Willy contracted to two women, we may nevertheless prefer Lee's solution and elect to believe that William Shaxpere and William Shagspere were two different people, but with the same first and last names, who appeared before the clerk at Worcester on successive days in the last week of November 1582, each of them needing a license in order to marry a woman named Anne who lived in a village in the extreme south of Warwickshire. Though this proposal may strain credulity, it is not beyond the bounds of possibility, and it has the conservative virtue of permitting us to valorize equally all the data in both the documents, and to make equally valid facts from them. Despite these advantages, however, and despite Lee's arguments, few contemporary scholars find any attractiveness in this virtue, or for that matter in the argument as a whole. The two documents in question, by general consensus (i.e., another incipient fact), refer to the same man and thus, by extension, to the same woman.

It will not be difficult to draw a moral from this much-discussed issue. Though the very topic of Anne Whateley is one that most of us prefer to ignore, she reminds us that we create and validate the facts that are most agreeable to us, or at least those that don't hamper our pursuit of our own hypotheses. Because of these preferences, poor Anne Whateley has become a nonperson, perhaps never to return. The registers of Temple Grafton parish have not survived from the period before 1695, and to my knowledge no one since the time of Chambers has been moved to search for her in other classes of documents. Mark Eccles accepted without question that Anne Whateley was a clerical error and not a real person, and

---

[14] The International Genealogical Index, under continuing expansion and revision by the Church of Latter-day Saints in Salt Lake City, lists almost a million and a half names from the county of Worcester in its 1984 edition, including over six hundred Shakespeares, but lists only one William Shakespeare in the entire county from the period before 1600, and that one is, of course, the playwright, cited because of his appearance in the very documents we are discussing. The presumed abundance of others must be set down to wishful thinking on Lee's part. Nor are matters any better inWarwickshire itself. The 1984 IGI lists over two million names from Warwickshire, including almost two thousand Shakespeares, but has only four sixteenth-century entries for a William Shakespeare. One of them is the playwright's baptismal entry, and the other three are, on grounds of age, not likely to be candidates for marriage in 1582.

he dismissed her in a few sentences.[15] But the record in which she is named may be as genuine and as accurate as any of the others, even though it is not currently fashionable to think so. Our present collective disposition, despite the efforts of Sir Sidney Lee, is to posit only one groom and only one bride. In this scenario, Shakespeare was not poised on the brink of marrying one of two different women, with the Hathaway family winning out; rather, there was never more than one woman in the case, the other being a mere slip of the pen. Thus we make, or do not make, facts from our evidence.

And such determinations soon achieve a momentum of their own, becoming paradigms of what Perrell Payne calls the "hypostatized proof," in which we confuse our conclusions about an event with the evidence for that event.[16] What began as a hypothesis, or claim, that Anne Whateley is a nonperson begins to coalesce in our minds with the notion that it is a fact, that there is evidence for her being a nonperson. That conviction having become implanted, we then cease looking for her, and she, like the authorship claimants, becomes a kind of shibboleth for the identification of members of the lunatic fringe.

The Anne Whateley story reminds us not only that the facts on which our preferred narratives are based are themselves subjective constructs, propositions about evidence rather than synonymous with evidence, but also that biography is a particularly vulnerable area for this kind of fact making, growing as it does out of our desire to build sensible lives out of scraps of data. Our awareness of this danger has produced one unfortunate remedy in our own time, namely the general avoidance of biographical study as a component of Elizabethan theater history. We prefer to approach our subject through the study of texts, or (increasingly) of buildings, rather than worry about the people who performed the texts or erected the buildings. Conjectural reconstructions of playhouses abound today, much as they did a hundred years ago; yet equivalent conjectures about the users of those playhouses—another popular Victorian pastime—are today regarded as unscholarly or romantic. The documentary evidence on which we erect our modern conjectures is no more substantial in the case of playhouses than in the case of players, yet we seem less comfortable with the unpredictabilities of

[15] Mark Eccles, *Shakespeare in Warwickshire* (Madison: University of Wisconsin Press, 1961), p. 64.

[16] Perrell F. Payne, Jr., "A Note on a Fallacy," *Journal of Philosophy* 55 (1958), 126; see also David Hackett Fischer, *Historians' Fallacies: Toward a Logic of Historical Thought* (New York: Harper & Row, 1970), p. 56.

flesh and blood than with objects of timber or brick or with geometric principles of design; when we do make use of biographical material, as a modern school of historical criticism likes to do, it is often in the service of some other agenda.

This biographical reluctance among Elizabethan theater historians is in sharp contrast to the practices of their colleagues who study eighteenth-century theater history, for whom a lively interest in the biographies of actors and managers is seen as appropriate, respectable, and legitimate. It might be supposed that one reason for this difference in attitude is that such information has survived in greater abundance from 1676 than from 1576. And indeed it has, but the same is true of information about playhouses in the two periods, and no correlative inhibition operates there. The source of the reluctance, I believe, lies elsewhere. Scraps of information about a playhouse—the Red Lion, for example—can be fitted into a preexistent construct far more readily than can scraps of information about an Elizabethan stage player. We have only the barest descriptions of a stage and tower at the Red Lion, yet modern scholars are already contending about the place and significance of those features in the ongoing narrative. We do less well with the scraps of information at hand about Elizabethan players and managers, because we have no equivalent hypotheses about the development of such roles in this period.[17] We find it easier to deal with Thomas Betterton's life than with Philip Henslowe's, and we are readier to construct versions of Charles Hart, Michael Mohun, or Cave Underhill than of John Garland, John Singer, or James Tunstall.

Tunstall is a useful example of a player about whom we know only random scraps. We know that in 1583 he was one of the earl of Worcester's players, a company with which Henslowe had intermittent dealings; we know that his name appears sporadically in various of Henslowe's records from 1585 to 1597, witnessing transactions involving Edward and John Alleyn and others. We know that by 1590 he had joined the admiral's company, that in 1592 he and John Alleyn were witness to one of James Burbage's splenetic outbursts against the widow Brayne at the Theater in Shoreditch, and we tell ourselves, in the formulaic phrase, that after 1597 he "disappears from the records." This is not quite true, though it says something about the size of the net we cast. Tunstall was already a married man when Henslowe began with him, and for Henslowe he

---

[17] Muriel Bradbrook's *Rise of the Common Player* (Cambridge, Mass.: Harvard University Press, 1962), despite its title, sheds no light on this matter.

was indifferently "Jeames donstall" and "Jeames donston," though he appears in other records as "Tunstall" or "Tonstall."[18]

It is tempting to accuse Henslowe of illiteracy in this as in so many other things, but the confusion was apparently widespread. The parish clerk where the Tunstalls lived was equally in the habit of using alternative names. Henry Tunstall the patriarch, a householder in the parish and a freeman of the Company of Saddlers, was a member of the parish vestry and a common councilor, so the clerk had numerous occasions to record his name, yet he spelled it indifferently as "Tunston" or "Tunstall." Sometimes these variants occur in the same entry, as seen in the clerk's notation from 1593 recording the burial of "Marguerit tunstonne" the widow of "henry tunstall saddler" upon her death of plague at the age of sixty-three.[19] Henry Tunstall himself, "cittizen and sadler of London . . . dwelling in the high striet" had died two years earlier and been buried in the church, "in the aley neare the fount . . . vnder the broken stone that the blocke dothe ly ouer where vpon the Minester dothe vse to stand at the funtt."[20] The probate records for both Margaret and Henry further substantiate the alternative names: he is recorded as "Henricus Tunstall alias Tunston," she as both "Margareta Dunston alias Tunstall" and "Margareta Dunston alias Tunston."[21]

Henry Tunstall and his family lived at the eastern edge of the city, in the parish of St. Botolph without Aldgate. Their parish clerk, Thomas Harridance, annotated his records of parochial affairs with a wonderful fullness, as seen by the record just cited. Unfortunately, the earliest surviving register for this parish begins in 1558, just too late to catch the baptism of James Tunstall, who was born in about 1555. James Tunstall the stage player was also a saddler, and of the right age (and mixture of name forms) to have been Henry Tunstall's son, though precise confirmation is lacking. Another parishioner, one John Dunston or Tunston or Tunstall, may have been James's brother. Early in 1584, Harridance made three entries in his daybook, once for each time banns were read for "Jeames tunstall and Jeane greene," and made still another entry for the day of their marriage. Tunstall was already a player by this time, but Harridance saw him and his family principally as parishioners. An assiduous recorder of

---

[18] *Diary.*, pp. 37, 49, 50, 239, among others; he is indexed in this edition as "Donstone" with a cross-reference to "Tunstall." The baptism of a "Dunston Tunstall" at St. Botolph Bishopsgate on 20 August 1572 suggests that two separate but confusable family names may be at issue here.

[19] GHL, ms. 9221.

[20] GHL, ms. 9234/1, 20 November 1591.

[21] GHL, mss. 9050/2, ff. 76ᵛ, 139; 9050/3, fo. 3.

details, Harridance noted the loss of a child in 1587: "Samvell Tunstall the sonne of Jeames Tunstall a player Dwelling in bell Alye being Beyond sparowes corner," he wrote, "was cristned the xx^{th} Daye of Aprill in ano 1587 by m^{r} Cowse Being the minister of creechurche ffor that m^{r} hayes [the regular minister] was not at home." After the appropriate interval: "The Wyfe of Jeam*e*s tunstall was churched the xij Daye of maye in ano 1587". But early the following year: "Samuell Tunstall the sonne of Jeames Tunstall a player Dwellinge in Bell Alye being near vnto sparrows cornar was Buried the xiij^{th} Daye of Marche ano 1587 [i.e., 1588] neare to the owter wall at the further ende of the sowthe yearde he was xij monethes owlde."[22]

The death of an infant was all too common an event in that period. For the Tunstalls, there was an earlier son, James, born in 1585 and still alive, who perhaps mitigated the loss. The parents may have comforted themselves in other ways as well, for another son, John, was born early in 1589, almost exactly nine months after the burial of Samuel: "Jhon Tunstall the sonne of Jeames Tunstall An Enterlude player Dwellinge in Bell alye beinge neare sparrows corner was cristned The xij^{th} Day of Januarie ano 1588 [i.e., 1588/89]"; subsequently "Jeames Tunstall*e*s wyfe was chur'd the therd daye of februarie ano 1588 [/89]"[23]

No other Tunstall children appear in Harridance's records, though James Tunstall the player lived for another decade and more. His absence from Henslowe's accounts after 1597 is explained by the abstract of a will preserved in the Guildhall Library, dated 8 December 1599. The will is nuncupative (from *nuncupare*, to declare), meaning that it exists not as a document written in the testator's presence and signed by him but as an affidavit, drawn up later and signed by witnesses who were at his bedside during his last moments, affirming the absence of a written will and reciting the dying person's last spoken requests. The James Tunstall who died shortly after 8 December 1599 wished to be identified as a citizen and saddler of London, perhaps reluctant to describe himself on the threshold of eternity as a stage player. He left everything to his wife, Jane. Two days later, on 10 December, Harridance noted the burial of "Jeames Tunstall Citt*iz*en & sadler of London & a player."[24]

[22] GHL, ms. 9234/1.
[23] GHL, ms. 9234/2.
[24] GHL: for the will, ms. 9051/1, Register of Wills of the Archdeaconry of London, fo. 145^{v}; for the burial, ms. 9222/1, the parish register. For the will probate on 15 December, see ms. 9050/3, fo. 121.

Tunstall thus appears to have been one of several Elizabethan stage players who were freemen of livery companies, such as Martin Slater, ironmonger, John Heminges, grocer, John Shanks, weaver, and Robert Armin and Andrew Cane, goldsmiths. One cannot track Tunstall in the records of the Saddlers' Company because the early records of that company were destroyed in 1666; but we know about the City regulation forbidding apprentices to marry, so if Tunstall earned his freedom by apprenticeship we can assume that he did so before 1584, the year of his marriage to Jane Green. As he was already playing with Worcester's company by 1583, likely he was a freeman even before then. He was forty-four years old at his death, thus twenty-four and eligible for freedom in 1579, and twenty-nine at his marriage. He might, of course, if he was Henry Tunstall's son, have taken his freedom not by apprenticeship but by patrimony, claiming it in right of his father, as a form of social insurance before going off to be a stage player. At the baptisms of his children, he is merely "player" to Harridance the parish clerk, but for his burial notice he is "sadler of London" as well. These social and economic linkages assume different degrees of importance at different times in a player's life—James Burbage was always "joiner" when it mattered—and we typically pay insufficient attention to such connections between the craft of playing and other City crafts.

A link of another sort may be seen between James Tunstall's youngest son, John, and the John Tunstall or Dunston who may have been the player's brother. This latter John died a violent death just two months after the burial of Samuel and seven months before the birth of the new baby. James may have given his new baby the name John as an act of memorial piety. Thomas Harridance recorded the details:

> Jhon Donston Cittizen and Bricklayer of London Beinge a howshowlder and Dwellinge at the signe of the blewe Anker neare vnto sparrowes corner was mvrdered By Thomas campion A Laboringe man who Ded Dwell in garden Alye and cominge Behynde the sayd Jhon Donstone sittinge at his owne Dore Ded throaste a knyfe in to his Backe vnder his lefte showlder Blade wch wente abowte v entchis Deepe into his Bodye and more where of he Dyed and the crowneres quest havinge gone vpon hem he was Buried in the sowthe alye in the churche vnder the Right syde of the greate stone that hathe so many pictures vpon it The xvij^th Daye of maye ano 1588. yeares xxxiiij.[25]

[25] GHL, ms. 9234/1.

Shortly after the death of this unfortunate John, who had been only a year older than James Tunstall, James and his family moved away from St. Botolph's, relocating in St. Katherine Coleman Street parish, where they remained for the next decade.

James himself, after being "long sick," died in December 1599, in more peaceable fashion than the murdered John, and Harridance set down his age at death as "year*es* xliiij." His body was brought back to St. Botolph's for burial, and he was interred "in the new Vault lately made in the Northesyd alley or Ile in the Church wch said vault was made at the chargis of the p*a*rish."[26] Among the St. Botolph's parishioners who attended his funeral one might have hoped to find fellow players William Augustine, Richard Darloe, Thomas Goodale, John Hill, and Robert Lee, all near neighbors of Tunstall's when he lived among them. Probably any one of them could have answered the questions we would want to raise about Tunstall. Why, for instance, had he turned from the prospect of a mercantile life in the City—which, as a freeman of the Company of Saddlers, he could have pursued in any manner he wished—to travel with the earl of Worcester's players? Was this the sort of thing only romantic young men did, or might it have made good business sense? What stature did he, as a City freeman, have among his fellows in Worcester's company? Were some of his fellow players also freemen of City livery companies? How many players like Tunstall, with wives and families in London, were members of troupes that played principally in the provinces, as Worcester's seemed to do? Why did Tunstall leave Worcester's and transfer to the admiral's company? Was it at his initiative, or did the admiral's players seek him out? Was he attracted because the admiral's players had a settled base in London at the Rose playhouse? Was playing in London more remunerative than playing in the provinces?

An earlier age would have thought the answer to that last question self-evident; our own age is not so sure, and rightly so. We might also wonder what happened to the rest of Worcester's company after Tunstall left and about the degree to which its fortunes in this period were related to the prosperity of other companies. We would also want to ask how much these shifts and alterations had to do with the theatrical "scene" in London at the turn of the century, and how much merely with individual prefer-ences about working conditions. Finally, we should inquire what it was like for the rest of these players, in 1599, to be pursuing the craft

---

[26] GHL, ms. 9234/5, fo. 190.

from which Tunstall had just made his final exit; why were *they* still at it? Such questions, and more, are prompted by the fragments of evidence we have been considering, though the fragments themselves address none of them. Narrative closure, if we are to achieve it in such matters, is likelier to result from our rhetoric than from our data.

In the chapters that follow, I have set myself a variety of similar questions, which I answer often provisionally and not always satisfactorily. Where possible, I try alternative rhetorical approaches; that is to say, I resituate the questions to make alternative answers possible. As new evidence comes to light, of course, the questions themselves have to be recycled; but I trust that, at least for the present moment, the questions I ask are the right ones. Susanne Langer reminded us long ago that our questions, rather than our answers, say who we are and what we value. I have devoted the latter half of this book to questions about events from the decade of the 1570s, and especially about the principal theatrical event, "1576." The earlier chapters are intended to set a context for the discussions that follow.

Economics and Narrative:
Stage Players in London

I

> Whether Henslowe was a good or a bad man seems to me a matter
> of indifference. He was a capitalist. And my object is to indicate
> the disadvantages under which a company in the hands of a
> capitalist lay, in respect of independence and economic stability,
> as compared with one conducted upon the lines originally laid
> down by the Burbages for the tenants of the Globe.
>
> —E. K. Chambers

In 1923, the year of publication of *The Elizabethan Stage*, the study
of economic history in Britain was in full career, paced by the
writings of W. J. Ashley, whose groundbreaking *Introduction to
English Economic History and Theory* appeared in 1888 and had gone
through four editions by 1906; of J. Thorold Rogers (*The Economic
Interpretation of History*, 1888); of Sidney and Beatrice Webb (*The
History of Trade Unionism*, 1894); of George Unwin (*Industrial Organization in the Sixteenth and Seventeenth Centuries*, 1904, and *The Gilds
and Companies of London*, 1908); and of R. H. Tawney (*The Agrarian
Problem in the Sixteenth Century*, 1912, and *English Economic History:
Select Documents*, 1914, which he helped edit). It was fueled from

---

The epigraphs to sections I, II, and III are from E. K. Chambers, "The Actor's
Economics" (*ES* 1:368); Barry Supple, *Commercial Crisis and Change in England 1600–
1642: A Study in the Instability of a Mercantile Economy* (Cambridge: Cambridge Univer-
sity Press, 1959), p. 2; and Fernand Braudel, *Afterthoughts on Material Civilization and
Capitalism*, trans. from the French by Patricia M. Ranum (Baltimore: Johns Hopkins
University Press, 1977), p. 75.

abroad by the writings of Werner Sombart, whose *Der moderne Kapitalismus* had appeared in 1902; of Max Weber, whose *Die protestantische Ethik und der Geist des Kapitalismus* first appeared in essay form in Germany in 1904 and 1905; and of other scholars published in the *Archiv für Sozialwissenschaft und Sozialpolitik* of which Sombart, Weber, and Edgar Jaffé were the founding editors. The British erected an even more durable monument with the establishment of the London School of Economics in 1895.

The Great War interrupted much of the intellectual discussion generated by this activity, but the questions hung in the air and were taken up again after the armistice. Tawney, perhaps the most visible of the British historians because of his appointment to civic and church committees, brought a vigorous spirit of ethical inquiry to both his public service and his scholarship, soon becoming known as one of the most influential spokesmen for the radical social criticism that came to dominate the Anglican church in the years before and during the war. His later writings followed the same path, leading perhaps inevitably to his celebrated exploration of Christian social thought after the Reformation, *Religion and the Rise of Capitalism*, published in 1926, just three years after the appearance of *The Elizabethan Stage*.

Chambers was busy with his own research while all of this was going on and was probably aware at some level of the intellectual ferment created by the new economics, but he seems to have been generally unmoved by it, or at least uncertain of its relevance to his own scholarship. Set against the large canvases of Weber or Tawney, his own subject must have seemed minuscule and highly particularized. Further, his instincts were agglutinative rather than analytical, his work a tribute more to accumulation than to insight. He probably found the ethical concerns of the Fabians or the Anglican socialists irrelevant to his principal interests, preferring to adopt the stance characterized by Arthur Marwick as "Tory empiricism."

Nonetheless, he was moved to incorporate into his work a chapter he called "The Actor's Economics," perhaps as a gesture toward this emergent school of historical thought. The unease with which he approached the topic, however, is evidenced not only by his reluctance to address it from a perspective congenial to the newly developing economic history of his day but also by his inability to settle on a coherent point of view for his argument.

Chambers opened his discussion of "the actor's economics" with a few observations about prosperity, the actual lot of a few players and the commonly perceived lot of all of them, and consequently the ground of much sixteenth-century ethical and social criticism, not all of it Puritan. He spent little time on this theme, however, apparently preferring to keep social and economic issues in their separate compartments. He quickly moved to a consideration of the relative status of hired men, sharers, and householders and thence, within the first ten pages, to the beginnings of an extended meditation on Philip Henslowe and his account book, which served as his principal text for the remainder of the forty-page chapter.

For Chambers, economics was simply bookkeeping writ large. The takings at the door and from the galleries, the payments for plays and for costumes, the making and collecting of loans, these were the building blocks of his study. The actor's economics and the actor's pocketbook, when seen from this perspective, merged imperceptibly into one another, delimiting each other's horizons and implicitly defining as external those larger economic issues that touched the life of the stage player when offstage, when out of the playhouse, except when the fame and demonstrable prosperity of an Alleyn or a Burbage warranted a digression into such territory. Otherwise, the offstage stage player was lost to view, along with such distant objects as wife and children, hired lodgings, and struggles for solvency, or the social and personal pressures of inflation, of want, of disease, of death. To include such considerations in a study of "economics" would have seemed to Chambers inappropriately sentimental, an unwarranted intrusion of twentieth-century social philosophy into a field of inquiry which must have seemed to him essentially a matter of arithmetic, free of any ideology.

Many of his contemporaries—prodded by Marx, whether persuaded by him or not—had come to feel differently about the role of economic activity in human affairs.[1] For Tawney, as for Unwin, economic history was a branch of moral philosophy, not merely a statistical study of prices and wages through the ages. This view was in the ascendant, and, galvanized by the intense social dislocations of the 1930s, informed a generation of economic historians whose intellectual heirs we may count ourselves to be. From our vantage point, Chambers's stance must seem blinkered and parochial; we

---

[1] "As interest shifted from the constitutional to the social and economic field, so the historical beliefs which act as driving forces are now mainly beliefs about economic history"; so Friedrich Hayek, neither a socialist nor a Marxist, in his *Capitalism and the Historians* (London: Routledge & Kegan Paul, 1954), p. 7.

can best understand it as a viable but rapidly failing position to which one could still adhere in the 1920s, but not much later. Its arguments and conclusions seem today of minimal utility: the major directions in which Chambers pointed his readers in "The Actor's Economics" were to an exploration of the structure of playing companies and the analysis of Henslowe's accounts, arenas in which subsequent scholarship soon overtook both his evidence and his conclusions without enlarging the scope of his inquiry. As a consequence, "The Actor's Economics" is probably the least-read chapter in the least-read volume of *The Elizabethan Stage*. Chambers's narrowed perspective on his subject served to purge it of all life and significance, reducing it to a tallying of pounds and pence, accompanied by an occasional moralizing aside about how the possession of money brings with it arrogance if you are Henslowe, advantage if you are Alleyn, true community if you are the Burbages. The matter was more complex, of course, and Chambers may have been aware at some level that he was not doing it full justice, that his comments were more reductionist than incisive.

We are now many years further down the path that Chambers sought to travel in the 1920s; we have had time to contemplate the landscape, in the company of various kinds of guides, and we have a better sense of where some of the main roads might lead us. In addition, we have far more information about the terrain, and modern technology enables us to configure information in ways Chambers and his colleagues, burdened with their innumerable slips of paper stuffed into envelopes, could only dream of. Despite this progress—if that is the right word—my own inclination is to wonder whether we are, in fact, approaching such matters very much differently than Chambers approached it. I suspect that, in the area of "the actor's economics" at any rate, the accumulated work of almost three generations of theater historians has produced little communal outcry for change.

True, the so-called new historicism in literary studies is characterized by an interest in the economic dimension of literary activity, indeed by a conviction that economics and history and literature are not separable contexts. But the claims of the new historicism did not develop out of the tradition in which Chambers worked, nor do any of its practitioners seem interested in continuing the discourse Chambers tried to start. In spirit the new historicists, and their colleagues the cultural materialists, are nearer to Tawney, and they prefer to espouse, or to contend with, the arguments of such writers as E. J. Hobsbawm, Peter Laslett, Maurice Dobb, or Christopher Hill in England, Marc Bloch, Lucien Febvre, Michel Foucault, or Fernand Braudel in France, Thomas Kuhn in the United States, Norbert Elias in Germany. The important issues for them are centered not on shillings and pence, in the narrow understanding put forth by Chambers, but on notions of subversion and containment, "history from below," *mentalités*, or the models or paradigms or protocols against which, it is claimed, events and their discontinuities can be interpreted. Braudel, an advocate of such models, opens his *Capitalism and Material Life* (1967) with an endorsement of Werner Sombart's 1902 remark, "keine Theorie, keine Geschichte," thereby stressing not only a common lineage but a shared distancing from the earlier Rankean documentary tradition in which "facts" would "speak for themselves."[2]

Chambers, I suspect, would have been appalled by all this. For him, the intrusion of hypotheses, of subjective points of view, into the historian's work would have seemed meddling. His task, as he had learned from Ranke's followers, was not to fictionalize or romanticize the past but simply to discover what had happened and to show the evidence for its having happened. The whole point of his own scholarship was to counter the subjectivity he felt to be the fatal contaminant in the works of Churton Collins, of Collier, of Fleay. His allegiance was to facts and evidence, but the relativist tide was rising even as he wrote; he had taken shelter under the old pieties, but just in time. When he ventured into print again seven years later, with his *William Shakespeare* (1930), some readers claimed that a change of tone, a readier acceptance of intelligent conjecture, was detectable.

It would be idle to speculate how Chambers, if he were alive today, might rewrite his chapter "The Actor's Economics"; in any event, such guesswork has little utility. It is enough, I think—following E. H. Carr's injunction to study the historian before you study the history—simply to suggest the kinds of considerations which led him to deal with the topic as he did. But the topic remains to be addressed.

---

[2] Hayek, who scorned Sombart's socialist bent, nevertheless joined Braudel in agreeing with him on this point: "The idea that one can trace the causal connections of any events without employing a theory, or that such a theory will emerge automatically from the accumulation of a sufficient amount of facts, is of course sheer illusion. The complexity of social events in particular is such that, without the tools of analysis which a systematic theory provides, one is almost bound to misinterpret them" (pp. 23–24).

II

[In England in 1600] the existing technology and the shortage of capital (to name only two of a host of interacting factors) kept standards of living at, or below, a level today associated with underdeveloped or backward economies. Most people would seem to have been employed in supplying the rudimentary wants of a poor society.

—Barry Supple

Earlier I cautioned against the snare of finding parallels in our own society for the contextualizing of sixteenth-century events, but economic comparisons such as Supple's require mediation. Chambers tried his hand at it in *The Elizabethan Stage*: "The purchasing power of money in the seventeenth century," he wrote, "is variously reckoned at from five to eight times as much as at present" (*ES* 1:370). Statements of this kind inevitably have a short usable life; they must constantly be reformulated, and probably should have expiration dates attached to them. Chambers's estimate is now so incorrect as to be dangerous. We know that during the Elizabethan period, when wages were set by parliamentary statute, an unskilled laborer might earn five to six pence a day, a figure that, if extrapolated to six days a week and fifty-two weeks a year (assumptions that imply a state of constant employment, itself a highly dubious premise), will still yield only £6 10s. to £7 16s. per annum. A simpler and likelier figure is a straight £6, to be seen as a kind of bare-minimum annual wage. We need only contemplate the equivalent figures in our own society to realize that the proper multiple is not five to eight times—indeed, I doubt that it was so low even in 1923[3]—but rather more like five hundred to eight hundred times.

Perhaps it is even more; as I write this chapter, entry-level employment in London in such minimally paid categories of unskilled labor as busboys or chambermaids is compensated at the normative rate of £2.80 an hour, or about £125 for a forty-four-hour week, which comes to about £6,500 for a year, presuming constant employment. If this is our own age's minimum wage, it suggests a multiplying factor nearer to a thousand. If in turn we use

---

[3] A decade before the appearance of *The Elizabethan Stage*, Ellis Powell (*The Evolution of the Money Market* [London: The Financial News, 1915], p. 33) reckoned the multiple at about double the figures given by Chambers.

this factor to discover the correlative modern prices of late-sixteenth-century goods, we find that the Elizabethan penny—for which one might have gotten a loaf of bread, a pot of ale, a dozen eggs, or a standing in a playhouse—converts to somewhat more than £4. The two-penny price of a small chicken or a pound of mutton works out to be almost £9; the sixpence that would buy a small quarto, or the attentions of a Bankside prostitute, or a pound of sugar, or one lemon, would come to £25. The First Folio, priced at £1, would today cost £1,000. And so on. The authors of the play *Sir Thomas More*, perhaps chiefly memorable to us for their cutting and pasting, would have understood the four-penny cost of a quire of writing paper, or the seven-shilling cost of a whole ream, as translating into the equivalent of about £2 for three sheets at modern prices. The paper alone in the *Sir Thomas More* manuscript thus represents an investment, in modern terms, of almost £20.[4]

These are startlingly high prices. But it is by now a truism that the Elizabethan age was a period of steady inflation, with prices rising out of all proportion to wages.[5] As early as 1549 John Hales lamented that "wheare xl[s] a yeare was good honest wages for a yeoman afore this tyme . . . nowe double as much will scant beare theire charges";[6] and matters were still worse by Shakespeare's day. The inflation was not uniform, however; it was led by grain and other food prices, which rose more rapidly even than the cost of goods. We now know that a combination of factors caused this rise in food prices, chief among them the pressure of an increasing population upon the means of subsistence.[7] Further, we know that

---

[4]This kind of extrapolation may strike some readers as unjustified; but see, for a modern analogue, the essay "Prices down the years," *The Economist*, 22 December 1990, p. 116.

[5]B. A. Holderness (*Pre-Industrial England: Economy and Society, 1500–1700* [London: J. M. Dent, 1976], p. 204) remarks that "it is not unlikely that real wages declined by 50–60 per cent between 1500–20 and 1590–1630" and, further, that in the latter period "most wage-incomes were often at or below subsistence level" for they "reflected local supplies of labour, not the prevailing price of food and clothing." For a comprehensive survey of these matters as they relate to London, see chapter 5 of Steve Rappaport's *Worlds within Worlds: Structures of Life in Sixteenth-Century London* (Cambridge: Cambridge University Press, 1989).

[6]John Hales, *A Discourse of the Common Weal of this Realm of England*, cited in R. H. Tawney and Eileen Power, *Tudor Economic Documents* (London: Longmans, 1924), 3: 307.

[7]Some people were aware of this even at the time: Richard Hakluyt advocated colonization as a way to relieve the pressure because "wee are growen more populous than euer heretofore" (*A Discourse Concerning Western Planting* [ms., 1584], ed. Charles Deane [Cambridge, Mass.: John Wilson, 1877], p. 37).

this increase was caused by a variety of factors, even, as some have suggested, by such imponderables as the dissolution of the monasteries and the abolition of clerical celibacy, actions that enlarged the size of the marriageable population by some percentage points within a few years and thus produced its own small increment to the birthrate a generation later. But this curious change in the social fabric went largely unremarked in its own time; other issues, more highly visible and more socially charged, presented themselves as likelier targets for blame. It had been fashionable, even in Chambers's day, to echo the popular sentiment of the age itself and to blame the high price of grain on the human wickedness and greed that led to enclosures, then to the evil practices of forestalling and regrating. Oblique references to these social ills can be found scattered through the drama of the period, testimony more to how things seemed than to how they were.[8] Tawney's study of the agrarian problem provided our own age with a clearer view of these matters, but the urge to find a moral rather than a statistical cause for secular events is still strong. What was crystal clear to the Elizabethan mind was that the times were hard, that some sort of poverty was a norm, and that under such circumstances honest labor was more deserving of reward than the various kinds of parasitism evident in the land. One did not have to be a Puritan to hold such views.

Unfortunately, some of the most grievous social abuses were no more than the characteristic behavior of persons in high places, and therefore largely immune from attack because of the stringent penalties (slit ears and noses if not worse) visited on imprudent moralists who chose to inveigh against such targets. At the other extreme, few segments of society were at once so accessible for derogation and so seemingly deserving of it as were stage players. In our own age the professional athlete occupies much the same morally ambiguous position, his prosperity seeming out of all proportion to his social worth or in some cases even to his individual desert, and quite unrelated as well to the generally acknowledged aims and goals of our society, except by recourse to pieties about character building; nonetheless, we rush to watch him display his skills. "I speake not howe little pollicie it is to suffer so muche mony to be so ill spente, whiche might be employed to better uses," said John Stockwood in 1578, speaking of the earnings of stage players.

---

[8] "The evidence on land enclosed for sheep farming shows it to have been small in extent and regionally localized"; so D. C. Coleman, *The Economy of England, 1450–1750* (London: Oxford University Press, 1977), p. 35.

Stockwood, preaching at Paul's Cross, attacked stage plays not on moral but on social grounds: at a time when there was so little money to go round, and so much clear need for it to be spent wisely, spending it at the playhouse was wasting it, "the suffering of whiche waste muste one daye be answered before God."[9]

Other voices sounded the same note of social concern. An unknown correspondent wrote to Sir Francis Walsingham in 1587 that "yt is A wofull sight to see two hundred proude players iett in theire silkes wheare fyve hundred pore people sterve in the Streat*es*";[10] and Samuel Cox, Sir Christopher Hatton's personal secretary, wondered that "we should suffer men to make professions & occupacions of playes all the yere longe, whereby to enryche idle loyterers wth plenty, whyle many of our poore brethren lye pitifully gasping in the streates, ready to starue & dye."[11]

All these remarks follow the same rhetorical path, so much so that it is difficult to tell whether we are in the presence of genuinely felt moral indignation or merely witnesses to the exercise of a conventional literary *topos* about the inequitable distribution of the world's goods. But if the motives of these writers are unclear, their premises are straightforward enough: they not only shared the common perception that such inequity prevailed but argued (as later socialists would also argue) that its roots lay largely in the greed or at least the deficient social awareness of the economically better favored. Once the sufferings of the deprived could be seen as caused, at least in part, by the attitudes and practices of a more favored group—rather than as merely being a result of God's will or of their own lack of merit—then the prosperous group could be targeted for vilification. Attacks on landlords, on cloth merchants, on foreign artisans, on moneylenders, on stage players, can all be found in the period. Whether a later age of economic historians would see the grounds for these attacks as sophisticated or simplistic is beside the point. Cox's starving wretches may or may not have been a consequence of capitalism, but the rhetorical force of these arguments created a psychological beachhead in the ideology of the age, and their

[9] John Stockwood, *A sermon preached at Paules Crosse on Barthelmew day, being the .24. of August 1578* (STC 23284), p. 137.

[10] BL, ms. Harl, 286, fo. 102[r]. The letter is excerpted, and mistranscribed in places, in *ES* 4:303–4.

[11] Cox's letter, written in 1591 to an unknown recipient, is one of a collection of letters formerly belonging to the Hatton family, now in the British Library [ms. Add. 15,891, ff. 184[r]-85[v]]. This extract is from fo. 184[v]. The letter is summarized in *ES* 4:237. See also Chapter 1, n. 4, above.

premises became truths to the extent that men believed them and acted on them.

Chambers found the attacks on stage players interesting enough that he took their prosperity, or at least the common clichés about it, as the starting point for his chapter; but he quickly slid off onto less controversial matters. He declined, for example, to pick up on the provocative comment of Henry Crosse in 1603 that "these copper-lace gentlemen" the stage players not only "growe rich" and "purchase lands by adulterous Playes" but also that "not fewe of them" were "vsurers and extortioners."[12] In Chambers's day such a comment would have seemed jarring and discordant, at odds with his age's sense of Shakespeare's fellows as objects of admiration, and thus easy to dismiss as vituperative or merely misguided; today we struggle, though not always successfully, to extend more tolerance and credit to such texts. We know, for example (as Chambers did not), that James Burbage and his brother-in-law John Brayne were engaged in moneylending as early as the late 1560s, concurrent with their involvement in the Red Lion playhouse.[13] And E. A. J. Honigmann has recently raised the interesting possibility that Shakespeare himself may have engaged in moneylending, but his inquiry has generated the predictable raised eyebrows. Some readings of the evidence are apparently still deemed inappropriate.[14]

I imagine that in our own day anyone addressing the topic of the stage player's economics would have to deal more fully with popular perceptions of stage players, or with the articulation of those perceptions in the various attacks on, and defenses of, their way of earning a living. We have long been familiar with the antitheatrical statements of the period and have gotten into the habit of dismissing them as products of the religious right, as the splenetic rantings of an intolerant and dyspeptic Puritan minority (or of opportunist professional writers exploiting the market). Only lately have we come to see that this view, too, is reductionist and that complaints against stage players and their supposed prosperity were motivated by concerns at both ends of the ethical and political spectrum. Some of the more articulate grievances were centered on

---

[12] Henry Crosse, *Vertues Commonwealth: or, The high-way to honour*, sig. Q1ʳ. The text is excerpted in *ES* 4: 247.

[13] For a loan of £60 made to Richard Dycher in 1568, see PRO, K.B.27/1229, memb. 136.

[14] E. A. J. Honigmann, *Shakespeare's Impact on His Contemporaries* (London: Macmillan, 1982), chap. 1.

social rather than doctrinal issues, were economically grounded, empathetic to the poor and dispossessed, and identifiable with sentiments that in our own time might be called leftist or liberal.

Of course there *were* attacks from the religious right; the earliest of them drew formulaically and impartially from both classical writers and church fathers, and their rhetoric constructed a stage player who was dissolute (Bavande, 1559), dishonest and wicked (Agrippa, 1569), infamous and blasphemous (Fenton, 1574), filthy and fleshly (Northbrooke, 1577), a dissembling hypocrite and a painted sepulcher (Stubbes, 1583). John Northbrooke, though early introducing the argument from cash, couched it in moral rather than social terms; in his view, giving money to stage players "is right prodigalitie, which is opposite to liberalitie . . . for the which no great fame or memory can remayne to the spenders or receyuers thereof."[15]

The impoverished masses themselves, the principal concern of the more socially oriented polemicists, fared poorly at the hands of the religious right. Crosse wrote of the "many poore pincht, needie creatures, that liue of almes, and that haue scarse neither cloath to their backe, nor foode for the belley, yet will make hard shift but they will see a Play, let wife & children begge, languish in penurie, and all they can rappe and rend, is little inough to lay vpon such vanitie."[16] That such people, rather than join with their betters in the condemnation of stage players, should actually want to patronize the plays was sufficient proof to Crosse and his fellows that the poor were morally little better than those who were the causers of their misery. In the midst of these ad hominem excoriations of wretched and prosperous alike, one comes with relief upon Stephen Gosson's temperate comment about stage players that "it is well knowen, that some of them are sober, discreete, properly learned honest housholders and Citizens well thought on amonge their neighbours at home, though . . . somewhat il talked of abroade."[17]

Subsequent defenders of stage players followed the path indicated by Gosson. They addressed the attacks of the religious polemicists by taking the moral high ground, refuting the charges of immorality

---

[15] John Northbrooke, *A Treatise wherein Dicing, Dancing, vain Plays or Interludes, with other idle Pastimes, etc., . . . are reproved . . .* (1577), p. 58. The standard text for this argument, to be cited again and again in the antitheatrical tracts, was a remark attributed to St. Augustine, *pecunias histrionibus dare, vitium est immane, non virtus* (to give money to players is a grievous sin, and no virtue). For Bavande, Agrippa, Fenton, Stubbes, et al., see *ES* 4:190ff.

[16] Crosse, sig. Q1ᵛ.

[17] Stephen Gosson, *The School of Abuse* (1579), fo. C6ʳ⁻ᵛ.

and licentiousness by arguing that the calling was virtuous, educative, and of service to the state. By contrast, the charges of the social critics—that stage players, in their prosperity, were not only insensitive to social problems but were in part one of the causes of those problems—remained unanswered. It would have been particularly difficult to refute the charges of prosperity; its opposite, want, was not a Calvinist virtue and thus hard to defend; and mere denial of prosperity would have carried little suasive force. It certainly carried none for Cuthbert Burbage in 1635, when certain members of the king's company petitioned the lord chamberlain to be admitted to shares as housekeepers in the profits of the Globe and the Blackfriars. Burbage, arguing against their claim, was hobbled in his response by the inadequacy of his rhetoric to the task of making himself into a pauper. His only defense was to rehearse "the infinite Charges, the. manifold lawsuit*es*," and so on, "that did cutt from them [i.e., himself and the other householders] the best part of the gaines that y^r hono^r is informed they haue receaued." He recounted how his father, James, had built the Theater in Shoreditch "wth many Hundred pound*es* taken vp at interest" and how he and his brother Richard "at like expence built the Globe, wth more summes of money taken vp at interest, which lay heauy on vs many yeares." He recounted also how their father had purchased Blackfriars "at extreame rates, & made it into a playhouse wth great charge and troble." Continuing at some length in the same plangent vein, he urged the lord chamberlain to deny the request of the petitioners so that he and his fellow householders would "not further bee trampled vpon then their estates can beare, seeing how deerly it hath beene purchased by the infinite cost & paynes of the family of the Burbages"; for (he added in a fit of excess) "it is onely wee that suffer continually."[18]

Cuthbert's appropriation of the rhetoric of despair was a clumsy effort, reminiscent of his father's earlier posturings. It was, finally, unsuccessful, for Cuthbert could not persuasively relocate himself in the moral terrain formerly held by Cox's starving wretches. But his paradigm was the same; like them, he too wanted to be seen as a victim of the avarice of stage players. And Cuthbert found it relatively easy to document the immoderate prosperity of the players who were complaining against him: during the previous twelve months, he pointed out, "each of these compl^{tes} gained

[18] The so-called Sharers' Papers, PRO, L.C.5/133, pp. 50, 51.

seuerally as hee was a Player & noe Howskeeper, 180^{li}, Besides Mr Swanston hath receaued from the Blackfriers this yeere as hee is there a Houskeeper above 30^{li}, all which being accompted together may very well keepe him from starveing."[19] But neither Cuthbert's reckonings nor his acerbic conclusion had the desired effect on the lord chamberlain, who found him and his fellows to be in even less danger than their colleague Swanston of starving. He decreed in favor of the petitioners and against the Burbages. The ghosts of Stockwood, Cox and the rest would have applauded his action.

The ghost of the unscrupulous James Burbage, however, must have groaned in Senecan anguish at this posthumous rapine of his estate. Cuthbert had no doubt inherited some of his father's acquisitive instincts and upwardly mobile aspirations—he had early attached himself to the household of Sir Walter Cope, and thus by extension to Lord Burghley—but he may have lacked the tradesman's cunning and street wisdom that James seemed to possess in abundance. A man not esteemed for uprightness and probity even among his friends, James Burbage had been heard to say, when taxed for his unconscionable behavior, "that he cared not a tord for Conscience."[20] He had been charged in his own day with everything from fraud to horse theft[21] and would have served as a useful model for an antitheatrical polemicist of either persuasion. When caught pilfering money from the collection box at the Theater, he had replied, with calculated remorse, that "it was the Deuill that led him so to do."[22] This response did not persuade his hearers, who saw in it only a self-serving attempt to plead inadequacy against the force of external confusions. This is not to say that a more modern explanatory platitude, such as "the capitalist system drove him to it"—positing a penniless James Burbage redressing his own poverty by redistributing some of the income of his partner John Brayne, —would be any more helpful. The desire of Swanston and his fellows to redistribute Cuthbert's income a half century and more later makes for a pleasant symmetry, though the forces underlying both such urges may elicit varying responses among us.

The fact is that sixteenth-century Londoners in great numbers were pushed by the profit motive into maximizing their incomes.

---

[19] Sharers' Papers, p. 51.
[20] PRO, C.24/221/12, the interrogatory; see C. W. Wallace, "The First London Theatre: Materials for a History," *Nebraska University Studies* 13 (1913), 58.
[21] For the horse theft, see PRO, C.24/239/11.
[22] PRO, C.24/226/11; see Wallace, p. 143.

The rhetoric of the age afforded them few nonderogatory labels for their activity; the term "profit motive" itself was still in the future. Some of them found a post-hoc justification for their behavior in the Calvinist approbation of prosperity; others found the activity to be its own reward. A contemporary centrist view (encapsulated in Ben Jonson's *Alchemist* and *Bartholomew Fair*) was that all of them, whatever their stance, had their integrity compromised or distorted in the process. Perhaps, if we may credit Honigmann or the tradition of the Stratford tithes, not even Shakespeare's soul survived the pressures intact.

The temptation to draw parallels with our own age is strong, and should be resisted. The means and extremes of economic behavior in the later sixteenth century were of a different order from those we are accustomed to today, even though our own system produces televangelists and arbitrageurs not unlike their predecessors in Jonsonian absurdity or greed. Free trade, the principal pillar of urban prosperity in Shakespeare's and Jonson's day, was still an equivocal activity, a new and not fully understood way of marketing—indeed, of living—centered on money and profits, yet still partially engrafted onto an older, essentially feudal system whose structures of kinship and service were largely intact, though hopelessly inadequate to the new burden. The cart was pulling the horse, and confusion was inevitable. John Wheeler attempted in 1601 to subsume metaphysics into economics ("all that a man worketh with his hand, or discourseth in his spirit, is nothing els but merchandise"),[23] making the disjunction even more evident. The resistance of groups and of individuals to the pressures of the new urban ethos, to the imposition of protocapitalist modes of thought and behavior, gave rise to various intolerances, of stage players as well as of cloth merchants, which today have largely disappeared from our consciousness.

Tawney believed that the Englishmen of the sixteenth and seventeenth centuries had left, in their responses to the clash between traditional views on social justice and newer notions of economic expediency, an important legacy of ideas which the economic historians of his own generation needed to explore. For Tawney, newly emergent capitalism "involved a code of economic conduct and a system of human relations which were sharply at variance

---

[23] John Wheeler, *A Treatise of Commerce* (STC 25330), p. 7; see also Marc Shell, *Money, Language, and Thought* (Berkeley: University of California Press, 1982), p. 179.

with venerable conventions, with the accepted scheme of social ethics, and with the law, both of the church and of most European states. So questionable an innovation demanded of the pioneers who first experimented with it as much originality, self-confidence, and tenacity of purpose as is required to-day of those who would break from the net that it has woven."[24]

Unlike the new urban morality, however, the feudal structures inherited by the Elizabethan Londoner placed little value on "originality, self-confidence, and tenacity of purpose"; the *Mirror for Magistrates* and Jacobean tragedy alike are filled with portraits of people who ended badly as a consequence of manifesting those very qualities. But though we know these things about the literature and the drama, we know less than we would like to know about how stage players, the abstract and brief chronicles of the time, were themselves affected by such issues. We should try to understand— better than Chambers did, or wished to—how the stage player, as free entrepreneur, was caught up in the clash of these attitudes, finding himself both used and abused, and how these circumstances shaped his sense of himself and of his calling. Walsingham's anonymous correspondent cited above, after having made his obligatory declaration that plays were abominations, turned deftly from moralist to pragmatist, allowing that "yf needes this misschef must be tollorated" then "lett every Stage in London pay a weekely pention to the poore, that *ex hoc malo, proueniat aliquod bonum.*"[25] These two arguments, of denunciation and exploitation, ought to have sat uncomfortably beside each other, yet they cohabited without difficulty in the new rhetoric of accommodation, itself a byproduct of the new economics of urban marketing.

The churchwardens of St. Saviour's parish, on the Bankside, had early found themselves caught in the same dilemma. They regularly assessed the playhouses in their jurisdiction for tithes for the poor, and their minutes show a continuing vacillation between the conflicting desires to be rid of the abomination in their midst and to hang on to the income. And in 1600, in the face of actual or anticipated opposition to the erection of the Fortune playhouse, some Finsbury

[24] R. H. Tawney, from "Max Weber and the Spirit of Capitalism" (1930), reprinted in *History and Society: Essays by R. H. Tawney,* ed. J. M. Winter (London: Routledge & Kegan Paul, 1978), p. 190.

[25] The writer of this letter seems not to have known that, over a decade earlier, the Common Council of the City of London had enacted just such a levy on stage plays. For a fuller discussion of this, see Chapter 5 below.

inhabitants petitioned the Privy Council that construction of the playhouse should be allowed to proceed, not only because it would be sited "neere vnto the Feildes" and thus not a trouble to the residents, but also because the builders "are contented to give a very liberall porcion of money weekelie, towardes the releef of our Poore."[26] Stage playing, like usury itself, was too scandalous to be tolerated and too useful to be suppressed. And stage players, regular contributors (like all Elizabethans) to tithes, subsidies, and other assessments and sometimes even "sober, discreete, properly learned honest housholders" as Gosson had characterized them, could hardly have enjoyed being cast by their neighbors in the simultaneous roles of responsible ratepayers and dissembling hypocrites, good citizens and painted sepulchers. Because we are not accustomed to being vilified in our profession of academic, or of having our publications or our lectures denounced as ungodly, or of having public attention invited to our pride, our prosperity, our dissolute wickedness, or our infamous fleshliness, we perhaps are insufficiently attentive to the cumulative psychological pressures that the attacks from both right and left must finally have brought to bear on the social attitudes of the players themselves, and thus by extension—because social issues and economic issues are not easily separated—upon "the stage player's economics." Crosse thought (fo. Q1^r) that "a Play is like a sincke in a Towne, wherevnto all the filth doth runne"—a strong and vivid image that, if applied frequently enough to our own teaching and lecturing, might well upset us, perhaps even affect our teaching and lecturing.[27] Did Shakespeare laugh off such diatribes?

But it will be objected that an answer to all such questions is properly to be found in the plays themselves and not in tangential inquiries about social and economic conditions. This was surely Chambers's own sense of the matter, and I suspect that it is still the prevailing view. The plays are our central concern, and the rest— playhouses, players, the larger social matrix—is context. Chambers could hardly have known that the very notions of text and context would soon be called into question; in our own day, critical theorists not only are uncomfortable about the isolating of text from context, they even resist the notion that such isolation is possible. For them,

---

[26] Greg, p. 50; *ES* 4:327.

[27] The expression is conventional, though nonetheless forceful for that; in Thomas Dekker's *1 Honest Whore* (1604), Hippolito tells Bellafront that her body "is like the common shore [i.e., sewer] that still receives all the town's filth."

the bird in the hand is a distortion, the bird in the bush your only true subject of study. Literary texts, they argue, are not only contexts for, but also influences on, other aspects of cultural and material life. This is not a new notion: Plato, who also believed it, banished poets from his ideal state. The antitheatrical polemicists of Elizabeth's time, working from the same premises, hoped for a similar power in their own writings, intended as instrumental in the proper shaping of social attitudes and thus of society itself. Their arguments were consciously dependent on the strategy of isolating and emphasizing moral and religious factors at the expense of a larger and more comprehensive view. Their implicit invitation to their readers was (in Hayden White's phrase) to look at the complex and see only the simple.

The literary attacks on stage players, and the actual lives of stage players, should in this view form two sets of "texts" whose points of congruency and opposition, when held in balance, may provide the occasion for a more rewarding study than would a concentration on either set by itself, with the other employed merely for validation, for "context." The latter course will make for a seemingly easy demonstration of whatever we wish to prove, but the proofs will be partial. In such cases, as Dominick LaCapra points out, "what is often taken as a solution to the problem should be reformulated and investigated as a real problem itself. An appeal to the context does not *eo ipso* answer all questions in reading and interpretation. And an appeal to *the* context is deceptive: one never has—at least in the case of complex texts—*the* context. The assumption that one does relies on a hypostatization of 'context,' often in the service of misleading organic or other overly reductive analogies."[28]

Unfortunately, the very notion of context is often a chimera in our study of the lives of stage players, the chief obstacle to any extended analysis being the deficiency of hard evidence about them, except for such prominent figures as Edward Alleyn or the Burbages, who are hardly representative. Stage players were not, on the whole, very litigious, though this ought not be construed as an argument for their general decorousness or civility; it means merely that they were not frequently involved in lawsuits, those best kinds of documents for the theater historian. Indeed, for most of them, little of substance is currently known, though a fair number of accidentals

---

[28] Dominick LaCapra, *Rethinking Intellectual History: Texts, Contexts, Language* (Ithaca: Cornell University Press, 1983), p. 35.

survive, providing bare evidentiary details shorn of perspective. Even an accumulation of such details is often insufficient to afford us any real sense of certain players as individuals. Often we have, at best, a sense of identifiable lives that were lived, yet seem uninhabited by real people. On rare occasions, however, we are allowed a glimpse of something richer and more ambiguous, full of the qualities of a good text. In the next section I discuss two such instances.

III

> Capitalism does not invent hierarchies, any more than it invented
> the market, or production, or consumption; it merely uses them.
> —Fernand Braudel

Early in his chapter "The Actor's Economics," in one of his infrequent ad hominem musings, Chambers offered an interesting explanation for the varying degrees of prosperity of different players. "Doubtless," he speculated, "there is a certain instability of temperament, which the life of the theatre, with its ups and downs of fortune, its unreal sentiments and its artificially stimulated emotions, is well calculated to encourage." One cannot help but wonder if Chambers penned these lines without noticing how they shared certain underlying premises with the more strident claims of the antitheatrical pamphleteers. Continuing his speculation, he wondered if "we may perhaps find the victims of such a temperament in certain actors who, although clearly of standing in their profession, seem to have been constantly shifting from company to company, without attaining any secure position or, as one may conjecture, reaping any substantial harvest from their labour and their skill." In support of this thesis, Chambers offered hasty thumbnail sketches of the careers of Richard Jones and Martin Slater and concluded by suggesting that "perhaps it is merely another way of stating the same issue to say that the financial success of a player depended on his obtaining an interest, not merely in the day-to-day profits of a company, but also in the permanent investment represented by a theatre."[29]

[29] *ES* 1:349–50.

Having thus linked, in his reader's mind, the two notions of temperamental instability and failure to become a sharer—in a fashion that would have joyed the heart of Cuthbert Burbage—Chambers found it easy to take up the conservative vantage point from which he would explore the relative fortunes of sharers and nonsharers. His ensuing discussion, ostensibly of economics but actually of ethics (a conjunction that Tawney would have approved), unfortunately led him to undertake not an inclusive overview of a complex set of issues but rather a narrow consideration of the respective virtues of the Henslowe autocracy at the Rose and the Burbage fellowship at the Globe. Chambers's own affinities are not difficult to discover in his discussion; the epigraph that opens this chapter, while in the form of a disclaimer, makes his position clear.

As disclaimers of my own I ought to state that I have no argument with one who prefers the Burbage model to the Henslowe model; nor do I mean to suggest that the calling of stage player had less than its fair share of persons of unstable temperament. But any picture drawn solely along those lines is incomplete. We know enough about Henslowe as a pawnbroker, about James Burbage as an owner of a livery stable, about Andrew Cane as a working goldsmith, about Martin Slater as an ironmonger, about Richard Tarlton as an innkeeper, and so on, to know that not all stage players or others connected with playhouses looked to stage playing as their sole source of income. Supplementary earnings might be generated in a variety of ways, from participation in recognized trades to the darker shores of usury and fraud. Some players, Tarlton and Robert Wilson among the earliest, even went home and wrote playscripts. The moral is simply that the offstage player cannot be ignored in considering the economics of the onstage player. All the world's a stage, as one playwright of the age remarked; my unpoetic corollary is that *homo economicus*—a character periodically discredited in our own day—was not a minor or negligible role played on that stage by him and his fellows. Depending on one's sense of the script, such a role might be variously seen as motivated by materialist concerns or shaped by their absence, governed by either abhorrence or acceptance of poverty, a compassion for others or a selfish need to exploit, a varying level of involvement in a market economy, the presence or absence of entrepreneurial proclivities, or simply an interest in the acquisition of, or the benefits of, wealth. Any of these readings may be apposite to the following account of the life of John Garland.

Garland was a well-known Elizabethan stage player; he had been chosen as one of the original members of the queen's company in

1583, and remained with them well into their twilight in the later 1590s. After the death of the queen in 1603 he (and perhaps the remainder of his company as well) played under the patronage of the duke of Lennox, and subsequently with Prince Charles's players. He was still active in playing in 1615, when the prince's men visited Norwich. Garland was named in the town records on that occasion as one of the principal players of the company. This much can be learned from any potted biography of Garland, such as those found in Chambers or Edwin Nungezer; these few details have been known for many years. They are not much to build on.

In an undated entry, perhaps from 1604, Henslowe noted in his *Diary* that his nephew Francis Henslowe was a member of the duke of Lennox's company along with "owld garlland," Abraham Saverey, and one Symcockes;[30] and in 1605 the same Saverey granted Francis Henslowe power of attorney to recover £40 from John Garland "of the ould forde" on a defaulted bond.[31] Henslowe's epithet "owld" in the first item is curious. Garland was probably no older than Henslowe; indeed, he may have been younger, for he was still having children ten years after Henslowe made his entry. Henslowe may have had the "old" of Old Ford in mind as he wrote. The reference to Old Ford in Saverey's document has been, until now, our only indication that Garland lived anywhere other than in London or on the Bankside.

Old Ford is near Hackney Marsh, some three miles east and north of London Bridge, certainly a rural setting and far removed from the daily activity of players and playhouses. Why was Garland living there in 1604? Had he gone into temporary retirement on the death of Elizabeth? These appear to be reasonable enough questions; we know where a great many players lived during their active lives, and they invariably lived in the city or on the Bankside in order to be near the playhouses. If Garland—especially if he is "owld" Garland— was living at Old Ford, he may well have withdrawn there to rusticate.

We come to such conclusions on the most reasonable of grounds. It is salutary, therefore, to find that on occasion we can be wrong. Evidence that we are wrong in this case is provided by an original document in the keeping of the Stepney Central Library, and there known as Deed no. 5; it is an indenture of agreement to levy a fine in

---

[30] *Diary*, p. 194.
[31] Greg, p. 62.

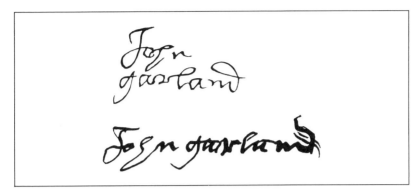

Figure 1. The signatures of John Garland. *Above,* John Garland the yeoman of Stratford at Bow, 1 March 1590 [Stepney Central Library, Deed no. 5]. *Below,* John Garland the stage player, from his will, 10 September 1624 [GHL, Commissary Court, Original Wills 9172/34, item 328].

the Court of Common Pleas in the conclusion of several transactions by which one Thomas Shaa of Ealing, Essex,[32] sold various pieces of land to five others. The indenture is dated 1 March 1589/90, and one of the parties is "John Garland of Stratford at Bowe in the County of Midd' yoman." The indenture bears the signatures of all the parties, including Garland's (see Figure 1).[33]

Here we find not only that John Garland had purchased his Old Ford holding while still in his prime as a player—while he was still playing with the queen's men—but that even at this time he was living not in London or in Southwark but at Stratford Bow, a village neighboring to Old Ford. Garland's purchase was described in detail in the document: "the said John Garland hath purchased to him and his heires one Close of Land and pasture wth thap*pur*tenaunc*es* in or neere the Hamlett of Olde foarde in the *pa*rishe aforesaid [i.e., of Stebunhythe or Stepney] conteyning by estimac*ion* ffyve Acres." No sale price is mentioned in the document, but that Garland's resources were evidently equal to the purchase suggests that he was no

---

[32] Ealing is (and was) of course in Middlesex; the scrivener (or more likely the scrivener's apprentice) who prepared the document made an error. Such document-able slips of the pen teach us to be on our guard against other, less readily demonstrable, errors, such as faulty dates or wrong names, that scriveners (or even bishops' clerks) may be equally prone to.

[33] This signature matches the signature on his will; see Figure 1.

impoverished vagabond. His desire to live outside the City, even at the height of his success as a queen's player, may suggest other things about him as well, and we take the first steps toward inventing his personality if we pursue such a tack.

Other kinds of evidence invite us to run the same risk. The great plague of 1593–1594 was a major dislocation in the lives of playing companies; forced into provincial touring, many of them went bankrupt, others were forced to reorganize, and when the pestilence subsided most of the old fellowships were in disarray. Garland elected to remain with the queen's players in 1595, at a time when other of his fellows apparently found it prudent to relocate elsewhere; in the same year the queen granted him an annuity for his natural life of two shillings per day, payable quarterly.[34] This is a generous award, amounting to some £35 per year; a man might live quite comfortably in Old Ford, or indeed wherever he liked, on such a sum. Was the annuity a reward for Garland's freely declared allegiance, or was it the price he exacted for his continued membership? Whatever mental picture we are forming of him might lead us to either of those choices, or to others in between.

Having established that Garland lived in Stratford Bow and Old Ford, we can turn to the appropriate parish registers for more information. Old Ford was only a hamlet, and lay within the bounds of Stratford Bow parish; fortunately, the registers of St. Mary's Church at Stratford Bow have survived from 1538, and the earliest of them[35] contains a few relevant entries. A burial is recorded on 16 June 1598 of "Elizabeth Smith widdow a Poore wooman travelling By pasporte from Whitchappell to Ipswich" who "here died in ye house or Barne of John Garland." Such entries of wayfaring deaths are not at all unusual in this period.[36] "Elizabeth ffeilder servant to m^r Garland of old ford" was buried on 25 September 1603 of "Plauge," perhaps a consequence of her having journeyed unwisely into the City a few days earlier at the height of the severe pestilence of that year. No evidence suggests that the plague itself had reached

---

[34] PRO, C.66/1426, memb. 35.

[35] GLRO, ms. P88/MRY1/1; subsequent citations of christenings, marriages, and burials at St. Mary's are from this register.

[36] Deaths by misadventure appear as well, suggesting some of the hazards of country life. "William Garland and John Evans both of Whitchappell Glovers servant*es* to William Nipinge of the same & were Drowned betweene Oldforde & Bowe the 4th day of June & Buried the 6th day of June 1628"; four years later, in 1632, "William Kempe of St Marie Matfellon als Whitchappell was Drowned att ye Oldford."

as far east as Old Ford or that any other member of the Garland household was afflicted.

A probate document from five years later, in 1608, provides us with evidence about what must be the most curious circumstance to have survived about John Garland. He was apparently touring with Lennox's company in the autumn of that year when his wife, for reasons unknown, determined that he had died—or perhaps only determined to assert that he had died. She applied for, and was granted, letters of administration from the Commissary Court of the bishop of London. Subsequent testimony before the court by one Joan Stephens, a poulter's wife, established that Garland was not dead after all but was playing in the provinces, and the letters were withdrawn.[37] Elizabeth Garland's motives in all this are lost to us, as is any clue about the role Joan Stephens played in the story, but the range of possibilities is rich, and tempting as well.

A patent for the already-active Prince Charles's company was formally issued on 30 March 1610, under the name of the duke of York's players, licensing "Iohn Garland Willyam Rowley Thomas Hobbes Robert Dawes Ioseph Taylor Iohn Newton and Gilbert Reason . . . with the rest of their company to vse and exercise the arte and quality of playing Comedyes, Tragedies, histories, Enterludes, Moralles, Pastoralles, Stagplayes, and such other like as they haue already studdied or hereafter shall studye or vse" (*ES* 2:242).

Four years after Garland's false death, on 26 February 1612, a genuine death occurred in the family. "Elizabeth Garland wife of John Garland Player was buried in ye Church in ye south Allie." The parish clerk, like James Tunstall's parish clerk a stickler for detail, provided (as was apparently his habit) this fascinating addendum about the placement of the body in the grave: "[her] feate came a littell past thend of ye Pewes towards ye Pulpit." A compulsive concern with the allocation of mortal space, perhaps; no doubt such annotation was useful when room for a new grave needed to be found, but I have not seen this kind of interest in burial details manifested by any other parish clerk of the period.

---

[37] GHL, ms. 9168/16, fo. 73v. "Vicesimo septimo die *[of September 1608]* emanauit Commissio Elizabethe Garland relicte Johannis Garland dum vixit de Stratford Bowe in Comitatu Middlesex abintestati defuncti." In the margin: "comparuit Joanna Stephens uxor Johannis Stephens in Gracious street poulter et allegavit dictum Garland iam mora gerere in partibus extranijs et ideo introducte sunt littere &c." A further marginal note reads "vacat quia vivit."

We might presume that an appropriate period of mourning ensued. There is no record of children baptized from this first marriage, so Garland may have experienced a solitary bereavement. Two years later, in 1614, he journeyed to Mile End to take another wife. "John Garland of Stratford bowe gent & Marye Miller of the same" were married on 17 October 1614 in St. Dunstan's Church.[38] It is not clear why the journey was felt to be necessary, or why they did not want to be married in their own parish church. We might allow such behavior to arouse our suspicions, but this temptation may merely lead us to more inventing. Garland must have been, by this time, at least fifty years old, perhaps more. Who was Mary Miller? The parish clerk at St. Dunstan's was usually quite responsible about entering "widow" against the names of women marrying for a second time; no such entry appears against Mary Miller's name. Perhaps he simply didn't know; after all, she was a stranger. But this may well have been her first marriage; as she began bearing children shortly after the wedding, she was likely a good many years younger than her new husband. We might speculate on that as well, if only to reveal our biases.

The Garlands returned to Old Ford to live, and in the following spring John Garland went on tour with his company, the prince's players. On 29 October 1615 "John Garland sonne of John Garland yeoman & marie his wife" was christened in the Stratford Bow church. But his was a short life; the parish clerk recorded fifteen months later that "John Garland sonne of John Garland Player & Marie his wife was Buried the 28th day of January in ye South Allie whose head doth lie att ye vpper end of ye stone & his ffeeate doth reach with in 2 feete of the Pewes." John Garland seems to have given over his trade of stage player at about this time, possibly motivated by his son's death; an agreement between the prince's company and the Alleyn-Meade syndicate from this period does not include his name.

A year after the burial of the son, in 1618, "Elizabeth Garland daughter of John Garland yeoman & Marie his wife" was christened. Unlike her brother, Elizabeth survived infancy; but this was the last child of which we have a record. Six years after Elizabeth's birth, on 19 September 1624—having lived through probably all of Queen Elizabeth's reign and nearly all of King James's—John Garland

---

[38] GLRO, ms. P93/DUN/265.

himself died. In his will, dated 10 September 1624,[39] he described himself as "John Garland of Stratford Bowe in the County of Midds gent" and asked to be "decentlie Buried in the Chappell of Stratford Bowe so neare my wife [i.e., his first wife Elizabeth] as may best be done"; he left "vnto Marie my wife" several parcels of land, at Stratford Bow, at Old Ford, at Mile End, and elsewhere, properties suggesting that he was a man of some substance at his death; he made bequests to his six-year-old daughter, Elizabeth, to be paid when she was eighteen, and to "John Garland of Burnt Wood [i.e., Brentwood] in the County of Essex Gardener." The two witnesses to the will signed themselves as "Thomas Skoryer" and "Walter Hutchinson." No other persons are named in the will; most conspicuously, no references are made to the players with whom Garland had spent all his working life. Such an omission might well lead us to wonder if this was indeed John Garland the player; the matter is resolved for us by the burial entry in the Stratford Bow parish register: "John Garland gent being a Player was Buried in the Church whose feate reacheth to y[e] second pillor one y[e] South side close to y[e] wall & so deepe y[t] one may be laied vppon him vppon y[e] 19th day of September." The entry evokes resonances from the gravedigger's scene in *Hamlet*, and from Shakespeare's own epitaph as well. Life and art are here inextricably mingled.

These, then, are the bare bones of a biography, or of a variety of biographies—little enough to go on. We are left to reflect upon "owld" Garland's life in Stratford Bow and later in Old Ford with his first wife, Elizabeth, possibly childless, later with his presumably young wife, Mary; to all outward appearance he was a family man of rural inclination, known indifferently to his parish clerk as yeoman, gentleman, or player. No invidium or opprobrium there, so far as one can tell. And yet there is a mystery at the center that invites our musing and tempts us to construct an occupant for these events. At one extreme we might devise a John Garland of gentle and rustic instincts, respected by his neighbors, fond of children, modest about his fame, preferring to live away from the press of business; at another extreme, an acquisitive John Garland, eager at an early age for a country estate, eager in his advancing age for a new young wife, eager to be known as yeoman or gentle-

---

[39] GHL. The register copy is in ms. 9171/24, fo. 328[r–v]; the original will is in ms. 9172/34, item 328. The will was proved on 29 September 1624.

man wherever possible. Either of these creations will serve our turn, depending on the use to which we wish to put it. But however we construct him, we must accommodate the evidence that, at the end of his life, he chose not to remember the professional colleagues with whom he had spent most of that life. A perplexing note on which to end.

Somewhat more circumstantiality awaits us in the next narrative. The roots of this second story lie not in the parched soil of parish registers and probate courts, out of which we must raise up our own narrative frame, but in the rich contestatory rhetoric of a lawsuit; we may thus be more indulgent in our attention to it.[40] Here follows what, for lack of a better title, might be termed "The Tale of William Downell."

William Downell and Frances Francis were married in St. Saviour's Church in Southwark on Monday, 24 March 1600, the day after Easter. Downell was a tailor, and by his own modest estimation "a younge man of smalle abillitye"; he took it as a particular blessing that "by the gratious providence and goodnes of god" he had come to know the young woman he was to marry, "the daughter of one Peeter ffraunces deceased," for she was not only "of good Parentage" but "had a good porcion left her." He was candid enough to acknowledge that marriage with her would be "a verye happie and readye meanes to his preferm^t."

They had met in the previous autumn, and by midwinter William Downell had persuaded Frances Francis to marry him. But he lived frugally, he said; his resources were thin and his single lodging inadequate. He "had noe greate acquaintance in London, beinge but a batcheller, and wanted an howse of his owne to entermarye the said ffraunces in." In late February an acquaintance named Oliver Russell learned of Downell's need for a place to live and spoke of it "vnto one John Singer, and vnto Alice Singer his wiffe." The Singers had a house on the Bankside, just beyond Southwark, in the parish of St. Saviour's. They may have been moved by compassion on hearing Oliver Russell's description of young Downell and his difficulties, or their ends may have been more self-serving; in any event, they offered to rent a portion of their house to the two young people. Downell and his betrothed moved in with the Singers "some fortnight before Easter" (that is, early in March 1600), "the howse of

---

[40] PRO, Req.2/70/47. Subsequent quotations, unless otherwise attributed, are from this source.

the said John Singar beinge on Southwarcksyde neere the playe howse Called the Swan in a Court Called Hobsons Court."

The independent evidence of the St. Saviour's parish register, and of the annual token books for the Bankside, corroborate Downell's location of the Singer household and confirm that the John Singer in question was the venerable and well-known stage player, author of the jig (now lost) known as "Singer's Vallentary" and a public performer with more than two decades of service in the profession. Singer had been, along with John Garland, one of the eight original members selected for the queen's company in 1583 and had played with John Bentley and Richard Tarlton in their heydays. After the great plague of 1593-1594 he joined the lord admiral's players, and his name appears regularly in Henslowe's *Diary* in the company of Edward Alleyn and others. For some years he had lived with his wife in the house in Hobson's Court where Downell found him in 1600, and he was still, at that time, active as a stage player with the admiral's company. The Singers were probably in their late thirties at the time; in the spring of 1600 Alice was pregnant with their son John, who would be born in September. They had at least two other children already and would have two more by the summer of 1603.[41]

The terms by which the Downells lodged with the Singers were simple and straightforward. They were to pay sixpence apiece for each meal taken with the Singers, and in return the Singers "would allow them their lodginge for that monye and vpon that agreem^t." It is not clear why Downell assented to this arrangement—unless he was dazzled by the prospect of lodging with a local celebrity—for these are not inconsiderable charges: assuming that Frances would take two meals each day, and her husband one, the cost of their lodging at the Singer household would have exceeded the daily wages of most of the workmen in London.[42] But Downell did take the lodging on those terms and did not, in his later recounting of the terms, remark on their exorbitance, even though he and his bride

---

[41] The St. Saviour's parish register (GLRO, ms. P92/SAV/3001) records the baptisms of "Thomas Singer S of John a player" on 1 August 1597, of "William Singer s of John a player" on 17 June 1599, of "John Singer s. of John a player" on 21 September 1600, of "Elizabeth Singer d. of John a player" on 30 August 1601, and of "Jane Singer d of John a player" on 1 May 1603.

[42] According to the wage schedule published by the government on 3 August 1587 (Paul L. Hughes and James F. Larkin, *Tudor Royal Proclamations* [New Haven: Yale University Press, 1969], 2:536), the wage for a journeyman goldsmith, joiner, founder, skinner, and so on, without food or drink, ranged from eleven pence to sixteen pence per day. The Downells must have paid from twelve pence to eighteen pence daily for their room and board.

did not stay with the Singers for more than a few months. With the arrival of summer, the Downells moved to better quarters, and William Downell said that he showed his appreciation at that juncture by giving to John Singer "two siluer beakers wch then Cost . . . five pound*es*," to Alice Singer "fiftye shilling*es* in monye," and to Alice's sister, who lived in the household as a servant, "tenn shilling*es* in money."

These gifts at parting suggest an astonishing generosity on Downell's part; clearly they are meant to signal an amicable, even cordial, relationship between the Downells and the Singers, even though Downell's later account indicates that such was not the case. All had not been well during their stay; indeed, their early summer departure may have been due in part to their sense that they could no longer lodge with the Singers. The Downell nest egg, amounting "to the som*me* of two hundred pound*es*, or two hundred and fiftye," was in the Singer house with them, and Downell, arriving with only his meager bachelor furnishings, claimed that he "had not a Chest" to put it in. Trustingly, or in his own words "throughe simplicitye and want of Judgm^t," he "was driven to laye vpp his money in the Chest of the said John Singar." It was hardly the safest of arrangements, and Downell later claimed that it was not long before Alice Singer had taken several pounds of his money, which "as shee then said shee had leant to a Neighbour of hers vpon a good quantitye of plate pawned and engaged for that money." Alice assured him that "the daye followinge or not above two or three dayes at the most he should haue it againe."

As the weeks went by and his remonstrances with Mrs Singer about the return of the money proved fruitless, Downell found himself "driven to ymparte the matter wth the said John Singar himselfe"; but Singer, on hearing the tale, "pretended so greate ignorance of the matter as thoughe he had neuer heard thereof before, and as thoughe he scarse beleeued yt to be true, that his said Alice had anyewaye made or entermedled therew^th." Downell, feeling misused, soon conceived a more sinister view of the events; he concluded that John and Alice Singer must have confederated against him, "Colludinge and Combyni*n*ge togeth^r of purpoze to defraude" him of his money. He pressed them both, throughout the summer, to repay the money, which "they somtymes faithfully pro*mised*" but "nowe att the last vtterlye refuze & denye to doe." Downell finally proceeded against them in the Court of Requests in the following autumn; his bill of complaint was entered in Michaelmas term, and the recital of his grievances therein form the basis of my narration.

And there, frustratingly for us, the matter seems to have died. No record of Singer's response to this lawsuit is extant, and it may well be (if Downell's grievances were legitimate) that the affair was settled out of court.[43] Despite its scantiness, however, the incident has its uses. Downell's version of the events invites us to imagine the following: (a) a John and Alice Singer who were willing to have the Downells lodge with them, but at curiously exorbitant rates; (b) a William Downell who acquiesced in the arrangement, apparently without protest; (c) an Alice Singer who "borrowed" Downell's money in order to make a loan to an unidentified neighbor; (d) alternatively, an Alice Singer who took the money outright and invented the neighbor; (e) a John Singer who was both ignorant of his wife's activities and unable to credit Downell's account of them; (f) alternatively, a John Singer who feigned the ignorance or who might even have been the instigator of the whole matter.

The image of the Singers which emerges from this account, whichever permutation we choose, is not a very attractive one. Though we will likely never understand the full dynamic of the Singer-Downell misunderstanding or even have Singer's version of the events, we can imagine the kinds of alternatives which might have been presented by the Singers in a law court had the suit been continued: (a) a claim of great inconvenience in lodging the Downells, undertaken only at the request of their mutual friend Oliver Russell; (b) a claim that the Downells were difficult and demanding lodgers and that the charges levied for their food and lodging were just and appropriate; (c) a claim that Downell had himself lent the "missing" money to Alice Singer, for a fixed term that he later sought, most unethically, to shorten; (d) a claim that the "gifts" of silver beakers on parting were merely the return of the Singers' own property, offered earlier as collateral for the same loan; (e) alternatively, a claim that the silver beakers were Downell's own collateral, offered as security for a loan made to him by the Singers, and that Alice Singer's "theft" was merely her way of ensuring Downell's repayment of a contracted sum; (f) a claim that all Downell's accounts of the Singers' venality were misguided and that many were his own inventions.

---

[43] Only a few leaves of the Decree Book for this year (PRO, Req. 1/20) have survived, and they contain no reference to any proceedings in this suit.

But with or without such hypothetical additions to the narrative, we can easily recognize the basic issues and also understand the facility with which the entire incident might be moralized into an emblem of greed or avarice (Downell's view of the Singers), or conversely of foolishness or simplicity (the Singers' possible view of Downell). It is to Downell's credit that he resisted casting one stone society had made readily available to him; in the recounting of his complaint he nowhere took notice of Singer's profession. This is unusual; denunciations and sneers were far more the norm in courts of law, as litigants tried to score easy points by appealing to common prejudice.[44] Had Downell been more sanctimonious, or more of an opportunist, he might have found it easier, in his plea, to locate the grounds for the Singers' vile behavior in the degrading influence of John Singer's means of livelihood. But then, had he been easily scandalized, he probably could not have brought himself to lodge with the Singers in the first place.

The "William Downell" of this account may equally be a construct, a conveniently naive young man of principle and integrity, whose sense of fair dealing was offended by immoral behavior from an unexpected quarter; the real William Downell may have been someone quite different. Pleadings in lawsuits are by nature partisan, and so likely to be of little utility in the clear delineation of character or motive, though they have to be reasonably accurate in their presentation of the actual events if the case is not to be thrown out of court. Downell's tale is more restrained than many another would be, and his account of life in the household of a prominent stage player may therefore be reasonably near the truth. If this should happen to be the case, then the possibility invites us to speculate on the appropriateness of Chambers's proposals about instability of temperament and to reflect on John Singer's—and also John Garland's—possible placement on the Chambers spectrum: neither successful, in that they were not sharers in a playhouse, nor unsuccessful, in that they did not lead a "constantly shifting" life like Richard Jones or Martin Slater, but occupants of that middle ground that the Chambers paradigm leaves largely unexplored.

---

[44] A single instance may serve. In 1577 Richard Hickes went to law against the stage player Jerome Savage and described Savage in the suit as "a verrie lewde fellowe" because "his Cheiffe staie of lyvinge is by playinge of interludes"; Hickes's partner in the lawsuit, Peter Hunningborne, was equally formulaic; he said of Savage that he was "a verrie lewed fealowe and liveth by noe other trade then playinge of staige plaies and Interlevdes" (PRO, Req.2/266/8; a fuller discussion of this lawsuit appears in Chapter 6 below).

Singer's readiness to exchange food and lodging for a sufficient amount of cash, and his subsequent involvement in a controversy over money, both serve to reinforce my claim that the player's economics cannot be bounded by the walls of the playhouse. Henry Crosse claimed in 1603 that some stage players were usurers and extortioners; if Downell's account is to be trusted, perhaps John Singer fits into one or the other of these categories. If so, he may not be the only stage player to do so.

But in the absence of further evidence, we cannot afford even that much speculation. We have, in this exemplar, a teasing glimpse of what might be either an unfortunate misunderstanding or else a genuine case of exploitation or manipulation, all the more intriguing because the account is partial and the bias of the observer unknown. It is just from such partial accounts, however, that popular mythologies are made, and neither the writers of antitheatrical tracts nor the ready audience for their works would have been balked by the scruples we are required to observe. From such instances as these, we must learn to see "the stage player's economics" as a compound of fact and fiction, of ineluctable economic processes and irrational social beliefs, all of which must be taken into account, along with the simpler matter of tallying receipts at the playhouse door. The rich narrative of Singer's doings and the comparatively less emotive account of Garland's serve equally as material for our sustained meditation on the stage player's offstage life. If we do not set for ourselves this larger view of the subject, we deny ourselves access to the best features of current social, economic, and historical thinking and will be left with an outdated set of perceptions, an empty and antiquated structure into which our fancy is all too likely to rush, with the predictable outcome.

PART TWO

PLACES TO BEGIN

PROLOGUE

For most historical realities the very notion of a starting-point remains singularly elusive.

—Marc Bloch

With a happy mixture of whimsy and earnestness, Philip Henslowe opened his account book to one of its middle pages and began to "Caste vp all the acowntes frome the begininge of the world vntell this daye beinge the 14 daye of marche 1604."[1] His impulse on that day will surely find a sympathetic resonance among others of us who record and chronicle, for there is manifestly no better place to begin than at the beginning, if one hopes to provide a proper and adequate accounting—whether it be in the economics of shillings and pence or in the more personal kinds of transactions, debts, obligations, and relationships which constitute our daily social exchange.

Unfortunately, any "beginning" as definitive as Henslowe's will surely elude our reach, and common sense will teach us to take a shorter view. In the field of Elizabethan theater history we have before us, as a cautionary exemplar, a massive monument to the Henslowe Impulse in the work of E. K. Chambers, who, wishing to write "a little book . . . about Shakespeare," soon found compelling reasons to "put first some short account of the origins of play-acting

---

The epigraph is from Marc Bloch, *The Historian's Craft*, trans. Peter Putnam (Manchester: Manchester University Press, 1954), p. 29.

[1] *Diary*, fo. 110 (p. 209).

63

in England and of its development during the Middle Ages."[2] The "little" book on Shakespeare (*William Shakespeare: A Study of Facts and Problems*, 2 vols., 1930) eventually got written, but only after Chambers had gotten *The Medieval Stage* (2 vols., 1903) and *The Elizabethan Stage* (4 vols., 1923) out of his system. His study of Shakespeare thus begins with the collapse of late Roman drama, which, though not quite the beginning of the world, is near enough to it for the purposes of most Elizabethan theater historians.

There is little danger that anyone, in the closing years of the twentieth century, will be inclined to replicate this performance. We are now likelier to go to the other extreme, starting our histories of Elizabethan theater too late rather than too early, beginning as if by reflex at 1576 or 1587; the former year supposedly denoting the point when "real" theater began, the latter marking the birth of "real" drama. The implicit sequencing in these dates—the notion that playhouses came first, then plays—is often inadvertently enshrined in our teaching as well, its patent illogic duly noted by our students and usually left unremarked, though they would surely object if we implied that birdhouses engender birds, or doghouses dogs. The recent discovery of new documents about the Red Lion playhouse or playing structure in Stepney, a precursor of such later and better-known buildings as the Theater and the Curtain, has encouraged movement toward a new consensus among theater historians that 1567 is a more appropriate starting date for any new history. Welcome as the new evidence is, however, the new response may, if unmediated, serve merely to perpetuate the old confusion by creating an even larger gap between the presumed first appearance of playhouses and our conventional notions about the first appearance of real plays.

The building of a stage in Stepney in 1567 is thus a problematic event. It signals something new, though we are hard pressed to say just what. The evidence indicates that the structures involved were minimal—a stage, a tower, and galleries—so its significance is probably not architectural. We know that a play called *Samson* was to have been performed there, but we know nothing else of its intended repertory—indeed, we know of very few plays of any sort from the year 1567—so claiming for it a significance in the history of dramatic literature is difficult. Our recourse is to argue that its significance is innovative and entrepreneurial, that it represents a

[2] *MS* 1:v.

"conceptual" or "psychological" advance in the development of the Elizabethan theater.

But playhouses, and the mental advances for which they may be the signifiers, don't grow in a vacuum. Two decades separate 1567 and the Red Lion and *Samson* from 1587 and *The Spanish Tragedy* and *Tamburlaine*, and that interval is characterized by a remarkable lack of surviving information about the early drama. The *Annals* of Harbage and Schoenbaum lists so few extant commercial play texts from the earlier part of those two decades that the need for investment in purpose-built playhouses must appear highly unlikely. The new evidence about the Red Lion thus forces us to look further back for its causes, for the simple reason that the erection of a playing structure in 1567 is the culmination of something antecedent as well as the beginning of something yet to come, and to understand its significance properly one must understand why it was needed, not simply take pleasure in contemplating what it heralded.

But this line of reasoning, if unchecked, leads imperceptibly into the Henslowe Impulse, and its twentieth-century variant the Chambers Obsession, the conviction that there is always something a bit farther back that will explain how we got to wherever we are at any given moment. This conviction may be a reflection of the degree to which we have internalized certain Darwinian notions of evolution, or perhaps only certain Aristotelian notions of cause and effect; but there is no easy or graceful exit from the dilemma. One must simply take a stand somewhere. And all such decisions about where to start (except for Henslowe's) are of necessity arbitrary: as Heraclitus understood long ago, we inevitably step into an already-flowing stream wherever we enter our chosen subject, and we leave a still-flowing stream behind when we exit. Our treatment of beginnings and of closures is thus little more than a set of rhetorical devices for focusing attention upon our traverse, and our wet feet, rather than upon the water.

Two hundred years ago, in his *Historical Account of the Rise and Progress of the English Stage*, Edmund Malone asked similar questions about beginnings. Surveying the evidence available to him—scanty in the extreme by our standards—he speculated on the likeliest point of commencement of theatrical activity in the sixteenth century. He concluded that the drama of that period bespoke a traditional rather than an innovative practice and that its chief feature must have been continuity rather than abrupt change. He thought that what seemed true of drama must have been true of its theatrical setting as well. "At a very early period," he suggested (by which he meant earlier than the 1570s) "we had regular and established players, who obtained a livelihood by their art."[3]

Like many of Malone's other intuitive hunches, this one does not seem out of place among our own contemporary formulations. Despite the intimations, in his title, of a proto-Victorian interest in ameliorative history, or at least in the resonances of its vocabulary, Malone seems to have had little interest in advancing the claims of an organically developmental model of the early stage. He was as comfortable with notions of continuity as with those of progress and so was not unhappy to discern evidence of preexistent roots for the practices that interested him. Scholars of the later nineteenth century, standing midway between Malone and us, more readily conceived of themselves as historical social scientists of the theater and so quite reasonably preferred a more Darwinian perspective, imagining the genius of the English theater to have emerged from its bottle some time during the reign of Elizabeth, making the dramatic world anew by transfiguring earlier practices and readying the stage for the arrival of its greatest poet. There is some truth in this view as well, though our own modern notions about what caused such changes are likely to be far more prosaic and mundane than those envisioned by Furnivall and his colleagues.

But neither of these positions is fully habitable at the present time. I suspect that most theater historians today would hesitate to argue for a history of the Elizabethan theater which was either overly conservative, and anchored in the notion of slow growth and development, or in some nineteenth-century sense evolutionary or even revolutionary in its perceptions. Our own age prefers a middle course, in which we might argue, like our more recent predecessor Chambers but for other reasons, for a developing change, sometimes sudden, within the context of continuity. On the conservative side we have, thanks to the efforts of modern researchers, ample evidence (and the likelihood of more to come) that the kind of commercial theatrical activity with which we are all familiar in the later years of the sixteenth century was in full career before the middle of that century. In the two chapters that follow, I consider some of that evidence.

[3] Edmund Malone, *A Historical Account of the Rise and Progress of the English Stage* (London, 1790), p. 33.

CHAPTER THREE

The Politics of Control:
Playing at Mid-Century

I

The development of an institution . . . must be explained partly in
terms of the opportunities offered and strains imposed by the
environment in which it functions.

—R. H. Tawney

It is a matter of consternation among certain theater historians
that, in contrast to the increasing quantity of specific evidence being
brought to light about playing in the provinces before the 1570s—
names of patrons, dates and places of performance, sometimes even
names of plays and of players—there is still so little correspondingly
specific evidence about playing in the City of London during that
same period. Chambers assembled what scraps he could find and
published them in the fourth volume of *The Elizabethan Stage*; since
his time very little has been added to the store, and in the aggregate
it doesn't add up to much, especially when compared to the
abundance of evidence now being published from provincial records.
The fact is that there simply are not many direct references to plays
and playing in the City from the middle third of the century. A
historian concerned with events in the City will have to find
alternative kinds of evidence to consider, hoping like Polonius that
by indirection he may find direction out. And such alternatives do

The epigraphs at each section are from R. H. Tawney, "A History of Capitalism"
(1950), reprinted in *History and Society: Essays by R. H. Tawney*, ed. J. M. Winter
(London: Routledge & Kegan Paul, 1978), p. 208, and Karl Marx, *Grundrisse*, trans.
Martin Nicolaus (London: Allen Lane, 1973), p. 110.

67

present themselves. We can, for example, learn something about playing in the City of London from the records of the Office of the Revels, the branch of the royal household charged with responsibility for royal entertainments. Ever since the publication of Albert Feuillerat's transcriptions of certain sixteenth-century documents relating to that office during the reigns of Edward, Mary, and Elizabeth, we have had before us bits of evidence which indicate that such activity was widespread.

One of the principal responsibilities of the master of the Revels was to supervise the mounting of holiday masques at court, and to that end he maintained, in his storehouse, props and costumes ready for use, at least in theory. As the royal masquers were understood to be members of the royal court or its retinue, and not professional players, there might seem to be little connection between the master's activities on behalf of his monarch and the more vulgar traffic of innyards and taverns. But let us consider a few examples, all taken from a set of inventories made by the clerk of the Office of the Revels in 1560, shortly after the accession of Elizabeth, and reflecting no doubt the costume acquisitions during the reign of her predecessor, Mary, and perhaps even during part of the reign of Edward. In his accounting of the costumes and accessories still on hand as of that year, the clerk listed, among other costumes, six gowns made of blue velvet and cloth of gold which had been sewn originally for a masque of Albanese warriors, then modified to serve in a masque of Irishmen, further modified for a masque of fishermen, and thence into mariners' costumes, and finally "into players garmen*tes*"—that is, being no longer usable in masques for the court, the garments were made available for hire or sale to local players. These six gowns, having undergone such usage and such transformation, or in the clerk's own words having been "so often shewen and forworne," were in his view no longer serviceable and were so entered into his account.[1]

Accompanying the gowns were undersleeves of purple velvet and cloth of silver and capes[2] of the same, similarly translated into Irish capes, then cut and fringed, "and since often vsed by players and nowe not chargeable"—that is, to be written off the account as a

[1] These and the following examples are from *Documents relating to the Office of the Revels in the Time of Queen Elizabeth*, ed. Albert Feuillerat (Louvain: Uystpruyst, 1908), pp. 21, 24, 27.
[2] The word in the manuscript is "cappes," but the nature and amount of alteration described makes it unlikely that caps are meant. See *Taming of the Shrew* IV.iii.140.

loss. As the chief function of the Revels office was to furnish costumes for revels at court, and not for plays put on elsewhere by local players or minstrels, such innocent-seeming phrases as "often vsed by players" strike one as anomalous. That such phrases occur at all is fortunate for us, for they constitute bits of evidence from the Revels' records themselves of the office's common practice of accepting fees from outsiders for the use of its garments. The yeoman of the Revels, the office's second in command, was the person commonly involved in this practice; it was not, strictly speaking, a contravention of the office's charter, though one could certainly argue that it was inappropriate, as it subverted the master's principal charge of preserving the office's costumes and props for royal use.

Other entries from this same set of inventories give us further information; I cite only one or two as additional instances. Some fifteen yards of red velvet, originally made up as six great pairs of almain sleeves, were similarly converted into costumes for the torchbearers in the masque of mariners, and afterward "often vsed by players"; as a result they were by the time of the 1560 inventory "so knowen and worne" that they were neither "seruiceable nor chargeable"; a testimony, perhaps, to the assiduity of the yeoman in hiring out his wares. Similarly, some forty yards of crimson damask, made up as frocks and priests' gowns with wide sleeves, were modified into costumes for torchbearers "and vsed by players and to them geven by Composicion" along with some cloaks and "slops" (i.e., baggy breeches) for torchbearers "which was altered agayne for players and to them geven by the m^r by composicion and so therof nil Chargeable." This latter entry reflects another kind of practice by the yeoman (and even of the master), that of settling the occasional fees owed to commercial players "by composition," that is, by giving them costumes in lieu of cash. Perhaps the players were happy with such an arrangement, perhaps not; but it was an efficient way for the Revels Office to rid itself of superannuated garments.[3]

The practice of hiring out the royal costumes by the yeoman of the Revels was not without its critics. A prosperous London haberdasher named Thomas Gylles complained to the master of the Revels in

---

[3] Nor were the players the only ones so compounded with. Elsewhere in the records for this same year one finds worn garments given by composition to the drum and fife players and taken for their fees (Feuillerat, pp. 25, 27, 28) and even, in one instance, "translated into Sloppes for children to playe in" (p. 21).

1572 that the queen's stock was being abused by the yeoman. Costumes were not given to players only after becoming worn out in the queen's service, Gylles claimed, but rather became worn because they were hired out to others from the beginning, even while new. He charged that the yeoman "dothe vsuallye lett to hyer her sayde hyghnes mask*es* . . . to all sort of parsons that wyll hyer the same" and that the garments so hired out took "more harme" from "werynge Into the cytye or contre where yt ys often vsyd" than from "werynge In the cowrt," because of "the grett presse of peple & fowlnes bothe of the weye & wether & soyll of the werer*es* who for the most part be of the meanest sort of mene." Gylles noted that he had "often complaynyde heroff to other*es*" in years past about these abuses, "yett there hathe byn no redresse of the same"; the yeoman, "havynge alloen the costodye of the garment*es*," still continued to lease them to outsiders "at hys plesuer." Gylles was the more aggrieved because he felt the abuse in his own purse; he was himself, he declared, a purveyor of costumes in the City and found the misused prerogative of the yeoman inimical to his own trade. He claimed to be "grettlye hynderyde of hys lyvynge" by the yeoman's practice, for he himself had "apparell to lett" and he "canott so cheplye lett the same as hyr hyghnes mask*es* be lett."[4]

Gylles appended to his complaint a list showing "for on yere last past"—that is, "syns the fyrst of Ianvarye last past 1571"—all "the tymes & places wher the sayd mask*es* [i.e., costumes] hathe byn seen & vsyde" outside of the court; his list contains twenty-one instances of lendings, almost once a fortnight on average. The occasions range from a set of yellow cloth-of-gold gowns sent "to the horshed tavern In chepsyde" to a set of copper-colored gowns lent for an interlude at "the maryage of the dowter of my lorde montague." The import of his grievance and of his list is twofold. First, it suggests that the letting of costumes had been a thriving business in the City in 1572, and perhaps for several years past, sufficient to attract the interest of a variety of entrepreneurs—not only of the yeoman of the Revels as a sideline but also of such men as Gylles himself, who, as a prosperous haberdasher, is unlikely to have bothered with such trade unless it had been profitable. The requisite premise for this notion is that the City contained a number

---

[4] Feuillerat, p. 409. For the measure of Gylles's prosperity, see his will (PRO, Prob.11/65, ff. 300^v–301^v).

of players—or at least a number of performers, if "players" seems too specialized a term—and that these persons required costumes with something approaching regularity. The grievance also suggests that the groups of players (or at least many of them) who comprised the City's free-lance theatrical activity in this period were not sufficiently organized to own or to control their own garments.

But this state of affairs was not new even in the 1560s: we have evidence of the same sort of thing going on forty years earlier. Scholars have known since the beginning of this century about the lawsuit brought by John Rastell the printer in the 1520s against his friend Henry Walton over the issue of playing costumes. Rastell, like Thomas Gylles a half century later, seems to have owned a number of such costumes, perhaps in connection with his playing enterprise in Finsbury. At one point in the early 1520s Rastell had to go overseas for six months, and he arranged to leave the costumes with his friend Walton during his absence. One presumes that Rastell might simply have packed the costumes away in his chest if security was his only concern; his leaving them with Walton suggests that he intended them to be used during his absence. And Walton did indeed take advantage of the opportunity to lease them out—at least twenty times during Rastell's absence, in both winter and summer (that is, almost once a week on average), according to the testimony offered during the lawsuit. These leasings were to a variety of people, including private groups of players, for the performance of plays in the London area. The resultant wear and tear on the costumes was apparently excessive, and on his return to London, Rastell, professing to be appalled at their condition, sued Walton.[5]

Some of the persons who had leased the costumes from Walton were called on to be deponents in the lawsuit; they described the costumes, and the extent to which they had become used and worn. The men who gave this testimony were not connected in any way with the court; they were such people as George Mayler of London, merchant tailor, age forty, and John Redman of London, stationer, age twenty-two, both of whom acknowledged being players and having played in the garments "dyvers tymes." One concludes from this kind of testimony that independent theatrical activity in London

---

[5] PRO, Req.2/8/14; a transcription appears in A. W. Pollard, *Fifteenth Century Prose and Verse* (London: Constable, 1903), pp. 307–21. For details of Rastell's stage in Finsbury Fields, see A. W. Reed, *Early Tudor Drama* (London: Methuen, 1926), pp. 230–33.

even during the middle years of the 1520s was lively enough to provide a clientele for anyone with costumes for hire. It seems clear that Thomas Gylles, owner and leaser of costumes in the 1570s, was by no means engaged in a recent or novel activity but was rather part of a long tradition; the only thing new in the 1570s was the unwelcome intrusion of the yeoman of the Revels (a post that did not exist in the 1520s) onto what Gylles considered his own turf. Gylles may have chosen the wrong argument when he claimed that the market for costume rental was not big enough to sustain the entry of the Revels Office into it. Not only did this appeal, grounded on his own economic disadvantage, clash with his other and better arguments about the general good, but he was probably wrong as well: it would appear that in the early 1570s the market *was* big enough.

We have, then, from these kinds of documents alone, bits of evidence which accumulate to suggest a steady level of demand for stage costumes in the City of London from the reign of Henry VIII onward. The records suggest that the typical hiring was for a short time rather than for an extended period, so that one might assume that the players who needed garments, especially in the earlier years, were local people with short-term needs. Players who traveled regularly in the countryside would have needed costumes for longer stretches of time; for them the services of the City leaser of costumes might have been less useful, or perhaps his charges for longer periods would have made permanent acquisition a reasonable alternative. From this assumption we may perhaps make the further assumption that playing in the City, especially in the earlier years, was—in contrast to touring in the countryside—much more an avocation or sideline than a principal activity for the men who did it.

Though the evidence of surviving play texts might lead us to believe that there was relatively little dramatic activity through much of this period, the corollary evidence of costume rentals indicates that playing was a thriving business in the City of London well before the first appearance of playhouses. For further corroboration, let us consider some other kinds of evidence drawn from the decade of the 1560s alone and consisting of items that, like the Revels items, have long been known. Bishop Grindal's letter to William Cecil in 1564 should probably have pride of place, for in it he speculated that the plague of 1563, one of London's worst, was probably caused by players:

By searche I doo perceive, thatt ther is no one thinge off Late is more lyke to have renewed this contagion*n*, then the practise off an idle sorte off people, wch have ben infamouse in all goode com*m*on*n* weales: I meane these Histriones, com*m*on playo^rs; who now daylye, butt speciallye on holydayes, sett vp bylles, whervnto ye youthe resorteth excessiuely, & ther taketh infection*n*: besydes y^t goddes worde by theyr impure mowthes is prophaned, and turned into scoffes. for remedie wheroff in my iugement ye shulde do verie well to be a meane, y^t a proclamation*n* wer sette furthe to inhibitte all playes for one whole yeare (and iff itt wer for ever, it wer nott amisse) w^thin ye Cittie, or 3. myles compasse, apon paynes aswell to ye playo^rs, as to ye owners off ye howses, wher they playe theyr Lewde enterludes.[6]

Grindal's sentiments about a better society in which plays were inhibited "for ever" found their echo in the City of London. In the autumn of the following year, 1565, the Court of Aldermen in a fit of zeal prohibited playing in any "taverns Innes victualinge houses or in enny oth^r place or place*s*" where money might be "demaunded collected or gathered" of anyone "for the heringe or seinge of enny such playe or enterlud."[7] And in the following spring, Robert Fryer, a goldsmith, was required to sign a performance bond with the lord mayor binding him for the remainder of the summer not to "*permyt or suffer any maner of Stage Play or Interlude to be playd w^thin any parte of his mansion" before the hour of "iiij of the Cloke in the after none," or to permit "any maner of people to enter or come into his seid house . . . before the houre of iij of Cloke . . . to se or hire any such play or interlude," on any Sunday or holiday, on pain of 10 fine.[8]

In the same year the lord mayor softened the earlier and more absolute ruling of the Court of Aldermen by prohibiting all plays and interludes at any time or place "w^thout o^r pryvetee and assent first had and obteyned for the same."[9] And in 1569 the Court of Aldermen bound themselves in another strict ruling that neverthe-less permitted playing to continue. The lord mayor, on their instruction, ordered them to ensure that no householder in any of their wards should allow plays in his house "but only in the daye time And that only betwene the houres of three & fyve of the Clock

[6] BL, ms. Lansd. 7, fo. 141; extracted and lightly edited in *ES* 4:266–67.
[7] CLRO, Jor. xviii, fo. 362; see *MSC* 2, pt. 3:300–301.
[8] CLRO, Rep. xvi, fo. 42^v; see *MSC* 2, pt. 3:301.
[9] CLRO, Jor. xix, fo. 10^v; see *MSC* 2, pt. 3:302.

in thafternone"—the statutory origin, perhaps, of the cliché about two hours' traffic—and that such householders should permit no persons coming to see a play "to haue or enter into anny Chamb^r or other secrete or close place or places wthin anny of there said houses" during the time of the play, but must require them "to remayne & stond in the open . . . duryng all the tyme of the same playes And then honestly to depart." Bonds of forty pounds were to be taken of all such householders for their good performance on this latter head.[10]

Forty pounds was a staggering sum in the 1560s; the intent of the enactment must surely have been in part to deter all but the economically secure, or the stringently well behaved, from offering the occasion for plays in their establishments or elsewhere. The degree to which the ruling did in fact act as a deterrent is unclear; though we know that playing continued, we don't know how much more vigorous it might have been without this decree. The evidence we have been considering thus far, from the Office of the Revels, the Court of Aldermen, and other City agencies, indicates a widespread and thriving activity. This evidence is the more crucial because it stands against the literary evidence, which is cumulatively very scant. And we have been conditioned to value the literary evidence. In *Tudor Drama and Politics*, his careful study of sixteenth-century plays in relation to their times, David Bevington has shown how the surviving plays from this middle period, taken year by year, can be seen to fit the larger political agenda of those same years. One might add that this is surely one reason for their publication and survival. We proceed uncritically, however, if we presume that the plays that did not survive from this period were just like the ones that did. For the middle years of the century, the survival of a text may well argue its relevance to a given faction's political ambitions and thus be grounds for suspicion on our part. Plays whose argument ran counter to official purpose are unlikely to have been preserved. Despite our awareness of these things, we may nevertheless feel at some subconscious level that the failure of plays to survive is synonymous with their failure to have been very good, or to have existed at all.

Another danger in our overvaluing the literary evidence, even in its absence, is that we run the risk of assuming that if there were no plays then players did not perform plays or performed only the few

---

[10] CLRO, Jor. xix, fo. 143^v; cf. Rep. xvi, fo. 442^v; see *MSC* 2, pt. 3:303–5.

that have survived and spent the rest of their time miming or engaging in "activities" of an essentially unsophisticated sort. These ideas are the result of a nineteenth-century attitude that we have inherited from Furnivall and Collier and Fleay and that ought to strike us today as patronizing. It presumes that, since the theater was in its infancy, so its activities must have been infantile. The later Darwinian "growth" of the drama into "maturity"—which was for these scholars a synonym for "Shakespeare"—was both the rationale and the chief subject of their inquiry, as we have seen.[11]

But the evidence seems to indicate that throughout the middle years of the sixteenth century the City of London was full of stage players doing more than simply juggling, tumbling, and rope dancing. The subject matter of their activities attracted the attention of officials in both the City and the court, periodically arousing concerns about heresy or sedition, but despite a variety of attempts at repression or control the players continued playing, making their presence felt, finding a ready audience, making some kind of money for themselves and presumably making money for their landlords as well, the owners of taverns or inns, or for private individuals such as the goldsmith Robert Fryer, who made space available for playing. And, on the other hand, the City's regulations from the 1560s, repressive though they may sound to us in the abstract, and harsh though they may have been in isolated instances, were on the whole not unreasonable—they required licensing and set the hours of business, not inappropriately—and in any event, regulation by the lord mayor and the Court of Aldermen seems not to have had any adverse affect on the continuing expansion and prosperity of the enterprise.[12]

---

[11] We are not free ourselves of this kind of romanticizing. It pleases us to remember early television as having been infantile, and we are inclined to dismiss, with varying degrees of contempt, the Ed Sullivans and Milton Berles and Henny Youngmans whom we may remember as its staples, while we forget the early pioneering work of John Frankenheimer and Rod Serling, the innovations of Playhouse 90, and the inspired lunacy of Sid Caesar, the Richard Tarlton of his day. Caesar improvised; the rest worked from scripts written by professionals, and the traditions within which they worked were constantly being reshaped under the very pressure of their inspiration. Imagine a case in which all our tapes of early television shows were lost except for a few documentaries on social issues and that our historical archive began with the first Masterpiece Theatre productions. That is essentially the state we are in with regard to the players of the 1560s and 1570s.

[12] Exception might be taken to this last statement. For example, one might want to query why, if the 1560s offered such a thriving market in the City as I am suggesting, a grocer should have decided in 1567 to build a stage and scaffolds in Stepney, a mile and

II

In the case of the arts, it is well known that certain periods of their flowering are out of all proportion to the general development of society, hence also to the material foundation, the skeletal structure as it were, of its organization.

—Karl Marx

The presence of this burgeoning theatrical activity in London during the middle years of the century is itself a phenomenon requiring explanation. The currently favored thesis is that the beginnings of the ferment lay in the political tensions associated with the final stages of Henry VIII's break with Rome, when certain ministers of the crown attempted to move public sentiment in their favor by making use of play texts embodying regulated points of view. Their aim, presumably, was to elucidate certain defensible positions about church government and thus to endorse the official posture of the crown with regard to the newly discovered English church. Though the evidence for this scenario is relatively scant and not readily detectable in denotative readings of the conventional documents, it still bears considering. Certainly the break with Rome ushered in a period of reformist zeal that Henry had neither desired nor properly guarded against, and the fortunes of stage players in that troubled period fluctuated with each change in the level of official tolerance.[13]

Henry VIII was himself quite active, at least nominally, as a patron of stage players in the later years of his reign; surviving records show royal support for three companies active in the 1530s and 1540s, said to belong to the king, the queen, and (at first) Princess Mary, though all three were probably under the more direct control of Henry's vice-gerent, Thomas Cromwell. The "patron" of the queen's company changed as frequently as Henry's queens changed, and Princess Mary's company was quickly reassigned to her brother as soon as he was born. These three troupes, though attached to the royal household, spent much of their time playing in the provinces. The company known after 1537 as the prince's players, appearing under that name when agitation for religious and political reform

---

more out of town, or why, less than a decade later, given these same working conditions, three permanent buildings should suddenly be built in the suburbs.

[13] See Susan Brigden, *London and the Reformation* (Oxford: Clarendon Press, 1989), p. 255.

was at its height, took to the road more as a standard-bearer for public notice than as a troupe for the pleasure of the young heir. Between 1538 and 1547 the prince's players appear in provincial records as regularly and as frequently as do the king's players, and all such public appearances were no doubt approved and encouraged by the crown for reasons having nothing to do with love of the drama. Henry, or perhaps more correctly Cromwell, thus kept before the public eye the names of the monarch, his consort, and his heir and associated them all with pleasure and entertainment, even as he used these troupes for the careful dissemination of new political and ecclesiastical ideas along with an endorsement of traditional pieties in the plays and interludes they performed.

And the repetition of those pieties was necessary, as we learn from a letter written to Cromwell by the duke of Suffolk, reporting on events in his county on May Day in 1537. "Apon Mayday last," he wrote, "was played A play whiche playe was of a kinge how he shuld Rulle his Realm And Amonges other thynges there came in oon & Playde hussbandry which said many thynges Agaynst gentillmenn myche more thenn was in the boke of the playe." In the letter, Suffolk reported his attempt to have the player arrested, but the player had fled; Suffolk then proposed to Cromwell that "yf it myght stande w^t the kynges pleasure that there shuld nother games nor playes be vsde in theise partyes this som^r whereby the Idell people shuld haue Acassyon to assemble."[14]

But there are plays and plays, sanctioned plays and unsanctioned plays. Suffolk's letter makes plain the dilemma that would be faced by a government wishing to support or promote certain plays and players while inhibiting others. We also learn from Suffolk's letter that there is such a thing as "the boke of the playe" even for unsanctioned plays by unauthorized troupes in the 1530s. Indeed, it seems to have been an unstated assumption throughout the period that plays required books, that they were not simply unwritten improvisations or skits. In June 1557 the Privy Council wrote to John Fuller, the mayor of Canterbury, thanking him "for his dilligence in thapprehending and committing of [certain unidentified] players to warde," whom he is to keep close until further order from the council; they also note that "their lewdd playe booke is committed to the consyderacion of the King and Quenes ma^{tes} learned coun-

---

[14] PRO, S.P.1/120, fo. 100^v–101^r. Suffolk was not opposed to playing in general; he had a troupe of his own, which played at York three years after this incident, in 1540; see *York*, REED (Toronto, 1979), 1:269.

sayle, who are wylled to declare what the same wayeth vnto in the lawe."[15] And, later in the same year, when the Privy Council inquired into a rumored performance they understood to be called *A Sackful of News* at the Boar's Head, they instructed the lord mayor to apprehend the players "and to take there playe booke from them and to send the same hither."[16] The council's assumption in this latter case, based on its own experience, was that a written text would of course underlie any such performance. Unhappily for us, the confiscation of such a text would virtually guarantee its disappearance; thus it is that of many plays in this period we know nothing more than a title, or an allegedly offending incident, sometimes no more than the bare fact of its having once existed.

But with such a multitude of "playe books" and of playing companies abroad in the land in the late 1530s, some authorized, more not, a certain tendency to ideological entropy was bound to manifest itself. Against such a pull, even three royal troupes would make scant headway in the promulgation of the official discourse. If the crown's intent in this period was to make active use of players and playwrights in their propaganda war against popery, the king's ministers, and Cromwell in particular, must have known they were taking a calculated risk. Suffolk's suggestion to Cromwell that there should be "nother games nor playes" during the summer of 1537 so that "the Idell people" should have no "Acassyon to assemble" crystallized the problem neatly. If the existence of authorized plays made difficult, or impossible, the control of unauthorized plays, then better to prohibit all plays.

But Cromwell was apparently unready to give over his use of the stage. Concurrent with the formation of the prince's players he had set up a company of his own[17] and in that same year had taken into his service John Bale, recently released from prison, to which he had been committed in 1536 for his extreme and outspoken Protestantism. Bale apparently wrote plays for Cromwell's use—by his own account in later life, some twenty-two comedies, principally on religious themes, "in idiomate materno, sub uario metrorum ge-

---

[15] PRO, P.C.2/7, p. 640, meeting of 27 June 1557 at Westminster.

[16] PRO, P.C.2/7, p. 695, meeting of 5 September 1557 at Westminster.

[17] They were known principally as the players of the lord privy seal—one of Cromwell's titles—and they appear in the records of Shrewsbury, Leicester, Oxford, Cambridge, Canterbury, Barnstaple, and elsewhere during these years. See W. T. Davies, "A Bibliography of John Bale," *Proceedings and Papers of the Oxford Bibliographical Society* 5 (1940), 210, and Paul White's forthcoming book *Theatre and Reformation*.

nere," of which five are still extant.[18] He also became associated
with a company of players and said that he wrote fourteen of his
plays "Presentim ad illustrissimum Dominum Ioannem Ver, Oxonie
Comitem," seeming to imply the patronage of John de Vere,
fifteenth earl of Oxford.[19] But the company that appears in Cromwell's account books in 1538 and 1539 is listed merely as "Bale & his
ffelowes," and most students of Bale's life have presumed that
Cromwell was himself the patron.

The extent of Cromwell's support of partisan drama and stage
players may never be known. His association with Bale may have
been the whole of it, or, more ambitiously, he may have been the
guiding spirit behind all the royal troupes. I incline to the latter
view. Had he stayed longer in power, he might have left more
evidence on this head. But his active role in advocating the king's
marriage with Anne of Cleves served to hasten his downfall. He was
executed in July 1540, and his conservative opponents moved back
into the king's favor. Bale was perceptive enough to see the danger
to himself and to flee the country; from Basle he wrote an impas-
sioned letter to "the pompouse popyshe Byschoppes" who had
taken over the country's affairs, accusing them of disrupting the
progress of Protestantism and harassing innocent Christians. Among
those suffering under their strict regime, according to Bale, were the
players of stage interludes. By this he may have meant only his own
former fellows, or he may have meant other groups as well; his
syntax leaves the matter open to question. "Non leaue ye vnuexed
and vntroubled No not so moch as the poore mynstrels and players
of interludes but ye are doynge with them. So long as they played
lyes and sange bawdye songes blaspheminge God and corruptinge
mennes consciences [you] neuer blamed them but were verye well
contented. But sens they persuaded the people to worshyp theyr
Lorde God aryght accordinge to his holye lawes and not yours and
to acknowledge Jesus Christ for their only redemer and sauer
without your lowsye legerdemaynes ye neuer were pleased with
them whan they tell you as the truthe is that youre Romishe father
hath played the cruell Antichrist and you his false phesicyanes
. . . ye take it vnpacientlye sekinge theyr destruccion for it."[20]

---

[18] Honor McCusker, *John Bale, Dramatist and Antiquary* (Bryn Mawr, Pa.:[n.p.], 1942),
p. 72.

[19] PRO, S.P.1/111, fo. 182; McCusker, p. 74.

[20] *Epistle Exhortatorye of an Englishe Christiane [to] the pompouse popyshe Byschoppes*, 1544
ed. (*STC* 1291), fo. 16^{r-v}. The author named on the title page is one Henry Stalbrydge;
most scholars have taken this to be Bale's Swiss pseudonym.

This is a vigorous defense of stage players as the vanguard of the new protestantism. Bale's outcry against their repression by the "pompouse popyshe Byschoppes" suggests that Cromwell's experimental use of the drama for political ends had come to an abrupt halt with his fall from favor. Suffolk's wish, that there be no more plays, had in the end been forcibly, if ephemerally, granted. (Bishop Grindal's wish, twenty years later, "to inhibitte all playes for one whole yeare," noting that "iff itt wer for ever, it wer nott amisse," is evidence not only that Grindal was the spiritual heir of Bale's antagonists but also that the repression of players, a perennial theme, was never wholly effective.) To the conservatives in power after 1540, it must have seemed that Cromwell's theatrical initiatives had awakened in the land a streak of reformist zeal broader and more dangerous than his own, one that quickly gave voice to a far wider range of religious and governmental complaints than the crown had any intention of addressing. These complaints, embodied in a variety of plays that were apparently too outspoken on such topics for official taste, by playwrights and players who were outside the circle of official support, had to be suppressed; Suffolk's complaint about the company of unknown players and their provocative play "of a kinge how he shuld Rulle his Realm" proved in the end to have more pragmatic force than Bale's arguments on behalf of theology.

With Cromwell gone, the crown took the easiest route to a settlement of the matter, giving up its own involvement in political drama and rejecting Cromwell's activist policies so that it might better and more vigorously repress the unauthorized activities of others. John Foxe recorded that in Shoreditch in 1541 one "*Shermons*, keper of the Carpenters Hall in Christes parish, was presented for procuryng an interlude to bee openly played, wherein Priestes were rayled on, and called knaues." He also noted that "about the same tyme also a certeine Priest was burned at Salisbury, who leauyng his Papistry, had maryed a wife, and became a player in interludes."[21] Still further repression seemed to be in store, or at least the report of further repression; at a meeting on 10 April 1543 the Privy Council committed to ward "Certayne ioyners to the nomber off xx" who had "made a disguising vpon the sonday morning wythowt respect

---

[21] John Foxe, *Actes and Monuments*, 1570 ed. (STC 11,223), 2:1378, 1376; these references are abstracted in *MS* 2:221. The priest, one Richard Spencer, was joined on the pyre by two other men named Ramsey and Hewet; all three were condemned for playing "matter concernyng the Sacrament of the altar."

ether off the day or the ordre whiche was knowen openlye the king*es* highnes entended to take for the repressing off playes." From another item of business at that same meeting, we learn that the City was more than ready to join in this undertaking; the council noted that "Certeyne players to the no*m*bre of iiij. belonging to my lorde warden" were committed to the Counters "for playing contrary to an ordre taken by the mayo^r on that behalf."[22]

Despite this increase of vigilance, voices were still raised in defense of stage plays. In his *Discourse touching the Reformation of the Lawes of England*, Richard Moryson claimed, much as Bale had, that plays "ar to be born withal, though they payn*n* and vexe som*me*." Moryson argued that plays were useful to the crown, "specyally when they declare eyther the abhominacion of the bisshop of rome and his adherent*tes*, or the be*n*efitt*es* browght to thys realme by yor grac*es* tornyn*g* hy*m* and hys out of it." Though plays may have been the occasion of abuses in the past, "They ar to be born*n* with all, yea thowghe so*m* thy*n*g in them be to be misliked neu*er*thelesse." Moryson, addressing his remarks presumably to the king, recalled that before the Reformation papist notions had been "daily by all meanes opened inculked and dryuen into the peoples heddes, taught in scoles to children, plaied in playes before the ignoraunt people, songe in mynstrell*es* songes and bokes in englisshe purposley dyuysed to declare the same at large." But the current suppression of playing had taken matters too far in the other direction, for "He that hath an ache in hys arme, my*n*ding to put it awaie, dothe not cute of tharme, but Laboureth to expell the ache pres^{r}uyng the arme for many good and necessary vses: the good husbondman, when he seethe his corne put out faire, and wedes emong it ofte tymes dothe suffer the weades to growe, least he shulde distroie bothe: so rulers so*m*tyme do and must wynke at the small faultes of suche ther subiectes as be indued w^t excellent vertues, bycause they will not lose the vse com*m*odyte and benyfite of thother: playes, songes & book*es* ar to be born withal," and so on.[23]

---

[22] PRO, P.C.2/1, p. 471; summarized in *APC* 1:109. The lord warden in this year was Sir Thomas Cheyney, a member of the Privy Council and the king's household treasurer. Imprisoning his players was a bold act by the City, probably not lightly undertaken; perhaps the rumored imminence of a royal decree helped to firm the resolve of the aldermen.

[23] BL, ms. Cotton Faustina C.ii, calendared in *L&P* 17:707. Moryson was one of the king's privy chamber. The treatise is undated but is assumed to be after 1536; I take it to be after 1540.

There is no evidence that pleas such as Moryson's effected any change in the official rigor or any improvement in the fortunes of stage players who were not royally patronized, during the remaining years of King Henry's life. While the three companies patronized by the crown continued to play during the 1540s, their repertories may have become less controversial; the tolerance extended to plays during the early years of the Reformation had worn thin.[24] With Henry's death in 1547 and the translation of the young prince into King Edward VI, the king's players and the prince's players suddenly found themselves with the same patron, while the queen's players suddenly had no patron at all. Despite this abrupt change, there seems to be some evidence that the three companies continued to exist, if only for a short time. We know that the queen's company stayed together for a while after the accession of Edward. They played at Dover a year or more after Henry's death, under the name of "the latte quyne Katerynges players,"[25] and were perhaps enabled in this by the duke of Somerset, the new lord protector, though they seem to have disappeared by 1549. Queen Katherine Parr outlived her royal husband and married again, but there is no evidence that she attempted to maintain the playing company on her own. Perhaps she never really thought of it as her own company. If the decision to maintain the royal troupes was Somerset's he may have toyed briefly with the idea of taking up Cromwell's experiment once more. Somerset had his own players when he was only the earl of Hertford during Henry VIII's reign, and now he pressed them into the royal service: "*the* King*es* players" and "my lord protectors players" played back to back at Norwich on 11 and 14 December 1548.[26] But there is little evidence for any more activity than this.

Somerset may also have maintained two sets of king's players for a year or two; but by 1549 at the latest some sort of reorganization must have taken place. We know that there was only a single company with that name in the 1550s. That company may have been formed by a merger of the two earlier troupes, or even of all three troupes. But mergers are always problematic; such a sudden inflation of the size of a company to twice its previous size, or even larger, would create more problems than it would solve. Would the newly

[24] For more on this point see Patrick Collinson, *From Iconoclasm to Iconophobia: The Cultural Impact of the Second English Reformation* (Stenton Lecture for 1985; Reading, England: University of Reading, 1986), pp. 9–15.

[25] MSC 7:40.

[26] *Norwich*, REED (Toronto, 1984), pp. 24, 25.

merged players require new play texts with more roles to accommodate their enlarged number? If so, would they discard as useless all
the old play books from their earlier days? When they traveled,
would all of them go? If not, would they need special versions of
their play books for traveling? Or would they simply split up into
their premerger groupings and take to the road with their old texts?
If they chose the latter course, then "merger" becomes a meaningless
term.

A more persuasive narrative, I think, would presume that the best
players of the two or three companies were carried over into the new
king's company. The creation of one new troupe, of the optimum
rather than the maximum size (whatever the former might have
been thought to be), would have made possible a continued use of
the most successful plays from all three repertories (assuming
different repertories for the three companies, which may not have
been the case). Those players who were suddenly redundant as a
result of this shuffle may have found professional homes elsewhere,
or they may have become part of the pool of common players in the
City.

If Somerset had briefly experimented with the use of playing
companies after the fashion of Cromwell—and the evidence either
way is virtually nonexistent—he may have found, as Cromwell's
opponents had, that matters could quickly get out of hand. Certainly
Somerset's interest after 1549 was in regulation and control, and this
interest was reflected in the City as well. In that year the City
authorized itself to "pervse all such enterludes as hereafter shalbe
pleyed by eny comen pleyr of the same within the Citie or the
liberties therof."[27] It also decided to ask the lord chancellor for help
in "the steyinge of all comen interludes & pleyes within the Citie &
the suburbes therof."[28] Both these items make it clear that playing
was going on both within and without the jurisdiction of the City. In
another action in the same year, the aldermen ordered John Wilkinson, a currier, "who comenly suffreth & meynteyneth interludes &
playes to be made and kept within his dwellyng house," to stop on
pain of imprisonment.[29] The singling out of Wilkinson is not unlike
the City's binding of the goldsmith Robert Fryer twenty years later;
indeed, the tenor of all of these documents from the 1540s is
strikingly like that of their counterparts from the 1560s, or even—

[27] CLRO, Rep. xii pt. 1, fo. 162ᵛ; printed in *ES* 4:261.
[28] CLRO, Rep. xii pt. 1, fo. 100; printed in *ES* 4:261.
[29] CLRO, Rep. xii pt. 1, fo. 92; printed in *ES* 4:261.

noticing the reference to playing "within the Citie & the suburbes therof"—from the 1580s. The complaints of the City were fairly consistent across this whole period, arguing that the occasion for the complaints—the steady presence of playing companies—was a constant as well.

In 1550 the Court of Aldermen issued a decree binding certain "common" players of interludes not to play in the City without license. The decree named eighteen otherwise unaffiliated players.[30] No doubt there were other such men who slipped through the City's net, but these eighteen are a considerable number, sufficient for three or four troupes, given the usual size of playing companies at mid-century. That the aldermen listed eighteen individuals, rather than the names of three or four companies, is further evidence of the transient nature of common troupes in this period. Such looseness and flexibility may well have been one of their great strengths, as it was for early jazz groups in our own century; but by the time of Edward and Somerset their days were numbered, and the official pressures against them were so strong that the term by which they were distinguished—"common players" as against "my lord so-and-so's players"—quickly became a term of opprobrium.[31]

The requirement of licensing that the decree of 1550 imposed may reflect a new sense in the City of strategies for control. The aldermen, though not always repressive in the matter of stage plays, had always been *pro forma* disapproving and thus always a potential ground for repression. After 1550, however, their rigor seemed to intensify. The same situation obtained in most of the other towns where players might wish to perform. Increasingly players were required to have some form of certification, usually by the governing bodies of those towns, before they would be allowed to play; the granting of this certification often had as its prerequisite the evidence of the playing company's sanction or protection by a patron. The loose and informal associations of players in the City of London,

---

[30] *ES* 4:261–62. The players are William Clement, John Crane, Robert Drake, Richard Gyrke, Richard Jugler, John Nethe, John Nethersall, Oliver Page, Richard Parseley, Robert Peacocke, Richard Pokely, John Radstone, John Rawlyns, William Readyng, John Ronner, Robert Southyn, Edmund Stokedale, and Robert Sutton. Several of these men later became royal interluders, appointments suggesting that their quality as players was not negligible.

[31] "Common player" was never a general synonym for "stage player" in this period, despite the mistaken assumptions in such works as Muriel Bradbrook's *Rise of the Common Player* (Cambridge, Mass.: Harvard University Press, 1962). The later sixteenth century witnessed the fall, not the rise, of "common players."

such as those who played for Rastell at Finsbury in the 1520s, began to disappear by mid-century under the pressure of official licensing requirements.

City and Court seem to have been in agreement at mid-century that a way had to be found to control the staging of inappropriate texts, and certification of the stage players who presented the texts may have appeared to be the most reasonable solution. Such certification, it might have been argued, would regulate as well as privilege the stable, continuing, patronized companies, whose identity could be ascertained and recorded and who might be held accountable for their conduct. As for the others—the occasional, the transient, the unaffiliated or "common" companies, which may have been perceived as the principal offenders in these matters—they soon came to be increasingly at risk.

Patronage, and the stability that accompanied it, must thus have come increasingly to be seen by players operating out of London as the key to survival at about mid-century. As a result, the quest for patronage burgeoned, as local players sought to protect their livelihoods. Hindsight makes the resultant confusion seem eminently predictable. Where the earlier problem had seemed to be unregulated players, with patronage and its attendant accountability proposed as a remedy, so it was not long before unregulated patronage itself came to be seen as a problem, increasingly complex as the century moved toward its end, with periodic attempts at control by the Privy Council in the 1590s and with final closure provided by King James in 1603 when he limited the privilege to members of the royal family.

James's intuition in this matter seems to have been sound. He understood the kind of power and the range of political possibilities inherent in the exclusive control of public players. But he was not alone in this understanding: the efforts at control in the last decade or so of Elizabeth's reign provide us with ample evidence that even by the 1580s both players and nonroyal patrons had come to understand this potential. A half century earlier than that, Henry VIII, or perhaps Cromwell, had also grasped the point but, unlike James, had seen no need to restrict the practice, for in the 1530s the extension of patronage, especially among those peers who were royal supporters, must have seemed no more than an extension of the tools of propaganda.

By mid-century that situation had changed, as the number of playing companies under royal patronage dropped from three to one. The one surviving company was destined to see various service over the subsequent two decades or so of its active life. As the king's players, during the six or so years that Edward reigned, the company toured regularly and frequently, showing the flag in the name of Protestantism. With Edward's death in 1553, these same players became the queen's company; and with Mary's marriage to the king of Spain they became the king's and queen's company and showed themselves each year in the countryside, and presumably in the City, under their new title and under the flag of Catholicism. With the accession of Elizabeth in 1558 they became once again the queen's players. But Elizabeth seems to have had ideas of her own with respect to the politics of patronage and the uses to which playing companies might be put. Having inherited a company of royal interluders, she kept them dutifully on the payroll but seems to have made no use of them. They played fitfully through the 1560s, though probably not in the name of any ideology, and died out finally for lack of replacement in 1571. They may have served no overt political function at all during her reign, though we have, from 1559, reference to the remark of the Spanish ambassador in London that William Cecil "was supplying playwrights with material for plays making mock of Philip of Spain."[32] If this is true, the vehicle may well have been companies other than the royal one. Elizabeth seems not to have changed her mind on this point until 1583, when she once again formed a company of royal players; but the agenda of this latter company seems to have centered on comedy rather than propaganda.

Royal patronage, then, which must have set a kind of standard in the 1530s and 1540s, had dwindled to nothing by the 1570s. There is no correlative evidence that the number of players in the City or the level of playing activity had correspondingly dwindled; if anything, the opposite is true. It is perhaps not surprising that the City found itself increasingly pestered at mid-century by what it took to be groups of unaffiliated and unregulated players, some of them not above falsifying the certifications needed to pursue their craft. In 1552 Cecil's agent, Richard Ogle, wrote to Cecil to report, "I have sent a feyned lycence to the councell whych we toke ffrom players";

---

[32] *ES* 1:244. Conyers Read (in "William Cecil and Elizabethan Public Relations," a chapter in the festschrift *Elizabethan Government and Society: Essays Presented to Sir John Neale*, ed. S. T. Bindoff, J. Hurstfield, and C. H. Williams [London: Athlone Press, 1961], p. 27) continues: "This may have been true, but there is no other evidence to support it."

Ogle thought the offense was "a thyng moche to be loked too and the offendo^{r}s worthy punysshement."[33]

But as the new wisdom was coming to understand, even patronized players could be a problem. A Privy Council memorandum from 1546 records the apprehension of "v persons naming themselfes Therle of Bathes s^{r}u^{a}ntes Who had played Lewde playes in the suburbes in London," for so doing they had been "committed to the counter in London", though only four days later—perhaps because of their patron's intervention—they were "ordered to be put to Libertie vppon bond not to play w^{t}out special Lycence of the counsail."[34]

Bath's players and the players with the feigned license are but a small part of the theatrical picture at mid-century. From 1535 to the accession of Elizabeth in 1558, companies of traveling players with nonroyal patrons appear regularly in the records of provincial towns. In addition to Bath's troupe, players traveled during this period under the patronage of dukes (Norfolk, Northumberland, Somerset, Suffolk), duchesses (Suffolk), marquesses (Dorset, Northampton), earls (Arundel, Bedford, Oxford, Sussex), barons (Bray, Chandos, Grey, Herbert, Seymour), and knights (Sir George Somerset). This is but a partial list; names of other patrons occur in the records, and no doubt still others have gone unrecorded. There seems to have been no shortage of patrons; what is less well understood is whether patronized troupes such as those listed here were provincial, domiciled at their patron's country seat and traveling only when he or she traveled, or whether they were principally resident in London, maintained in the City by their patron. If the latter, then the City was far more full of playing companies than we have formerly imagined. Either way, the presence of these players would have been felt in the City even as the presence of their patrons was.

Many of these groups continued under the same patrons into Elizabeth's reign. Other patrons disappear from the records, however, and, perhaps inevitably, new patrons appear in the first years after 1558, such as the earl of Derby and the brothers Ambrose and Robert Dudley (shortly to become the earls of Warwick and Leicester). The last two men seemed to understand, as Henry VIII had,

---

[33] PRO, S.P.10/15, fo. 75, item 33, 27 October 1552.

[34] BL, ms. Add. 5476, a Privy Council register from 10 May 1545 to June 1547 (one of the few such registers not deposited in the PRO), fo. 197^v, meeting of 6 May 1546 at Greenwich. Calendared in *L&P* 22, pt. 1:373.

that troupes of players could be politically useful; though their own fortunes were precarious and their prospects uncertain in the new reign—or perhaps because of those considerations—troupes playing under their patronage appeared seemingly within minutes after the coronation of Elizabeth.[35] Ambrose Dudley's players were at Bristol in September 1559, where Dudley was described in the town records as "m^r of the interlude players,"[36] whatever that may mean; and Robert Dudley, three months earlier, had occasion to write to the earl of Shrewsbury requesting license for his players to perform in Yorkshire. In this well-known letter, Dudley spoke of the players as "my servauntes," who "be suche as ar plaiers of interludes" and who "have the Licence of diverse of my Lords here . . . to plaie in diverse shieres within the realme."[37]

Dudley's letter seems to have been a response to Elizabeth's proclamation of 16 May 1559, in which licensing was declared to be a necessary prerequisite to playing.[38] The proclamation, a restatement of similar regulations by Elizabeth's predecessors, constituted no new message for its intended recipients. In straightforward and direct language, it held sheriffs and lords lieutenant responsible for the good conduct of all who played, with authority to imprison offenders. The subject of concern, according to the language of the proclamation, was "common Interludes in the Englishe tongue," and the danger was that "some that haue ben of late vsed, are not conuenient in any good ordred Christian Common weale to be suffred." The licensing officers were charged—"euery of them, as they will aunswere"—to "permyt none to be played wherin either matters of religion or of the gouernaunce of the estate of the common weale shalbe handled or treated."

In addition to these "common Interludes," the proclamation addressed, at its close, the matter of patronized players. "And further her maiestie gyueth speciall charge to her nobilitie and gentilmen, as they professe to obey and regarde her maiestie, to take good order in thys behalfe wyth their seruauntes being players, that this her maiesties commaundement may be dulye kepte and obeyed."

---

[35] Their father, John Dudley, created duke of Northumberland in 1551, had similarly taken a company of players to himself on the instant and kept them until his death in 1553.

[36] J. T. Murray, *English Dramatic Companies* (London: Constable, 1910), 2:209.

[37] In *ES* 4:264.

[38] *ES* 4:263–64.

Dudley's letter, complying with the intent of the proclamation, serves as good evidence for two related matters. It shows, by example, that the proclamation was being taken seriously, that licensing was now seen to be an important matter, and that a patron might facilitate the process for his players; and it further shows that, in Dudley's view, it was important that his players be free to travel and perform in the provinces—important enough that he would intervene on their behalf if necessary. I take this latter notion as another instance of the use of players as a means of showing the flag, and one might easily speculate on a variety of motives impelling Dudley to such action on his own behalf.[39]

In the larger view, the royal proclamation and the letter from Dudley also suggest that, in the new climate of licenses and restrictions, playing companies would fare badly without patrons. The theatrical excesses that followed on well-intentioned official policy in the late 1530s, and again during the first two years of Edward's reign, were sufficient warning to the new queen that players must be kept firmly in check. It may be no accident that in the 1560s, judging from the few plays that have survived from this period, playwrights turned from political and religious contentiousness to a concern with more generalized social ills.[40] From this point on, the history of public playing in London is a history of patronized companies; and in the provinces, though common troupes managed to survive for another decade or two, the same outcome eventually prevailed. The patronized company was no doubt stronger, in that it had assurance of a degree of stability: in exchange for the adoption of a certain decorum in presentation and the acceptance of certain obligations of fealty, the players might expect a continuing association and an affiliation that would work to their benefit. If their patron saw a benefit to himself in the maintenance of players, so much the better. By contrast, the more mutable kind of common troupe that might have survived and even flourished in London in the 1530s and 1540s, answering to the needs of a less centralized and less sophisticated clientele, was now effectively dealt out of the marketplace.

---

[39] The earliest concrete evidence we have about Dudley's players as a group, dating from 1572, indicates that they were, at least by that date, a fully London-based company. James Burbage had been living in London since 1559, the year he married Ellen Brayne; his fellows, John Perkin and the rest, seem also to have been City players. More on all of this in the next chapter.

[40] See David Bevington, *Tudor Drama and Politics* (Cambridge, Mass: Harvard University Press, 1968), chap. 10, for more on this head.

Had the City and the crown not attempted, each for its own reasons, to regulate the terms and conditions of playing during the middle years of the century, then common players might have continued to flourish, operating as free agents and perpetuating an economic viability based on topical interludes, rented garments, and temporary playing spaces. Not pressured to do anything differently, they would have felt little need to grow or develop. But the evidence does not permit such a narrative. The licensing regulations and the increased governmental assertion of control impelled the players in turn to consider their own self-interest and to devise new ways of managing their affairs. Some of them were up to this challenge, others were not. The acquisition of patronage was the first step by which a London-based group of players might hope to get a better grip on its economic lifeline; in this the players would merely be following the pattern set down earlier by their provincial brethren in the great houses. The next step was to find ways to control, or even to take into their own hands, the terms and circumstances under which they played. But both these steps required an unfamiliar venturesomeness, a reaching out for new relationships. Step one brought the patrons into the picture, the Leicesters and Warwicks and others—some of them willing participants in the new arrangement; and step two brought in the businessmen, the John Braynes and Philip Henslowes and the rest—some of them even more willing.

This, at any rate, is the narrative I assemble from the data at hand. In some places, as I have acknowledged, the surviving evidence is so scanty that my arguments are largely hypothetical; in other places there are more documents available than I have used, but none, I hope, which will damage my construct. The burden of my argument has been that one might see a development in the economic status of the London-based playing company from the 1540s to the 1570s and that the growth of the Elizabethan theater, or its "rise and progress" as Malone termed it, would not have happened in quite the way it did without the governmental exploitation of plays under the late Henry and possibly again under the early Edward, the undesirable consequences of such activity, and the resultant shift toward licensing at mid-century. I think it possible to see in retrospect that players who were not members of permanent companies, who did not have permanent playing places, who did not even own their own costumes, were as a consequence not economically circumstanced to bring about the remarkable development of Elizabethan drama which we know took place. The future was to be in the hands of players with more aggressive instincts, of performing entrepreneurs who sold their vision of active drama to patrons on the one hand and to investors on the other. As I read the evidence, the erection of the Red Lion in Stepney in 1567 (or something like it) was but the inevitable next step, once the constraints of licensing had been internalized. The later developments—the Theater, the Rose, the Swan, the Globe, and all that happened within those structures— would not have come about under either the laissez-faire playing conditions that served for Rastell and his companions in the 1520s or the privileged servitude of Bale and his company in the 1540s.

CHAPTER FOUR

John Brayne, Grocer:
Stepney, 1567

I

Let them show the former things, what they be, that we may
consider them, and know the latter end of them.

—Isaiah 41:22

With the accession of Mary Tudor to the English throne in July
1553 the Protestant experiment that had flourished under Edward VI
was brought to an end, and the Catholic faith and liturgy reinstituted.
Radical Protestant fervor, so praiseworthy in the earlier reign, was
now treasonable, and the guardians of the newly returned faith
were alert for signs of anti-Catholic fanaticism, which, they suspected
might lurk beneath any stone or bush.

Henry Machyn, a Londoner and a purveyor of funeral trappings,
kept a diary during this period, though in its pages the turmoil of
the times is largely invisible. Narrowly parochial in its concerns, a
document that only an antiquarian could love, the diary records
little more than a series of processions, not only funeral processions
but also royal processions, religious processions, lord mayors'
processions, and many other kinds of processions, the descriptions
often verging on the formulaic. Machyn's entry for Corpus Christi
Day in 1554, however, contains an arresting account. The feast of
Corpus Christi is tied to Easter and is therefore a movable feast; in
1554 it fell on 24 May, near the end of the first year of Mary's reign,
and so its celebration was Romish in tone and format for the first
time in two decades.

Every parish was to have its festivity on that day, and according to
Machyn there were "mony goodly prossessyons in mony par-
ryches," with "stayffe torchys bornyng" and rich liturgical canopies
"borne a-bowt the strett." In particular, the men of "sant Pulcurs
parryche [i.e., St. Sepulchre without Newgate] went a-bowt ther
owne parryche" and also processed, with their neighbor parishes,
"in Smythfeld," where, "as they wher goohyng, ther cam a man
unto the prest that bare the sacrament, and began to pluke ytt owt of
ys hand, and [*in*]contenent he druw ys dager, and [*in*]contenent he
was taken and cared to Nuwgate."[1]

It is not clear that Machyn even saw the event he described, but
his version of the story was the same as the one circulated by the
new Marian authorities as proof of their wisdom in worrying about
lingering Protestant disaffection. The annalist John Stow, repeating
the story in his chronicle, made it somewhat more particular. The
anonymous "man" of Machyn's account was identified as "a joyner
that dwelt in Colman streete called John Strete"; and Stow added the
detail that, once in Newgate, the man "fayned him selfe madde."[2]

It must have been a popular story, for it did not go away. A few
years later, when Mary had been succeeded by Elizabeth and the
Protestants were again in power, a different narrative emerged.
John Foxe, the martyrologist, found the then-current version a
willful distortion and "not to be credited." In Foxe's view the poor
man of the account, far from being a madman or even a radical, was
but another of God's poor martyrs. Here is Foxe's alternative
account of the incident:

> vppon Corpus Christi day, the procession being made in Smithfield,
> where, after the manner the Priest with his boxe went vnder the
> Canapy, by chaunce there came by the way a certaine simple man,
> named John Streate, a ioyner of Coleman streete, who hauing some
> hast in his busines, and finding no other way to passe through, by
> chaunce went vnder the Canapy by the Priest. The Priest seeing the
> man so to presume to come vnto the Canapy, being belike afraid, and
> worse feared then hurt, for feare let his Pixe fall downe. The poore man
> being straight wayes apprehended, was had to the Counter, the Priest
> accusing him vnto the Counsayle, as though he had come to slay him,
> when as the poore man (as he himselfe hath since declared vnto vs)
> had no such thought euer in his mind. Then from the Counter he was

---

[1] *The Diary of Henry Machyn*, ed. John Gough Nichols, Camden Society, o.s. vol. 42
(London, 1848), pp. 63–64.

[2] *Machyn*, p. 338. The notes to the Street passage include the citation from Stow.

had vnto Newgate, where he was cast into the Dongeon, there
chayned to a post, where he was cruelly & miserably handled & so
extremely dealt withall, that being but simple before, he was now
feared out of his wit altogether, and so vpon the same had to Bedlem.[3]

Simple John Street thus became an unwitting witness for the faith,
a liturgical antihero, admitted to the fellowship of suffering martyrs
when all he wanted to do was cross the road. Foxe might secretly
have wished that the account had more vigor to it; in a more
well-made story, the man's attack on the relics of heathenish
idolatry would have been deliberate, as it was some twenty-five
years later in Anthony Munday's account of one "Richard Atkins" in
his curious tract called *The Englishe Romayne Lyfe*. According to
Munday's narrative, this "Atkins" found himself in Rome in the
summer of 1581, "And one day going in the streete, he met a Preest
carying the Sacrament, which offending his conscience, to see the
people so croutch and kneele to it: he caught at it to haue throwne it
downe, that all the people might see what they worshipped."[4]

Nicholas Ling, who published Munday's book in 1582, must have
been taken by the symbolism of this narrative incident, for he spent
the extra money necessary to embellish it with a full-page four-part
woodcut (see Figure 2). Such stories, and such illustrations, about
the destruction of popish icons became in their turn the narrative
and pictorial icons of a strengthened Protestantism. John Street
might well have had a larger place in such a tradition, or in the
panoply of English martyrs, had he been more violent, or more of an
ideologue.

But such was not John Street's style. He was, as Foxe said he was,
a simple joiner, a family man in his early thirties at the time of his
sudden notoriety. He had been married for eight years, and two of
his four children were still living, the youngest, Peter, being a bare
nine months old. The family lived in the parish of St. Stephen's
Coleman Street, just east of the Guildhall, where John had his shop
and kept his apprentices, one of whom was buried in the churchyard
in 1551. John Street was poor; at no point during his life did the

---

[3] The passage from Foxe's *Actes and monuments* is taken from the 1583 edition (*STC*
11,225), where it appears on p. 1473. A convenient modern source is *The Acts and
Monuments of John Foxe*, 8 vols., ed. J. Pratt, 4th ed. (London, 1877), where the relevant
passage is in vol. 6, p. 560.

[4] Anthony Munday, *The Englishe Romayne Lyfe*, 1582 (*STC* 18,272), p. 73. The modern
edition by Philip Ayres (Oxford: Clarendon Press, 1980) reproduces the woodcut.

Figure 2. Upper left quarter of the woodcut in Anthony Munday's *English Romayne Life* (London, 1582), STC 18272. Published by permission of the Folger Shakespeare Library.

collectors of the subsidy find his worldly goods to be worth as much as three pounds.

St. Stephen's was one of the City's larger parishes, extending some five hundred yards in its greatest dimension, but so narrow that no parishioner lived more than a hundred yards from the parish boundary. Perhaps three thousand people lived in the parish at this time, most of them of the poorer sort.[5] For reasons of proximity as well as trade, John Street, from the mid-1550s onward, would surely have known his fellow parishioner and fellow joiner James Burbage. Burbage was some ten years Street's junior, having been born (by his own testimony) in about 1531;[6] in 1554, the year of John Street's

[5] See Edwin Freshfield, "Some Remarks upon the Book of Records and the History of the Parish of St. Stephen, Coleman Street, in the City of London," *Archeologia* 50 (1865), 17–57. The St. Stephen's Coleman Street registers are at the Guildhall Library, mss. 4448 and 4449/1.

[6] The mandatory keeping of parish records did not begin until 1538, so it is un-

sudden notoriety, Burbage would thus have been in his early twenties, nearing the end of his apprenticeship, and living at his master's house.

A fanciful narrative would posit James Burbage as John Street's apprentice; he might have been so, as the dates fit (Street was free by 1546 and could have taken an apprentice at any time thereafter), and Street seems to have been the only married joiner living in St. Stephen's parish for the whole of that time.[7] An alternative narrative would have Burbage serving under another master, then being taken on by Street as a journeyman after achieving his freedom. Either of these versions would account for Burbage's continuing presence in the parish as a freeman.

But John Street was not the only possible parish connection for James Burbage. There was, as it happens, a whole other Burbage family traceable in St. Stephen's parish before 1559, and this family may possibly be James Burbage's kin. If James was not living with John Street's family as an apprentice, he might have been living as a young unmarried freeman with a parishioner named Daniel Burbage. In 1546, the year of John Street's marriage to Margaret Bullace, Daniel Burbage was also married at St. Stephen's, to Helen Parker, and Daniel and Helen had five children over the next eight years. Once again, a fanciful narrative would propose a connection; the difference in ages between Daniel and James was probably less than fifteen years; they could have been cousins, even brothers. There is, however, no evidence either in the register or elsewhere to suggest a family link between this Daniel Burbage and our James Burbage, other than the repetitive and teasing entries in the register about Daniel's trade: he was a minstrel.

Had Daniel lived longer, he might have left more clues about himself. But he died in the spring of 1563, probably in his early forties, leaving no will; two of his children died later in the same

---

likely we will find an official birth or baptismal record for James or anyone of his generation.

[7] Parishioners got their names enrolled in the parish register by getting married, having their children baptized, or being buried; apart from such events, their daily lives went by unnoticed in such a document. The first of those recordable things happened to James Burbage in 1559; prior to that time he was formally invisible. There may have been other invisible joiners in the parish as well; but those joiners (indeed, those guildsmen in general) who took apprentices into their homes were likely to be married, thus likely—as John Street was—to be traceable because of family baptisms or burials. A joiner named Edmund Tuckney makes an appearance in the St. Stephen's parish register after 1551, but he may well have been a new freeman that year, as Burbage would have been by 1555 or 1556.

year, no doubt victims of the bad plague that summer, the same plague that carried off poor John Street and three of his children. Daniel's widow, Helen, died a dozen years later, in 1575, and did leave a will,[8] but in it she mentioned no relatives, only her surviving children, Anne and Lawrence. The son had aspired to be a carpenter, even as did John Street's son Peter, who was of the same age; but Lawrence gave up midway through his apprenticeship and disappeared from view, while Peter, as we know, went on to a greater glory.

There are also other Burbages for our notice besides Daniel, and happily for us their relationship to James is clearer, though the other information about them is just as scanty. James, it seems, had two brothers, Robert and William, both of whom lived as adults in the parish of St. Giles Cripplegate, a large parish that adjoins St. Stephen's. Robert became a carpenter; he was apprenticed in 1566, on the same day that Daniel's son Lawrence was apprenticed, and he secured his freedom in 1573. At first glance these dates would seem to suggest that Robert was considerably younger than his brother James. A youth apprenticed in 1566 would likely have been born in about 1550. If this is the case with Robert, he would have been twenty years younger than James.

And he may have been; one notes, however, from an inspection of the apprenticeship records of the Carpenters' Company (made easily accessible by the company's admirable editing and publishing program[9]) that the typical age of apprenticeship in that guild, once such information began to be recorded in the 1570s, was considerably higher than in other London companies. Rare is the apprentice in his mid teens; the average age is twenty. The work may simply have been too demanding for the average young boy. Lawrence Burbage was sixteen when he was indentured; Peter Street was seventeen.

---

[8] The will of Helen or Ellen Burbage ("Elen Burbytch") is in the Guildhall Library, ms. 9172/9A, fo. 162. It is an original will, not a register copy, and is nuncupative.

[9] The records of the company are on deposit in the Guildhall Library and are being transcribed and published under the general title *Records of the Worshipful Company of Carpenters*. The first four volumes (1913, 1914, 1915, and 1916) were edited by Bower Marsh and published by Oxford University Press; the next two (1937, 1939) were edited by John Ainsworth and published by Phillimore; volume 7 (1968) was edited by A. M. Millard and published by Pinhorn's on the Isle of Wight. Further volumes are to come. The existing volumes are fully indexed for proper names, less well indexed for other categories such as place names, trades, or subject headings. For example, the Red Lion (mentioned in the records in 1567, and discussed later in this chapter) does not appear in the index.

They were both on the young side.[10] Robert Burbage, on these analogies, could have been born anywhere from 1550 at the latest to 1540 as a possible earliest. Even the earliest of these dates, however, would make him a decade younger than James.

James's other brother, William, was of an indeterminate age. William had a son John who was baptized in the church of St. Giles Cripplegate in 1578; in that year James would have been forty-seven, Robert possibly as old as thirty-seven. William could easily have been near to either of these ages. James Burbage himself had sired a daughter two years earlier, in 1576; so the baptism of William's son John is of little help in establishing his age.

The evidence for all of these relationships is to be found in Robert's will, made in 1583 and preserved in the Guildhall Library.[11] In it he spoke of his mother, Margaret, as still living; he named his brother William and William's son John, and he named his brother James and James's children Ellen, Alice, Cuthbert, and Richard, along with James's friend, John Brayne. There is unfortunately no evidence here of a connection with the minstrel Daniel, nor is it likely that there would be, for Daniel and his wife were both long dead. But Robert's mother was still alive, and we need to remember that she is not necessarily James's mother; she may have been a second wife for their father. This circumstance might account for the seeming gap in years between James's birth and Robert's and also explain how she was still alive in 1583, when any mother of James would have been in her seventies if not older.

Robert's membership in the Company of Carpenters is documented in the records of the company. We are on shakier ground with James Burbage's profession of joiner. Burbage would have belonged to the ancient guild of joiners centered at the church of St. James Garlickhithe, which functioned as a sort of fraternity for both

---

[10] Here, for example, are the age figures taken from the apprentice entries for the accounting year 1575/76, the year in which the Theater was built. There were fifty-three apprentices that year (a lower number than usual). The two youngest apprentices were Thomas Nightingale, age twelve, and Jonas Lawrence, age thirteen. Each of them was indentured for a full twelve years, to bring them to the necessary age of twenty-four, the minimum age for a freeman. One can only wonder what their duties were during the early years of their servitude. At the other extreme, the oldest apprentice was Randolph Pinchback, age thirty, who indentured himself for the minimally requisite seven years, so that he would have been thirty-seven when he earned his freedom. Between these outer limits were one boy indentured at the age of 14, three at 16, seven at 17, eight at 18, four at 19, six at 20, five at 21, six at 22, two at 23, three at 24, and thereafter one at each age up to 30.

[11] Ms. 25,626/2, fo. 273.

joiners and wood carvers. The guild, founded in 1375, replaced whatever organization had existed earlier. In 1401 the guild received its license from the lord mayor and the Court of Aldermen, and by the early fifteenth century had its formal stages of apprenticeship, freedom, and livery, as well as an official standing in the City. John Street was described in his father-in-law's will in 1546 as "citizen and joiner of London," the traditional formula for a freeman of a recognized guild. Such guilds had a monopoly of the trades they represented; one could not practice joinery in London except under the auspices of the guild of joiners. The Carpenters' Company itself regularly called in "a Joyner" to mend tables and trestles, windows and doors in Carpenters' Hall. As James Burbage was by occupation a joiner—we have ample testimony to that—he must have been a freeman of this company. The parish clerk at St. Stephen's knew him for a joiner and so described him in the entries for his wedding in 1559 and at the baptism of his first child, Mary.

But the guild of joiners, although a monopoly, apparently did not have the full range of powers to license, examine, and control which most other companies had, for it operated without a royal charter. The guild was not formally chartered by the crown as a livery company until 1571, when James Burbage would have been about forty years old. The royal charter empowered the newly reconstituted company from that year forward to make searches, to certify or penalize workmanship, and to levy assessments, much as the more established companies—goldsmiths and mercers and grocers —had been doing for years. Anyone working as a joiner in the City in 1571, even James Burbage, who "reaped but a small lyving by the same" (as an opponent in a lawsuit said of him some years later), would have come under the new company's more stringent purview. The incorporation of the company may have forced marginally successful joiners to rethink their allegiance to their craft; the new terms were sure to make their life more rigorous. Unfortunately for us, the earliest records of the new Company of Joiners have all perished; the charter, a grant of arms, some bylaws, and a few deeds are all that survive.[12]

It is possible, however, that by 1571 James Burbage had already relinquished the trade for other reasons. The parish clerk at St. Stephen's, who was not a model of consistency even in the best of

---

[12] For information about the early years of the Joiners' Company, see *Annals of the Worshipful Company of Joiners of the City of London*, ed. Henry Laverock Phillips (London: privately printed, 1915).

times—he regularly got Burbage's name wrong[13]—stopped referring to James Burbage as "joiner" after 1560, though he continued to describe John Street as a joiner until his death. This absence may suggest, though it need not, that Burbage had turned to another trade by the early 1560s. We do know that he identified himself as a joiner and not as a player in the lease of the Shoreditch property for the Theater from Giles Allen in 1576; but we have learned, from the example of James Tunstall, saddler, John Heminges, grocer, Martin Slater, ironmonger, and Philip Henslowe, dyer, that these appellations provide a kind of shorthand social identification that may have nothing to do with a person's actual means of livelihood.

Yet another set of neighbors in St. Stephen's parish was the family of Thomas Brayne, a tailor by trade though a freeman of the Girdlers' Company. Thomas Brayne and Alice Barlow had been married early in 1541 and had two children, John and Ellen.[14] At the age of thirteen John was apprenticed to a grocer, the aptly named John Bull, and spent nearly a dozen years of servitude living and working in Bull's house and shop in Bucklersbury, a small lane at the eastern end of Cheapside.[15] Sometime between 1560 and 1565 the apprentice received his freedom; one can't be more precise about the date because the wardens' accounts for that five-year period

---

[13] The clerk seemed unable to remember whether the name was Burbidge or Bridges. Here are all the entries from the earliest register (ms. 4448) relating to a James Bridges or James Burbidge; it seems unlikely that they refer to more than one person. If they are two people, then they have the distinction of marrying the same woman (or perhaps two sisters with the same name), and having children with the same first names.
1559: "Weddynge of James Brydgys Joynner And helen Brayne the dowghter of thomas brayne Taylor the xxiij[th] day of Aprylle"
1559: "Chrystenynge of Marye Brydgys the dowghter of James Brydgys Joynner the xxiiij day of decembre"
1562: "Christeninge of Richard Burdbidge the sonne of James Burdbidge the xxviij of maye 1562"
1563: "Christening of Adam Bridges the childe of James Bridges the same daie" (as the previous entry on the page, i.e., 5 September)
1563: "Burying of Adam bridges the childe of James Bridges ye xiiij[th] of septemb[r]"
1563: "Burienge of marie Bridges the xix daie of november"
1565: "Christenynge of cvtbart bvrbidge ye child of James bvrbidge ye 15 of June"
1568: "Chrystninges of Rychard briggys the child of James brygges the vij daye of July A° 68"
1574: "christerninge of Elen breges the child of James breges the xiij day of June"
[14] Thomas married Alice in her parish church, St. Michael Bassishaw (the parish immediately to the west of St. Stephen Coleman Street), on 22 January 1541. I am grateful to Mary Edmond, who found this entry, for communicating it to me. Thomas died in 1562; his widow, Alice, died in 1566; both are buried at St. Stephen Coleman Street. For his will, see GHL, ms. 9172/4B, fo. 91.
[15] He was apprenticed on 13 March 1554; GHL, ms. 11,571/5.

have perished.[16] As apprentices were required by statute to be at least twenty-four years old when they took up their freedom, John Brayne had to have been born in 1541, the year of his parents' marriage, in order to have been of legal age by 1565.

James Burbage made his first appearance in the St. Stephen's register when he married John Brayne's sister, Ellen. If the dates just mentioned above posit John Brayne as the first-born child of his parents, then Ellen must have been John's younger sister (I have found no baptismal record for either of them) and thus seventeen years old at the most when she and James Burbage were married in St. Stephen's on 23 April 1559. Seventeen was an unusually early age for a girl to marry in this period.[17] If James was indeed born in 1531 he would have been about twenty-seven years old on his wedding day. The day is also, by tradition, Shakespeare's birthday, but that event was still five years in the future.

John Brayne's own marriage, to Margaret Stowers, took place some six years later at St. Dionis Backchurch in 1565. The marriage must have been one of Brayne's first actions upon receiving his freedom in the Grocers' Company; he was twenty-four. St. Dionis was apparently Margaret Stowers's parish; the register entry for the wedding describes the groom as being of St. Stephen's Wallbrook, the parish in which Bucklersbury is located. After gaining his freedom, Brayne seems to have stayed in the Bucklersbury area, perhaps taking over his master's shop. All the Brayne children were subsequently baptized at St. Stephen's Wallbrook, while the children of James and Ellen Burbage were baptized at St. Stephen's Coleman Street until 1576.

Here, then, we have an initial cast of characters, made up of relatives, friends, and neighbors, who had known one another since the 1550s. It remains to notice the arrival of the two Burbage children who were to play such a prominent role in the history of the English stage. Cuthbert Burbage was baptized at St. Stephen's on 15 June 1565. The churchwarden that year was Cuthbert Beeston, a wealthy benefactor of the city and a prominent member of the Company of Girdlers, the company to which James Burbage's father-in-law had

---

[16] The next surviving volume of records commences with the 1565/66 accounting year, by which time John Brayne is already on record as a freeman.

[17] The average age for girls not of the upper classes was about twenty-five. See Lawrence Stone, *The Family, Sex, and Marriage in England, 1500–1800* (New York: Harper & Row, 1977), pp. 50–51. Ellen could of course have been John's twin, and thus eighteen, but this is still quite young.

belonged. Perhaps Cuthbert Beeston stood godfather to Cuthbert Burbage; it would have been a politic, and not uncharacteristic, move on James Burbage's part to invite him to do so, and the baby's name might thus be accounted for. Three years later, on 7 July 1568, James's son Richard was baptized. There had been an earlier son Richard born in 1562, who must have died soon thereafter, though I have not found the burial record. These baptismal dates tally reasonably well, though not exactly, with information we already have. In a series of lawsuits in 1590 and 1591 concerning the Theater, published over half a century ago by C. W. Wallace,[18] we learn from the depositions of John Alleyn and others that Richard Burbage was James Burbage's youngest son, perhaps nineteen or so in 1590, and that Cuthbert, by his own testimony, was twenty-four in 1591. We can now adjust these estimates by the necessary year or two to make them correct. James Burbage also deposed in this lawsuit, stating in 1591 that he was about sixty years old. No doubt this figure needs adjusting by a year or two as well, though we will probably never know how to do it. This single statement remains our only evidence for his age.

II

> . . . He that has wit, let him live by his wit; he that has none, let
> him be a tradesman.
>   —*Eastward Ho*, II.ii.

But the births of Cuthbert and Richard Burbage are not the most significant theatrical events of the mid-1560s. More important, surely, is a curious playhouse venture about which we know almost nothing, commencing nine years before the erection of the Theater, and which may have involved James Burbage and which certainly involved his brother-in-law John Brayne. The locale was a place called the Red Lion; the time, the summer of 1567. By then John Brayne was about twenty-six years old, married, living with his family in Bucklersbury, and working at his trade as a grocer. His name occurs regularly in the company records for this period; on

---

[18] Charles William Wallace, "The First London Theatre: Materials for a History," *Nebraska University Studies* 13 (January, April, July 1913), 1–297.

one occasion he was fined for selling rotten rhubarb.[19] By 1567 Brayne and James Burbage had been brothers-in-law for over eight years. Burbage was still living in St. Stephen's Coleman Street with his family: his son Cuthbert was two years old that summer and Richard was still a year away. Brayne had apparently entered into some sort of agreement with the landlord of a property called the Red Lion—"in the parishe of Stebinyhuthe" as it is described in its best known, and until recently its only known, citation[20]—to erect a stage and some galleries in order to mount a play about Samson. The landlord must have found the terms agreeable. Brayne contracted first with a carpenter named William Sylvester to erect the galleries, and later with another carpenter named John Reynolds to build the stage.[21] It seems that Brayne's desire was to have the whole structure completed by mid-July, but complications arose.

Brayne found fault with Sylvester's scaffolding almost as soon as it was set up, and found reason to sue Reynolds over the stage work a year or so later. The controversy with Sylvester is the one with which we are all more familiar. On 15 July 1567, with "the storye of Sampson" waiting to be staged, the wardens of the Carpenters' Company heard Brayne's complaint about the alleged deficiencies in Sylvester's scaffolds and set up a jury to view the workmanship and make a judgment. Four impartial freemen of the company were named, and both Sylvester and Brayne agreed to abide by their decision. The entry of this agreement, and its terms, in the court book of the Carpenters' Company was for many years our only evidence for the whole Red Lion enterprise, and one of the few surviving examples of Brayne's signature. Unfortunately, the details of Brayne's complaint were not recorded, nor is there an addendum noting the jury's decision. My guess in the latter case is that Sylvester's work was substantially approved as done. Sylvester was by all accounts competent in his craft; he had been a freeman of the

---

[19] The records of the Grocers' Company are in the Guildhall Library. Brayne appears in the wardens' accounts in virtually every year from 1565 (the first extant accounts after his freedom) until his death in 1586. The reference to the "evill ruberb" is ms. 11,571/6, fo. 401.

[20] *Carpenters' Company Records*, 3:95–96, 15 July 1567.

[21] The Sylvester information comes from the records of the Carpenters' Company, as above. The information about John Reynolds is contained in a lawsuit brought before the Court of King's Bench in Hilary term 11 Elizabeth (1569), discovered by Professor Janet Loengard. See her essay "An Elizabethan Lawsuit: John Brayne, his Carpenter, and the Building of the Red Lion Theatre," *Shakespeare Quarterly* 34 (1983), 298–310, for a transcription of the full text of the document.

company for eighteen years, was a member of the livery, and would rise to be warden of his company within eight years of this incident.

The controversy with Reynolds, detailed in a lawsuit recently discovered by Janet Loengard, provides us with much more substantive information. Reynolds signed a performance bond for Brayne on 17 June 1567, in which he promised to build "one Skaffolde or stage for enterludes or playes . . . in height from the grounde fyve foote," and to build upon that stage "one convenyent turrett" to stand "in heyghte from the grounde . . .thirtie foot." In what must appear to us as an inverting of priorities, Brayne required that the turret be completed by 24 June, and the stage by 8 July. Reynolds agreed to meet these deadlines or to forfeit twenty marks. The bond, presumably drawn at Brayne's own direction, noted that there were "galloryes nowe buyldinge" at the site, apparently a reference to Sylvester's work in progress. Sylvester's own deadline must have been within a week or so of Reynolds's final date, for Brayne appeared at Carpenters' Hall on the fifteenth of July with his complaint against Sylvester.

When Brayne sued Reynolds in the Court of King's Bench some eighteen months later, in January or February of 1569, he hoped to collect his twenty marks on the bond, claiming that Reynolds had defaulted. Reynolds in turn argued that Brayne's claim was groundless because the stipulated work had all been completed on time, indeed ahead of time, the turret on 20 June and the stage by 1 July. But the work had not gone smoothly, according to Reynolds: he contended that Brayne had continually interfered with him during the course of the construction. Sylvester may have told a similar tale to the wardens of the Carpenters' Company. One cannot help but wonder what Brayne's private agenda was that summer. We must remember that he was only twenty-six years old; if the playhouse undertaking was his first major investment, he may have been nervous about the expenses and thus needlessly contentious about many phases of the project. We must be grateful for this state of affairs, however, for without it we would have none of the present evidence.

It is safe to conclude that, as the work of erecting the scaffolding for both the stage and the galleries was undertaken by freemen of the Carpenters' Company, any other workmen would have also been members of that company, or their apprentices; guild rules would have prohibited taking on an outsider like James Burbage, despite his possible skills with hammer and saw. Nor is it likely that Burbage would have been interested in such labor, for by 1567 he had no doubt already given over his erstwhile trade. But other possible connections present themselves. One may wonder if Burbage was involved as a player in the play about Samson that was to be performed on the new stage. Perhaps it was Burbage's desire to mount the play which brought about Brayne's involvement in the project. One can perhaps conclude, from the statements made in the 1590 lawsuit between the Burbages and the widow Brayne, that John Brayne was unlikely to have had an independent interest in the stage. Like his later interest in the Theater, his interest in the Red Lion may well have been a product of his brother-in-law's importunities. Even his attempt to decry the finished carpentry work as incomplete or defective, perhaps in an effort to reduce his charges, may have been inspired by Burbage's suggestion. We will never know; but such behavior was certainly not beyond Burbage, as the records unearthed by Wallace amply testify.

The precise location of the Red Lion is an equally puzzling matter. To say merely that it was in the parish of Stepney, as the entry in the Carpenters' records does, is only slightly more helpful than to say that St. Paul's is in London. Stepney proper was a small village a half mile or so east of the city; but its church, St. Dunstan's, served a much wider area, commonly known as Stepney parish or (more simply but more confusingly) as Stepney. This larger notion of "Stepney" embraced a community that began at the eastern edge of the City, near Aldgate and the Tower, and extended eastward nearly a mile downriver, enclosing not only the village of Stepney but also the hamlets of Mile End, Shadwell, Ratcliff, and Limehouse. Some of these smaller communities had their own places of worship, constituted initially as chapelries attached to St. Dunstan's but later achieving independence. One such chapel that had already become a separate entity by Elizabeth's reign was the church (and parish) colloquially known as Whitechapel, more properly the parish of St. Mary Matfellon.

The term "Stebinyhuthe," or Stepney Heath, is a Londoner's term, referring indifferently to any one of the open areas in that part of "Stepney" which was adjacent to the City. There are, unfortunately, no maps or surveys of Stepney parish, or even of the western end of the parish, from the 1560s; as a result, with only the entry in the Carpenters' records as our guide, we have hitherto been quite unable to locate the Red Lion. But the Reynolds lawsuit gives more circumstantial information; it tells us that the scaffolds were to be erected "wythyn the Courte or yarde lying on the south syde of the Garden belonginge to the messuage or farme house called and

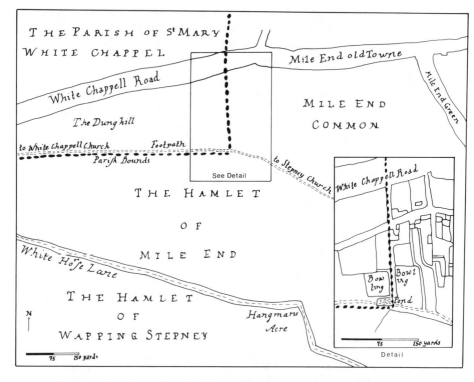

Figure 3. Location of the Red Lion playing structure, based on the map of Mile End Old Town by Joel Gascoyn, surveyor, 1703 (exemplar from the Stepney Central Library collection)

knowen by the name of the Sygne of the Redd Lyon . . . scituate and beinge at Myle End in the Paryshe of Seynt Mary Matfellon otherwyse called Whyte Chappell without Algate of London, some-tyme called Starks House."[22]

This description is filled with useful details, but it requires a certain amount of decoding. Mile End is one of the Stepney parish hamlets; its center, no more than a few dwelling houses, lay some quarter of a mile or more beyond the easternmost edge of the St. Mary Matfellon parish boundary (see Figure 3). The open areas surrounding the village could, apparently, also be thought of as

[22] From the lawsuit, PRO, K.B.27/1229, memb. 30.

"Mile End," just as they could in another context be thought of as "Stepney Heath" or "Stebunheath." These options of nomenclature continued even if the open areas extended across the bounds of a neighboring parish. Our first task, then, is to understand where a structure that stood in Stebunheath (as in the Sylvester account) and also both in Mile End and in St. Mary Matfellon parish (as in the Reynolds account) might have been located.

We might begin by noting that the stage and galleries were to be built on the grounds of a messuage that was already known as the Red Lion, or as Red Lion Farm, and that had formerly been known as Stark's House. It is helpful to know that the name belonged to an existing messuage and was not simply Brayne's invention, for it is thus likelier to appear in other records. The survival of deeds and ground leases from this period is highly erratic, and one must be grateful for whatever scraps remain. I have found no references at all to a Stark's House[23] and no deeds to the Red Lion property itself; but there are three deeds from the later seventeenth century, currently on deposit at the Stepney Central Library, which describe a piece of ground standing just to the north of the farm.[24]

The first of the deeds (no. 2687) describes the ground in question as lying "on Mile End Greene in the parish of White Chappell," thus confirming the possibility of the two similar details in the Reynolds lawsuit. The piece is rectangular, some fifty feet east to west and some two hundred feet north to south. Its northern boundary fronts on the main highway leading from Aldgate past Whitechapel Church to Mile End and thence to Bow; on the south the ground "ffronteth the Redd Lyon." It would appear from this deed that the Red Lion property was set some distance south of the main road. The next deed (no. 2688) describes the same piece of ground, stating that the land "fronteth the Redd Lyon Inne" and is bounded on the

---

[23] There were some Starkeys in London who held property in Stepney in this period, but nothing connects them with the Red Lion Farm. See the 1545 will of Roger Starkey, mercer (PRO, P.C.C. 41 Pynnyng, now Prob.11/30, ff. 319^v–20^v), who left to his wife, Katherine, during her widowhood "All that my house or place withall thappurten^{a}nces being in Stebinheth which I late bowght and pourchased of James Awdeley Esquyer the house gardeyne orchyarde and the closes paled adyoynyng to the same Whiche I late bought and purchased of Thomas Marrowe gentilman." See also the 1552 will of Thomas Starkey, mercer (PRO, P.C.C. 1 Tashe, now Prob.11/36, ff. 4^v–5^r): "Item I gyve and bequeth to my said wieff a parcell of Lande which I bowght of John Starkey liynge at Stebynhith in the County of middelsex and one other percell of Lande whiche I bowght of mistres Nesterfeild also Lyinge at Stebenithe."

[24] The three deeds are as follows: no. 2687, 4 February 1688, Thomas Whitehead to John Mitchell; no. 2688, 14 February 1688, John Mitchell to William Morgan; no. 2689, 13 July 1689, John Mitchell to John Jackman.

west by "a Cart way or passage Leading from the Kings Highway there to the Redd Lyon Inne aforesaid." The last of the three deeds (no. 2689) describes the piece of ground as lying "on the Southside of Milend Greene neere the Red Lyon Inne or farme in the parish of St. Mary White Chappell" and separated from the farm by "the ffoote Path or Cawsway Leading from White Chappell to Stepney Church."

Thus we have, in these three deeds, independent confirmation of the continued existence of a property at Mile End called the Red Lion Farm, known at the time of the deeds as the location of an inn. While the property at issue in the deeds is—like the playhouse site itself—described as lying both in Mile End and in St. Mary Matfellon or Whitechapel parish, no description of the farm itself suggests that it shares this double location. From the deeds we learn that the farm had a cartway leading to it from the main road and that it lay to the south of the footpath to Stepney Church. The earliest maps of the area show many of these details clearly, as in Figure 3: the highway, the footpath, the parish boundary. From these maps it is clear that the footpath served as the parish bounds, so that property south of that line would not be in Whitechapel but in Mile End or Stepney only. Yet the courtyard "belonginge to the . . . farme house" where the scaffolds were to be erected was unambiguously in both places. Figure 4, based upon the earliest of the surviving maps, shows my conjectural location of the Red Lion Farm and of the playhouse site. This is a preliminary sketch, based on inadequate evidence; I do not recommend putting overmuch trust in it, but at some point one has to make a tentative first assumption.

There is no mention of an inn in the earlier evidence. The Carpenters' records speak simply of "the house called the Red Lyon in the parishe of Stebinyhuthe"; in the Reynolds lawsuit the property is described as a "messuage or farme house." Perhaps the farmhouse served as an inn in the 1560s, perhaps not. E. K. Chambers decided in 1923 that Brayne's Red Lion was a "playing-inn" and we have followed his lead ever since. The Reynolds evidence saves us from continuing in this assumption, for the bond is quite clear on that point. It says that the scaffolds were to be erected "wythyn the Courte or yarde lying on the south syde of the Garden belonginge to the messuage or farme house called and knowen by the name of the Sygne of the Redd Lyon." So a piece of land "belonging to"—the phrase is significant—the farm contained a garden plot, and there was an open yard to the south of the garden; in that open space a stage and galleries were to be erected. Brayne's

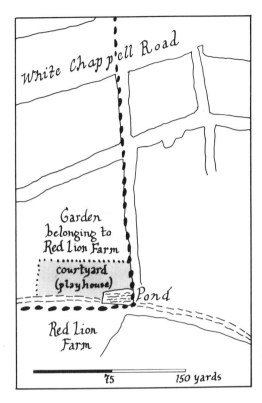

Figure 4. Conjectural location of the Red Lion playing structure, detail

venture was thus not even a "playhouse" in the strict sense of the term, as there was no building enclosing the stage and galleries. Both stage and galleries are described as "scaffolds," which suggest a kind of construction different from that found in playhouse buildings after 1576.[25]

It seems, then, from these bits of evidence that the structure that engaged Brayne's (and probably Burbage's) attention in 1567 was

---

[25] I am grateful to Professor Herbert Berry for sharing with me the pieces of evidence he is accumulating from the records of the Carpenters' Company regarding the nature of "scaffolds," which appear from the documents almost invariably to have been structures made up of poles and lashings rather than of timbers and nails. Thus a stage and a set of galleries might both have been "scaffolds" to a carpenter (as Brayne's structures were to both Sylvester and Reynolds); the term denotes the nature of construction rather than the intended use.

built to standards more characteristic of temporary than of permanent structures. Further, it was built a fair distance from the City—as far to the east as the later Newington Butts playhouse would be to the south—and on a site near, though not on, the main eastern highway out of the City. One ought to speculate on the possible reasons for these choices.

Mile End, the settlement just beyond Brayne's playing place, was itself best known during the period for its famous green, not only a traditional place of resort in warmer weather but the site of the annual assembly of the trained bands of the City militia when they gathered each May for drill and muster. Stow speaks of these events and alludes to the huge muster of 1539, not equaled in his lifetime, when all the trained bands were given orders "to goo owt at Algat to myllend grene, & the ffeylde ther abow t", then back in formation to the City; and then, as though that were not enough, to march onward to Westminster, then back to the City again.[26] The more normal pattern for a muster was much less ambitious; the trained bands assembled and disbanded at the green, making their way there and home on their own time, often with friends and families in tow as in any ordinary summer excursion to the same place. On all such occasions, no doubt there were demands made on the local population for some ale and some entertainment.[27]

In the earlier years of the century the Red Lion Farm, just off the main road to the green, may have been one of the places functioning as a tavern or place of refreshment for citizens on excursion or muster. If playing was also a traditional activity in the area, the landlord of the farm may have seen the development of an open air

[26] A collateral account of the 1539 muster can be found in BL, ms. Harl. 3741, printed in *Archeologia* 32 (1847), 33. An excerpt: "euery alderman w^t hys warde yn good order of batayll before vj of the clokke yn the mornyng came ynto the comon felde betwene myle ende & Whyte chapell / And than all the gonners sortyd theymselffes ynto one place / lykwyse dyd the pykes & the archars & the byll men Than euery company by hymselff rynged & swayled yn the felde, whiche was a goodly thynge to be holde ffor all the feeldes from Whyte chapell to myle ende / And from Bednall grene to Ratclyff & stepney were all coueryd w^t men yn bryght harnes w^t glysteryng weponn /." According to this account, there were minstrels in the muster, marching with the standard-bearers and, like them, dressed all in white.

[27] Nor would this have been an Elizabethan development; alehouses stood there from early times, and records show the presence of "players" at Mile End from the beginning of the century. The account book of John Heron, Henry VII's treasurer of the chamber, records on 6 August 1501 "Item to the pleyers at Myles Ende iij^s iiij^d" (PRO, E.101/415/3, fo. 61^v). See Sydney Anglo, "The Court Festivals of Henry VII: A Study Based upon the Account Books of John Heron, Treasurer of the Chamber," *Bulletin of the John Rylands Library* 43 (1960), 12–45.

playing space of his own as a reasonable extension of the facilities. The playing may well have been seasonal, and so a set of temporary scaffolds, to serve as stage and galleries, may have sufficed to test the profitability of such a venture over the first couple of seasons. The summer of 1567 was half over by the time the stage was ready for the Samson play, so the May muster of that year could not have been the primary purpose for its erection; but the structures probably survived for a few more years. It seems unlikely that they were later converted to a more permanent installation.

What happened after the play of Samson was finished? One possibility is that the scaffolding was removed and that the courtyard beside the garden reverted to its original use—whatever that might have been. Such a hasty dismantling makes little sense to me. The scaffolding for the galleries must have been moderately costly, else the wardens of the Carpenters' Company would not have troubled themselves to adjudicate the dispute between Brayne and Sylvester in so formal a manner. Entries of this sort are rare in the court book of the company, and when such disputes do appear they are normally adjudicated by two arbiters rather than the four assigned in this instance. It seems unlikely that a structure that called forth such attention should have been intended for a life no longer than the run of a single play. The alternative is that the scaffolding stayed up and that playing continued at the Red Lion for a few more years. Nine years after the Red Lion venture, in 1576, Brayne and Burbage were ready for a much more ambitious undertaking. It is perhaps safe to assume, from the greater magnitude of the Theater project, that their earlier experience at the Red Lion had been satisfactory and perhaps even profitable. I say "their" experience because I have already persuaded myself that Burbage was directly involved in the earlier affair. I do not see how he could have avoided being so. My own conjecture is that two attitudes emerged from the Red Lion experience: the first was that Brayne and Burbage confirmed their earlier belief that there was a substantial audience ready to support such a playing establishment; the second was that the road to Mile End was the wrong place for such an enterprise.

The first appearance of James Burbage in our standard reference works is in the year 1572, when he signed his name, along with five of his fellows, to a letter imploring the earl of Leicester to take them into his household service.[28] The letter makes it clear that Burbage

---

[28] *MSC* 1:348; *ES* 2:86.

was already one of the earl's players, and the prominence of his name in the letter—he was the first of the six signatories—has suggested to some scholars that he must have been the leader of the troupe and therefore that his association with Leicester was not new that year. His name is likewise mentioned first in the royal patent of 1574. Placing these dates beside the Red Lion dates, one verges on an interesting conjunction: if we allow ourselves to assume that Burbage's service as one of Leicester's players had begun some years earlier than the 1572 letter, and if we also assume a continuing use of the scaffolds at the Red Lion as a playing place for a few years after 1567, then the possibility arises that the Red Lion was one of the places where Leicester's men played.

This is an attractive idea, and a novel one, for which explicit evidence is entirely missing. We must remember that the Privy Council never mentioned the Red Lion as a place of playing, in any of its numerous letters to the Middlesex justices; the lord mayor never complained to the council about a playing place near Mile End just beyond his legal reach; nor is the Red Lion named in a letter or decree or proclamation of any sort as a place of playing. I take comfort, despite this litany of negatives, in the knowledge that we know very little about any of the early playing places in and about London. The four famous playing inns in the City—the Bell, the Bull, the Cross Keys, and the Bel Savage—were often the object of unwelcome civic attention from the lord mayor and the Court of Aldermen, for those inns all lay within the City's jurisdiction. Remove from the early history of those inns the documentary evidence from that one source, and almost nothing is left. The earliest known references to any of these inns, I should add, are a decade or more later than our 1567 references to the Red Lion. One must regret, from a documentary point of view, that the Red Lion lay outside the City's jurisdiction, for the result is that it attracted little notice. But I have no doubt that part of its appeal for Burbage and Brayne consisted in just that fact.

Taken all in all, we know perhaps as much about the Red Lion today as Edmund Malone knew about the Theater two centuries ago, though we know far more about the people involved in the enterprise than he did. The story line I have constructed for the Red Lion thus resembles his for the Theater, in being a mixture of interesting information and unproven possibilities; and my narrative, like his, may in the end be testimony principally to its author's proclivities. In this we share a kinship with the startled priest in the

Corpus Christi procession in 1554 who, seeing a confused John Street bearing down upon him, had to devise a hasty interpretation. All such early assessments, though destined to be modified by subsequent accounts, are essential as points of departure and thus serve a useful purpose in their own moment.

PART THREE

1576 AND
ITS NARRATIVES

PROLOGUE

A belief that historiography is a purely documentary or descriptive reconstitution of the past may be prone to blind fictionalizing because it does not explicitly and critically raise the problem of the role of fictions (for example, in the form of models, analytic types, and heuristic fictions) in the attempt to represent reality.

—Dominick LaCapra

The preeminent "story" in Elizabethan theater history tells of James Burbage and his building of a playhouse in Shoreditch in 1576. In the dominant nineteenth-century version of the story, the force behind this activity was James Burbage the stage player, a servant of the earl of Leicester, reacting to and responding to the needs of his fellow stage players for a playhouse of their own, in which they might pursue their craft free of the interference of the City. In this version of the story, the building known as the Theater had its conceptual and spiritual origins in the creative imagination of Burbage and in the fellowship of Leicester's players, the same men who had petitioned the earl in 1572 for his protection and livery and whose names were listed in 1574 in the royal patent affirming their privilege. The story tells how the collective wisdom of these players, based on their earlier experience with innyards, was sufficient to generate ideas about a basic structure for the new playhouse

The epigraph is from Dominick LaCapra, *Rethinking Intellectual History: Texts, Contexts, Language* (Ithaca: Cornell University Press, 1983), p. 62.

building, and how Burbage and John Brayne contrived to put up the cash to underwrite the project. The glorious result of this early community of effort was a structure that soon became its own emblem, symbolizing the birth and nurturance of the Elizabethan drama and, in its later days, nurturing as well the nation's greatest poet.

This is an attractive story line, Whiggish in its intimations of progress and improvement, eschatological in its anticipation of Shakespeare, and lucid in its easy identification of the forces of good and evil. Its attractiveness enabled it to persist as a viable account long after the vogue for such narratives had waned, and versions of it can still be heard in classrooms across the land. Wallace—whose romantic view of history was by no means incompatible with his passion for documents and "facts"[1]—came upon it as a young man and found it irresistible. He embellished his own version of the narrative by observing that the story of the playhouse was suffused with "a human interest of its own," from "its inception by James Burbage in 1576 to the full florescence of Shakespeare in 1599," and positing the origins of the Theater in a collegial Burbage, "a builder, a planner," who "was a good organizer, and was not without support at Court," who "saw possibilities" in the new project, who in 1576 "talked the situation over with his brother-in-law and others," and who "showed them that the erection of a building devoted solely to play-acting would be profitable."[2]

Wallace's recension of the story formed part of his introduction to a massive set of transcriptions which he published in 1913, providing scholars with an abundance of new material about the early history of the playhouse. Few of the documents he published bore out the

---

[1] Wallace happily embodied such ambiguities; in the same breath he could be a Comtean positivist, vowing to do his best "to maintain that new scientific attitude of modern historical research," and a Rankean empiricist, affirming; "In all my work I have had no theme to maintain, no theory to defend, and no hypothesis to propose. My sole guide has been the simple desire to find the truth and to tell it as I find it" (from an unpublished essay, "Shakespeare as a Man among Men," typescript on deposit at the Henry E. Huntington Library, Wallace Papers B2.i.24).

[2] C. W. Wallace, "The First London Theatre: Materials for a History," *Nebraska University Studies* 13 (1913), 1, 3, 4, 11. Malone was not aware of these notions, because Burbage's connection with the Theater had not been established at the time he wrote his *Historical Account of the Rise and Progress of the English Stage* in 1790. The story is very much a product of the nineteenth century, and the Burbage-as-colleague paradigm still persists. Here is Glynne Wickham in 1963: "In . . . 1574 the Earl of Leicester's Players were granted a royal Patent . . . and in 1576 a member of that company of players, James Burbage, erected a building principally, if not exclusively, to enable these players to exploit the financial advantages of this Patent to their fullest extent" (*Early English Stages, 1300–1660* (London: RKP, 1963) vol. 2, pt. 1:xii).

claims made in his introduction; rather, many of them suggested that collegiality was not a chief, or even a detectable, virtue of Burbage's. Wallace himself had clearly resisted the implications of this testimony, for his devotion to the Burbages ran deep, but later tellers of the story, making better use of the documents, found it easier to devalue the role of James Burbage the stage player and to focus instead on James Burbage the entrepreneur, whom they saw as responding to a private urge to get in on the profits of playing, to be a landlord and collect rents, and ultimately to become rich, even at the expense of his own fellows if necessary. In this alternative version, Burbage and Brayne were the only ones involved in the erection of the Theater; there was no community of interest, no fellowship of players, no altruism. Chambers was more comfortable with this later and less idealized account of the events and occasionally seemed to want to go even further, to devise a narrative centered on James the capitalist, a man in the grip of social and psychological forces of which he was only dimly aware and whose enterprise was rescued from the dangers of such an orientation only by the later and larger humanity of his sons, Cuthbert and Richard.[3]

Wallace and Chambers thus conveniently emblematize the two principal alternative constructions of the story—in essence, the two versions that most of us have inherited—and in so doing they make clear the implicit hazards of such schematizing. There is probably no way to adjudicate between the two positions, for they rest upon authorial predisposition rather than upon data; and it may be that a properly balanced account of this significant undertaking in the development of the English theater will never be written, for the simple reason that the overwhelming preponderance of available evidence about the details of the enterprise is in the form of legal pleadings, in which Burbage and Brayne (and later their respective heirs) contended with one another to establish the "true" account of what had actually happened. The historian wishing to attempt the story yet again is thus faced not only with the differing interpretations of later scholars but with the competing truth-claims of the participants themselves, the ostensible subjects of the investigation.

It is perhaps also inescapable, given the primary interests of most researchers, that the stories about the Burbages which emerge from these legal proceedings should be attended to more assiduously than the stories centered on Brayne or the other participants.

---

[3] Chambers did not pursue this vision of James Burbage; his interest was perhaps deflected by the greater ease with which Henslowe's career might be made to fit such a paradigm.

Brayne's unhappy experience at the Theater, his later disastrous adventures at the George Inn, his subsequent impoverishment and early death, apparently the result of a beating, receive scant notice, for such occurrences can hardly be milestones in the life of one of the elect. By contrast, the image of an antic young Richard Burbage— reveling in an affray in the playhouse yard, tweaking Nicholas Bishop's nose, brandishing a broomstick in the widow Brayne's face (or, more correctly, in his aunt Margaret's face), and then "in laughing phrase" recounting all to Edward Alleyn's elder brother John—becomes a kind of icon for besieged virtue, an emblem of all the dash and verve that we admire, perhaps even that we require, in our honorific first family of the stage.[4]

Indeed, the very circumstantiality of the testimony in some of these lawsuits—the broomstick episode is perhaps the most salient example—may serve to deflect our attention from the less dramatic but more essential structure that a larger narrative about the Theater needs to have if it is to cohere in a useful way. We have ample data from which to make a story, more than either Wallace or Chambers had, and the temptation to do just that, to make the story again, in a newer and more up-to-date version, full of revealing details, is very strong, especially as the story of the Theater is generally assumed to be so central to the larger history in which it participates.

But such a strategy, by its very assumptions, puts the coherence of that larger history at risk; there are, after all, two other playhouse enterprises with an equal claim to our attention, and as well a partly discoverable common ground on which to situate the three stories that may emerge. The very complexity of one of those stories, and the contradictoriness of many of its parts, gives it a richness and texture unattainable at present by the others. The difficulty of extracting a balanced and coherent account from such disparate materials might well make a reductive approach seem not only tempting but almost inevitable. I hope to resist both the pleasures and the pitfalls of this siren call and content myself instead with looking at the raw materials of all the stories, with an eye to laying out the ingredients from which a larger narrative, or alternative larger narratives, might be put together.

---

[4] E. A. J. Honigmann, in his Arden edition of *King John* (4th ed.; London: Methuen, 1954), suggests that Shakespeare himself was inspired by the broomstick incident, using its underlying dynamic to structure his confrontation scene between Constance and the Bastard ("Introduction," pp. xlvii–l).

CHAPTER FIVE

New Economies for the 1570s:
The City of London, 1574–1576

I

Many of us have got so preoccupied with analysis and argumenta-
tion that we are in danger of forgetting how to tell a story and
even of forgetting that telling a story is the historian's real
business after all.

—J. H. Hexter

Perhaps, as J. H. Hexter urges, "the story" is different from the
argument and analysis, perhaps not. In any event, these elements
will form a major part of this chapter as I attempt to lay some
groundwork for a narrative about three playhouses built on the
outskirts of London within a year or so of one another. Our marker
for this event is the year 1576, a year that, on the analogy of 1066 or
1492, has achieved inevitability in the annals of theater history and
become its own symbol. But we should rightly be curious about that
date; we should wonder why the three playhouses were built in that
year, rather than a year or two earlier or later, and should also
wonder whether the appearance of three of them at what is
effectively the same moment in time is merely coincidental. A
narrative properly addressing these issues should explore not only
the arrival of the buildings but the possible motivating forces that
underlay their appearance.

The epigraph is from J. H. Hexter, *Reappraisals in History* (Chicago: University of
Chicago Press, 1979), p. 21.

In raising these propositions I am not doing anything novel. The Victorian outlines of the antecedent action were generally agreed upon a hundred years ago: though Collier and Fleay quarreled about the details, they both took the principal preliminary milestones to be the parliamentary Statute against Vagabonds in 1572, the royal patent for Leicester's players in 1574, and the City's restrictive regulations of playing later in the same year. These three events are undeniably important, and if they are viewed in isolation—rather than seen as three moments among several hundred in the life of the court and the City during those four years—they will seem to form a continuum and thus will appear to provide a coherent and self-evident run-up to the main event, the erection of the first public playhouses.

The first of these events, the Statute of 29 June 1572, "An Acte for the punishement of Vacabondes," contained provisions one might easily construe as being inimical to the welfare of the playing profession (though I have argued in Chapter 3 that such official restriction on playing was salutary as well as punitive). Among its other provisions, the statute declared that any able-bodied persons, including "all Fencers Bearewardes Comon Players in Enterludes & Minstrels, not belonging to any Baron of this Realme or towardes any other honorable Personage of greater Degree," who "shall wander abroade and have not Lycense . . . shalbee taken adjudged and deemed Roges Vacaboundes and Sturdy Beggers"; that is to say, if any such persons, while playing without license or even while traveling without license, were to fall into the hands of the authorities they were to be considered automatically as "vagrant wandring and misordering themselves contrary to the purport of this present Acte" and were to be "presentlye commytted to . . . Gaole."[1]

Following hard upon this action—or so it seemed to Collier and Fleay, though in fact there was an interval of almost two years—the first royal patent to players was issued to Leicester's men, on 10 May 1574; the record copy of this document noted in its margin that it was intended "pro Iacobo Burbage & aliis," and it licensed them "to vse, exercise, and occupie the arte and facultye of playenge Commedies, Tragedies, Enterludes, stage playes, and such other like as they haue alredie vsed and studied, or hereafter shall vse and studie," and further "to shewe, publishe, exercise, and occupie to their best commoditie" these stagings "aswell within oure Citie of

---

[1]Statute 14 Eliz. cap. 5, extracted in *ES* 4:269–71.

London and liberties of the same" as elsewhere in the realm, "any acte, statute, proclamacion, or commaundement heretofore made, or hereafter to be made, to the contrarie notwithstandinge."[2] As the earl's players were, by virtue of his patronage alone, exempt from the strictures of the statute of 1572, this patent is unlikely to have been issued as a counter or response to that statute; the wording of the final provision—"heretofore made, or hereafter to be made"— may have been framed to anticipate other dangers.

One such perceived danger may have been the City itself. In the early months of 1574 the aldermen had made another of their periodic attempts to restrict stage plays; on this occasion, however, the queen's officers stepped in. Meeting at Greenwich on 22 March 1574, a scant six weeks before the issuance of Leicester's patent, the Privy Council dispatched a letter to the lord mayor requiring him to declare "what causes he hath to restrain plaies," so that the councilors "may the better aunswer suche as desyre to have libertye for the same."[3] The letter offers no hint about the identity of those desiring such liberty, though one might plausibly imagine James Burbage and his fellows among their number, given that the patron of their playing company was a privy councilor. But so were the patrons of four other playing companies—the earls of Arundel, Lincoln, Sussex, and Warwick—and those four were present at the meeting when the letter was drafted, while Leicester was not.

The lord mayor's response to the Privy Council's query has not survived, but echoes of it no doubt appear in a long and circumstantial Act of the Court of Common Council entered into the record on 6 December 1574. This fuller statement, articulated half a year and more after Leicester's patent had been issued, began by noting, in the usual formulaic terms, the "greate disorders and inconveniences" that "ensue to this Cittie" because of the "inordynate haunting of greate multitudes of people specially youthe, to Plays, enterludes, and shewes"; such gatherings were the "occasions of ffraies and quarrelles, evill practises of incontynence," and so on. The council decreed that "from hensforth no play comodie tragedy enterlude nor publique shewe" was to be presented in inns, private houses, or elsewhere, not even in open spaces, if "publique or commen collectionn of money of the auditory or beholders therof" would be a part of the presentation, until the person sponsoring or housing the

[2]PRO, C.66/1116; *ES* 2:87–88.
[3]PRO, P.C.2/10, p. 210ᵛ.

presentation first secured the express permission of the lord mayor and the Court of Aldermen and gave bonds to the chamberlain of the City.[4] These last provisions represent a new stringency; by their means the City gave notice that the licenses of others—nobleman, Privy Council, or the monarch herself—would henceforth not be sufficient in themselves to permit playing for profit in the City; the lord mayor's approval would have to be added to them.

Here, then, are the preliminary steppingstones to the Tale of the Playhouses in its Victorian form, with the stage set, the contending roles of court and City delineated, the lines drawn for the conflict to come, James Burbage and his fellows singled out for special attention, and the imminent appearance of the Theater scripted as a kind of epiphany.[5] But a closer look at these materials reveals cracks in the structure. We have a parliamentary statute addressing the national issue of vagabonds or unattached adults, in which players were but one of several classes of persons mentioned; a royal patent issued twenty-two months afterward granting special privileges to the players of the queen's favorite; and, seven months further along, a document from the City which, as I hope to demonstrate, has less to do with the suppression of stage playing, and more to do with City finances, than may at first appear. My own sense is that the thread of relationship among these three items is pretty thin; though the three all have to do with players, they have little to do with one another. The last of these documents, the Act of the Court of Common Council of 6 December 1574, is arguably the only one of the three that has a direct bearing on the appearance of playhouses

---

[4]CLRO, Jor. xx, pt. 1, ff. 187ʳ–88ʳ. Some ten years later, in November 1584, the entire act was copied out again by the town clerk and sent to the Privy Council as part of the City's effort to counter an appeal made by the queen's players in that year; the copy made at that time, along with the supporting papers of the City's argument, passed intact with many of Burghley's other papers into the collection now known as the Lansdowne manuscripts (BL, vol. 20, item 10, ff. 23–33), where they were found by Collier, Fleay, and others; all modern transcripts of the act, including the ones in *MSC* 1, pt, 2:175–79) and in Chambers (*ES* 4:273–76), are taken from this source. There are differences between the two versions, though not significant ones; to my knowledge, however, no one has sought out the text of the original in the Journals. I use it here as the source of all my citations in this chapter.

[5]The scenario had great staying power. As late as 1962 Muriel Bradbrook was still urging it, describing the patent to Leicester's players as a "magnificent riposte" to the City's repressions, to which the aldermen "could retaliate only by laying down minute regulations." In consequence, "emboldened by the support of the great," a generic entity described as "the players" took "the next and decisive step" in the sequence and built the Theater, at which point "the history of the London stage had begun" (*The Rise of the Common Player* [Cambridge, Mass.: Harvard University Press, 1962], pp. 55–56).

in 1576 and is, as well, probably the only one of the three that will repay our sustained attention.

II

> What country, friends, is this?
> This is Illyria, lady.
>
> —*Twelfth Night* I.ii

For a number of years now we have had relative ease of access to information about the activities of Elizabeth's court and of the various agencies of her central government, by virtue of the existence of numerous published calendars of state papers both domestic and foreign, of Privy Council minutes, of various assemblages of official correspondence such as those found in the Lansdowne, Harley, and Egerton manuscript collections, and additionally in other collections such as those catalogued by the Historical Manuscripts Commission. All these calendars are guides to the contents of original manuscript material, much of it in the Public Record Office or the British Library; and the documents themselves (far more than the calendars) help us to understand the many different matters that claimed the attention of those charged with managing the country's affairs.

In contrast to this convenience—and its attendant hazard for the unwary, of inviting the assumption that the calendars are always accurate or complete or that they can substitute for the originals—the situation with regard to the City's documents is much less congenial. Except for a valiant effort in the closing years of the last century to provide an index to the books of letters in the town clerk's office[6] and abstracts of wills proved in the Court of Husting there has been no program of publication for the calendars or summaries of the official records of the City of London for this same period, and as a consequence, theater historians whose circumstances preclude

---

[6] The most useful of these for our period is W. H. and H. C. Overall, eds., *Analytical Index to the Series of Records Known as the Remembrancia, Preserved among the Archives of the City of London, AD 1579–1664* (London, 1878). There are also some published abstracts of wills proved in the Court of Husting through the sixteenth century (*Calendar of Wills Proved and Enrolled in the Court of Husting, London, AD 1258–AD 1688*, ed. Reginald R. Sharpe, 2 vols. [London, 1889, 1890]). In the main, though, the Corporation of London's publication program has centered upon its medieval holdings.

access to London archives are often forced to overlook or ignore the activities of the various City agencies as they may relate to an inquiry. True, certain City documents relevant to theater history were transcribed and published early in this century by the Malone Society,[7] but the very specialization of these collections, their narrow focus on only those documents having direct relevance to theatrical affairs, induces a kind of tunnel vision in scholars who rely on them alone.

The original documents show that the men responsible for governing the City had as many different pressing matters on their agenda as did the Privy Council, though on a local rather than a national or international scale. One cannot, for example, scan the volumes of Repertories, or minutes, of the Court of Aldermen for this period, or even for the brief span of months between the end of 1574 and the summer of 1576, as I propose to do here, and fail to notice how large a portion of the aldermen's time was spent monitoring the workings of their own Orphans' Court, the organ through which the City discharged its obligation to care for the minor children of deceased freemen.[8] The general sense of responsibility shown by the aldermen for the welfare of the children, and equally of their estates, is impressive. The aldermen also cared for the elderly incapable; in the summer of 1575, for example, they charged themselves with the support of a widow Hallywell, "lately become Lunatycke and dystraught of her wytt*es*," and they determined that she should be "Comytted to Bedlem and there kepte."[9]

There were also periodic concerns about the state of the River Thames and frequent meetings with the City commissioners who comprised the Courts of Conservancy of the Thames, most of whom were simply aldermen wearing different hats. At the other extreme, in the summer of 1576 some aldermen were deputed to go and investigate "A certeyne fowle poole of water wch standethe at

---

[7]See, for example, *MSC* 1, pt. 1: 43–100, "Dramatic Records of the City of London: The Remembrancia" and its continuation in *MSC* 4:55–65, "More Records from the Remembrancia of the City of London"; and *MSC* 2, pt. 3:285–320, "Dramatic Records of the City of London: The Repertories, Journals, and Letter Books."

[8]The standard work on this topic is Charles Carlton, *The Court of Orphans* (Leicester: Leicester University Press, 1974). Carlton observes on p. 39 that the affairs of orphans took "a disproportionately large amount of time and energy of the Court of Aldermen," and my own reading in the documents certainly confirms his assessment.

[9]CLRO, Rep. xviii, fo. 406, court of 21 July 1575. In our present enlightened age we might not regard such a disposition of the matter as compassionate, but this is to apply inappropriate standards.

thende of Goldinge Lane."[10] There was a riot on Tower Hill in late February 1576, the investigation of which occupied them for a period; there were solicitations for various worthy causes, including a collection authorized in all the City churches "for & towardes the dyschardge & redempcion of certayne Englysshemen nowe beinge Captyves in Barbarye."[11]

Among their more bureaucratic matters of business, the aldermen regularly contended with what they took to be royal encroachments on the prerogatives of the City. There were numerous public offices in the City to which the lord mayor and aldermen held the right of election and reversion, among them such posts as the town clerk and the town crier, the common serjeant and the common hunt, the city waits, the keepers of Newgate and the Counters, the attorneys in Guildhall and in the sheriffs' courts, the clerk of the bridge house, the bailiff of Southwark, the garbler, the ganger, and the collector of scavage; by one count, there were some 140 such offices.[12] Various noblemen, particularly those on the Privy Council, used their strongest arts of suasion (the aldermen might have said "coercion") to push their own nominees for the more lucrative of these posts whenever a vacancy, or a reversion, came to their attention. These appeals arrived with such predictable regularity that the aldermen may be forgiven for perceiving some grand design lurking behind them.

Sometimes the encounter took the form not of an appeal but of a fait accompli. The issue that exercised the aldermen in 1575 was the issuance of a royal patent to one Richard Candler which licensed him to draw up writs and other documents in the City scriptorium attached to the Court of Arches in Cheapside, the mercantile heart of the City. In March 1575 a delegation of fourteen of the most senior aldermen called in person on the Privy Council to invite them to "revoke the patente lately gravntyd by the Quens Matie vnto Rychard Candler consernynge the makynge of pollycies, and other wrytinges w^tin this Cytie, As a thinge contrarye to the lyberties of this Cytie."[13] And as ammunition for subsequent visits on the same

---

[10]CLRO, Rep. xix, fo. 89, court of 21 June 1576.

[11]CLRO, Rep. xix, fo. 25, court of 16 January 1576.

[12]Valerie Pearl, *London and the Outbreak of the Puritan Revolution* (London: Oxford University Press, 1961), p. 61. Frank Freeman Foster, by including such others as servants in the lord mayor's household, reaches a total of some five hundred offices in the City's gift (*The Politics of Stability: A Portrait of the Rulers of Elizabethan London* [London: Royal Historical Society, 1977], pp. 173–79).

[13]CLRO, Rep. xviii, fo. 362^v, court of 22 March 1575.

topic, the aldermen directed their clerk to make a list of all offices granted during the previous seven years specifically "at the request of the Quenz Maties Lettres or any of her highnes pryvie Cownsell."[14] These periodic conflicts over prerogative may have been measured steps in a "struggle between court and City," as some readers of the evidence would have it, or they may have meant merely that opportunism was alive and well among the nobility, and territoriality equally so among the aldermen. Whatever the explanation, such conflicts had been going on for years and would continue for many more; in 1575 Richard Candler was simply the most recent point of irritation.

Additionally, much of the aldermen's time in 1575 and 1576 was spent investigating reported abuses in the wine trade, principally widespread complaints about overpricing. Their inquiries having established that matters had indeed gotten out of hand, the aldermen were quick to arrest a number of vintners in May 1576 and clap them into prison.[15] On another occasion they imprisoned a number of bricklayers, including two wardens of the company, "for Certeyn dysorders by them Comytted."[16] Apart from these particularities, the more general maintenance of order was also a matter of constant concern. Periodically the aldermen issued directives "for the apprehendynge and takynge of all sortes of Roges ydle and suspecte persons bothe men women and Chyldren . . . and them forthwithe to comytte vnto brydewell."[17] The statute of 1572 for the punishment of vagabonds gave them further grounds for action, and sometimes their orders reflected the very phraseology of the statute, authorizing "the apprehendinge of Roges vagabo^undes and maysterles men . . . Contrary to the forme of the Statute in that Case lately made and provyded."[18] These steps may well have been reasonably successful; Mr. Recorder Fleetwood, writing to Lord Treasurer Burghley in August 1575, was ready to declare that "M^rles men Rogges ffencers and suche like" were now under control in the City; even such trouble spots as Holborn and St. John's Street, he said, were "neu^r so well and quiett, for neither Roge nor masterles man dare ones looke into those partes."[19]

---

[14]CLRO, Rep. xviii, fo. 364^v, court of 31 March 1575. The aldermen were not successful in this match; Candler stayed on, a thorn in their sides, for some time.
[15]CLRO, Rep. xix, fo. 82^v, court of 29 May 1576.
[16]CLRO, Rep. xix, fo. 72^v, court of 3 May 1576.
[17]CLRO, Rep. xviii, fo. 389, court of 9 June 1575.
[18]CLRO, Rep. xix, fo. 4, court of 10 November 1575.
[19]BL, ms. Lansd, vol. 20, item 8, ff. 20–21, 13 August 1575.

Fleetwood may have believed this; more likely he sensed that it was what Burghley wanted to hear. The aldermen must have had a somewhat different view of things. They were indeed gathering people off the streets; as a result, Bridewell Hospital, founded by the aldermen in 1553 as a house of correction, was quickly filled with apprehended rogues and vagrants who required their constant attention, and it was not long before many of the "ydle and suspecte persons" who had been taken there were released again into the streets for lack of room. And on 16 June 1575 "yt was orderyd that Mᵣ Recorder Mᵣ Mershe Mᵣ Morton and Rychard yonge grocer shall heare and examyn the matter of A rape supposed to be Committed at the signe of the bell in gratyowse strete, and of their doynges therein to make reporte vnto this Coᵣte."[20]

It was, in short, a busy time for the aldermen, and stage players occupied little of their attention during that time. There is no mention specifically of plays or players in any of the minutes of the twice-weekly meetings of the Court of Aldermen during all of 1575 or 1576;[21] nor is any greater concern about players to be found in the records of the City's other chamber, the Court of Common Council, which, though it met far less frequently than the Court of Aldermen, was equally engaged with a variety of matters of business during the same period.[22] After addressing the matter of plays and interludes

[20]CLRO, Rep. xviii, fo. 394. Such reports rarely survive, and this one has not. Reports to the Court of Aldermen were invariably submitted in writing, and outside of meeting time; one almost never encounters a mention of their contents, or even of the fact of their submission, in the subsequent Repertory entries. The Bell in Gracechurch Street was, of course, one of the four famous playing inns in the City in the 1580s, though it may not yet have become a playing inn in 1575; the alleged rape was probably not connected with the performance of a play in any event, for the aldermen would have been unlikely to omit mention of such a coincidence.

[21]The last time they had been concerned with such matters was at the meeting of 2 March 1574, when they opposed a request from the lord chamberlain that one Mr. Holmes should have "the role gouerment & Appoyntment of all plaies & enterludes to be plaied wᵗʰin this Citie aswell for the players & for there matters as places" (CLRO, Rep. xviii, fo. 169ᵛ). The aldermen sent a letter to the lord chamberlain arguing that "this case is suche & so nere touchings the gouernance of this Citie in one of the greatest matters thereof namely the assemblies of multitudes of the quenes people and regard to be had to sondry inconveniences whereof the perill is contynually vpon euery occacion to be forseene by the rulers of this Citie that we can not wᵗʰ oᵣ dueties beside the president far extendinge to the hurte of oᵣ liberties well assent that the said appoyntment of places be committed to any private person for wᶜʰ & other reasonable consideracons it hath longe synce pleased yoᵣ good L amonge the rest of her maᵗᵉˢ most honorable counsell to rest satisfied wᵗʰ oᵣ not grantinge the like to suche persons."

[22]Histories of the London theater in the sixteenth and seventeenth centuries, even those of quite recent origin, often fail to discriminate among actions originating in Common Hall, the Court of Common Council, the Court of Aldermen, the Lord

in their act of 6 December 1574, referred to above, the councilors, like their colleagues the aldermen, dealt no more with the subject throughout 1575 and 1576; indeed, the council did not record another item of business on this topic until 1580.[23]

But the act of 1574 was a lengthy one; it ran to nearly fourteen hundred words, occupied three whole pages of the Journal, and comprised the longest single entry in the Journals on any topic between the previous April and the following March.[24] Given the dearth of other evidence that stage plays constituted a serious concern at this period, we may feel hard pressed to explain the copiousness or complexity of this particular response and may appropriately wonder if there might not be more here than meets the casual eye. The act as recorded in the council's minute book incorporated a number of points which had appeared in earlier statements by the councilors or aldermen, so that much of its rhetoric will have a familiar ring; nevertheless, it is a new document, careful in its structure and grounded on a series of innovative premises which the councilors and the aldermen must have seen as central to their new intent. Their focus, from the outset, was on the social consequences of playing and not on plays or players as such. One recognizes the cadences of their opening statement that "greate disorders and inconveniences haue bynne found to ensue to this Cittie by the inordynate haunting of greate multitudes of people specially youthe, to Plays, enterludes, and shewes"; we have encountered these sentiments before, along with the more titillating claims of "evill practises of incontynence in greate Innes" during times of playing, brought about by the "inveglinge and alluringe of maydes specially orphans" to the "chambers and secret places adyoininge to their open stages and gallarys." We also know about the "w^{th}drawinge of the Quenes Maties Subiectes from divine s^{r}uice on sondaies and hollydaies," though we may here encounter for the

---

Mayor's Court, the Sheriffs' Court, the Husting Court, the town clerk's office, the city chamberlain's office, or other organs of City governance, preferring instead to describe the activities of these various bodies generically as the indifferent behavior of an amorphous entity called "the City Fathers"; as a precise and informative label this phrase is as useless as its correlative would be in our own day.

[23]CLRO, Jor. xxi, fo. 7, meeting of 11 January 1580; a precept for the suppression of playing in the evening and at night. *MSC* 2, pt. 3:310.

[24]The former addressed at great length the marketing of billets, faggots, and coal (Jor. xx(1), ff. 131^v–32^v); the latter prohibited with equal copiousness the introduction of tallow into soap (Jor. xx(1), ff. 198–99^v).

first time their social concern about the "vnthrifty wast of the money of . . . poore and fond p*ersonnes*" who patronize plays.

But we must not be lulled by this familiarity, even though we know that, except for the last mentioned, these sentiments were not newly minted in 1574. Thirty years earlier the Common Council had prefaced an earlier proclamation against playing with essentially the same arguments, noting that plays were being put on "in dyuers & many suspycyous darke & inconvenyent plac*es*," with increasing frequency "vpon the Sondaye & other hallydayes in the tyme of Evensonge & other deuyne s uice," and that they brought "a greate p*arte* of the youthe" of the City in undesirable contact with "manye other light Idle and evyll disposed p*ersones*," to the inevitable corruption of the former.[25] Indeed, certain portions of the official rhetoric were becoming quite predictable; but in the document of 1574, in addition to voicing their concerns about the poor, the councilors added a new argument, that of personal hazard: they alluded in passing (teasingly for us) to the "sondry slaughters and mayhem*inges*" that were known to result from the periodic "ruynes of Skaffoldes fframes and Stages and by engynnes weapons and powder usad in plaies." The imagination leaps at such a statement, of course, but can do little more than wonder at its roots; one cannot say whether these remarks were grounded in actual events now lost to us or were only rhetorical flourishes based on hearsay and common rumor. The latter is by no means unlikely, especially as one of the aims of the councilors in this document was to portray playgoing as hazardous in as many ways as possible.

The suppressing of playing was a recurrent affair in the City, most easily justified in times of plague, and the suppressions decreed at those times—so the councilors affirmed in the present document—grew not only on their own initiative but also in compliance with the "severe and earnest admonicion" of the Privy Council, reflecting "her Ma*ties* expressse pleas*r* and com*m*aundem*t* in that behalf." Indeed, a mild plague, and a suspension of playing, were upon them even as they constructed this document.[26] Their ambition went further, however, and the plague was to be one of their points of entry. They feared, or so they explained, that "vpon goddes

[25]CLRO, Jor. xv, ff. 241*v*–42*r*, court of 6 February 1545.
[26]Because of the plague the Privy Council, at its meeting of 15 November 1574, had ordered the sheriffs and justices of Middlesex, Essex, and Surrey "to restraine all plaiers . . . w*th*in x miles of London untill Esther next" (PRO, P.C.2/10, p. 285*v*).

mercifull wthdrawing his hand of sicknes from vs . . . the people &
specially the meaner and moste vnrulye sorte" would, with "sodden
forgettinge" of the evil times just past, "returne to the vndewe vse of
suche enormytes" as stage plays.

Having thus used some old and some new arguments to establish
a rhetorical grounding for their intention to gain and keep control of
playing, the councilors moved to a consideration of the arguments
likeliest to command assent in maintaining the welfare of the City.
Their first theme was the twin vices of unchastity and sedition, and
on that head their determination was that "no play comodie,
tragedy enterlude nor publique shewe shalbe openly played or
shewed . . . Wherein shalbe vtteryd anny wordes examples or do-
inges of anny vnchastitie sedicion nor suche like vnfitt and vncom-
mly matter"; for anyone transgressing this restriction, the penalty
was to be "Imprisonment by the space of xiiij days of all personnes
offendinge in anny suche open playinge or shewinges and v^{li} for
euery suche offence." This was an unexceptionable position, leaving
little room for criticism. Occasions of sedition and unchastity could
hardly be defended even by the most ardent playgoer, and the Privy
Council itself maintained a healthy interest in the former if not the
latter; the councilors aligned themselves correctly on this issue,
setting penalties not for all plays but only for those which trans-
gressed the bounds of moral or political decorum. Other plays (so
ran the implication) would be at less risk. To ensure against the
point's being lost, at the end of the document the council affirmed
again its desire to safeguard the "Lawfull honest and commely vse of
plays pastymes and recreacions in good sorte."

But we must not be taken in by this posture of good will and civic
mindedness. The subsequent provisions of the act come closer to
showing us the real intent of the council. After taking their stand on
sedition and unchastity, they moved on to the first of their serious
provisions, the City's right to prior perusal of play scripts. They
decreed "that no Inkeper Tauernekeper nor other personne What-
soeuer wthin the Liberties of this Cittye shall openly shewe or play
nor cause or suff^r to be openly shewed or playd wthin the hous yard
or anny other place Wthin the Liberties of this Cittye anny play
Enterlude comodye tragedy matter or shewe wch shall not be first
perusad and allowed in suche order and forme and by suche
personnes as by the L Mayo^r and courte of Aldermenn for the tyme
beinge shalbe appoynted." Furthermore, anticipating Hamlet's ad-
vice to the player not to speak more than is set down for him, they

added that no innkeeper, tavern keeper, or other person (a useful catch-all) "shall suff^r to be enterlacyd added mynglyd or vtterid in anny suche play enterlude comodye tragidy or shewe anny oth^r matter then suche as shalbe fyrst perusad and allowed as ys aboue said."

The cautionary perusal of play texts, thus positioned to appear a logical consequence of the council's concern for sedition and unchastity, opened the door both to the collection of fees for licensing and to the limitless possibilities of harassment—not of players, let it be noted, but of those who would offer them playing space. It was to be the innkeeper, tavern keeper, or generic other person who had the obligation to present the book of the play to the responsible authority for perusal; we may imagine the response of a company of players upon being told that they must surrender their play book to an innkeeper or tavern keeper so that he might in turn pass it on to some City functionary for additional approval.[27]

But the approval of the text was not the only hurdle; the innkeeper himself had to be approved, and also his inn, the lord mayor thus being assured that there were good reasons for allowing the play to proceed. This consideration was made clear in the next provision of the document, which specified that "no personne shall suff^r anny plays enterludes comodies, tragidies or shewes to be playd or shewed in his hous yard or other place Whereof he then shall haue rule or power but only suche personnes and in suche places as apon good and reasonable consideracions shewed shalbe therunto permytted and allowed by the Lorde Maio^r and Aldermenn." Another layer of permissions, of course, meant more fees and more hassle.

But the bureaucratic tangle was not to stop even there. Those wishing to host plays, even after complying with all the above restrictions, still had to post bonds with the chamberlain for their good performance in all these matters. The act informed them that, though they might have gotten permission from the lord mayor, they might not "take or vse anny benifite or advantage of suche permission or allowaunces before or vntell suche personne be bound

---

[27]The Proclamation of 16 May 1559 authorized such licensing by the "Maior or other chiefe officers" of the City, but the City had not previously spelled out its rights in such detail; in any event, the function was soon to pass into the hands of the Master of the Revels.

to the Chamberlen*n* of london . . . wth suche suert*es* and in suche sum*me* and suche forme for the keping of good order and avoidinge of the discord*es* and inconvenienc*es* abouesaid As to the L Maio^r and courte of Aldermen*n* . . . shall seme convenient."

So the person, be he innkeeper or otherwise, who might wish to sponsor a performance of a play to which spectators might come and for which an admission fee might be charged or a collection taken would henceforth be required to submit the text of the proposed play to one of the lord mayor's appointees for certification, with his guarantee that the text so approved would be, word for word, the text actually played; to demonstrate to the satisfaction of the lord mayor his own probity, the suitability of the venue, and the appropriateness of having such a performance; and to post bond with the chamberlain for the maintenance of good order of the proceeding. But even after traversing all these steps, and finally receiving license and permission, the proprietor would still not be assured of his performance, for the act reserved the City's right to suspend "anny suche licence, or p*er*mission at or in anny tymes in W^{ch} the same for anny reasonable consideraci*on* of sicknesse or otherwise shalbe by the lorde Maio^r and Aldermen by publique p*ro*clamaci*on* or by precepte to suche p*er*sonnes restrayned or comaunded to staye and ceasse, nor in anny vsuall tyme of dyvine s^ruice in the sonday or hollyday nor receyue anny to that purpose in tyme of s^ruice to see the same apon peyne to forfeite for eu*er*y offence v^{li}."

And there is yet more; an open-ended, variable fee to be paid. If by now we are benumbed by the rhetoric of the act, we may well miss the significance of this passage, yet it lies at the very heart of the City's intention: "eu*er*y p*er*sonne so to be lycenced or p*er*mitted shall during the tyme of suche contynewaun*n*ce of suche Lycence or p*er*mission pay or cause to be paid to the vse of the poore in hospitalls of the Cittye or of the poore of the Cittye visited wth sicknes by the discression of the said Lord Maio^r and Aldermen such som*mes* and paymen*n*tes and in suche forme as betwen the lord Maio^r and Aldermen . . . on thonne p*ar*te and suche p*er*sonne so to be lycencyd or p*er*mytted on thoth^r p*ar*te shalbe agreed." A potential proprietor would surely be aghast by now; the nature of the "agreement" to be reached in each case about the level of contribution was no doubt to be based upon the lord mayor's assessment of the landlord's available resources, that is to say, of the worth of the establishment, so that the larger and more sumptuous inns would have been assessed the larger and more sumptuous payments.[28] And the penalty for failing to comply with this "contribution" was that "in Want of euery suche payment / or if suche personne shall not fyrst be bound wth good suertes to the chamberlen of london for the tyme beinge for the trewe payinge of suche sommes to the poore that then euery suche Lycence or permission shalbe vtterly void and euery doinge by force or cullo^r of suche licence or permission shalbe adiudged an offence against this acte in suche mann^r as if no suche licence or permission had bynne had nor made."

That this enactment was to have overriding jurisdiction was made clear by the next statement: "anny suche licence or permission to the contrary notw^tstanding." And that their motives were lofty was attested by the immediately sequent sentences, reiterating their statements made earlier: "And be it lykewise enacted that all sommes and forfeitures to be incurryd for anny offence agaynst this acte and all forfeitures of Bondes to be taken by force meane or occasion of this acte shalbe imployed to the releif of the poore in the hospitalls of this Cittye or the pore infectyd or disesyd in this Cittye of london as the lorde Maio^r and Courte of Aldermen for the tyme beinge shall adiudge mete to be distributyd."

This focus on the needs of the poor, the infected, and the diseased, and of the hospitals charged to care for them, may strike a modern reader of the text as both commendably compassionate and oddly puzzling in its context. A generation earlier, in the aftermath of the Dissolution, the City had acquired from the crown in separate transactions the five hospitals—St. Thomas's, St. Bartholomew's, Bethlehem, Bridewell, and Christ's—which had become, by 1575, its chief resource for the care of the ill, the impoverished, the deranged, and the orphaned.[29] The institutions were both socially necessary and financially draining. By the various terms of acquisition, the City had obligated itself to maintain the hospitals, at a cost of five hundred marks annually. It was a heavy obligation; in subsequent

---

[28]We do not know the size of the inns commonly used for players in this period, though it seems unlikely that they would have been among the grandest and best appointed; the so-called four great playing inns of the 1580s and 1590s (the Bell, the Bull, the Cross Keys, and the Bel Savage) were certainly not the most sumptuous inns in the City, but neither is there any evidence of their use as a venue for plays before the date of this act. The earliest record that names a specific City inn (the Bel Savage) as a playing inn dates from 1575.

[29]The process had begun in 1539, when the City petitioned the crown for a grant of three of them; see CLRO, Jor. xiv, ff. 129–30.

years "the pou*e*rtye of the Same Citie" was "moche burdoned &
grevyd" by it, and "hathe not a littel grutched & Repyned ffor
Remedy."[30] One remedy that presented itself in 1548 was to shift the
burden of the statutory debt from the city chamberlain's coffers to
the livery companies. But even by that time, costs had mounted far
beyond the five hundred marks of the original grant.

The various hospitals met their financial needs in different ways.
St. Thomas derived much of its income from rentals and other
revenues; Bridewell from the profits of the labor of its inmates; and
so on. Of the five, only Christ's Hospital survived, and precariously,
"wholly . . . by y[e] Liberal Devotions of good Citizens."[31] The City
did what it could to assist; to help finance St. Bartholomew's
Hospital, for example, the Court of Aldermen transferred to it the
monopoly of certain fees, such as the gauging of wine and fish and
the use of the great beam for weighing; proceeds were to be used "to
the vse Releiff & Sustentacion of the pore people w[t]in the house of
the poore foundyd in westsmythfeld . . . for eu*e*rmore & to none
other vse or p[r]pose."[32] But the hospitals were increasingly costly to
run, and by the 1580s they were all so badly in arrears that special
audits and commissions had to be ordered.[33] Glimmerings of this
fiscal drain were becoming evident even in 1575, though the
relevance of these problems to the control of stage plays, or to the
act of 6 December 1574, may not be immediately apparent.

The act concludes with a final disclaimer, to keep the City from
unnecessary trouble at the hands of the powerful: "Provided alway
that this acte (otherwise then towching the publisshinge of vnchast
sedicious & vnmete matters) shall not extend to anny plays enter-
lud*es* comedys tragidies or shewes to be playd or shewed in the
pryvat hous dwellinge or lodginge of anny nobleman Cittizen or
gentilman*n* w[ch] shall or will then haue the same their so played or
shewed in his presence for the festyvitie of anny marriage assembly
of ffrend*es*, or other like cause w[th]out publique or com*m*en collec-

---

[30]CLRO, Jor. xv, ff. 398–400[v].

[31]GHL, ms. 6.

[32]CLRO, Jor. xv, fo. 399; specifically, "Custodye of the greate Beame or balaunce
com*m*enly called the kyng*es* beame / the beame of the Styllyard / the yron beame / the
Pakkyng / Gawgyng of wyne & ffishe / Garbelyng / the Small beame / & for weyng of
Sylk*es* / the Mesures or mesurage of Sylk*es* / Wollen Cloth / Lynen*n* cloth / Corne /
Grayne / Salt / Cole / Seldage of Lether & such other Lyke / And also of the Custodye &
Kepyng of the Com*m*en m[r]kett place for Wollen clothes & Lynen clothes com*m*enly callyd
Blackwelhall."

[33]See, for example, CLRO, Rep. xxii, ff. 3, 18, 151[v], 155, 163; Jor. xxii, fo. 389.

tion*n* of money of the auditory or beholders therof reservinge alway to the lord Maio^r and Aldermen*n* for the tyme beinge the Iudgem^t and construc*c*ion accordinge to equitie what shalbe counted suche a playing or shewing in a pryvat place."

There, then, is the Act of Common Council of 6 December 1574. One month later, just after the Christmas holidays, the Court of Aldermen affirmed the council's action and instructed Mr. Dalby of their secretariat to "drawe *preceptes* according to an Acte of co*m*en Cownsell heretofore made and provyded Consernynge Enterludes and playes w^tin this Cytie" so that the "Acte and Conten*tes* thereof" might be "putt in due execution."[34] One might expect, given the stringency of the measures which the act enunciated, that playing in innyards and in other public places in London would have ground to a virtual halt in its aftermath. Did it do so? Evidence is scant, of course, but it seems a reasonable guess that innkeepers and others addressed by the act, anticipating its enforcement and the penalties for noncompliance, would have had second thoughts about offering their premises to players in light of the sudden escalation of costs and of bureaucratic hassle as well. No doubt some innkeepers for whom the continuance of playing was important would have tried to pass these costs on to the players, so that their own profits might remain intact; but the players would surely have been equally reluctant to have themselves assessed for weekly contributions to hospitals based not on their own resources but on an arbitrary valuation of the establishment in which they were playing. Nor would they have wished to lay themselves open to the fines—five pounds for each offense—which might be levied against them because of their host's inattention or dilatoriness.

An alternative construction, of course, is that the promulgation of the act was itself a political maneuver by the councilors, their principal aim being the enactment and recording of a strong and vigorous legislation. They may have intended no more than an ordinary commitment to the strict and universal enforcement of its provisions. The penalties of the act, once affirmed, could be invoked at the pleasure of the lord mayor, the aldermen, the councilors, the sheriffs, or any of their agents, or as easily overlooked, as the occasion might demand. One of the traditional uses of prohibitions has been to provide a context for the profitable granting of exemptions and for the equally profitable issuing of licenses authorizing

---

[34]CLRO, Rep. xviii, fo. 328^v, meeting of 13 January 1575; *MSC* 2, pt. 3, item xxxviii.

others to grant exemptions. Given what else we know of City governance, this is a plausible, and not an unnecessarily cynical, construction to place on the act, especially in light of the evidence that companies of players did continue to play in the City after 1574 and that playing in innyards seems, if anything, to have increased after that date. Perhaps certain innkeepers felt less intimidated by the new legislation than did others, or perhaps merely felt comfortable about continuing to offer a venue for players while others did not. Correlatively, certain companies of players, moved by their own self-interested understanding of the act, may have felt more strongly than others that they were among the intended targets of the legislation.

But though they may have been the ostensible targets, players were not the rhetorical object of the act; the shrewdness of the councilors in constructing their text lay in their choice of addressee. Royal patents to players, a new development in the summer just past, lay beyond the City's power to ignore or to discount, and it was becoming increasingly evident to the aldermen that even the sponsored playing troupes of the more powerful nobles, whether graced by royal patent or not, might begin to cause difficulty for the City if it were perceived that the aldermen or the councilors were taking aim at them directly, and thus by implication at their patrons.

The change of strategy evident in the 1574 document was thus a new departure for the City's governing legislators, whose previous tactics had consisted primarily of impounding players themselves. Thirty years earlier, for example, during the latter years of the reign of Henry VIII, the Court of Aldermen, having decreed that there were to be no plays in any of their wards, instructed themselves to "attache & com*m*ytt vnto warde all & eue*ry* suche *per*son & *per*sones as will take upon theym to play & make int*er*ludes . . . there to remayne vntyll they shall fynde good suretyes that they shall no more so vse theym self*es*."[35]

Perhaps the aldermen were more fearless in those earlier days. Toward the end of Henry VIII's reign, "certeyn co*m*en pleyers of ent*er*ludys belongyng (as they seyd) to the Erle of hertf*ord*"—that is, belonging to the man who within three years would become duke of Somerset and lord protector—"were enioyned no more to pleye eny suche ent*er*ludys herafter wythin this Cytie excepte it be in the howses of the lorde mayer Shreves aldermen or other substancyall

---

[35]CLRO, Rep. x, ff. 322^v–23^r, court of 2 April 1543.

Co*miners*."[36] And within a month of that reprimand the Common Council issued a proclamation requiring, among other things, that "no maner of p*erson*e or p*erson*es . . . of what soeuer estate degree or Condic*ion* . . . presume or take vpon him or them at any tyme hereafter to play*e* . . . any maner of Enterlude or co*m*en play*e*" in the City.[37]

The aldermen and the councillors continued the theme, replaying it each year; in the following winter (1546) they determined that "the proclam*ation* herbefore made ageynst the Co*m*en Pleyers of enter-lud*es* w*t*in the Cytie shall to morowe be proclaymed ageyn"[38] and affirmed in the next winter after that (1547) their determination "to pull downe vpon sundayes in the mornyng all suche byll*es* of int*er*lud*es* as the co*m*en players of the same int*er*ludes shall cause to be affyxed or sett vp vpon eny post or other place."[39] In 1554 they were still aiming their artillery at the players; in that year the Common Council declared, among other prohibitions, that "no maner of p*erson* or p*erson*es" should "make prepare or set fur-the . . . eny enterludes or Stage playes."[40] And ten years later, well into Elizabeth's reign, the lord mayor was using virtually the same language, in a precept which decreed, among other things, that "no maner of p*erson* or p*erson*es" should "take vpon hym or them to sett fourth or openly or pryvately play*e* . . . eny maner of enterlude or stage play*e*."[41]

All this changed with the 1574 document; the City's new posture was the essence of conciliation. The councilors affirmed, in language quite unusual for them, their readiness to encourage "Lawfull honest and com*m*ely vse of plays . . . in good sorte" and their care to exempt from all the just-announced strictures "anny plays . . . to be playd . . . in the pryvat hous . . . of anny nobleman Cittizen or gentilman*n* . . . [and] played or shewed in his presence." Indeed, the act as a whole could arguably be defended—surely the councilors must have had this in mind—as conducing to the better exercise of the players' craft, by ensuring that only reputable and responsible sponsors and sites would be made available to companies of players. Thus, they might have argued, her majesty's service would be

[36]CLRO, Rep. xi, fo. 135, court of 12 January 1545.
[37]CLRO, Jor. xv, ff. 241ᵛ–42ʳ, court of 6 February 1545.
[38]CLRO, Rep. xi, fo. 244ᵛ, court of 25 February 1546.
[39]CLRO, Rep. xi, fo. 315ᵛ, court of 17 March 1547.
[40]CLRO, Jor. xvi, ff. 287ᵛ, court of 19 April 1554.
[41]CLRO, Jor. xviii, fo. 184, court of 12 February 1564.

strengthened, and the noblemen who patronized the players could confidently rely on the City's assured care on their behalf. The act—so this rationale would posit—was designed actually to enable, rather than to suppress, the responsible presentation of stage plays in the City.

And this may indeed have been the final legacy of the act, whatever the intentions of its framers. My fascination with the three playhouses erected outside the City's jurisdiction in 1576 has led me to pay less attention to the concurrent rise, within the City, of such establishments as the Bell, the Bull, the Cross Keys, and the Bel Savage. According to the Victorian formulation, such playing inns should have ceased, not begun, their active lives in the wake of the act. Nor should we conclude, from the later prominence of these four inns, that they were the only ones so utilized; there may have been others, less prominent, less frequently used, which may yet turn up in the records.

By mid-March 1575 the governors of Christ's Hospital had taken their first official notice of the new act's existence. They instructed one of their number "to take out of the mairᵒˢ courte the ordeʳ taken for the Inholders and howses wher plaies be frequented" and to make a full note of its provisions, "to thintent that ordeʳ may be taken in that behalf accordinge to theffect of the said act of comon counsell in that behalf."[42] New fees seemed poised to come their way, and they were interested.

III

> Yea, but not change his spots.
> —*King Richard II*, I.i

The Act of the Court of Common Council of 6 December 1574 articulated what appeared to be a new alignment of sympathies and stringencies on the part of the common councilors; the swift ratification of the Act by the Court of Aldermen suggests that the new attitudes it embodied were widely shared in the City's halls of governance. The focus of the City's attention had shifted from

---

[42]Court Minutes of Christ's Hospital, GHL, ms. 12,806/2, fo. 121ᵛ, court of 12 March 1575.

companies of stage players, which, because they were itinerant and often nobly patronized, did not come clearly under the City's control, to the owners or proprietors of playing places in the City, which, because they were fixed, remained constantly under the City's jurisdiction. Whether the motives of the councilors and aldermen were sincere or calculated, whether enforcement of the act was to be rigorous or partial, whether playing in the City would thenceforth be nearly impossible or merely more difficult, whatever the new conditions might prove to be, it must have seemed to the players themselves that the rules of the game, if not the game itself, had been subtly changed and that a new set of attitudes on their own part might be called for.

The summer of 1575, the first summer following the act, was possibly the last summer in which all the major playing companies played in inns or other houses that lay under the lord mayor's jurisdiction. The companies active in London in that summer included, to the best of our knowledge, not only the group under Leicester's patronage (James Burbage, John Perkin, John Laneham, William Johnson, and Robert Wilson, as they were listed in the Patent of 1574), but also others belonging to the earls of Warwick, Sussex, Oxford, Lincoln, Pembroke, and Essex, and perhaps still others belonging to Lord Howard, Lord Rich, Lord Abergavenny, and Sir Robert Lane. No doubt there were additional groups as well, which have left no trace. When a company was invited to play at court, a record of the payment was made, and these records have for the most part survived. When a company had the misfortune to attract the attention of the lord mayor or aldermen, some notice of this event would usually appear in the City records. When a company traveled in the provinces, showing—or failing to show— its letters of authorization to the appropriate town officials, some record of the company's appearance, or even of the rejection of its request to play, would often be entered in the town's record books; often, as well, the visits of players were entered in the record books of great houses. By contrast, a company might spend its entire existence playing in innyards and open fields and never appear in anyone's record book. Even companies that played always and only in London could well have attracted no documentary notice at all, if they were never involved in disturbances or other infractions and never invited to play at court. Hence any list we might construct of playing companies active in the City in 1575 is bound to be incomplete; but the list we have, even with this defect, is sufficient to suggest that a sudden constriction in the availability of playing places in the summer of 1575, such as the Act of Common Council may either intentionally or inadvertently have created, would have produced an economic crisis for a rather large number of players.

Information about individual players in 1575 is as scanty as might be expected, but bits of data survive from which we may, with a modicum of license, construct a plausible story to help illuminate the summer season in question. In this period the brothers John and Lawrence Dutton were citizens of London, freemen of the Weavers' Company, and stage players. Lawrence may have been the elder; he achieved a moment of notoriety in the records of Bridewell Hospital in 1577 when one John Shawe, a brothel keeper, told the governors that Margaret Goldsmith, one of his working women, had been taken from him in 1576 and set up elsewhere by one or both of the Dutton brothers. Shawe, no mincer of words, told the Governors that "m*a*rgarett is nowe at one Horspoll at the Bell beyond Shorditche chirche and there one Lawrence Dutton*n* kepes her he is a player & there is two brethere*n* and by reporte both their wyves are whores."[43]

Lawrence had been with Sir Robert Lane's men in 1571-1572, and was probably their leader; John had likely been with them as well. The Statute against Vagabonds of 1572 may have raised questions in their mind about the security of this affiliation and moved them to seek a patron better situated than a mere knight and better able to offer them protection. In this they may have anticipated Leicester's men, who did not appeal to their patron for his protection until 1574. By late 1572 the Duttons had moved to the service of the earl of Lincoln, apparently bringing the rest of Lane's players with them. In that same year the brothers, along with Thomas Gough, one of their fellow players who was also a citizen and barber surgeon of London, entered into a contract requiring one Rowland Broughton of London to supply them with some eighteen plays over the course of the next thirty months, apparently for a company of boy players which the Duttons and Gough intended to set up.[44]

Nothing further is known of this projected company of children. Probably it was intended, like its adult counterpart, to serve under

[43]GHL, Bridewell Hospital Court Minute Book, vol. 3, ff. 118–25, court of 2 January 1577. These minute books are at the King Edward School in Witley, Surrey; I consulted the microfilm copy in the Guildhall Library in London. I am grateful to R. Mark Benbow for drawing my attention to this item.

[44]PRO, C.2/Eliz./D.11/49; for a transcription and brief commentary, see R. Mark Benbow, "Dutton and Goffe versus Broughton: A Disputed Contract for Plays in the 1570s," *REED Newsletter* (Toronto, 1981), 2, 3–9.

the protection of the earl of Lincoln; but the collapse of the contractual arrangement with Broughton may be one of the signs of the project's failure. The brothers themselves remained with Lincoln's players until 1575, when, moved perhaps by the difficulties erected by the Act of Common Council, they shifted their service yet again, joining Jerome Savage in the earl of Warwick's company. Savage, the leader of Warwick's group, may have attracted their interest by his greater success in finding a place to play in 1575 or perhaps by his intriguing suggestion that a strong company—which Warwick's would certainly be with both Savage and the Duttons among its members—might find a way to set up its own playing space.[45]

Elsewhere in the City the players who served Warwick's brother the earl of Leicester may have been entertaining the same notions. It is possible, however, that the dilemma was not an immediate issue either for Leicester's players or for Warwick's, for they may not have been in the City during most of that summer. The queen had been on progress through her realm since the latter part of May; the brother earls of Leicester and Warwick were both part of her retinue, and their players in turn may have been a part of *their* retinue. It is generally taken for granted that Leicester's players were present at Kenilworth for the famous festivities there, which occupied twenty days in July, and we know that Warwick's players played before the queen at Lichfield at the beginning of August, and publicly in the city of Leicester some time earlier.

But the queen's progress occupied nearly 150 days, and it is perhaps unlikely that companies of players attended her courtiers for all that period. Her Privy Council did follow her throughout the progress, however, and its membership included four major patrons of playing companies, not only Leicester and Warwick but also Sussex (the lord chamberlain) and Lincoln (the lord admiral). The dates and places of council meetings, and the names of those in attendance, are easily ascertainable from the published record of their proceedings.[46] The council met some fifty times during the progress, with Leicester present for over forty of the meetings, and Warwick present for almost that number. Sussex was present for not quite thirty, Lincoln for barely ten.

---

[45]For the story of Savage's playhouse, see the next chapter.

[46]*The Acts of the Privy Council*, ed. J. R. Dasent, n.s., vols. 8 and 9 (London, 1894), contains transcriptions of the relevant entries. For a summary of the progress itself, see *ES* 4:91–92.

The queen did not return to the vicinity of London until mid-October, but evidence of plague in the City, which had already forced a fortnight's deferral of the opening of Michaelmas term, kept her sequestered at Windsor into November. Probably there was a cessation of playing as well, though we have no record. Companies of players—as perhaps Leicester's and Warwick's—returning with their patrons to London at that time and hoping to take up playing in the City must have found their circumstances uncertain. Perhaps the players attended on the progress only intermittently, spending the rest of their time in London; alternatively, they may have attended the progress fairly steadily—or followed on its heels, playing in nearby towns—because the late summer plague had closed London to them. Either way, their return to the City in the late autumn of 1575 may have provoked another crisis about space.[47]

In the closing months of 1575, virtually at the first anniversary of the act, the aldermen had occasion to recur to it, in an exchange with the governors of Christ's Hospital which allows us greater insight into the City's perceived relationship between the staging of plays and the financing of hospitals.[48] The act, as we have seen, contains repeated assertions that its projected revenues "shalbe imployed to the releif of the poore in the hospitalls of this Cittye," but it contains no correlative statement that support from the City's own coffers was to be simultaneously withdrawn, and the new revenue source to stand in place of the old. Yet that is what seems to have happened. And when the money from the new source failed to materialize, the governors of the five hospitals found themselves in a quandary.

Late in 1575 the governors of Christ's Hospital openly questioned the Court of Aldermen on the matter. The aldermen's response was

---

[47]I do not mean to imply that these companies were all "London companies," for the term is relatively meaningless in this period; but the members of the major companies—indeed, most of the stage players for whom we have any biographical information at all—had their homes and families in London, and for them "return" is the appropriate word.

[48]The aldermen had in fact perceived a relation between staging plays and financing hospitals some months before the framing of the act. In their letter to the lord chamberlain of 2 March 1574, defending their rejection of the claim of Holmes to "haue the appoyntm^t of places for playes & enterludes w^thin this Citie" (see note 21 above), they claimed that within the City "great offices haue bene & be made for the same" by their own initiative, the primary purpose of which was "the releif of the poore in the hospitals," an objective "wch we hold vs assured that yor L will like well that we preferre before the benefit of any pryvate persone."

to instruct "the M^rs and Governo^rs of x̄pies hospytall" to call together "all suche persons beinge Inneholders and kepers of Innes within this Cytie and the lybertyez thereof, or any other person in whose howsez, any enterludes or playes are Commenly vsyd to be played and kepte," and to require that these same people "doe trulye answeare and paye to thuse of the poore of the same hospytall, all suche sommez of monye as by an Acte of Common Cownsell lately made and provyded ys lymited and appoynted."[49] The governors of the hospital were told, in so many words, that they might take upon themselves the responsibility of enforcing the act if they wished to benefit more fully from the revenues it was supposed to provide.

The strategy of the aldermen is here quite clear. The innkeepers and others who were supposed to be paying regular fees "to the vse of the poore in hospitalls of the Cittye" were identified as somehow failing to meet their obligations, and the intimation was that they were withholding payment. No notice was taken of the alternative possibility that there may have been no fees to begin with, either because the innkeepers were declining to make their establishments available to players or because the players themselves were largely absent from the City during much of that year. The governors of Christ's Hospital, the first to complain to the alderman about the missing income, won thereby the dubious honor of being selected to confront the innkeepers on this issue and to see that thenceforth they "doe trulye answeare and paye" the money they were presumed to owe— not an enviable position for the governors, but nonetheless a development with implications for the players. Our expectation that the City would have been enforcing its own decrees during this period, and would thus have had some sense of the true extent of playing in innyards in 1575, may be no more than a consequence of our own modern sensibility about legislative convention; the Common Council and the Court of Aldermen may have seen this legislation from the start as a means of escaping from, rather than intensifying, their own role in overseeing stage playing within the City. That someone should be monitoring plays and players was clear, but it might as well be someone with a direct financial interest in the matter.

---

[49]CLRO, Rep. xix, fo. 18^r,v, meeting of 8 December 1575; *MSC* 2, pt. 3, item xxxix.

Indeed, one might read the 1574 act as doubly targeted, intended to free the aldermen and the city chamberlain at once from the twin burdens of supporting the hospitals and regulating playing. The hospitals were offered a presumably steady and reliable external source of revenue, the collection of which would involve them inevitably in the close supervision of stage playing, and thus two administrative birds might well be taken care of with one legislative stone. The principal concern of the act of 1574, therefore, may not have been plays and players at all; as a perennially ubiquitous and therefore taxable activity, playing may have been merely the handiest perceived solution to a quite separate problem of municipal funding. The governors of Christ's Hospital, to whom the authority was now delegated, might well have brought a greater attention to the enforcement of the decree for the simple pragmatic reason that they needed the money. Would this have meant a more stringent enforcement than might have obtained under the aldermen? Perhaps. Coming as it did, just before the holiday season in December 1575, the elevation of the governors to the position of fee takers for stage plays may well have had mixed consequences for all concerned with playmaking and playgoing during the winter months of that year.

There were plays at court during the Christmas holidays, as usual, but otherwise the City may have been inhospitable. On the evening of 26 December, Warwick's men (the Duttons and Savage) played before the queen, but on that same day Leicester's men were performing in New Romney, Kent. Burbage and his fellows returned the next day, playing at court the evening of 28 December, but such traveling can hardly have been congenial or desirable at that time of year. Warwick's men played at court again on New Year's Day at night, and we know of no other court entertainment until Candlemas (Sussex's men), Shrove Sunday (4 March, Leicester's), and Shrove Monday (5 March, Warwick's). What else these players were doing during the winter of 1575/76 is at present unknown.

There are, as noted earlier, no further entries in the records of either the aldermen or councilors for 1575 or 1576—none, that is, for two years after the passage of the act of 1574—to suggest that control of the drama was a continuing concern to them during this period; but this is not to say that the act of 1574 did not occupy their attention after its first passage. The aldermen made a serious and determined effort to get their new legislation to work, but all their subsequent discussions of it were in the context of hospital funding, not of stage playing. They put their own official weight behind the hospitals for the better enforcement of the act, while still insisting that the hospitals play the major role in its enforcement. The governors of Christ's Hospital, having first looked into the provisions of the act in the previous March, were by this point quite dissatisfied with the arrangement, and in mid-December 1575 they instructed five of their number "to repayre to my Lorde maior on tuesday next to declare the opinion of this courte towchinge the takynge of monie of thinholde^{rs} wheare plaies be frequented towardes the Releif of the poore." The governors found it "a matte^r very vnconvenient" and recommended "rathe^r that they [i.e., plays] shold be altogethe^r restrayned, and that in any wyse they [i.e., the governors] wold not haue any monie so gotten to releue the poor w^tall."[50]

This move was a calculated gamble; the posture assumed by the governors was firm and properly moral, yet not devoid of possible political value. By claiming that revenue from stage plays was tainted, they perhaps hoped to embarrass the aldermen into devising an alternate source of funding and thus escape the present impasse. But the aldermen were themselves quite familiar with the ramifications of such rhetoric, and in this instance they were not to be put off. In mid-January 1576, a month after their meeting with the delegation from Christ's Hospital, the aldermen directed the hospital's treasurer, Thomas Hall, to "delyver vnto every Alderman of this Cyttye in wrytinge the names and surnames of every suche persons as do refuse to be contrybutoryes to the poore of the same hospytall."[51] An appeal from the governors to be freed of this inappropriate burden met with little sympathy; in the following week the aldermen appointed a committee of twelve distinguished citizens (four aldermen, one common councilor, and governors of three of the City's hospitals among their number) to "heare & examyne the contentes of the supplycacion exhybyted vnto this Courte by the M^r and governours of x͞p͞ies hospytall and . . . to take suche ordre therein as to theyre good dyscrecions shall seeme convenient."[52] With the appointment of this committee the issue was effectively relegated to limbo, and nothing further is heard of the matter.

[50]Court Minutes of Christ's Hospital, GHL, ms. 12,806/2, fo. 140, court of 17 December 1575.
[51]CLRO, Rep. xix, fo. 28, court of 19 January 1576.
[52]CLRO, Rep. xix, fo. 33^v, court of 26 January 1576.

So the Act of Common Council, and the subsequent disagreements about its enforcement, became something of a political football in the City in the early months of 1576. It is tempting to see a connection between these matters and the imminent erection of playhouses in the suburbs.[53] One might wonder, for example, if the impulse to have premises of one's own—the impulse that we assume motivated Burbage and Savage and the others at about this time—might not have antedated the act, might not have found its initial expression in a desire to have premises in the City, perhaps to be one's own innholder. An exemplar was to hand in Edward Alleyn's older brother John, who had inherited the lease to the family inn in Bishopsgate and styled himself "innholder," but who was also a sometime stage player and is not likely to have overlooked the possible intersection of these two activities. Burbage might equally have entertained such a thought. If so, the act of 1574 did not create, but by its intricacies merely redirected, the desires of certain stage players about owning a building.

This redirection would in itself have been, I suggest, an unforeseen consequence of the act of 1574, especially if (as I conjecture) the intent of the act was not, in any sense, the suppression of stage plays but rather the conversion of playing—now that royal patents to players made suppression of playing a dubious rather than a desirable goal—into a fee-producing activity. If the cost of maintaining the City hospitals might thus be defrayed, the City might find it possible to tolerate, even discreetly to support, playing; but it would be at others' cost, either of the innkeepers or of the players themselves. Absent from this equation in the minds of the councilors was the possibility that certain groups of players might subvert the process by doing something hitherto unheard of.

In another section of the same order in which the governors of Christ's Hospital were sent out to collect their own fees, the aldermen recorded their awareness that "one Sebastian that wyll not commvnycate wth the Church of England" (by whom they meant

---

[53]Glynne Wickham finds little connection between the two: "This Act," he says, "far from being the immediate cause of Burbage's decision to build the Theater in the suburbs, is simply a compendium of all the variants which had been used during the past thirty years in vain attempts to define the words 'substancial commoners' and 'in their houses' and thus enforce the letter of the City Proclamation of 1545" (*Early English Stages, 1300–1600* [London: RKP, 1963], 2, pt. 1:196). My own understanding of the document differs from Wickham's, but I share his sense that it is less instrumental than tradition would have it.

Sebastian Westcott) "kepethe playes and resorte of the people" at St. Paul's, "to great gaine"—the Common Wisdom about the profitability of playing—"and p*er*yll of the Corruptinge of the Chyldren wth papistrie." The City remembrancer, Thomas Norton (better known to posterity, though not to his colleagues, as the joint author of *Gorboduc*), was appointed "to goe to the Deane of Powles" (this was Alexander Nowell) "and to gyve him notyce of that dysorder, and to praye him to gyve suche remeadye therein, w^{t}in his iurysdycc*io*n, as he shall see meete, for Christian Relygion and good order."[54] The studied ambiguity of the final phrasing leaves us in much uncertainty about the nature of the "dysorder" and about the sort of "remeadye" the aldermen intended that the dean should give; was the disorder that Westcott was a papist or that he "kepethe playes"? Were the aldermen suggesting their readiness to make an issue of the recusancy, but equally to overlook it if the playing were brought under control? Would an acceptable "remeadye" be for Nowell to get rid of Westcott, to terminate the playing, to offer to post bond for the playing, or merely to assuage the aldermen's unhappiness with the playing by making a contribution of some sort to the City's coffers? The yoking of this communication to Nowell with the instructions to the governors of Christ's Hospital suggests that in the minds of the aldermen, at least on this day, stage plays and the recovery of fees were seen as related topics.

Once such a state of mind is reached, the vision of monetary relief may well ameliorate the object to which it is attached; earlier notions of hostility to stage plays may well turn imperceptibly into a kind of fiscal toleration, in which the necessary evil comes to be seen more as necessary than as evil. The councilors had managed, with their act, to turn playing to their own uses, though the first year of their new legislation had not apparently brought them the revenues they had anticipated. No doubt they hoped the income would increase in the future; probably they neither expected nor anticipated the imaginative remedy the players themselves were about to launch in 1576. Three groups of players, at least, were on their way to undermining the council's money-raising scheme, and in the process freeing themselves from the jurisdiction of the lord mayor, the Court of Aldermen, and the Court of Common Council.

---

[54]CLRO, Rep. xix, fo. 18^{r,v}, meeting of 8 December 1575; *MSC* 2, pt. 3, item xxxix.

POSTSCRIPT

There is a bit more to the funding history of Christ's Hospital.
Throughout 1575 and 1576 the hospital remained overextended, as
the Court of Aldermen continued to send young children there to be
"vertuouslye brought vp at the Cost*es* and chardges of the sayd
hospytall."[55] In October 1576 the Court of Common Council,
seeking to alleviate this pressure with additional funding for the
hospital, legislated that the fees currently collected from the defective
measure of cloth offered for sale at Blackwell Hall were to be
redistributed by the city chamberlain according to a new formula;
one-third of the money so collected was to go to the use of the mayor
and commonalty, another third was to be paid to the informers who
enabled the collection in the first place, and the final third was to go
"to the releef of the poore in Cristes hospital in this Citty."[56] The
Court of Alderman seconded this legislation on 23 April 1577,
empowering the masters of Christ's Hospital to proceed at law
against all persons offending against the act and to inquire after "the
harboringe of the same [defective cloths] in com*m*on Innes and other
places of this Cytie."[57]

But the officers of the hospital did not need this additional
burden; by the previous summer their lives had already become
complicated enough. In June 1576 the Court of Aldermen had felt it
necessary to decree that "thoffycers belonginge to the seu*er*all
hospytalls" were under no circumstances to "be beaten or mysvsed
by eny p*er*son or p*er*sons w[th]in this Cytie" while they were engaged
in "thexecutinge of their offyces."[58] Whatever the specific circumstance that motivated this ruling, relations between innkeepers and
the governors of Christ's Hospital were likely already strained, as a
result of the powers given to the governors in the wake of the act of
6 December 1574. The further legislation in the spring of 1577
seemed likely to produce yet more friction between them. By the
end of 1577 the innkeepers had apparently had enough; they
protested formally to the Court of Aldermen, who in masterful
fashion sent them directly to the source of their unhappiness: on 11
December 1577 the aldermen ordered "that the byll of complaynte

---

[55]For example, "A poore Chylde lately lefte in the night tyme in the entrye of A
howse in Lymestrete"; see CLRO, Rep. xix, ff. 31, 145.
[56]CLRO, Jor. xx(2), ff. 312[v]–13[v].
[57]CLRO, Rep. xix, fo. 195.
[58]CLRO, Rep. xix, fo. 89[v].

exhibetyd vnto this Co^r^te by the M^r^ wardeyns and companye of the Inholders of this Cytie shalbe referryd to the hearynge and examynacion of the M^rs^ and Gouerno^rs^ of x̄p̄ies hospytall, and they to take suche order therein, as to their dyscreacions shall seame good And thereof to make reporte vnto this Co^r^te wth conveniente spede."[59]

The bill of complaint itself has not survived, but the innkeepers may well have included, as one of their grievances, a falling-off in custom as a result of the disappearance of certain popular companies of stage players from their premises. In the eyes of the innkeepers, the governors of Christ's Hospital may well have seemed to be the villains in the piece—an unfortunate conclusion, if it were so, for the governors were as caught up in the machinations of the aldermen as were the innkeepers. Among others who might have suffered as a result of this spate of legislation were those companies of players who still preferred to, or who were constrained to, rely on the hospitality of innkeepers.

[59]CLRO, Rep. xix, fo. 272.

CHAPTER SIX

A Playhouse at Newington:
Jerome Savage, 1576

I

There is a story of a drunkard searching under a street lamp for his house key, which he had dropped some distance away. Asked why he didn't look where he had dropped it, he replied, "It's lighter here!"

—Abraham Kaplan

Of the three playhouses erected in "1576," the one built at Newington Butts has traditionally been the easiest for scholars to neglect. Where the Theater and Curtain stood virtually side by side in Shoreditch, a short walk beyond Bishopsgate, the playhouse at Newington Butts stood alone, a mile below London Bridge, as far to the south of the City as the earlier Red Lion had stood to the east (see Figure 5). It was the most distant playhouse administratively as well; south of the Thames, it was in a different county and in a different diocese, answerable to a different sheriff and under the jurisdiction of different sessions and assize courts. Whether despite these distances or because of them, it was probably the first of the three playhouses to be begun and may have been the first completed.

That we know so little about this playhouse has sometimes seemed sufficient evidence of its insignificance. The well-known

---

The epigraphs to the two sections are from Abraham Kaplan, *The Conduct of Inquiry* (San Francisco: Chandler, 1964), p. 11, and Stephen Gosson, *The School of Abuse, containing a pleasant invective against poets, pipers, players, jesters and such like caterpillars of a commonwealth* (1579), sig. C3ᵛ–4.

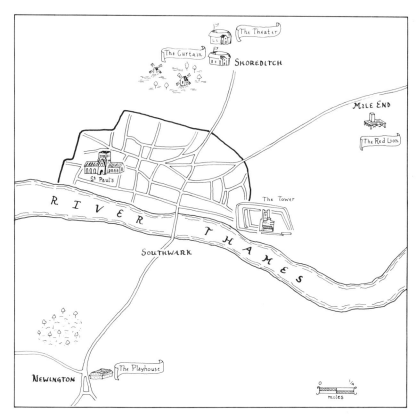

Figure 5. Location of London's earliest playhouses

memorandum of the Privy Council acknowledging the remoteness of its location and the "tediousnes of the waie" there has served as a convenient rationale for our assuming that the Butts playhouse was an ill-considered venture from the start, badly located, doomed to failure and early extinction, and hence not likely to reward our sustained inquiry.[1] All but the last of these assumptions may well be true. Indeed, the playhouse, which may have been the first of the three built in 1576, was certainly the first to be dismantled and forgotten. Further, the building does not appear on any contempo-

---

[1] Memorandum in *ES* 4:313.

rary map or perspective view, as both the Theater and Curtain do; hence we have been able to make no responsible claims about how it looked or where it stood. The playhouse seems not to have been the subject of any litigation, so we are denied those details of structure, ownership, and deployment which have for so long been a part of our awareness of the Theater and which have lately enriched our knowledge of the Boar's Head playhouse in Whitechapel. The Newington Butts playhouse was as remote from the Theater as the Curtain was proximate, geographically as well as financially. While we know that Henry Laneman, the proprietor of the Curtain, made an appearance as a deponent in the Theater litigation and had some sort of profit-sharing arrangement with Brayne and Burbage (more on this in the next two chapters), the person or persons who built the playhouse at Newington Butts remained quite outside that charmed circle. Finally, unlike the other two playhouses, the playhouse at Newington Butts seems not even to have had a name. On the analogy of the Theater, it may have been called the Playhouse, though more likely its name, whatever it might have been, was simply not current enough to have found its way into the written records.

Our knowledge of the Butts playhouse is thus meager, founded on a few statements affirming its existence, still fewer about its characteristics, proprietors, even occupants. Given all these handicaps, it is little wonder that this thoroughly marginalized playhouse should survive only on the fringes of our consciousness. We know that Philip Henslowe entered in his *Diary* some receipts for the admiral's and chamberlain's companies, which were playing there together for a week or so in June 1594, and we know that the Privy Council sent directives to the Surrey justices to suppress illegal playing there in the summers of 1580 and 1586. We know also that among the Henslowe papers at Dulwich is an undated Privy Council warrant, possibly from 1592, in which a petition from Lord Strange's players to abandon Newington Butts and return to the City was approved. But aside from these four items with their scanty facts, there has been until recent times little to go on. The presence of two companies at the Butts in 1594 under Henslowe's auspices led Chambers to muse that "possibly the theatre had come into Henslowe's hands" by that time,[2] and Wallace claimed in 1913 to have

---

[2] *ES* 2:405.

seen a document confirming that the playhouse had disappeared by 1599.[3]

Other bits of information have been available to us as well, though not in what we might think of as our standard sources, and perhaps for that reason easily overlooked. For the Butts playhouse, some very useful information has been at hand for over a generation. In 1955 Ida Darlington, then archivist of the Greater London Record Office, announced her discovery of a pair of leases indicating that the playhouse at Newington Butts had been "built by a Richard Hickes, one of the Queen's Yeomen of the Guard, at some date between 1566, when he had a lease of ground there from the Dean and Chapter of Canterbury, and 1580, when the playhouse is first mentioned.[4]

"Richard Hickes" is a name not generally known among theater historians, and the Darlington clue, with its Gilbert and Sullivan overtones, would have been more than sufficient to pique one's interest, if only it had come to someone's attention.[5] Who was Richard Hickes, "Yeoman of the Guard", and why would he build a playhouse at Newington Butts? Fair questions, even as they reveal the state of our unknowing. Had we known nothing of the Theater, we might have been equally perplexed to come upon the Red Lion documents with their mention of one John Brayne, a grocer, and we might equally have wondered what could be known about him. Hickes, like Brayne, can be pursued through the records, where his appearances are fitful but consistent.

Like Brayne, Hickes entered upon his mercantile life as a grocer's apprentice, attaching himself in about 1547 (the records are inadequate at this point) to the grocer Thomas Norton.[6] On 14 October

---

[3] Wallace said that the playhouse "was in 1599 only a memory, as shown by a contemporary record to be published later" ("The First London Theatre," *Nebraska University Studies* 13 (1913), 2). He never followed through on his promise—unfortunately a frequent failing of his—but the document he had in mind is most probably the one from the Surrey and Kent Commissions of Sewers cited below, note 50.

[4] Ida Darlington, *St George's Fields*, vol. 25 of *The Survey of London* (London: London County Council, 1955), p. 86.

[5] An early attempt of my own to pursue the matter (*Shakespeare Quarterly* 21 [1970], 385–98) is superseded by this chapter.

[6] This Norton is not to be confused with the younger man of the same name who was a playwright, poet, translator, lawyer, and Remembrancer of the City of London. Norton the grocer was nearly fifty years old by the time Hickes, one of his last apprentices, achieved his freedom. This Norton had earned his own freedom in 1530 but did not advance in his company, seemingly never making it out of the yeomanry and into the livery. The entry for Norton the poet in the *Dictionary of National Biography* speaks erroneously of a connection with the Grocers' Company, and confusion on this

1553, somewhat before the end of the statutory seven years, "Richard hyck*es* late Apprentice with Thomas Nortone" was "Receyved and sworne" into the freedom; the clerk noted of him "that he was made ffree within his terme of yeres"—an event usually, though not always, a sign of precocity and therefore auspicious.[7] Thereafter Hickes disappears from the records of the company for some four or five years. Unlike John Brayne, who was an active grocer from the day of his freedom until the late 1570s, Hickes seems to have moved off in other directions as soon as he became free. After an absence of five years, however, something impelled him to renew his connection with the Grocers' Company; in the accounts for 1557 his name reappears, the company clerk noting that "Richard hick*es*" had for the first time made his annual payment of two shillings "brotherhood money" in that year. For some years thereafter he paid these annual dues regularly. In 1558 the clerk entered his name against this contribution as "Richard Hick*es* on of y*e* ga*r*de" and noted that he was living in Southwark. Hickes continued the payments for some ten years, until 1567, when his name appears on the list for the last time.[8]

Hickes's decision to maintain his connection with his livery company may have had something to do with his new career as a member of the royal retinue. The curious Grocers' entry from 1558, "on of y*e* ga*r*de," is clarified for us on a certificate of residence issued

---

head is made worse by the presence of yet another grocer of the same name and by the failure of the clerk of the Grocers' Company to construct prose that distinguished clearly among the three. The company did have occasion to remember the Remembrancer from time to time: in 1572 they granted him a benevolence for his "paynes . . . abowte thaffaires and sutes of the Companie," particularly a contested legacy, and in 1576 they did so again, this latter time in particular "agaynst a Lycence graunted to an Italyan being hurtfull to the hole body of this cytie and specyally agaynst this company" (GHL, ms. 11,588/1, Court Minutes of the Grocers' Company, 1556–1591, ff. 233, 272*v*).

[7] GHL, ms. 11,571/5, Wardens' Accounts of the Grocers' Company, 1534–1555, ff. 430, 435. All new freemen had to pay their two-shilling entrance fee, and Hickes did so promptly, as did another apprentice, William Jeffrey, made free on the same day. The company clerk entered Jeffrey's payment and immediately below it, in a moment of inattention, wrote: "R*es* of Jeffrey Hickes late Apprentice w*th* Thomas Norton." The scribal context for this entry makes it easier to argue that "Jeffrey Hickes" was a ghost name; other instances, "Anne Whateley" among them, have no such clarifying context. Cases like these teach us to be on our guard, as they can easily make for erroneous history.

[8] GHL, ms. 11,571/6, Wardens' Accounts of the Grocers' Company, 1555–1578, ff. 52 ("Richard hick*es*," 1557/58), 89 ("Richard Hick*es* on of y*e* ga*r*de," 1558/59), 118 ("Richard Hickes of y*e* ga*r*de," 1559/60), 150 ("Ric Hick*es*," 1565/56), 176*v* ("Ric Hickes," 1566/57). Wardens' accounts for the five years between 1560 and 1565 have not survived.

in 1563 by the commissioners of subsidies to "Richard Hickes one of thordinary yeomen of the quenes ma^ties chamber."[9] Hickes was rated in that year, in his capacity as yeoman, to the value of £24 in annual wages and lands, a not inconsiderable sum. In 1567 he appeared in an Exchequer lay subsidy roll in a full list of yeomen under the general heading "The ordinary yeomen of the Quenes ma^tes chamb^r." There were some 135 names in this list, most of them rated at the level of their annual wages of £18, and assessed 24 shillings on that amount. But "Richard Hick*es*" was again rated "in wages and Land*es*" to the amount of £24, and assessed 32 shillings. Only about ten other names on the list are so highly remunerated, or so highly taxed.[10] Hickes, having achieved this level fairly early in his career, stayed there for the remainder of his life. Early in 1585, probably not much beyond his fiftieth year, Hickes died intestate, a widower, with his married daughter Margaret Hunningborne as his only heir. On 9 February 1585 the administration of his estate was granted to her.[11]

This, then, is the man who was alleged to have built the playhouse at Newington Butts. Our next step is to locate him there more firmly by turning our attention to the plot of ground itself and to Ida Darlington's information about the leases. In the 1560s and 1570s the "town" of Newington was little more than an intersection where the roads from Camberwell and Clapham joined on their way to Southwark;[12] it lay about a mile south of London Bridge, and the settlement at the intersection numbered perhaps a hundred souls. The church, St. Mary's, was there at the intersection, but the parish of Newington extended beyond the limits of the town to embrace the whole of the manor of Walworth, in which the town and its surrounding lands lay.[13] The lords of this manor, since before the Conquest, were the dean and chapter of Christ Church, Canterbury.

[9] PRO, E.115/221/8, 8 May 1563.

[10] PRO, E.179/69/82, 8 March 1567

[11] PRO, Prob.6/3, fo. 132^v (old 129^v). "Peter Huningburne and Margaret Hickes" had been married at St. Mary Woolchurch Haw on 18 February 1572 (GHL, ms. 7644).

[12] "Newington Butts" was either the full name of the town of Newington or the name of that segment of the queen's highway, with its intersection, where the town sat. It was not the name of a nearby archery field, as one finds confidently asserted in older histories; Darlington notes that in the "very voluminous" records relating to Newington there are no references of any sort to archery butts. She suggests that the name referred to the shape of the triangle of land at the road junction; there are, she says, many instances from Surrey and elsewhere of the use of the word "butts" for odd corners or ends of land (p. 85).

[13] Darlington, p. 81.

Darlington's notes in her 1955 book indicate that Hickes's leases were to be found in the archives of Christ Church, better known as Canterbury Cathedral, and so they are, along with the other records of the dean and chapter. From those records we learn that the lords of the manor periodically leased out bits of their demesne lands in Walworth, a chief parcel of which was comprised of six discrete but contiguous fields, leased as a unit and collectively referred to in their records as "Newington 35 Acres."

All of these lands lay eastward from the highway and intersection of Newington Butts. One of the fields, called Stewfen, was an osier ground, bounded on all four sides by a common drainage sewer, and Darlington notes that they were "for the most part underwater during nine months of the year."[14] To the west of Stewfen lay a small holding of two acres called Little Pightel, and west of that, abutting the highway, lay a ten-acre plot called Lurklane, where we will eventually be able to situate the playhouse. There was another field called Flexcroft and a divided or two-part close called Horse-mongerland. On 26 November 1566 the dean and chapter of Christ Church, Canterbury, demised these six pieces as a single parcel to "Richard Hickes one of the yeomen of her ma^{tes} garde."[15]

Hickes's original lease was for sixty years, but on 29 September 1573 the entire parcel was redemised to him, for reasons unspecified in the records; there was apparently no change in the rental, though in the new version Hickes bound himself to maintain the common sewer and the bridge or bridges over it "if any be."[16] There are no further leases to Hickes, but there are subsequent leases of the property to other persons, and the later leases are full of useful information. On 30 November 1590, Hickes having died some years earlier and his lease apparently having been surrendered, the dean and chapter demised the same parcel of six pieces to Richard Cuckowe of Southwark, an innholder.[17] The six pieces in the parcel, their boundaries and contiguities, are described in a manner and form identical with the description in Hickes's earlier leases, except

[14] Darlington, p. 82, note c.

[15] Chapter library, Canterbury, Register V3, ff. 172^v–73^v. The property was still being leased as six fields bearing these names as late as 1801; see deed 69,584, Church Commissioners, chapter library, Canterbury.

[16] Chapter library, Canterbury, Register V3, ff. 172^v–73^v.

[17] He was called both Cuckowe and Cuckuck in different assessment lists for the same property. He was the son of Thomas Cuckowe of Southwark, also an innholder, who was buried on 16 June 1589 in St. Olave's parish. Richard seems to have moved to Newington shortly after the execution of the second lease. He was a vestryman and later a churchwarden of St. Mary's Church in Newington, and a member of many presentment juries for that part of Surrey.

(important for us) for one "enclosed" segment of the piece called Lurklane, which was to be withheld from Cuckowe and reserved to the use of Hickes's son-in-law Peter Hunningborne: "except and allwaies to the saide deane and Chapiter and theire Successors reserued one messuage or tenem^t heare to foare by one Richard Hickes deceased errected and builte vppone p*a*rcell of the saide land*es* nowe called the plaie howse wth all howses gardens or ortchard*es* theare vnto adioyninge as they be now in closed and in the occupac*i*on nowe or late of one Peter Haningburne or his assignes."[18]

As they had done earlier with Hickes, the dean and chapter redemised this property to Cuckowe on 1 November 1596, specifying the same terms, exempting again the segment of Lurklane and describing the playhouse once again as having been built by Hickes. (The 1596 lease was for the most part simply copied from the 1590 lease; whoever drew it up did not know, as we now do, that by the time of its execution the playhouse was no longer standing. More on this below.) Cuckowe remained the leaseholder of record to the end of the century for all of the lands in "Newington 35 acres" except for the parcel with the playhouse on it. Another pair of leases touches more circumstantially on the small piece of ground withheld from Richard Cuckowe in the foregoing two indentures. On 5 April 1595 the playhouse land itself was leased to one Paul Buck of Southwark. Apparently Buck had earlier obtained the reversion of the property, for in his lease it was stated that the "terme and interest" of the lands had come by good and lawful succession to him.[19] As part of the contract, Buck surrendered the lease to the dean and chapter, and it was straightway redemised to him. By its terms, the dean and chapter leased to Buck the "howse and tennem^t latelie builded by the foresaide Richarde Hickes vpon a parcell of [*land lying*] scituat and beinge in Newington neere Southwarke in the countie of Sur*rey* called Lurklane [*which parcel was*] letten as aforesaide to the saide Richarde Hickes amonge other landes togeither w[*ith one garden*] or garden plott as it is nowe inclosed out of the saide lande called Lurklane."[20]

---

[18] Chapter library, Canterbury, Register W23, ff. 36^v–37 and 292$^{r–v}$. The citation is from 292^v. These are the two leases referred to by Darlington.

[19] Buck apparently entered the premises at once; on 27 October 1595 the subsidy commissioners found "Paule Buck gent" in Newington and rated him at £6 "in good*es*."

[20] Chapter library, Canterbury, Register W23, fo. 266.

A description of the property follows immediately; with its later emendations, it remains the only description we have of the ground on which the Newington Butts playhouse stood. "All [*which said*] howse and garden conteyneth in length alonge by the landes of the saide Deane and cha[*pter now in*] the tenure of the saide Richarde Hickes or his assignes towardes the northe fortye and six y[*ards And*] like length alonge by the common Sewer there towardes the south ffortie fower yardes [*And in*] bradth alonge by the Queens high waie there towardes the west thirtie six yardes And [*in*] breadh alonge by the landes of the saide deane and Chapiter towards the East twentie [(*some words perished*)] To haue and to houlde," etc.[21]

Buck must have been well prepared for his dealings with the dean and chapter, for almost immediately upon accepting the lease he observed that the dimensions of the property were faulty. Accordingly, the next day (6 April 1595) a new lease was drawn. The dean and chapter acknowledged the errors of the former lease, "in wch lease certaine content*es* of the lande therein enclosed are set downe wch doe not conteyne the whole lande as it was inclosed by the saide Richard Hickes." In the amended lease the new dimensions were to show "the full content of the landes inclosed in [*the*] saide garden and garden plott not fullie set downe in the saide former lease as it was inclosed and taken in by the saide Richarde Hickes in his lyfe time bearing the content of ffortie and eight yardes towardes the north and south and in breadth towardes the East ffortie and twoe yardes and in like breadth to the west thirtie and three yardes be it more or less."[22]

These six documents, with their interlocking descriptions, enable us to construct for the first time a fairly precise picture of the environment of the playhouse. We may now determine with some accuracy that the land on which the playhouse stood was the southwest corner of the field called Lurklane; its northern side was about 144 feet in length and its eastern side about 126 feet, and on both these sides the adjoining land was the remainder of Lurklane. The western edge of the property was about 99 feet long and fronted on the queen's highway, or the Butts of Newington. The southern edge was about 144 feet long and defined by the common sewer that

---

[21] Chapter library, Canterbury, Register W23, fo. 266. The right edge of the page has crumbled; readings in brackets are supplied from other documents dealing with the property. The missing eastern dimension cannot be supplied, but as it is erroneous (see below) there is no loss.

[22] Chapter library, Canterbury, Register W23, fo. 266^{r-v}

flowed along it toward the east. The entire property was "inclosed out of" Lurklane, that is, walled or bounded from the remainder of the field.[23] The property contained "howses" or a "howse and tennem^t," one of which was the playhouse and the other presumably a dwelling. The property also contained a garden and an orchard. The total area involved was less than an acre.

These specifications give us for the first time an accurate siting for the playhouse. Further, the details in the leases make possible a number of connections with information in other documents in which only partial descriptions of the property are given and in which the playhouse itself is not mentioned. One such document, in which the highway, the sewer, and the orchard are the only clues, is important because it tells us the identity of the man who lived in the dwelling on the property in 1576. The document is the volume of Court Minutes of the Surrey and Kent Commissioners of Sewers; the man on the premises was Jerome Savage, the leading player with the earl of Warwick's company. Sewer records may seem an unlikely source for information about players and playhouses; a brief explanation of the document itself may be in order.

In Shakespeare's day the southern side of the Thames opposite London consisted chiefly of flat, open country, large areas of which were below the river's daily high-water mark. These low-lying lands were preserved from regular inundation at high tide by a line of reinforced embankments along the river which were inspected at regular intervals. But the ground behind the embankments often became soggy from other causes. Much of it was swampy to begin with, like Lambeth Marsh (or like the osier ground called Stewfen, a parcel of Hickes's land at Newington); and after a heavy rain the marshes and other low areas would be covered with water that might remain for weeks. Drainage of this recurring surface water was accomplished by a variety of small ditches leading into a system of common sewers, and from the sewers into one or another of the main sluices that emptied into the Thames at various points along its southern bank, protected by barriers to prevent backflow. These sluices—Whitewall sluice, Heath's Wall sluice, Duffield sluice, Boar's

---

[23] The details of the enclosing are not given, but it may be instructive to compare the description of the Curtain property in Holywell as it appeared in the deed of 18 March 1581; there the property was described as "that parcell of ground and close walled and inclosed with a bricke wall on the west and Northe part*es* and in parte with a mudde wall at the west side or ende towardes the southe called also the Curtayne close" (PRO, C.54/1098).

Head sluice, Earl's sluice—were vital to the welfare of the region, and their maintenance was a matter of continuing concern.

By good fortune the early records of the Surrey and Kent Commissions of Sewers, commencing in 1569, have survived; and by reading through them one can see how the various sewer commissioners and their presenting juries set about identifying the landowners and tenants of the various parcels of land lying along these common sewers and how the commissioners required them not only to pay periodic assessments for the maintenance of the river embankments and the major sluices but also, under penalty of fine, to clean and maintain those portions of the common sewer which abutted their lands. One such sewer, on the Bankside, ran along Maiden Lane past the Rose playhouse; accordingly, about six rods of its length became the responsibility of Philip Henslowe, the owner of the Rose, and we find the commissioners repeatedly ordering Henslowe to clean and repair "the com*m*en sewer before his play howse."[24]

Newington Butts lay athwart one of these common sewers, a part of the Duffield sluice system. Several sewers in the Newington-Walworth-Camberwell area emptied into Duffield sluice, but the particular sewer that concerns us ran from Lambeth Marsh in an easterly direction past the church and parsonage at Newington, under the road at Newington Butts, and on through orchard and meadow land to the Lock Hospital, a leper house on Kentish Street (now Old Kent Road), where it joined the sluice system (see Figure 6). The lands lying on this sewer were assessed in detail in reports of the sewer commissioners on 13 July 1576, 5 July 1577, and 3 November 1578 and were listed in all three assessments sequentially

[24] GLRO, ms. SKCS 18, Court Minutes of the Surrey and Kent Commissioners of Sewers. Some early references to Henslowe and the Rose may be found on folios 153^v, 237, 239, 241^v, 247, 249^v, and 257^v. I did not search beyond 1600. The six rods for which Henslowe was assessed was, for an estimate, fairly close to the known dimension of 94 feet for that side of his plot (*ES* 2:406; 6 rods = 99 feet). It is well to remember that these sewers did not serve the functions of modern sewers. Their chief purpose was to facilitate drainage. They were for the most part open channels, bridged over for foot traffic in places, and occasionally covered over entirely, as in passing under a road. Such underground stretches were protected by grates at either end to prevent debris from accumulating in places difficult of access. The sewers were emphatically not for the removal of rubbish or waste. A starchmaker in Newington was ordered by the sewer commissioners to cease dumping the waste products from his starchmaking into the common sewer (fo. 143^v); an unfortunate farmer whose privy had been tipped into the common sewer was ordered to remove it or be fined (fo. 131^v); another man was ordered to make "a grate of Iron for the keeping of his doung & fylth out of the common sewer" (fo. 138^v).

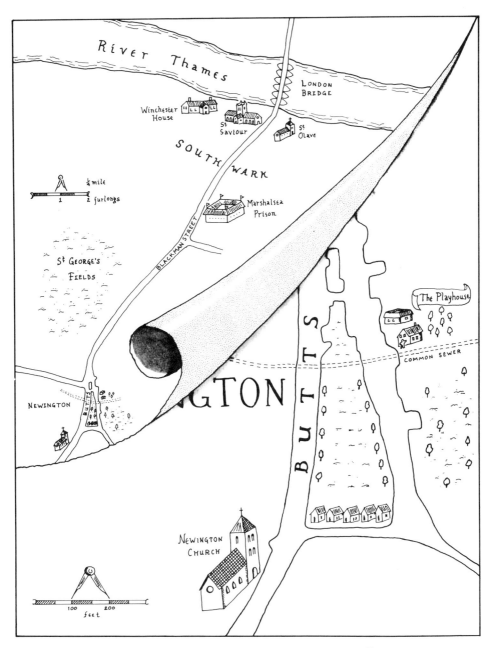

Figure 6. Location of the playhouse at Newington Butts

from west to east, as they occurred along the length of the sewer. From the Newington parsonage on the west side of the Butts, the sewer crossed the road into Richard Hickes's land. For the portion of the sewer which intersected the road, the sewer commissioners decided in 1576 that it was the responsibility of "thenhabitantes of the parishe of Newington to clense & cast deeper one rodde before the grate at Jerome Savadges doore." As the first tenants east of the road, it was the responsibility of "Jerome Savadge & John Hills to skowre & cast deeper x roddes of their common shewer leading from the grate at newington Buttes to the ende of Jerome Savages orchard corner" (fo. 87ᵛ).²⁵

Hilles must have lived to the south of Savage, since the sewer was Savage's southern boundary. In 1577 another survey of the sewer was made, "begynynge at the grate at Newington Buttes & so all alonge to the bridge at the Lasier howse," and Savage and Hilles were again listed first and charged with ten rods (fo. 95ᵛ). In 1578 the survey included "All the landhoulders from Newington bridge vppon both sydes the Commen sewer & so alonge to Duffildes sluce," and once again Jerome Savage and John Hilles led the list (fo. 105ᵛ).²⁶ The evidence that the grate of the common sewer was in front of Savage's door, and that the sewer ran to his "orchard corner," suggests that his dwelling, garden, and orchard must have occupied the southern portion of the lot, the playhouse therefore standing to the north.

The records do not indicate who, besides Savage, may have been living on the premises in 1576; no mention is made of a wife or family. But a detail from the parish register may be of interest. On the tenth of December in that year, a grave was opened in the burial

---

²⁵ The assessors were less accurate here than they were with Henslowe (see above); their estimate of 10 rods (= 165 feet) for the length of Savage's southern bound is more than a rod in excess of the known length of that side of the property, specified as 48 yards (= 144 feet) in Buck's lease.

²⁶ Hilles died at the end of March 1579 and was buried in the churchyard of St. Mary's, Newington. His will (P.C.C. 15 Bakon, now PRO, Prob.11/61, fo. 124ʳ⁻ᵛ) shows him to have been an extensive property holder, with a house in the City, tenements in Southwark, and a farm in Kent, but it unfortunately tells us nothing about his neighbor to the north in Newington. In the sewer surveys, the tenant immediately behind Savage, on the next piece of Richard Hickes's land, was Thomas Cuckowe in all three cases. Cuckowe probably farmed these lands, and may have held the reversion to them, in which case his son Richard's assumption of the lease in 1590 may be seen as a logical outgrowth of tenancy. It is important to note in this connection that Richard Hickes himself was never listed as a tenant on his lands; he lived elsewhere, probably in the City, and perhaps in Shoreditch near one of the other playhouses (more on this in the next chapter).

ground of St. Mary's Church in Newington, just across the road from Savage's property, and "ffrancis walker the sarvant of Jerom savaige was bvried."[27] No cause of death is mentioned.

II

> The carpenter raiseth not his frame without tools, nor the devil his work without instruments; were not players the mean, to make these assemblies, such multitudes would hardly be drawn in so narrow room. They seek not to hurt, but desire to please; they have purged their comedies of wanton speeches, yet the corn which they sell is full of cockle; and the drink that they draw, overcharged with dregs.
>
> —Stephen Gosson

The sewer records shows that Jerome Savage was Richard Hickes's tenant at Newington from the summer of 1576 to the autumn of 1578; from another source, a 1577 lawsuit in the Court of Requests, we learn that Savage's tenancy on the premises had begun even before the summer of 1576. Savage's tenancy was the very point at issue in the lawsuit; apparently from the first it had been fraught with complications.[28] All the parties to the suit—Jerome Savage the complainant, Richard Hickes and his son-in-law Peter Hunningborne the two defendants—agreed that on 25 March 1576 Hickes had given Savage a new thirty-year lease, to run until Lady Day 1606, as replacement for the older lease that Savage had purchased from one Richard Thompson, the former tenant, and under the terms of which Savage had already been living on the premises. Thompson's lease had been for nineteen years and thus would have been granted to him by someone other than Hickes, whose own proprietorship had begun only ten years earlier; accordingly Savage, in discussing his new lease, asked for assurance from Hickes that he

---

[27] GLRO, ms. P92/MRY/1, the parish register of St. Mary's Newington.

[28] The account that follows is taken from the lawsuit, PRO, Req.2/266/8. There is no date on the bill, but the two answers are dated 10 and 17 May 1577. There are no further pleadings, and no interrogatories or depositions. The books of decrees and orders for the Court of Requests do not survive for these years, so nothing can be known about the suit beyond the documents at hand.

was truly the legal landlord and empowered to bind himself in such an indenture.

Savage recalled in his bill of complaint that Hickes, defending his status as the legal landlord, had affirmed his readiness to give Savage a new lease "for terme of 30 yeres" if Savage so desired, and had further claimed "to have the verie fee simple of the premisses," which was overstating the case a bit, though neither Hickes nor Hunningborne objected to this assertion in their responses. The two defendants agreed that Savage had been sceptical about Hickes's status and had required that Hickes insert a clause in the new lease affirming "that he had full power right and Aucthoritie to Demise and graunt the saide Messuage" to Savage; in addition, Savage required him to "seale a bond of a Hundred Poundes" as earnest that Savage's new lease would be good. Hickes agreed to do so, and the new indenture was drawn and sealed on or about Lady Day 1576 (some three weeks before James Burbage and Giles Allen signed their own lease to the premises in Shoreditch where the Theater was to be built). Savage paid a ten-pound fee for his lease, with its inserted clauses and ancillary bond, and got in return what he thought was clear tenure of "the said messuage and one orchard and garden" until 1606, at a rent of four marks, or fifty-three shillings, four pence, per year, payable quarterly on the traditional quarter days.[29]

Hickes was, according to his son-in-law Peter Hunningborne, "a symple and plaine dealinge man," whom Savage had "greatlie abused" by such expressions of mistrust. Hickes concurred in this assessment of his own character. Yet Hickes and Hunningborne seem to have dealt obliquely with Savage, for shortly after the issuance of the new lease on 25 March 1576 they attempted to have it set aside and to have Savage evicted. Under pressure of Savage's lawsuit, the two men had to explain their reasons for this action, and they both recounted their own recent legal confrontation with one

---

[29] The specification of "one orchard and garden" hardly sounds like a description of the entire parcel called Lurklane, which was some ten acres in extent; more likely it was the smaller piece, the playhouse lot, on which both the orchard and the garden stood. One may perhaps infer from this phrasing that the lot in question had already, at some time before 25 March 1576, been defined as a separate piece, that is, already "inclosed out of" Lurklane by the appropriate bounding. Savage may have found the lot so enclosed when he bought Thompson's old lease, or he may have done the wall building himself. The new lease may thus have been an exchange; a surrender of a lease to the whole of Lurklane in return for a new lease to the playhouse plot alone.

another at the common law, whereby Hunningborne had sued his wife's simple and plain-dealing father, ostensibly for a debt of £50, though the matter may have been one of dower.[30] Hickes settled with Hunningborne out of court, so they both said, and the settlement had involved the granting to Hunningborne of a reversion of the Lurklane property, as well as of two other Hickes properties in the parish of St. Olave's in Southwark. This was "before" Savage's new lease, they said; both men also said that Savage, at the signing of the new lease, had been apprised of this circumstance and understood its implication, namely that Hunningborne had been inserted between Hickes and Savage in terms of rights to the property, "wherevnto the saide compl^t [i.e., Savage] consented." Hickes claimed further that Savage "did acknowledge the said Peter Honingborne as his Landlord," adding as an afterthought "as this defendant hath bene Credablye enformed."

Savage's version of these events is quite different. At the time he took his lease he "knew not of any such assurance as the said Peter now pretendeth"; he learned of the supposed reversion quite some time later, perhaps as late as the end of 1576 or early 1577, when Hickes came to him with a story "that the said Peter had & hath of the said Richard a former graunte" given to him "before the said second lease." But Hickes refused to show Savage any document affirming the grant of reversion, so Savage concluded that "eyther ther was no such lease or yf ther were any the same was ante dated." Fearing the worst, he speculated that the primary function of such a document (if it existed) might well be extortionary, "made only vpon trust betwen the said parties . . . by fraude & coven to deceive such to whome the said Richard should lett the premisses." Hickes was adamant, however, warning Savage that Hunningborne was his new landlord, that his continued tenancy would be at Hunningborne's pleasure, and that Hunningborne would be by shortly to collect the rent and to tell Savage his fate. Savage concluded from these events that the two men wanted him off the premises.

But there are some binds in this story. If the reversion had truly antedated Savage's lease, then Hickes had not delivered a good title in the lease, as Savage had required, and his bond of £100 to Savage

---

[30] I have been unable to find any evidence of this lawsuit in any common law court in the years in question.

would thus be forfeit. Hickes's claim that Savage had acknowledged a reversion that circumscribed his rights in the lease even as he was signing the lease seems unlikely on the face of it. The "reversion story," apparently an initial maneuver by the two men which failed to achieve its desired end of removing Savage from the premises, was quietly dropped as a strategy; when Savage introduced it as an item in his bill of complaint, however, the two men had to deal with it publicly.

But Savage was right: they wanted him off the premises. In his complaint he did not speculate on their reasons but recounted instead the devious manner in which, on Lady Day 1577, his new landlord Hunningborne contrived to get him to default on his rent. By the terms of the lease (which are quite conventional), Savage had fourteen days' grace after each quarter day for payment of rent, which was to be paid on the premises. Failure to pay the rent by the end of the grace period in any quarter, "in part or in all by the space of ffourteane Daies," was grounds for immediate repossession of the premises by the landlord. The procedure was that Hickes or his agent would come to the house to collect, and someone had to be there to pay him. For some reason Savage had to be away at the time of the payment on Lady Day 1577, but he left his friend Thomas Whase there, he said, with the money to pay Hickes.[31] By the afternoon of 8 April, the fourteenth day, Hickes still not having arrived, Whase set off to London "hopinge to mett ther wth the said Richard Hik*es* to pay the said some."

Peter Hunningborne of course arrived as soon as Whase had departed. By his account, he "gentlie demanded his rent," though he didn't say of whom he demanded it; the implication is that other people were on the premises even if Savage and Whase were not. No rent being forthcoming, Hunningborne waited there "one hole hower in the latter p*a*rte of the daie even vntell the sonne was set and the daie finished" and then he went home. Whase, returning "w[th]in half an houre after" and learning that Hunningborne had been and gone, immediately "retorned to the house of the said Peter in London," where he was shortly joined by Savage himself. As it was still the evening of 8 April they asked him to accept the rent, but he was adamant, claiming that the day had ended. Finally, said Savage, "his wif [that is, Hickes's daughter Margaret] receyved the

---

[31] Savage's need to leave a friend on the premises may suggest that he was unmarried at the time, a point to which I shall recur.

same Rent & she deliuered it to the said Peter," though Hunning-borne denied knowing anything of such a matter.

Shortly thereafter Savage must have gone to law. In his bill he claimed that Hickes and Hunningborne "seeke still to frustrate and make void" his lease, indicating by this phrasing that he was still on the premises and that Hunningborne had not followed through with his claim of forfeiture. Further, Savage claimed to fear "some perill in the p^rmisses may insue," suggesting that the two men were not above acts of sabotage to buildings or other property on Savage's land. Hickes himself had affirmed that any eviction would be not only of Savage but of "all others occupiinge the same premisses"— perhaps those same others of whom Hunningborne had "gentlie demanded his rent."

And Hunningborne was interested in what was on the land. One day, he said, he had arrived at Savage's place "wth workmen accordinge to a couenant and condicion conteyned in the saide lease." He had come "to view the reperacions," whatever he may have meant by that; presumably something had been built on the land, and he wanted to see it. But he "could not be suffered to enter and view," he complained, because "those that kepte the house vtterlie denied him so to doe and shutt the dore against him." The door that was shut against him may have been to the playhouse, and "those that kepte the house" may well have been Savage's fellows, the same "others" alluded to earlier. Savage himself was no more hospitable; Hunningborne complained that he had been "evill vsed and threatened" by Savage, who "giveth vnto the Defendant Threteninge wordes and fecheth his sword to thende, as this defend^t is induced to beleave, to stricke this defendant"— a bit of effective theatricality on Savage's part, no doubt, almost as good as Richard Burbage's later flourishing of a broomstick in the face of the widow Brayne, but equally good material for Hunningborne to present in court against him, claiming it as "another cause whereby the lease should be void."

Hunningborne claimed to have endured verbal abuse as well, asserting that Savage "braggeth and bosteth that he hathe suche freindes as shall Compell this Defend^t to deale in suche sort as pleaseth him." Hickes also affirmed that Savage "makethe great Bragges" and says that that he could "procure greate freindes to Counten^aunce his matter." Against that, Hunningborne could only plead weakly that "for his part" he "would be contented to allow" Savage to stay on the premises but that "he cannot Con-venientlie doe" this "because in trewthe this defendan^t is in great neede of a house"; Hunningborne "meaneth to dwell there him sealf."[32]

The "house" that Hunningborne was "in greate neede of" and meant "to dwell" in was of course not the playhouse but rather the other building on the premises, where Savage currently lived. None of the parties to the lawsuit proposed to solve the dispute by a division of tenancy, with Hunningborne in the dwelling house and Savage in the playhouse; each wanted the whole of the premises to himself. Savage claimed to have a valid lease to all of it, and defended his right; Hickes and Hunningborne, for reasons unstated, also wanted all of it, including the playhouse, for themselves. The "business" taking place on the premises was nowhere named or described in the lawsuit, though it was alluded to obliquely: "the Complainant farreth not greatlie thereof," said Hickes, "for he hath sett a Bill on the Dore to sell his interest"; Hunningborne's version was that "he did sett a Bill on the dore to sell or doe awaie the same." This remark (assuming that it is true) is open to various constructions. Savage may indeed have been faring badly with his playhouse and hoping to find a graceful way out, or he may simply have been advertising its availability for hire. Alternatively, the "Bill on the Dore" may not have been of Savage's doing at all.

Savage's character came in for a full share of attack as well, the remarks of the two defendants being crafted for maximum effect in court. "In trewthe," as Hunningborne declared, "the compl[t] himsealf is a verrie lewed fealowe and liveth by noe other trade than playinge of staige plaies and Interlevdes." The lewdness and the stage playing were of course complementary; Hickes seconded the deprecation, explaining that "for his lewde and loase life [Savage] hath ben presented to the ordenarie and is Comaunded by the Ordenarye as is saide to avoide the parrishe wth his lewde behavior." Hunningborne went on: "his lewed behavior would sone make an honest man werie of so wiked an idell livinge tenante and so much the more because the honest neighboures in that place doe so mislike his behavior as they will not suffer hime to Dwell there anie longer."[33]

---

[32] Hunningborne was married to Margaret Hickes by this time, though I have found no record of the baptism of children. As Savage was still on the premises in November 1588, according to the sewer assessments—and was himself married by then, as I shall argue below—the lawsuit may well have gone no further or been settled out of court.

[33] The phrases are conventional Puritan formulas; compare the contemporary attacks of Philip Stubbes or, thirty-six years later, Zeal-of-the-Land Busy's condemnation of players in *Bartholomew Fair*.

In all likelihood the more judgmental of these comments are overstatements, but they do furnish grounds for speculation. The defendants were at pains to establish that Savage's "lewde behavior" was well known at Newington Butts, that it had been going on for some time on Hickes's premises, and that the "honest neighboures in that place" were of one mind in misliking it. The vigor with which Savage defended his right of tenancy on the property suggests that more than simply a dwelling and an orchard were at stake; and the alleged action of the Ordinary[34] would be groundless if Savage's objectionable activities were carried on elsewhere than in Newington. The exact nature of the "lewde behavior" was, in Hickes's and Hunningborne's terms, sufficiently identified by their comment that he was a player "of staige plaies and Interlevd*es*."

It is possible that Hunningborne and Hickes accurately reflected the resentment of the good citizens of the Butts. From what one can learn of the inhabitants of the area, they seem to have been propertied, well-to-do, somewhat conservative, somewhat puritan.[35] Many of them (like Savage's neighbor John Hilles) plied their trades in London but preferred to live away from the City. Newington Town was only one mile from London Bridge, but St. George's Fields served as a buffer and made the whole area pleasantly rural—noted, in fact, for its peaches—so it ought not seem unlikely that Savage's neighbors were distressed by the "lewde behavior" of interludes and stage plays in their midst. What is important is the implication that his deplorable activity had been going on for some time. Indeed, if the playhouse lot had already been separated from Lurklane by the time of Savage's lease in March 1576, and if the community had already grown weary of Savage's activity on Hick-

---

[34] Most of Surrey was in the diocese of Winchester, but Newington was one of eleven Surrey parishes in the exempt deanery of Croydon, a peculiar in the jurisdiction of the archbishop of Canterbury. Thus the Ordinary was, in this case, probably the dean of Croydon acting as the archbishop's deputy in Newington rather than the archbishop himself.

[35] Many Newington wills survive for this period, most of them at the Public Record Office, where one can also find literally dozens of lawsuits, mostly about property and inheritance, involving the same people and their neighbors. The parson at Newington from 1569 until his death in 1584 was Stephen Bateman or Batman, a doctrinaire moralist, pedantic poet, heavy-handed allegorizer, and author of several learned tracts for the godly, among them *A christall glasse of christian reformation wherein the godly maye beholde the coloured abuses used in this our present tyme* (1569) and *The New Ariual of the three Gracis into Anglia, Lamenting the abusis of the present Age* (1580). That Bateman's moral earnestness fitted with the temper of his parish is evidenced by the numbers of his parishioners (among them Savage's neighbor John Hilles) who specified in their wills that Bateman himself, and not merely "some godly person," should deliver the funeral sermon.

es's premises, and if the Ordinary had already invited Savage to relocate, one can only presume that the playhouse had been on the site for a while before the lawsuit of April and May 1577, before the machinations of Lady Day 1577 which inspired the lawsuit, perhaps even before the winter of 1576/77 altogether.[36]

If Hickes himself had built the playhouse, as Ida Darlington proposed on the basis of her reading of the leases, it would have been disingenuous of him to take so righteous a stand against Savage for exercising the trade of player in that same playhouse. Equally, one might suspect that the opprobrium of an antitheatrical community would fall as much on Hickes for housing and promoting such lewdness as on Savage for exercising it. Yet Hickes seems to have been quite comfortable in his accusatory role, a comfort suggesting (at least to me) that despite the perfunctory mention in the leases about the structure being Hickes's work, Jerome Savage was the actual builder of the playhouse and further suggesting that Hickes and Hunningborne, once having seen the building in operation, had grown covetous. Hickes was, after all, an ordinary yeoman of the queen's chamber, who neither lived nor worked in Newington. Savage, on the other hand, was a stage player and the leader of a prominent company; he had a long lease on a serviceable piece of ground and lived there himself; he must have sensed that he was in a good location, and he was surely sensitive in 1575 and 1576 to the implications of the recent act of Common Council. He would have known, from his own experience as an inhabitant, that Newington, like Stepney, was an area popular with Londoners on outings, and he knew that there had been a playhouse of sorts at Stepney nine years earlier; though the Red Lion may not have been wholly successful, in that earlier time there had been fewer pressures by the City on playing companies, less need for them to think about alternative arrangements for their playing sites.[37]

---

[36] James Burbage presumably commenced building his playhouse in the early spring of 1576, and Savage perhaps started at about the same time; both their leases began in March 1576, though Burbage's lease was new while Savage's was a renewal and he had already been living on the premises. Both playhouses may well have been in use before the winter of 1576/77. James Burbage was called by his son Cuthbert—in 1635, when contrary witnesses would be hard to find—"the first builder of playehowses," and the Burbage lobby has held the field ever since. The primacy of the Theater has never been seriously challenged, but the two other playhouses in contention had no comparable champions and no comparably illustrious occupants.

[37] Newington Butts and the nearby St. George's Fields were, like Finsbury Fields to the north of the City (and unlike certain unsavory parts of the Bankside), respectable resort areas for Londoners. The suitability of Savage's location was attested by the later

Let me review for a moment what we have known heretofore of Savage and of his company, the earl of Warwick's players. Only two facts have been generally known about Savage: that he was listed, along with John and Lawrence Dutton, as payee for two performances at court by Warwick's men during the Christmas season 1575/76, and listed again, this time alone, as payee for a play in the Christmas season 1578/79.[38] These dates, 1575 and 1579, conveniently and tightly bracket what we have since learned about him at Newington in 1576, 1577, and 1578.

The history of his company is similarly confined. The first extant reference to Warwick's men in this period is for performing at court on 14 February 1575. The earl had earlier entertained a company of players who disappear from the records in the mid-1560s; they may have been rejuvenated when Savage joined them ten years later, or they may have been disbanded, so that Savage's company became a wholly new one. The payment record for the play they performed at court in February 1575 unfortunately includes no names of players or payees. Following this performance, the company played at court during every subsequent Christmas season and was frequently noted in the provinces as well, until 1 January 1580, its last recorded appearance. Thereafter, like its predecessor, this company too seems to have disappeared, and Savage with it; the commonly accepted explanation is that the collapse of the company was effected by the Duttons' pulling out to form a new company under the patronage of the earl of Oxford.[39]

---

success of the famous inn and coaching house, the Elephant and Castle, located only a few yards away from the site of the playhouse. Some scholars, considering the virtues of an inn in such a setting, have, like T. F. Ordish (*Early London Theatres* [London, 1899], p. 46), believed that the Butts playhouse must have been "a well-frequented inn, of the type familiar to us, with spacious yard and galleries round." This conjecture is attractive to those who wish to see the Newington structure as a less fully theatrical enterprise than the Shoreditch buildings. But the building was always referred to by the Privy Council, by the dean and chapter of Canterbury, and by the sewer commissions, as the "playehowse," and never as an inn. One Privy Council minute even referred to it as a "theatre." Comparable forms of reference do not occur for such known playing inns as the Bel Savage, the Cross Keys, the Bell, or the Bull.

[38] "To John Dutton Lawrence Dutton Jerome Savage &c therle of Warwick*es* players" (PRO, A.O.1/382/14); "To Jerom Savage & his company seruauntes to Therle of warwicke" (PRO, A.O.1/383/17).

[39] Chambers (*ES* 2:98) reproduces the text of a mocking poem that ridiculed the Duttons: "The Duttons and theyr fellow-players forsakyng the Erle of Warwyke theyr master, became followers of the Erle of Oxford." The Duttons seem to have drawn off enough men to destroy Warwick's company, but presumably Savage did not follow them.

Judging from their appearances at court, Warwick's men thus had a period of eminence, or at least a florescence, lasting about five years. One might wonder what occasion triggered the emergence of a company under Warwick's patronage in 1575, after a decade or so of no recorded activity. The career of the earl himself may offer a partial explanation. Five years older than his brother the earl of Leicester, Warwick was above all a professional military man; but his career in the field was cut short by a serious wound sustained in defense of the Protestants at Le Havre in 1563, which forced him to retire for a time from public life to recuperate. Though he retained the post of master of the ordnance granted to him in 1560, the middle years of that decade were otherwise fallow ones for him. The playing company he had patronized in the early 1560s faded into obscurity at about this time. When, after a few years, he was well again, he returned to court and made himself serviceable in other capacities. In 1568 he was made a member of the commission looking into the affairs of the queen of Scots, and in 1572 he was one of the judges at the trial of the duke of Norfolk. In the autumn of 1573 Warwick was admitted to the Privy Council, joining there (among others) his brother Leicester.

The more powerful of the privy councilors—Sussex the lord chamberlain and Lincoln the lord admiral as well as Leicester—were patrons of playing companies at the time Warwick joined them, and he may well have decided that the moment was appropriate for reviving his own company.[40] In 1575 he was made lieutenant of the Order of the Garter, but by then Savage and the Duttons were already his players (the Duttons having left Lincoln's service to join his). Savage functioned as their leader,[41] and his plans for the company may have included from the outset the provision of a new playhouse on his premises in Newington, a structure Savage may have commenced to build or modify as soon as the earl's patronage was assured. Savage's desire for a long lease (he requested the

---

[40] Others on the council, besides these four, included the earls of Arundel and Bedford, the lord treasurer (Burghley), the chancellor of the exchequer (Sir Walter Mildmay), the chancellor of the duchy of Lancaster (Sir Ralph Sadler), the treasurer and the comptroller of the queen's household (Sir Francis Knollys and Sir James Crofts), and the two principal secretaries (Sir Thomas Smith and Sir Francis Walsingham). Of these remaining members only Arundel, a former lord chamberlain, maintained a company of players.

[41] J. T. Murray (*English Dramatic Companies* (London: Constable, 1910), 1:285–86) thought that the Dutton brothers were the leaders of this company. Savage may well have brought them in with him, but he seems to have been solely in charge.

thirty-year term from Hickes, by his own testimony), and his assertions to Peter Hunningborne two years later that he had friends in high places, may be reflections of this relationship.

If we knew more about Savage's own career before 1575 we might have a better sense of the forces at play in his decisions. We do not know how old he was, or how long he had been a player before 1575, or in whose service. We may presume that he had been moved to build his playhouse by the new stringencies of the Act of 1574, but he may have been moved equally by his acquisition of a new company or perhaps inspired by the earlier Red Lion experiment, a venture he might have hoped to emulate or improve on. There is no way to know. As we do not know how long, before 1576, his tenancy in the dwelling house at the Butts had begun, we can't really say when he began planning for the playhouse, or even when he began building it; we know only that by the end of 1576, according to the testimony of Hickes and Hunningborne, it had been around for a while.

As a member of the Privy Council, Warwick would have periodically directed his attentions toward the social and political implications of having players and playing places in the City. The regular suspensions of playing in and around London which the Council intermittently decreed (so easily documented in later years because of all the violations) seem to have been accepted without incident by all the certified acting companies during the decade of the 1570s; if one may trust the surviving evidence, the annual orders to cease playing which were issued between 1575 and 1580 seem in no instance to have been followed by notices to the justices about observed or reported violations by these companies.

We know of four such inhibitions for this period. The first, in the Privy Council minutes for 15 November 1574, restrained all playing within ten miles of London until the following Easter because of the plague, but with no specific playing places named. The second, on 1 August 1577, was more precise, citing "the Theater and suche like" as examples of places to be closed. This is the first mention of the Theater, as many scholars have pointed out. It is also the first mention of at least one other playhouse, if I interpret "and suche like" correctly. The third, on 10 November 1578, gave authority to "restraine certen players" in Southwark and in other places "nere adioyning w^{th}in that parte of Surreye." The fourth restraint, on 13 March 1579, was in the same general terms as the one of 1574, with no playing places named. It was not until the summer of 1580, after the breakup of Warwick's men and Savage's presumed abandonment of the Butts, that the Privy Council took formal notice of the playhouse there; on 13 May of that year they wrote the Surrey justices that despite the inhibition of playing—apparently being observed by the other playing companies—"neuertheles certen players do playe sunderie daies euery weeke at Newington Buttes." Since none of the privy councilors seemed to know who these players were, the justices were directed "to enquier who they be that disobey their Commaundeme^t in that behalf" and to "forbidd them" to play any more.[42]

The presence of unknown players at the Butts in 1580 suggests that the moral fervor articulated by Hickes and Hunningborne in their lawsuit had served its purpose and that the two men no longer found it necessary to be scandalized by such unspecified "lewde behavior" as they had noted of their tenant in 1577. Their care, in the lawsuit, to mention nothing about the presence of a playhouse on the premises suggests to me a desire on their part to avoid any possible court directive that the structure be dismantled. They wanted to be rid of Savage, not of plays; whatever delicately circumscribed moral stance they had been forced to adopt to achieve this end, it must have seemed to them unacceptable to abandon the structure as the price of evicting Savage. In the event, though it had taken until 1580 to achieve their ends, by that year Savage was gone and the playhouse was still standing; indeed, a new company of players appeared on the site so promptly after Savage's departure in 1580 that it looks as though someone may have been anticipating its availability. The earl of Oxford's players, we know, were hastily assembled by John and Lawrence Dutton when they and some of their fellows abandoned Savage and Warwick's to set up on their own. Our earliest notice of them is in April 1580, when Lawrence Dutton and Robert Leveson, "servants to the Earl of Oxford," were imprisoned in the Marshalsea following a brawl at one of the Inns of Court. These may be the same men who were playing at the Butts in violation of the inhibition a month later.[43] If this is so, then most of the members of the company were simply returning to their old stage under a new name, a circumstance that would account for their ready appearance, and that raises the possibility of an earlier collusion between Hunningborne and the Duttons (perhaps formed as early as 1577) to squeeze Savage out. Hunningborne may have

[42] PRO, P.C.2/10, p. 285; /12, pp. 2, 300, 427; /13, p. 10.

[43] Chambers (*ES* 2:100) suggests on tenuous evidence that Oxford's men were playing at the Theater in Shoreditch at this time.

made a better financial arrangement with the Duttons, and his pleasure at Savage's departure may have been the sweeter for the three years' delay.

From this point on the history of the playhouse is more uncertain. The transfer of the property from Hickes to Hunningborne seems to have been a permanent arrangement, for a decade later the sewer commissioners found Hunningborne himself on the premises, where before they had found Savage. Richard Hickes had in the meantime died, and Hunningborne's wife, Margaret, assumed the administration of his estate.[44] The playhouse must have been at least intermittently active throughout this period, for when the Privy Council suspended playing in the early summer of 1586 "for thauoyding of the infection" they wrote the Surrey justices (11 May) to take special care to restrain plays "at the theater or anie other places about Newington"; the council also required the lord mayor to suspend playing in the City and took pains to tell him about their prohibition of playing at Newington, which was "out of his charge" or jurisdiction (see *ES* 4:302). Other playhouses also lay outside the lord mayor's jurisdiction; the singling out of Newington for special mention, or special reassurance, may mean that the playhouse there was particularly active at that time, or perhaps that it was a particular offender in this regard.

There is also no certainty about what company or companies used the playhouse during the 1580s. By the middle of 1583 the Duttons, or at least John Dutton, had abandoned Oxford's group for the newly formed queen's players. Unlike the earlier Warwick's company, which apparently collapsed with the departure of the Duttons, Oxford's men seem to have kept themselves together after the loss of their leaders, playing at court in 1584, touring in 1585 and 1586, receiving a reprimand for posting bills in London in 1587, and subsequently leaving scattered and discontinuous traces of their activity. The earl of Oxford may have written plays for them, and Anthony Munday may have acted with them. But there is no evidence to show how long they remained a permanent or continuing company.

In 1590, Richard Cuckowe took over the lease to Newington 35 Acres formerly held by Hickes, with the exception of the playhouse parcel, thereby becoming Peter Hunningborne's neighbor; and on 26 February 1591 the presentment jury for the Commission of

---

[44] PRO, Prob.6/3, fo. 129.

Sewers presented "Richard Cuckow to make a sluce or thorough at his gate leading into his feild next adioyning to the playhouse" and Peter Hunningborne "to open the sluce by the play house that the water may hav a fre passage."[45]

In 1592 a company of players belonging to Lord Strange may have played at the Butts playhouse; from the documents one learns that "of longe tyme plaies haue not there bene vsed on working daies."[46] Entries in Henslowe's *Diary* show that the admiral's men and the chamberlain's men played together at Newington for ten days in June 1594;[47] Henslowe's receipts on this occasion were quite small. One could argue that by the 1590s, with three other playhouses in existence, all of them nearer the City and thus easier of access, the playhouse at Newington was at an economic disadvantage. Nonetheless, it might well have gone on, but that its ultimate demise was decreed by other forces. On 6 July 1594, less than a month after Henslowe's brief and possibly unhappy tenancy, the dean and chapter took steps to remove the playhouse altogether: on that date they "agreed that Mr Paule Bucke shall have the leases of the ten*emente* and plaiehouse thereto adioyninge in Newington renewed vp to xxj yeares wth coven^{a}nt*es* as before and wth a clause that he shall convert the playehouse to some other vse vppon the saide grownde and not suffer anie plaies there after michelmas nexte."[48]

Buck seems to have lost little time in complying with this requirement. His lease to the grounds, formally renewed a year later on 5 April 1595, spoke only of the "mansion howse and tenneme^t latelie builded by the foresaide Richarde Hickes," along with a "garden plott . . . inclosed out of the saide lande called Lurklane"; there is no mention of a playhouse.[49] And on 5 October 1599, when next the presentment jury for the Sewer Commission visited the premises, they found "that the sewer leadinge from the houses where the old playe house did stand att Newington all alongest vnto the Bridge goyng from Barmondsey cross the high waye vnto sainct

[45] GLRO, ms. SKCS 18 (Court Minutes of the Commissioners of Sewers), fo. 172.

[46] In *ES* 4:313.

[47] Henslowe's note doesn't say "together," though most later scholars have presumed that to be his meaning; his own heading reads: "In the name of god Amen begininge at newing ton my Lord Admeralle men & my Lorde chamberlen men As ffolowethe 1594" (*Diary*, p. 21).

[48] Chapter Act and Minute Book, 1581–1607, fo. 153. See also the leases, above. I have been unable to find any connection between this Paul Buck and the stage player named Paul Buck who appears in the records of St. Anne, Blackfriars, during this period.

[49] Chapter library, Canterbury, Register W23, ff. 265^v–66.

Thomas Watering*es* is needefull to be cast clensed and scowred."[50] From construction to demolition, then, the playhouse at Newington Butts stood on its site for some twenty years. Its rival playhouse the Theater, after a similar span of years, was also dismantled before 1599, but for different reasons. The Butts playhouse stayed down, however, its timbers used as framing for some tenements (if I correctly understand the reference to "the houses where the old playe house did stand"), while the timbers of the Theater were destined for several more years of theatrical use on another site, perishing finally in a glorious blaze in 1613.

III

See, they forsake me!

—*1 Henry VI*, V. iii

But Jerome Savage probably saw none of this; I believe, on what I take to be strong circumstantial evidence, that he was dead by 1587. I have already made the assumption that the Jerome Savage named in the sewer records and in the subsidy assessments cited above was the stage player, even though neither the sewer nor the subsidy commissioners identified him in those terms. I want now to make the same assumption about another set of records in which a Jerome Savage appears, though with no identifying trade. These other records, in fact, comprise all the remaining references I could find, of any sort, to anyone named Jerome Savage; they all seem pretty clearly to refer to one man, and the circumstances they document seem consistent with what we know of the stage player.

At about the time of the breakup of Warwick's players in 1580, Savage the player disappears from the Newington records (and from theatrical records generally); this new Savage makes his first appearance with his family as a resident in Wood Street, near Cheapside, at about the same time.[51] The new Savage had been a single man in 1576, but a year later, while the Hickes-Hunningborne lawsuit was being contested, he and a woman named Anna Lansenberg had

[50] GLRO, ms. SKCS 18, fo. 294(bis)ᵛ. This entry must surely be the "document" that C. W. Wallace saw in 1913 (*ES* 2:405); see note 3 above.
[51] See PRO, E.115/343/52; GHL, ms. 645/1, fo. 112.

been married. Anna and her parents were members of the Flemish community in London whose social and spiritual home was the Dutch Church at Austin Friars. Many of the church's records have survived, and one of them shows that Anna's growing relationship with Jerome Savage had been a source of grave concern to her parents. They had forbidden her to see him; they may have preferred that she marry a countryman, or they may have been scandalized by Savage's way of life. But Anna, defying them, regularly stole away from her parents' home (*vvt haerder ouders huys ontstolen*), surreptitiously and at night (*by nachte ende ontyde*) and "followed her lover" (*is haeren vryer gevolght*). Despite repeated admonitions from her parents and the elders of her church, she held to her intention of marrying him (*is nochtans met der trovve voortgevaeren*), and her persistence was rewarded: Anna and Jerome Savage were married at the end of November 1577. As a consequence, she was excluded from the communion of her church as a form of "public shame" (*opentlike beschaemtheyt*).[52]

While it is possible that Savage may have continued as a player after the collapse of his Newington enterprise in 1580, he may equally have turned his hand to other, less frustrating, activities. If we still have the same Savage here, then this new phase of his life lasted only a bit longer than the playhouse venture; a few weeks after Christmas 1586 he sickened and died, leaving Anna, his wife of less than ten years, with five small children. He made his will on 30 January 1587;[53] his first bequest (and the only bequest to anyone outside his immediate family) was to his "aunt Levyna Mar-

---

[52] "Hierome Savidge & Anne Lancenbergae" were married at All Hallows Lombard Street on 28 November 1577 (GHL, ms. 17,613). Anna's excommunication was recorded at the Dutch Church, Austin Friars, on 15 December 1577 (GHL, ms. 7387, item 3108; for a somewhat misleading abstract of the document, see J. H. Hessels, ed., *Register of the Attestations or certificates of Membership, Confessions of Guilt, Certificates of Marriage, Betrothals, Publication of Banns, &c., &c., Preserved in the Dutch Reformed Church, Austin Friars, London, 1568 to 1872* (London, 1892), p. 223, where "Anna Lancenberghe" is mistranscribed as "Anna Launenberge"). I am indebted to Paul Hoftijzer of the Sir Thomas Browne Institute of the University of Leiden for translating this document for me. Anna was listed in a return of aliens prepared for Burghley in 1583 as "Anne Savage, bonelacemaker, the wief of Jerom Savage an Englishman" (Cecil ms. 210/11, in HuSocP 10, pt.2:268). A Willem van Lansenberghe, perhaps Anna's father, was listed as a member of the Dutch Church at Austin Friars in 1574 (GHL, ms. 7403), and a Willm Lansenbergus was recorded as a household servant in Whitechapel in 1571 (PRO, S.P.12/84, fo. 106). I have found no other occurrences of the name.

[53] PRO, Prob.11/70, fo. 80. For his burial in St. Peter Westcheap, see GHL, ms. 645/1, fo. 112.

quyne."[54] He left substantial bequests to his son, Daniel, (£60) and to his four daughters, Elizabeth, Anne, Faith, and Suzan (£30 each), and the rest of his estate, including "the profites of anye farme and other landes that I houlde within the parishes of Islington and Pancrase" to his wife, Anna.[55]

There are no other bequests, and notable among those not mentioned in the will are Savage's former associates the earl of Warwick's servants. Such an omission may seem a serious bar to any identification of this Savage with the stage player; but we have already seen, in Chapter 2, that the will of the stage player John Garland similarly contains no mention of fellow players. If, as I speculated earlier, the alliance of Savage's colleagues with the Duttons was the cause of the breakup of Warwick's players, then the absence of their names from the will is understandable; the rift must have been deep.

The bequests indicate that Jerome Savage of Wood Street was a man of some substance at his passing.[56] Had he, assuming he is the same man, been equally prosperous eleven years earlier, when his playhouse was being built? Or was he at that time, like Burbage, a

---

[54] "Aunt Levyna Marquyne" (née Lieven Honing) was the Flemish wife of Francesco Marchino (or "Francis Marquine," as he usually appears in the records); they lived near the Savages in Wood Street. The Marchinos were early members of the Dutch Church at Austin Friars and intimates of Jan Utenhove, its presiding spirit, and his wife, Anna; their son John Marquine was later a minister there. A Lombard who had worked for eleven years as a merchants' factor in Antwerp before settling in England in 1559, Marchino received his letters of denization in 1562, identifying himself at that time as a silk weaver; but once in England he had turned his hand to type founding and still later to running a school for "straungers sonnes" who had been "borne in England." He met his wife-to-be, Lieventken Honing, at the Dutch Church. See A. A. van Schelven, ed., *Kerkeraads-protocollen der nederduitsche vluchtelingen-kerk te Londen* (Amsterdam, 1921); Irene Scouloudi, ed., *Returns of Strangers in the Metropolis 1593, 1627, 1635, 1639*, HuSocP 57 (1985); and R. E. G. Kirk and Ernest F. Kirk, eds., *Returns of Aliens Dwelling in the City and Suburbs of London from the Reign of Henry VIII to that of James I*, HuSocP 10 (1900–1908). Savage's own origins, at present unknown, may equally have been Walloon or Flemish; the returns of aliens list several families named (sometimes interchangeably) Sauvage and deWilde.

[55] Some nine months later, on 2 October 1587, "Anna Savage widowe off this paryshe" was married to one Richard Wood (GHL, ms. 6502, register of St. Peter Westcheap).

[56] In 1576 the Surrey subsidy commissioners had found Savage the stage player to be worth £3 (PRO, E.179/185/310); in November 1586, just a few months before his death, the London commissioners found Savage of Wood Street to be worth £5 (PRO, E.115/343/52). The legacies in the latter's will make it clear that these figures bear little relation to his actual wealth. Francesco Marchino, equally prosperous, was perhaps less adept at hiding his prosperity. In 1572 he was rated at £20 (GHL, ms. 2942); four years later, in 1576, perhaps instructed by Savage, he managed to be worth only £15 (PRO, E.179/145/252).

man of modest means and in need of a moneyed partner? If the latter, then there is still more to be learned about the Jerome Savage story. A romanticized version would have Francesco Marchino (see note 54) cast as the moneyed backer, with Savage catching his first glimpse of the demure Anna Lansenberg, kinswoman to Marchino's wife, Lieven ("Aunt Levyna"), in the family parlor as they drew up their articles of agreement. For a number of reasons this is an unlikely scenario; and, in any event, guesses along those lines are grounded on the assumptions that Savage's playhouse was as elaborate and venturesome as the Theater in Shoreditch and that other symmetries might have been called for as well; and none of these may have been the case. We have no grounds for assuming that the Newington structure looked like the Theater or Curtain. Savage may well have embarked from the start on a much more limited project, one that lay within his own means. He had few exemplars; if his earlier inspiration had been the Red Lion project, then his vision of his own playhouse may have been not much more elaborate. If Peter Hunningborne's complaint—that "those that kepte the house" had "shutt the dore against him"—is a reference to the playhouse, then at minimum the structure had walls, but beyond that one can only conjecture.

If the finished playhouse was a smaller and less ambitious structure than its coevals in Shoreditch, it may the more readily have encouraged Paul Buck to take his lease of the property even if the rentals entailed dismantling the building. We know that the disassembly of the Theater in 1599 required a number of hands and that brick and plaster and lath remained scattered over Giles Allen's ground after the salvageable parts had crossed the river. Buck may have found the Newington playhouse easier to dismantle. Perhaps part of its relative lack of appeal, both for companies of players and for spectators, was that it was simply not as impressive as either the Theater or the Curtain. The "tediousness of the waie" there may have been a more forceful argument to present to an official, but the building itself could well have been part of the problem.

Three playhouses went up in the suburbs of London in "1576"; for a variety of reasons, I have chosen to deal first with the one at Newington Butts. In many ways it seems the most idiosyncratic of the three: it lay furthest from the City, a mile into Surrey, and was thus quite isolated from the other two, which were near neighbors in Shoreditch. It is the only one of the three which seems to have been built by a stage player out of his own resources, and the only one of the three for which no pictorial representation has been found. Some of the evidence suggests that it may have been the first of the three to be built. But principally I wanted to begin with a playhouse other than the Theater, whose story is so elaborate that it runs away with the larger narrative, making an imbalance in the way we "see" the theatrical scene in 1576.

I wished, also, to record what I could of the fragmented evidence from which we might assemble a life of Jerome Savage. One of the earliest of the playhouse entrepreneurs, Savage is also the least regarded; but to the extent that his circumstances were different from those of the men who put up the Theater and the Curtain—and at present we do not even have a candidate for the latter role—he is worth our attention. Knowing about him, even as slenderly as we do, helps us to avoid making facile generalizations about playhouse builders.

CHAPTER SEVEN

A Playhouse at Shoreditch:
The Theater, 1576

I

Let us from point to point this story know.
—*All's Well That Ends Well*, V. iii

What we know about the erection and early operation of the Theater is based almost entirely upon information derived from a set of legal documents dating from the late 1580s and early 1590s. Though the documents make it amply clear that Burbage and Brayne had been at odds virtually throughout the early history of the playhouse, they make it equally clear that the two of them had managed somehow to keep their antagonisms out of the law courts during that period. But when Brayne died in 1586, at the age of forty-four and in the Theater's tenth year of operation, litigation began almost immediately. Brayne's widow seems to have fired the first shot almost before the funeral baked meats were cold, with a suit brought at the common law; Burbage responded shortly thereafter with a countersuit in Chancery, and the widow Brayne brought another Chancery suit in retaliation.[1] All these suits took place between 1586 and 1590, though the proceedings in Chancery dragged on until some time after James Burbage's own death early

---

[1] The best account of the various documents bearing on the Theater is to be found in Herbert Berry's "Handlist of Documents about the Theatre in Shoreditch," in his *First Public Playhouse: The Theatre in Shoreditch, 1576–1598* (Montreal: McGill-Queen's University Press, 1979), pp. 97–133.

in 1597. We are lucky that they did so, for they brought us a wealth of detail without which we would know as little about the Theater as we do about the Curtain and the playhouse at Newington Butts.

A suit in Chancery is far likelier than a suit at the common law to leave a trail of paper and parchment, even though such a suit might be resolved at any point in its development. A complainant, or plainant, would begin a suit in Chancery with a written *bill of complaint*, which, if found by the Court to be a true bill or *billa vera*, would be countered by the defendant with a written *answer*; the complainant could then respond to the answer with a *replication*, and the defendant to the replication with a *rejoinder*. All of these documents would be in English. Many suits were settled before getting so far, and many others were settled at that point. The few that were not, however, proceeded to the next stage, the gathering of testimony from third parties by means of one or more lists of written questions (*interrogatories*) and transcribed answers to those questions (*depositions*), the latter signed, usually on each sheet, by the deponents and thus a valuable source of information about signatures. Interrogatories were constructed by the parties to the suit, in consultation with their attorneys, and were intended to elicit responses that would advance their own claims. Thus, some depositions would be on behalf of the complainant, others on behalf of the defendant. The lawsuits between the Burbage and Brayne factions generated seven different sets of interrogatories, which in turn produced twenty-five depositions by twenty different people. Sixteen of these people deposed only once, but John Alleyn, Ralph Myles, and Nicholas Bishop each deposed twice, once for Brayne and once for Burbage, and John Hyde deposed once for Brayne and twice for Burbage, noting rather wearily at his final session that "he hath been ex^d twyce alredye before now in this Co^{r}te in the matters in controuercye" between the two litigants (C.24/228/10; Wallace, p. 111).[2] In all, there are fourteen depositions on behalf of Burbage and eleven on behalf of the widow Brayne.

---

[2] Most of the information in the following account comes from the depositions here described. The occasional juxtaposing of pieces of information from different parts of different suits has resulted in a morass of citations which periodically makes the documentation intolerable; I regret this but see no responsible way out of the dilemma. References are to the documents themselves (in the PRO unless otherwise noted), followed where applicable by a citation of the relevant page number in C. W. Wallace's transcription in "The First London Theatre: Materials for a History," *Nebraska University Studies* 13 (1913).

The end product of all this questioning and answering is a set of narrative accounts that interlock in certain ways but not in others; sometimes the discrepancies, though trivial, are nonetheless in-explicable. For example, a soap maker named Nicholas Bishop, deposing for the widow Brayne in January 1592, said he was thirty-two years old (C.24/228/10; Wallace, p. 96); some ten weeks later, deposing for the Burbages, he said he was thirty (C.24/228/11; Wallace, p. 114). Other discrepancies may be more significant. John Hyde, a grocer, deposing for the widow Brayne in February 1592, said (as she must have hoped he would) that Burbage and Brayne "did Joyntlye morgage" the lease of the Shoreditch property to him (C.24/228/11; Wallace, p. 107); more than a year earlier, however (in December 1590), Hyde had deposed for the Burbages, and on that occasion (as they must have hoped he would) he said nothing about Brayne or about "jointly" but merely stated that the lease had been mortgaged to him by James Burbage (C.24/218/93; Wallace, p. 53). Some problems are caused not by discrepancies but by mere failures; for example, Nicholas Bishop and Ralph Myles were both asked unambiguously (on behalf of the Burbages) whether the players in the Theater "vse to plaie on the sondaies" or "vpon the sabothe day," and both managed to complete their depositions without answering the question, even though an impor-tant point hung in the balance (C.24/228/10; Wallace, pp. 112, 114, 117, 119-20).

Nonetheless, a kind of consistency does emerge from these documents. The issues in contention eventually become clear, even though they often fail to achieve closure. If one is willing to take the statements of the contending parties at face value, to tolerate reasonable hypotheses about the places where they conflict, and to presume that some sort of persistent purpose underlay the actions and testimonies of the participants, then the possible form or direction that a narrative account might have will begin to come into focus. In the previous chapter I attempted to offer such an account for the playhouse at Newington Butts, because the surviving data were scanty and not self-evidently interconnected; my aim was to tease a kind of coherence out of what there was. But in the case of the Theater the evidence, in its relative copiousness, suggests that one's first steps should be analytical rather than synthetic. So I take a different tack here: what follows is not so much a narrative as a chronology of the stages a narrative would have, but with all the ambiguities intact and unresolved.

25 March 1576—Leasing the Land

It is not clear (to start at what might be the beginning) how James Burbage came to know about Giles Allen's property in Shoreditch (see Figure 7); perhaps through his neighbor Hugh Richards. There was a large old barn on the premises, called by Allen the "great barn" to distinguish it from a smaller one in the tenure of the earl of Rutland. At the time of Burbage's interest in the property one end of the great barn was occupied by a butcher named Robert Stoughton, who used it as a slaughterhouse, and the other end by Richards, who was an innkeeper and who, like Burbage, lived in Coleman Street parish. It is not clear what Richards used his end of the barn for, but if he and Burbage knew one another he may have been the person who first drew Burbage's attention to the availability of the property, with its piece of vacant ground beside the barn.[3]

The barn was not the only occupied structure; other old buildings stood on the property as well, with several rent-paying tenants *in situ*. The barn was either "verie substantiallye builte" (Giles Allen's recollection), "very ruynous and decayed" (Richard Hudson's recollection), or "reddy to haue ffallen downe" (Thomas Osborne's recollection). Opinions about the other buildings were less contradictory, just about everyone agreeing that they were "decayed," "ruynous and ould," or "rotten."[4]

In addition to the great barn (or Great Barn, as Wallace and his followers preferred to dignify it) there was a millhouse, occupied by a weaver named Ewen Colfoxe, and a two-story divided tenement adjoining it, whose lower rooms were occupied by Richard Brackenbury and by Alice Dotridge, a widow, and the upper three rooms occupied by Thomas Dancaster, a shoemaker. There were two other tenements or houses, one occupied by John Dragon and the other by Joan Harrison, a widow, and another house, with an attached garden, occupied by William Garnett, a gardener. These details have been available to us for three-quarters of a century, and their very

---

[3] If this scenario should prove correct, then Richards the innholder, like the invisible owner of the Red Lion Farm in Stepney nine years earlier, might have seen some advantage to himself in the nearby presence of a playing place. If so, the benefit would have been short-lived, for Richards died in March or April 1578 (for his will, see PRO, Prob.11/103, fo. 46).

[4] The six quotations offered here are from Req.2/87/74 (Wallace, p. 194), Req.2/184/45 (Wallace, pp. 227, 233), C.3/222/83 (Wallace, pp. 76, 77), and Req.2/184/45 (Wallace, pp. 236, 240).

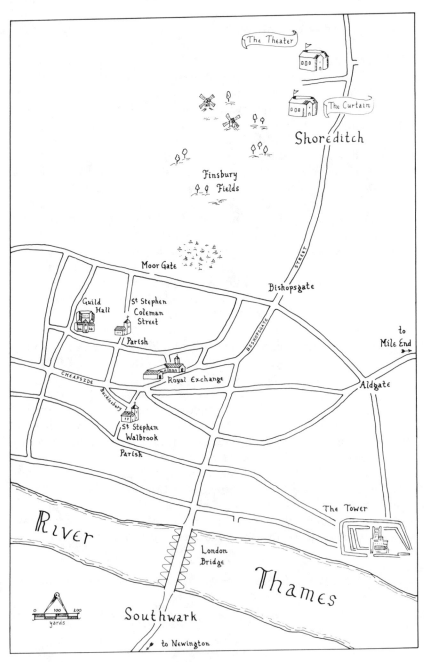

Figure 7. Shoreditch and the City

existence invites further pursuit. In my own case, such pursuit has proven fruitless; I have been quite unable to trace any of these people in any other documents.[5] No doubt other searchers before me have experienced the same frustration. It would have been useful, at the least, to have located wills for one or more of them, to see if any of them mentioned James Burbage or the new playhouse in their midst, but I have looked in all the relevant probate courts and come up empty-handed. Even Hugh Richards, the Coleman Street innkeeper and potentially the most useful of the lot, remains a virtual cipher. Giles Allen characterized these tenants as a group as being so poor that "they vsuallie begge in the feildes and stree*tes* to gett mony for the paiment of their rent*es*" (Req.2/87/74; Wallace, p. 193). James Burbage is not on record as having said anything about them at all, but his sense of their beggarliness, like his sense of the barn's sturdiness, may well have differed from Giles Allen's.

The formal starting date of Burbage's lease was Lady Day (25 March) 1576, but he did not sign the lease until 13 April 1576, nearly three weeks later. This delay is not unusual; most leases in the period were framed to commence and end on one of the four quarter days (of which Lady Day was perhaps the most commonly used) regardless of the actual day of signing. Perhaps the document itself took longer to draw up than anticipated; or perhaps the parties were unable to meet on the date specified in the document. Burbage may have been busy; it is not clear whether he was still a stage player in March 1576, but he may have been. He was named ("Burbage and his company") in a warrant for payment by the treasurer of the chamber on 14 March for a play presented before the queen on 4 March (see *MSC* 6:11), but this phrasing is inconclusive. He may well have been traveling with the company, whether playing or not, and thus prevented from concluding his business with Allen on Lady Day itself.

---

[5] There is one possible exception. The will of a Joan Harrison, widow, was proved in the London Commissary Court in 1594 (GHL, ms. 9172/17A, no. 81) though it contains no clues and may be for a different person. This widow Harrison bequeathed "the lease of my house [location unspecified] vnto my son Rychard harison & to my dawter susan harison [married name Susan Keale] to be equalley devyded between them & if aney of them will dwell in it then to paye the other half the rent it goeth for." This widow could not have been overly poor, for she left her two children two featherbeds with bolsters, two rugs, two coverlets, two blankets, four pair of sheets, two tablecloths, two drinking cloths, six napkins, two iron pots, a brass kettle, four platters, three pewter dishes, three quart pots, two pint pots, a table and stools, two chests and bedsteads. The original will, which survives, bears the testator's mark, not signature.

Giles Allen recalled in 1591, some fifteen years after the event, that Brayne had never been a party with Burbage in the securing of the original lease in 1576. He stated unambiguously that "nether the said Jo. Braynes nor any other for him" asked at any time "to be Joyned w^t the said James Burbage in the said lease"; indeed, "the said lease was suewed for by the said Burbage & not ment any way to the said Braynes" (C.24/226/9, *ex parte* Burbage; Wallace, p. 74). John Hyde recalled that when the lease of the premises was mortgaged to him in September 1579, it was mortgaged by "the said James burbage" alone (C.24/218/93, *ex parte* Burbage; Wallace, p. 53). These men reflect the position argued for by the Burbages; but John Griggs, deposing for the other side, offered an alternative version. Griggs, a twenty-four-year-old carpenter's apprentice in 1576, said that he had heard it "crediblye reported" that "it was agreed" between Burbage and Brayne "y^t the said lease shuld be made in the name onlye of the same James and yet to the vse of them bothe" (C.24/226/11, *ex parte* Brayne; Wallace, pp. 133-34).[6]

Robert Myles, a goldsmith and long-time associate of Brayne's, supported the view advanced by Griggs. Myles remembered Brayne's telling him "that he was advysed to suffre the said Burbage to take the said lease in his owne name and he to convey ou*er* to him the said Braynes his execut*o*^{rs} and assignes the moytie or half of all the profitt*es* growing by the playes & Rent*es* there and Burbage to haue the other moytie." Furthermore, according to Myles, "the said Burbage entred into CCCC^{li} bonde to the said Braynes to p*erforme* the same as by the same bond may appere." This course of action, according to Myles, was what "the sayd Braynes sayd he was advysed to do least yf the said lease had come in both ther names the Survyvo^r shuld go away wth all." The legal distinction is clear; had both their names been on the lease, Burbage and Brayne would have been joint tenants, with right of survivorship, and on the death of one partner all his interest would pass to the other partner. This was an eventuality that neither partner seems to have wanted. Their

---

[6] Griggs, later the builder of the Rose playhouse, appears in Henslowe's *Diary* as "John griggs cyttezin and Butcher of London" (*Diary*, p. 29) and was a freeman of the Company of Butchers by patrimony, being the son of Simon Griggs, butcher; but he was apprenticed in 1573, at the age of twenty-one, to Richard Smith, carpenter, then to Richard Holdgate in 1574 on the death of Smith, and then "transported from the companie of the butchers" to become a freeman of the Company of Carpenters in 1578 without formally finishing his apprenticeship. See Court Books of the Company of Carpenters, courts of 5 November 1573 (fo. 9), 25 November 1574 (fo. 20^v), and 8 July 1578 (fo. 49^v).

preferred arrangement was to be tenants in common, with distinct moieties and with no implications of survivorship. Myles urged the correctness of his own version of the events, insisting that all these details "the said James Burbage hath confessed to this Depo^t dyvers and sondrye tymes to be true" (C.24/226/11, *ex parte* Brayne; Wallace, p. 140).

The murkiness can be said to begin at this point, with the nature of the arrangement between Burbage and Brayne being itself a point of contention among the parties involved. Those of the Brayne faction maintained that Burbage's name standing alone on the lease emblematized a fiction implicit in the negotiations from the start, while those of the Burbage faction held that it accurately reflected the situation in 1576, regardless of how that situation might have been altered later. The claims on both sides seem about equally balanced.

There are a few more details. There was to be a "fine" or premium for the purchase of the lease, that is, a sum of money—£20 in this case—to open the proceedings. Giles Allen recalled that Burbage paid something toward this fine but could not recall how much: "he thinketh he had some therof in hand and A bonde for the paym^t of the rest." This bond, according to Allen, was "not fullye yet discharged," and "the said Bonde is now remayning at his house in the cuntrye." The debt for the fine was Burbage's alone: "the said Jo. Braynes paid no penny to this depo^t . . . nor promysed to paye this Depo^t any part therof." Further, Allen "never reconed or reputed any persone or persones whatsoever as his ten^{a}nt of the premisses syns the making of the said lease but onlye the said James Burbage." He recalled that the rent was about £14 a year (C.24/226/9, *ex parte* Burbage; Wallace, p. 75). By the terms of the lease, Burbage was to make two hundred pounds' worth of repairs to the existing buildings during the first ten years of his tenancy, in return for which Allen would offer Burbage a new twenty-one-year lease whenever such repairs were completed within those ten years (K.B. 27/1362, memb. 587; Wallace, pp. 167, 177).

1576: Spring-Summer-Autumn—Building the Playhouse

Possibly Burbage or Brayne, in anticipation of the signing of the lease, had begun to move some building supplies onto the grounds and even to commence construction on or shortly after Lady Day, though my guess is that they had not, such a move being potentially dangerous. If their intent was to have the building ready for occupancy that summer or (more likely) that autumn, they would wish to begin as soon as possible, but they were unlikely to have taken unnecessary risks. The interval between Lady Day and the signing of the lease was twenty days; perhaps they found the delay tolerable, perhaps not. Nothing in any of the records tells us when construction began.

Nor do the records tell us who built the Theater. William Sylvester and John Reynolds, who built the stage and scaffolds at the Red Lion, are hardly likely to have undertaken another job for the Brayne-Burbage syndicate, given their bad experiences in Stepney. Other carpenters, better known to later theater historians, are equally unlikely. John Griggs, who built the Rose playhouse for Philip Henslowe in 1587, was still a carpenter's apprentice in 1576, though his then master, Richard Holdgate, might have been hired to do the job. The same is true of Peter Street, who dismantled the Theater and built the Globe out of its timbers in the winter of 1598/99; Street was still an apprentice with Robert Maskall in 1576. But neither Maskall nor Holdgate appears in any of the litigation under review, though they were both still alive in the early 1590s, on the dates when others were making their depositions.[7] Had these two men worked on the playhouse, their testimony would surely have been as useful as that of the other tradesmen who were called in as deponents principally because of that connection. This absence from the records, when one might have expected their presence, makes their participation in the building of the Theater unlikely, and thus that of their apprentices as well.

But let us not forget the carpenter Robert Burbage, James's recently discovered brother, who in 1576 had been a freeman for three years. He is certainly a candidate, and his death in 1583 would account for his absence from the proceedings in 1591 and 1592.

Aside from the family connection, one or two more clues point to Robert Burbage as well. Sizable timbers would have been needed for the playhouse, perhaps more than for an ordinary dwelling, and such timbers were costly. They would arrive in London by barge and be unloaded at the wharf belonging to the Carpenters' Company, where the company auditor checked for proper sizes and dimensions. If James Burbage had been tempted to cut corners in the

---

[7] Holdgate died in 1592, Maskall in 1593 (GHL, mss. 9171/17, fo. 428^v; 9050/2, fo. 108).

building of his playhouse, we might find evidence of it here. The Wardens' Accounts of the Carpenters' Company for 1576 and 1577 show thirty-one fines levied "at the waterside for stuf not keping skanteling" (i.e., proper measure), most of the fines being for improper lath or quarter boards, the smallest fine being 9 pence. Only four freemen were fined for larger timbers: John Purnell, 12 pence; one Longhurst, 12 pence; Henry Store, 2 shillings; and Robert Burbage, with the largest fine recorded for those two years, 4 shillings, 8 pence.[8]

Another teasing piece of evidence can be found in Robert Burbage's will, made in 1583. "I leaue to my brother James Burbadge," he wrote, "all such dett*es* and dewties as he nowe oweth vnto me (except fower poundes whiche John Braynes and my said brother James doe owe vnto me ioyntly and seuerally." Four pounds was a not inconsiderable sum; it would have been almost a year's wages for one of Robert Burbage's journeymen. Robert did not forgive this joint debt as he did his brother's individual debts; the debt's existence suggests Robert's involvement in some formal dealing "ioyntly and seuerally" with the Brayne-Burbage partnership. The playhouse seems the likeliest occasion for such dealing, and the fact of the debt's still being unpaid by 1583 is quite consistent with other unpaid debts by James Burbage which the records affirm for us.

Robert apparently bore no familial grudge about this debt; he named his brother James one of the overseers of his will. (His feelings about John Brayne are not on record.) He named as the other overseer Bryan Ellam, a fellow carpenter, a man who would be one of the witnesses a few years later in the 1591 lawsuit between the Burbages and the widow Brayne. Ellam deposed in that lawsuit that he was fifty-eight years old and that he had known the James Burbages and the Braynes for about fifteen years, that is, since about 1576. Bryan Ellam was already a freeman in 1576 and may well have met the Burbages while working with Robert Burbage on the playhouse. Was Ellam the principal builder? Perhaps, though he nowhere identified himself as such; and in 1576 Burbage and Brayne, after their experience with Sylvester and Reynolds in

---

[8] GHL, ms. 4326/5, p. 332; see *Records of the Worshipful Company of Carpenters*, vol. 5 (London: Phillimore, 1937), p. 79. The Court of Aldermen had themselves taken notice of these offenses; at their meeting of 10 May 1576, shortly after the first timbers of the playhouse must have been delivered, they issued a warning to the Company of Carpenters that they not "offend in breakinge thacte of com*m*on Covnsell concernynge the buyinge of tymber Boorde or lathe at the water side" (CLRO, Rep. xix, fo. 75).

Stepney, might well have preferred a carpenter they knew to one they were just meeting. The evidence is thus inconclusive, though Robert Burbage may seem to advance the better claim.

1576, 1577—Paying for the Playhouse

James Burbage's debts to his brother Robert were not his only ones. He had, or professed to have, little money of his own; Henry Laneman, owner of the Curtain playhouse, said "that the comen speche went when the said Theater was in building that it was Braynes money & Credit that builded the same and that James Burbage was at y^t tyme verye unhable to Joyne therin" (C.24/226/11, *ex parte* Brayne; Wallace, p. 148).

John Hyde, a grocer and the man who lent them money on their lease in 1579, remembered that "when the said Braynes entred into the Accion of the said Theater he was wo^{r}th fyve hundreth poundes at the least and by com*m*en fame wo^{r}th A thowsand m*a*rkes and A man well thoght of in london"; Hyde further thought that Brayne "bestowed the same or the most part therof vp*p*on the same Theater to his vndoing" (C.24/228/11, *ex parte* Brayne; Wallace, p. 106).

John Griggs the carpenter said that Brayne was "A man of g^t welth, and of A welthie Trade"; he also knew that "suche promisses and speche as passed frome the said James Burbage to the said Braynes" concerning the "g^t welth and profitt that shuld ryse vnto them by buildyng A Theater or playe house & other buildinges" had been sufficient to fire Brayne's imagination, or perhaps his avarice. Brayne, once won over to the idea (so Griggs recalled), " provided A g^t some of money hyred wo^{r}kmen provyded Tymber and all other nedefull thing*es* for the building of the said Theater." Griggs thought that Brayne spent in all "the some of one thowsand m*a*rk*es* at the least." Further, "hoping of the g^t welth that shuld ryse vnto him by the same," he "gave vppe his trade sold his stocke his house he Dwelt in in Bucklers berye london & wholye ymployed all he could make towardes the said Building*es* and setting fourthe the same"; but the enterprise was, Griggs added, "to his own vtter vndoing at the last" (C.24/226/11, *ex parte* Brayne; Wallace, p. 134).

Robert Myles the goldsmith remembered that he had been present "at tymes whan the said James Burbage did earnestlie insynuate his brother in lawe John Braynes" to take a lease of the Giles Allen land for a playhouse which "wold grow to ther co*n*tynuall great profitt & com*m*odytie through the Playes that shuld be vsed there everye weke But the said Braynes being of A welthie trade alredye and A grocer in Bucklers Burye london & Ryche was verye lothe to deale in the matter of the said lease." Myles said that he "hath heard the said Jo Braynes many & often tymes saye that the drawing of him by his brother Burbage to deale in the matter of the said Theater was his vtter undoing" and that he would never have done it but for "the swete and contynuall persuasions" of Burbage. Myles heard Burbage tell Brayne that the playhouse cost "shuld not excede the some of CC^{li}" (£200). After Brayne had spent five hundred pounds or so he complained to Burbage about the excessive cost and (so Myles recalled) Burbage told him "it was no matter praying him to be contented it wold shortlie quyte the cost vnto them bothe" (C.24/226/11, *ex parte* Brayne; Wallace, p. 139).

The testimony by Myles is the fullest on these matters. Because he was of the Brayne faction, and all his depositions were on behalf of the widow Brayne, they provide a view of James Burbage which is perhaps not impartial. Myles remembered Brayne's saying that Burbage would have been unable to build the playhouse without Brayne's money "for it wold cost fyve tymes so moche as he was wo^{r}the." Myles rehearsed Brayne's commitment to the project and described his spending of money "out of his owne purce & what vpon Credit about the same to the some of vj or vij^C li [£600 or £700] at the least." By contrast, Myles described Burbage as being "nothing able ether of him self or by his credit to contrybute any like some towardes the building therof," with the result that Brayne, fearing all "to be lost that had bene bestowed vppon it alredye," was "dryven to sell his house he Dwelled in in Bucklers bery and all his stock that was left and gyve vppe his trade yea in the end to pawne & sell both his owne garmentes and his wyves & to ren [*sic*] in debt to many for money to fynishe the said Playe housse." Toward the latter end of the project, according to Myles, "the said Braynes and his Wyfe . . . were dryven to labo^r in the said wo^{r}kes for saving of some of the charge in place of ij^o laborers Whereas the said James Burbage went about his owne busynes and at sometymes when he did take vppon him to do some thing in the said wo^{r}kes he wold be and was allowed A workmans hyre as other the workmen there had" (C.24/226/11, *ex parte* Brayne; Wallace, p. 139).

Edward Collins was twenty-three years old in 1576 and apprenticed to Robert Kenningham, a grocer whose house and shop stood near Brayne's house and shop in Bucklersbury. Like Griggs, Collins had heard the common rumor of Brayne's wealth; he said that in 1576 Brayne "was reputed emonges his neyghbo^{rs} to be wo^{r}th one thowsand poundes at the least" and that after joining with Burbage in the playhouse venture "he began*n* to slack his own trade," giving his full attention to the playhouse "in hope of great welth & pro*f*itt during ther lease." Collins thought that Brayne had spent "one thowsand m*a*rke*s* at the least" on the project and knew that "at the last he was dryven to sell to this Depo^{tes} ffather his lease of the howse wherin he dwelled for one C^{li} and to this Depo^{t} all suche wares as he had left and all that longed therunto Remayni*n*g in the same for the some of one Cxlvj^{li} & od money." Part of Brayne's agreement with Collins involved the latter's paying forty pounds "to one Kymbre an Iremonger in london for Iron wo^{r}ke wch the said Braynes bestowed vp*p*on the same Theater." Once his house and shop were sold, according to Collins, "the said Braynes tooke the matter of the said building so vpon him" that he exhausted his own resources and "was dryven to borow money to supplye the same"; but, having made himself into a poor credit risk by these actions, "he found not towarde*s* it aboue the value of ffiftie pounde*s* some p*a*rte in money and the rest in stuff" (C.24/226/11, *ex parte* Brayne; Wallace, p. 137).

Robert Myles, Brayne's staunch supporter, said "he hath heard the said James Burbage confesse . . . that all the charge wch he was at in the accomplishing of the p*r*emisses from the begyn*n*ing to the end did not amount to the full value of one C^{li}." It seems unlikely on the face of it that Burbage should have said such a thing to Myles—unlikely, indeed, that Burbage should have taken Myles into his confidence on any of the matters that Myles claimed he "hath heard"—yet Myles "verylie thinketh [it] to be true ffor he never knew him but A po^{r} man & but of small Credit being by occupac*i*on a Joyner and reaping but A small lyving by the same gave it over and became A com*m*en Player in playes." Myles also said of Burbage "that his Credit was suche as nether m*a*rchant nor Artificer wold gyve him Credit for the value of x^{li} vnles his brother Braynes wold Joyne w^{t} him" because Brayne was "A man well knowne in london both of his own wellth and of good credit" (C.24/226/11, *ex parte* Brayne; Wallace, p. 141-42).

Myles claimed to have "heard the said Braynes by earnest othe afferme that all the readye money wch his brother Burbage brought fourthe to be ymployd towardes the building of the said Theater was but about xxxvij^{li}" in actual cash "and the rest that made vp*p*e about the some of fyftie & od pounde*s* [and] wch was in maner all that he bore towardes the said charge was in od peces of Tymber waynescott & suche like thing*es*" (C.24/226/11, *ex parte* Brayne;

Wallace, p. 142). This is a curious echo of Edward Collins's claim about Brayne's being unable to borrow more than "ffiftie pound*es* some p*ar*te in money and the rest in stuff." If Myles and Collins are talking about the same amalgam of cash and goods, amounting to some fifty pounds in the aggregate, then one of them has got the context wrong; either this figure represented Burbage's contribution or it represented what Brayne was able to raise elsewhere. There is no further evidence in the documents to permit a resolution of this dilemma.

Myles further recalled that Burbage used to require compensation for "his own labo^{r}" on the playhouse and remembered Brayne's telling him that "Burbage made him to allow him in some thing*es* the value of vj^{d} for A grote." Myles thus claimed to know "y^{t} the whole building of the p*re*misses in effecte and the taking of the said lease was done at the onlye charge of the said Braynes by his own goodes & credit." Myles also recalled that Brayne, just before he died in 1586, had said that Burbage not only owed him his share but also owed him for "the moytie of the value of certen tymber lead Brick Tyle lyme & sand left of the building of the said Theater" worth one hundred pounds. (C.24/226/11, *ex parte* Brayne; Wallace, pp. 142, 147).

It seems clear from these competing claims that the summer and autumn of 1576 were contentious times for Brayne and Burbage; perhaps their undertaking was hampered not only by their own disagreements but also by matters not mentioned in the lawsuits. For example, there was plague in the Tower in July 1576, and even as late as September the opening of Michaelmas term was deferred for a fortnight because of the pestilence. There is no evidence that playing was suspended in the summer or early autumn, but it likely was; when law terms are postponed, other civic measures usually appear as well. There is likewise no evidence that there was a pause in the building of the playhouse; no litigants or witnesses mention such a hiatus. If playing was suspended, playing companies would have taken to the road, and James Burbage, whose livelihood depended on playing but whose dreams of prosperity depended on finishing his playhouse, may have been uncertain whether to go or to stay. Unfortunately, the records tell us nothing of how he may have resolved that dilemma; nor do we know with any certainty whether he still considered himself a stage player by the summer of 1576.

In November the Spanish armies stationed in the Netherlands mutinied and sacked Antwerp, and the Dutch provinces united

under the terms of the Pacification of Ghent. If construction continued on the playhouse during this period, it escaped the formal
notice of the Court of Aldermen, whose attention may have been
taken by other matters, not all of them international in scope. On 11
December the aldermen ordered "that there be no more footeball
playe or other dysorderly exercyse vsed w^{th}in the Royall exchavnge
at any tyme hereafter" and, indeed, that "no more footeball playe be
hereafter vsed" anywhere at all in the City.[9] Warwick's, Howard's,
and Leicester's players comprised the court's Christmas schedule,
but no personal names are mentioned in the payment records for
Leicester's players.

1577—The Playhouse in Use

By August 1577 the Theater was in use, for it was mentioned by
name in a Privy Council injunction of 1 August (*ES* 4:276). With the
opening of the playhouse for business, the continuing disagreement
between Brayne and Burbage over the equitable sharing of costs and
profits of the venture became even sharper. Robert Myles, never one
to minimize James Burbage's shortcomings, said that after the
playhouse was built and operating, Burbage had "A secret key"
made for "the Com*m*en box where the money gathered at the said
Playes was by both ther consent*es* putt in" and that "by the space of
about ij° yeres" thereafter he contrived to "purloyne & filche therof
to him self moch of the same money." By this stratagem, according
to Myles, Burbage not only deceived Brayne "but also Disceyve[d]
his fellowes the Players." Furthermore, "many tymes [he] wold
thrust some of the money Devident betwene him & his said
ffellowes in his bosome or other where about his bodye Disceyving
his fellowes of ther due Devydent wch was equally to haue bene
devyded betwene them." Myles said that he "dothe verelie beleve
[this] to be true" because "he hath heard the said James Burbage
vp*p*on fynding of the same falce key confesse so moch in effecte to
the said Braynes praying him to forgyve him and he wold yf he
lyeved make him Recompence saying it was the Devill that led him
so to do" (C.24/226/11, *ex parte* Brayne; Wallace, pp. 142-43).

The various testimonies by Myles furnish vivid and circumstantial
details about the early history of the playhouse. Cumulatively they

---

[9]CLRO, Rep. xix, fo. 150.

suggest, by their authoritative tone, that Myles was present at many of the most intimate confrontations between Brayne and Burbage. A modern scholar is hard pressed to understand Myles's repetitive locutions that he "dothe verelie beleve" what he is saying; was this a variant form of "he doth know," or was it an acknowledgment that the source of his account was hearsay? The matter is not simple, though twentieth-century members of the Burbage faction have preferred the latter interpretation. Myles was the strongest deponent on the Brayne side of the dispute, and he was certainly not a disinterested witness; but this partisanship does not impeach his testimony. The picture he gives us of James Burbage is as plausible as any other we might form from these documents.

9 August 1577—The Lease at Pawn?

During the summer of 1577 Burbage and Brayne finally agreed to secure for themselves a written document spelling out the nature of their respective shares in the playhouse undertaking. I assume the initiative to have been Brayne's, for he rather than Burbage stood to benefit from the existence of such a document. William Nicoll, a notary public, recalled in the summer of 1592 that "about fiftene yeres past" Burbage and Brayne had come to his then shop in St. Olave in the Old Jewry "and required to have a lease & Coven^antes drawen betwene them of the moytie of certen howses or Ten*tes* barne stable Theatre gardeins and other premisses wch the said James Burbage then held by lease of one Giles Allyn of Hallowell." Burbage and Brayne explained to Nicoll "that though the lease was taken in the name only of the said James Burbage yet it was ment to be for both their vses and therfore he the said James Burbage was willing to assure the one moytie of the premisses to the said John Brayne." With this declaration, the ambiguity surrounding the original agreement is not so much resolved as superseded; it is still not clear whether Burbage's decision about sharing dated from the first taking of the lease or was of more recent origin.

Nicoll the scrivener, understanding the needs of tenants in common, drew up and engrossed "an Indenture of lease" between Burbage and Brayne dated 9 August 1577, which was apparently meant to be attached to the original lease. But Nicoll seemed to remember, in 1592, that the new lease, so engrossed, "was not sealed by the said James Burbage for that the originall lease made to him by the said Giles Allyn and Sara his wief was then at pawne for

money wch was borowed for the building of the said Theatre"
(C.24/226/11, *ex parte* Brayne; Wallace, p. 151).

This statement is our only evidence for the original lease having
been at pawn as early as 1577. Other statements in these documents
make it clear that the lease was pawned in 1579 to the grocer John
Hyde; if it had also been pawned in 1577 it must have been
redeemed before 1579, itself an unlikely event given the troubled
history of loan repayments throughout this narrative. Nicoll's recollection may be confused. At the time of his deposing in 1592,
however, he was only forty-four years old, thus only some twenty-
eight years old at the time he drafted the lease between the two men;
senility can hardly be invoked here. The case, then, for the lease's
having been pawned in 1577 is problematic.

22 May 1578—The Bond of Assurance

William Nicoll further recalled that a year later, in May 1578, John
Brayne—perhaps dissatisfied with the legal protection he had
secured for himself by the covenant of 1577—"did require" Nicoll to
draw an obligation binding James Burbage in four hundred pounds
to make Brayne "a good and lawfull lease graunt and other as-
suraunce of the moitie" of the Shoreditch premises. Nicoll accordingly drew up the document, "and afterwardes the said James
Burbage did seale and delyver" the same to Brayne, in the presence
of Nicoll and "one John Gardyner." Nicoll's memory of this later
document was refreshed in 1592 by its "being shewed vnto him" at
his deposing. There is no mention that the covenant of 1577 had
been produced as evidence by anyone in these proceedings; Nicoll
was the only person to mention such a document, and in the context
of a pawned original lease, a circumstance that perhaps makes the
whole claim suspect (C.24/226/11, *ex parte* Brayne; Wallace, p. 151).
The bond for four hundred pounds, however, apparently did exist
and was acknowledged by James Burbage in 1595 as his; he had
given it to Brayne as assurance of his good performance in "the
Assigninge over of the same moytie" (C.33/89, fo. 130; Wallace, pp.
156-57).

1 July 1578—Brayne Makes His Will

During the accounting year ending in the summer of 1578, John
Brayne was fined ten shillings by the Grocers' Company "for

making free of [his apprentice] Will*i*am Muschamp before thend of his terme."[10] The premature granting of freedom in any of the City livery companies was contrary to City statute, and thus an amerceable offense; it happened infrequently, if one can judge from the number of entries found in the wardens' accounts of the various guilds. Usually, a master unable to keep an apprentice for his full term arranged to "set him over" to another master for his remaining years. Brayne's offense, coming at this juncture, might be seen as the action of a man anxious to be rid of the encumbrances of an earlier life, at whatever cost.

Brayne also looked forward, in the summer of 1578, to the prospect of a next life. On the first of July in that year, he drew up his will. It is not clear whether he felt himself to be near death at that moment or whether he had been advised, in the light of his financial difficulties with his brother-in-law, that making a will would be a prudent step. In the will he claimed to be "syck in body," though this phrasing may have been no more than formulaic. He asked that his body be buried "wth in the p*a*rishe churche of Saynt Lenord*es* whereof I am a p*a*rishoner," thereby giving us our first firm evidence that by 1578 he had moved away from Bucklersbury and the parish of St. Stephen's Walbrook. Unfortunately the will—and it is the original will, with Brayne's signature on it, not merely a record copy—says nothing whatever about Burbage or about the Theater. It provides that his wife, Margaret, should have a house in Trumpington, Cambridgeshire, which he owns; his brother-in-law Edward Stowers is to have a similar house in Essex.[11] His wife is to be his executrix, and his "welbeloued frend*es*" Henry Watson and Robert Myles, goldsmiths, are to be the overseers.[12] There is nothing more of substance; in particular, there is nothing whatsoever about the playhouse or about Brayne's moiety thereof. Given the prominence of the playhouse in Brayne's life during the preceding two years, such an omission is curious indeed.

---

[10] GHL, ms. 11,571/6, fo. 476.

[11] For Brayne's purchase of the Essex property in 1572, see PRO, C.54/873, wherein Edward Stowers, even then a tenant of the property, is described as a blacksmith.

[12] GHL, ms. 9172/12C, fo. 125. The will was proved in 1586 in the Commissary Court of the Bishop of London. Three London parishes bore the name of St. Leonard—in Foster Lane, Eastcheap, and Shoreditch. Presumably Brayne had relocated in the last of these, the parish in which the Theater stood and where, after 1576, James Burbage and his family also lived. Of the three parishes, only St. Leonard's Foster Lane fell within the purview of the Commissary Court; but Brayne was domiciled in Whitechapel when he died, in the parish of St. Mary Matfellon, also under the probate jurisdiction of the Commissary Court.

12 July 1578—The Differences Taken to Arbitration

By the summer of 1578 the set of formal and informal agreements between Burbage and Brayne had broken down yet again. By midsummer Brayne had managed to require, and gotten Burbage to acquiesce in, the setting up of a board of arbitration to hear and determine their dispute. If Brayne was indeed "syck in body" this summer, he may have seen such a move as the last hope of securing his estate. Burbage's acquiescence, too, may have been motivated by the prospect of Brayne's imminent demise. But the agreement was not without its stresses. Brayne wanted to bind Burbage, in advance, to honor whatever decision the arbitrators would reach, and so he took him once again to William Nicoll the notary public. Nicoll recalled vividly their coming "both together in the shop of this deponent about bond*es* of arbitrament" and remembered how Burbage and Brayne "fell a reasoning together of the yll dealing of the same James Burbage" and how Brayne's "reasoning" so moved Burbage that he "did there strike him wth his fist and so they went together by the eares In somuch that this deponent could hardly p*a*rt them" (C.24/226/11, *ex parte* Brayne; Wallace, p. 152). Surely a wonderful moment, the equal of the broomstick episode in vigor if not in pathos—indeed in pathos too, Brayne being "syck in body" as he was—but unfortunately the documents do not tell us whether Burbage was truly angry and venting his anger in violence or was merely trying to intimidate his brother-in-law. The lame conclusion to all this activity was that Burbage gave Brayne a bond of two hundred pounds to perform his part of the arbitrament.[13]

Two men, John Hill and Richard Turner, were chosen to be arbitrators. Possibly one man was chosen by each side, though if so it isn't clear who chose whom. Hill and Turner seem to have been lawyers; Robert Myles said of them that they were "men of great honestye & credit" and of "great discression and indifferiencye betwene them bothe" (C.24/226/11, *ex parte* Brayne; Wallace, p. 143); such an endorsement from Myles might lead one to believe that they were partial to the Brayne faction or at least that their determination

---

[13] Robert Myles produced two bonds in Chancery in 1595 as part of his case against the Burbages. The first was the £400 bond of assurance given by Burbage to Brayne on 22 May 1578; the other was the bond for £200 made by Burbage to Brayne for the performance of the arbitrament. Myles claimed that they were both forfeit, but Chancery declined to take up the matter, referring him instead to a court of common law.

was in Brayne's favor. The arbitration itself was a formal affair, held in the precincts of the Temple on Saturday, 12 July 1578. Edward Collins, the young man who had bought out John Brayne's grocery stock, recalled that he "was Requested to say to the said Arbytrato^{rs} being in the Temple Churche what he could say of the habilitie of the said Braynes whan he & Burbage Joyned together in the foresaid lease & building of the Theater." Collins remembered that he had "declared truelye vnto them what he could saye of the said Braynes" (C.24/226/11, *ex parte* Brayne; Wallace, p. 138).

Robert Myles, the persistent advocate of the widow Brayne's case in these lawsuits, said that the central provision of the arbitrament by Hill and Turner had been that Burbage and Brayne should each have "the one half or moytie of the profit*tes* that shuld grow & ryse by the plaies to be vsed ther" and also "of the Rent*es* ffynes & other yerelie profit*tes* of suche other tenem^{tes} & places there as shuld yerelie grow due for the same." Further, if there should ever arise a need to mortgage the lease in order to raise cash, "then they both shuld Joyne in the same morgage" and the income from "the said Playes & the other said Rent*es*" should go only toward "the Redempc*ion* of the said lease" (C.24/226/11, *ex parte* Brayne; Wallace, p. 143).

Robert Myles had a son Ralph, who had been only eleven years old when the Theater was built but who had clearly inherited from his father all the requisite tales about the controversies between his friends the Braynes and those awful people the Burbages. Ralph Myles was called upon to depose in 1592, by which time he was twenty seven years old, free of the goldsmiths by patrimony in right of his father, but in actual practice a soapmaker. Ralph recalled that one provision of the arbitrament had been that all profits coming from the Theater were to be used "for the payment of suche deb*tes* as ether the said Brayne or the said Burbage were then in for the building and repayring of the said Theatre" and that until those debts were satisfied, neither Burbage nor Brayne "shuld haue nor enioye any p*ar*te or p*ar*cell therof to his or ther owne vse." Once the debts to others had been satisfied, then Brayne was to receive all the profits of the playhouse to his own use until he had repaid himself "suche somes of money wch he had lade out . . . more then the said Burbage had done." When that point was reached, the income was to be divided evenly between them. The only exception to this, as Ralph Myles recalled, was that, while the outside debts were being repaid, Brayne was to be allowed ten shillings a week "for & toward*es* his house keeping" and Burbage was to have eight shillings a week for the same, out of "the profittes of such playes as shuld be playd there vpon sundaies" (C.24/228/10, *ex parte* Burbage; Wallace, pp. 119-20).

This last point may prove to be important. Ten shillings a week to Brayne and eight shillings a week to Burbage makes a total of eighteen shillings, all of it to be paid out of Sunday gatherings. There would have been little point in arriving at such a settlement if it was unrealistic; the implication must be that, even in 1578, Sunday earnings at the Theater were in excess of eighteen shillings so frequently that the figure could be taken as a benchmark. This rather interesting conclusion depends entirely, of course, on the accuracy of Ralph Myles's testimony. Interrogatories administered in 1592 on behalf of James Burbage sought to establish whether such playing actually took place at all. Nicholas Bishop was asked "whither do the players of enterludes, vse to plaie in the said Theatre vpon the sabothe day yea or no," but he responded merely that there had been "wekelie playes & interludes" there. Ralph Myles was asked "whither do thei vse to plaie on the sondaies ther, yea or no," and his response was neither yea nor no, but rather the account cited above; he stated that the allowances were to come from Sunday playing but did not say that Sunday playing actually occurred (C.24/228/10; Wallace, pp. 112, 114, 117, 119-20).

The point is thus left hanging. One might speculate that the Brayne faction had been seeking to establish that there were no Sunday plays, hence no income to Brayne from the agreed-upon arrangement; the Burbages would of course have had to demolish such a claim by asking the question pointblank. But when challenged directly to say whether there had been Sunday playing, the two deponents, ostensibly of the Brayne faction, managed to fudge the issue, perhaps to avoid having to say "yea" rather than "no." This is a reasonable, though not inevitable, construction to place on these parts of the documents.

Thus even the arbitration, which must have seemed in 1578 to have resolved all pending issues, had proved by the early 1590s to be yet one more site of controversy, with conflicting answers, and even nonanswers, to the questions raised about it.

23 June 1579—Burbage Arrested

John Hynde, a haberdasher (not to be confused with John Hyde the grocer), recalled in 1592 that "about xiij yeres past," that is, on 23

June 1579 "in the after noon," he "did cause one Saunders then one of the S^{r}iaunt*es* at mace to the Shyreff of london or his yeomen to arrest and attache the body of the now compl^t [James Burbage] as he came down Graces street towardes the Crosse Keys there to a Playe." The arrest was for settlement of a debt of £5 13s, a sum Hynde had recovered against Burbage and Brayne "by a nisi prius tryed in the Guilde Halle london." That both Burbage and Brayne were parties to the debt suggests that it was connected with the playhouse. Hynde also remembered that on the same day, or soon after, Saunders the sergeant brought the requisite £5 13s to him in discharge of the recovery (C.24/226/10, *ex parte* Burbage; Wallace, pp. 89-90). The implication is that Burbage, or someone acting for him, had raised the money and paid Saunders in order to secure his release from prison. Further detail is lacking, but the incident suggests that Burbage was not without financial resources in the summer of 1579.

The wording of Hynde's recollection is ambiguous as well about the nature of Burbage's excursion "down Graces street towardes the Crosse Keys . . . to a Playe"; did Hynde mean that Burbage was on his way to perform at the Cross Keys, that Burbage's company was playing at the Cross Keys with Burbage in attendance upon them, or merely that Burbage was going as a spectator to a play? If the first of these, then perhaps our estimates of when Burbage gave up stage playing are too early; if either the first or second of these, we need to wonder why his company was playing at the Cross Keys rather than at the Theater; while the last option suggests a degree of disconnection between Burbage and Leicester's players which invites still further musing.

26 September 1579—Mortgaging the Lease

By the summer of 1579 it must have become clear to all that the rumors of Brayne's imminent death had been exaggerated. Burbage was perhaps disappointed. Brayne's death would surely have relieved some of the financial pressure on the enterprise, but it was not to be. By September 1579 he and Brayne were as much in debt as ever and needed to find other ways to raise cash. Their only collateral was the lease to the Shoreditch property. In mid-September they brought their case to "one Jo. Prynne a Broker," and Prynne in turn put them in touch with a grocer named John Hyde, who may have been known to Brayne from earlier days. Hyde, who deposed three times between December 1590 and February 1592, remembered that he had first been approached by Prynne, who had "offred the lease of the Theater in morgage" to him. In a subsequent meeting of all four parties, acceptable terms were "agreed on both sydes," and a few days before Michaelmas "Burbage & Brayne did Joyntlye morgage . . . the said lease" to Hyde for £125. Furthermore, "Joynt-lie they and the said Prvne . . . did entre into bonde . . . for the Redempcion therof" (C.24/218/93, *ex parte* Burbage; Wallace, p. 53; also C.24/228/10, *ex parte* Burbage; Wallace, p. 111).

The bond Hyde required of them was for £200. Conventionally, such performance bonds were for twice the amount of the debt; in this case the bond ought to have been for £250. Despite this seeming leniency, however, these terms taken all in all may have been heavier than the norm. Performance bonds were normally required in lieu of other collateral; that Hyde chose to exact both the bond and the collateral (i.e., the lease)—even though the bond was for a somewhat lower figure—suggests that he felt the loan to involve some risk.

The terms, as Hyde recalled them, were straightforward. Burbage and Brayne had a year and a day to repay the £125, after which the lease was to be forfeit, and the bond of assurance as well. Hyde affirmed that "nether the said James Burbage nor John Brayn" paid him "any part or parcell of the said money" during the year in question (C.24/228/11, *ex parte* Brayne; Wallace, p. 107); therefore the lease "was absolutely forfeited and lost" by them (C.24/218/93, *ex parte* Burbage; Wallace, p. 53).

12 January 1580—Leasing the George

Why didn't Burbage and Brayne make the payments to Hyde? One would imagine that Burbage in particular might have been concerned about the prospect of losing his lease to the grounds on which his playhouse stood, and thus losing the playhouse itself; how was it that he and Brayne could not manage to meet the requisite payments? Burbage seems to have had nothing else on his agenda during those years, and profligacy is one charge that even his enemies did not lay against him. Further, his ability to raise the necessary cash on those occasions when he was arrested—five pounds and more for Hynde in 1579, twenty pounds for another arrest in 1582—suggests that he maintained a kind of nest egg. John Alleyn, elder brother of Edward, who identified himself in 1592 as an innholder of St. Botolph's without Bishopsgate, thought "in his conscience that the said James Burbage did detayne the profittes of the premisses in his owne handes of purpose that the said morgage shuld be forfetted" (C.24/228/11, *ex parte* Brayne; Wallace, p. 99), though he offered no explanation of why such an outcome would be of benefit to the Burbages. Brayne was equally guilty of nonpayment, and he was no more destitute than Burbage; further, unlike Burbage, he was financially active on at least one other front during this period. On 12 January 1580 he took a lease from John Field of London, gentleman, to an inn in Whitechapel called the George, with its adjoining gardens.[14] The lease was for twenty-four years and the annual rent was thirty pounds, payable in four quarterly installments of £7 10s. The evidence suggests that Robert Myles had joined with him in this enterprise (C.2.Eliz./B.13/5).

The Burbages were not unaware of such activities on Brayne's part; in their earliest lawsuit against the widow Brayne, in 1588, they alluded to the leasing of the George, implied that they had been involved with Brayne in the negotiations for the lease, and claimed that Brayne had promised, in the presence of witnesses, to settle a moiety of the premises on them (C.3/222/83; Wallace, pp. 42, 43). In their later lawsuits they took steps to demonstrate that Brayne had other debts and obligations as well and that his impecuniousness was not due wholly to his investments in the playhouse. In 1592 they required a deposition of William James, who was at that time in his early forties and living near Dublin. In 1579 James, then twenty-eight years old, had been Lord Wentworth's bailiff of the manor of Stepney, and James remembered that he had been called upon in that year "to extend [i.e., to assess as a preliminary to seizing] the goodes of the said Jo. Braynes at the Sute of one Jo. Hynde"—not Hyde the grocer, but Hynde the haberdasher who had arrested James Burbage in the previous summer. Hynde was bent on recovering from Brayne a debt of £25 10s, a different debt, presumably, from the one of £5 13s which Burbage and Brayne jointly owed him and for which he had earlier ordered Burbage's arrest. James found, however, that Brayne's property in Stepney had been conveyed away by "a dede of gyft" to "one William Thomson of Ratcliffe," a man whose connection with Brayne was that he had "maryed the said Braynes wyves Sister."[15] William

---

[14] Wallace thought that Brayne had built, not leased, the inn (pp. 9, 14).
[15] William Thomson and Eleanor Stowers were married at St. Dionis Backchurch on

James concluded that the deed of gift was "of purpose to defeat and defrawde the said Execution," not only of Hynde's but also the executions of "others that afterwardes came" against Brayne (C.24/226/10, *ex parte* Burbage; Wallace, pp. 90-91). Four years earlier, in their lawsuit of 1588, the Burbages had also protested this subterfuge, calling Brayne "a verie subtell persone," deploring the "deed of gift to the said Tomson" and claiming that the contrivance was done on purpose to "impouerishe [Burbage] and depryve him of his interest and tearme for yeres" in the playhouse (C.3/222/83; Wallace, p. 41).

This is our first mention of any property in the manor of Stepney belonging to Brayne. It may well be a reference to the newly acquired George Inn, which lay in Whitechapel and thus within the jurisdiction of the manorial court. As "1579" extended in the popular consciousness until 25 March 1580, James's recollection of the date is not at odds with Brayne's lease of 12 January 1579/80. If these associations are correct, then Brayne's investment in the George Inn was carefully sheltered virtually from the moment of its inception. Perhaps the gift was Brayne's device for keeping at bay such creditors as John Hynde, who sought (legitimately) to recover debts from the playhouse in Shoreditch. It may equally have been a way of keeping this new investment out of the hands of James Burbage himself.

31 July 1580—Sharing the George with Myles

Brayne's partnership with Robert Myles was formalized in the following summer, when the two men signed an indenture by which Brayne leased a moiety of the George Inn, with its gardens and outbuildings, to Myles for an annual rental of 15, that is, half of Brayne's own rent of thirty pounds (C.2.Eliz./B.13/5). Myles was also to pay half of any costs of operation. Such an arrangement suggests by its very tidiness that a beneficial business arrangement might be in the offing. But Brayne had equally tidy agreements with Burbage and had little to show for them; the story of his relationship with Robert Myles is similarly more complex than this agreement might suggest.

---

31 August 1562. For Brayne's marriage to Margaret Stowers in the same parish three years later, see Chapter 4 above.

For a lawsuit she initiated in 1587 (C.2.Eliz./B.13/5), Brayne's widow constructed a story about the encounter between Myles and her husband which is a remarkable piece of narrative in itself. In her version, "one Robert Myles of London," a "Gouldsmythe" who had fallen on hard times, arrived at the doorstep of the George in the summer of 1580 with a "poore Wiffe and children" and claimed to be "in greate necessitie and calamitie"; he and his family "had not any convenient house or place to dwell and harbo^r themselves in." Myles "made knowne vnto the saide John Braynes his poor and bare estate that he was then lately fallen into" but nonetheless proposed to Brayne that they should become equal partners in the ownership and management of the George. Myles assured Brayne that it "would be profittable and gaynefull" to both of them "through the greate travell and dilligence by him and his sayde wief to be taken and sustained in the saide Inne." Myles persisted in his "greate and earnest suite and lamentable complaint and intreatie" until Brayne, apparently afflicted with poor judgment at this juncture, welcomed Myles and his family, agreed to the proposal, and professed himself "euerye waye willinge and readye to do hym good and pleasure hym."

The reality of the situation was less saccharine. To begin with, by the time of this supposed meeting in the summer of 1580, Myles and Brayne had already known each other for years; in the will he drew up in 1578, Brayne had named Myles as one of his overseers. There is little reason for us to believe that the George enterprise was Brayne's alone. Brayne and Burbage, we recall, had constructed a similar fiction in 1576 about the Theater's being Burbage's alone. Brayne's standard rhetorical posture in difficult situations seemed to be that he had become involved only because of the persuasions of others. Indeed, Brayne's relations with Myles seemed to be a reprise of his relations with Burbage, and like that other relationship this one had problems from the start. Travelers who stay at inns expect their horses to be fed, and hay was thus a regular necessity for the George. Myles had an uncle named George Scott who lived in Chigwell, some ten miles northeast of London, and who dealt in hay. Myles told his uncle that he was now the proprietor of the George Inn and asked him for forty pounds' worth of hay on credit. The uncle apparently demanded to see Myles's lease before agreeing to such an arrangement; accordingly, Myles and Brayne seem to have constructed a phony lease, in which Brayne purported to convey to Myles "his whole Interest and Terme of yeares" in the inn, rather than simply half of it as was the case with the real lease.

Myles showed this phony lease to his uncle, who was satisfied, and the hay arrived. Myles forgot to return the phony lease to Brayne.

April 1580—Brayne and Burbage Indicted

Meanwhile, playing was in full career at the Theater, and the activity did not escape official notice. The current lord mayor, Nicholas Woodroffe, wrote in mid-April to the queen's lord chancellor, Sir Thomas Bromley, complaining of a "great disorder" at the Theater the previous Sunday but offering to suspend a planned investigation of the incident upon his understanding that the Privy Council was taking the matter in hand.[16] Any "investigation" Woodroffe might have set in motion would of course have had little legal force, as the Theater lay beyond his jurisdiction; but the assertion of concern was creditable. What the Privy Council apparently did on this occasion was to alert the Middlesex justices to the problem posed by the playhouse, and the justices in turn apparently directed their presentment jurors to return an indictment. The jurors promptly presented "Joh*ann*es Braynes de Shorditche in com*itatu* Mid*d*le*sex*ie yoman et Jacobus Burbage de eadem yoman" for bringing together unlawful assemblies of people to see plays "at a certain place called the Theater" (*apud quendam locum vocatum the Theatre*) on 21 February 1580 and on "divers other days and occasions before and after" (*diversis aliis diebus et vicibus antea ed postea*).

The indictment itself is undated, but it must have been later than 21 February as it speaks of offenses committed both on and after that date. Probably it was issued in April, about the time of the lord mayor's letter. Going to a playhouse was not in and of itself illegal, and the document offers no explanation for its use of the phrase *illicitas assemblaciones*, but the date specified, 21 February, was not only a Sunday but in 1580 was the first Sunday in Lent. The lord mayor's complaint about another Sunday fracas at the Theater suggested to Wallace and Chambers that the true offense was Sunday playing, not merely playing. It may even have been, more narrowly, Sunday playing in Lent. The outcome of the indictment is not known, but the modern consensus is that the various ordinances

[16] CLRO, *Remembrancia* I.9.

already in existence prohibiting Sunday playing began to be more stringently enforced.

If so, then the agreement reached by Burbage and Brayne two years earlier would have been put in jeopardy. Part of that agreement had been that Brayne would get ten shillings a week, and Burbage eight, out of the proceeds of Sunday playing. If such playing were inhibited, that part of the agreement would have ceased to function, and one or another of the parties might have been tempted to claim that the entire accord had thus become void. Both of them being shrewd, they may have wanted it both ways, that is, to claim (on the basis of the indictment) that Sunday playing had been suppressed, yet to continue supporting Sunday playing to maintain their income. Such an inference presumes, of course, that their tenants the players (whatever group it might have been) were willing to collaborate in this disobedience. Were they? The refusal of Nicholas Bishop and Ralph Myles in 1592 to affirm "whither do thei vse to plaie on the sondaies ther, yea or no" may have been a simple reluctance to acknowledge this breach of the law in a formal deposition.

26 September 1580—Default on the Mortgage to Hyde

A year had gone by since the lease of the Shoreditch premises was mortgaged to the grocer John Hyde for 125. No repayment had been made by either Burbage or Brayne, and Hyde concluded on this date that the mortgage had been forfeited and was thus his. Hyde deposed in 1590 that "he was offended that the said burbage and Brayne did not repay hym"; he thought "to put the said burbage out of possession of the said Theatre" because the debt remained unpaid and he therefore "*received* no *profitt* thereby" (C.24/218/93, *ex parte* Burbage; Wallace, p. 54). But in some fashion not made clear, Burbage and Brayne reopened negotiations with Hyde and persuaded him to forbear his foreclosure. They reached a new agreement, the terms of which, as Hyde recalled them, were straightforward. Burbage and Brayne, "or ether of them," were to pay Hyde "v^{li} A weke till all the foresaid Morgage money were payd"; then "they shuld haue ther lease againe" (C.24/228/10, *ex parte* Burbage; Wallace, p. 111). Here, as in the case of the presumed Sunday takings of eighteen shillings, one might conclude that Burbage and Brayne entered into such a contract confident of a weekly income of five pounds or more from the playhouse. At that rate, they would have paid off the principal in twenty-five weeks. A few more payments for what Hyde called his "reasonable consideracion for the forbearing" of the loan beyond its original date of forfeiture, and in little more than half a year the lease would have been redeemed. Perhaps the winter season of 1580/81 bore out Burbage and Brayne's estimates of future income, perhaps not; Hyde recalled only that they did not adhere to this schedule of payment. Deposing for the Burbages in 1592, he recalled that for some "iiij^{or} or v w^{kes} after" the granting of the extension, Burbage and Brayne—or one of them— had indeed held up their end of the bargain, but thereafter "they performed no more" (C.24/228/10, *ex parte* Burbage; Wallace, p. 111).

June 1581—Losing the Lease to the George

Brayne and Myles, new partners in the George Inn, continued to need money. With Brayne's permission, Myles proposed to mortgage his lease—that is, his half-interest—to raise cash. He found one John Banbury of London, gentleman, who would lend him sixty pounds for six months but who did not find Myles's lease of a moiety to be an attractive collateral. Myles then offered him the phony lease of the whole inn, and he took it. At the end of the six months Myles asked for an extension and Banbury said that he would grant one if Myles produced better sureties. Myles persuaded George Scott (the uncle with the hay) and his cousin Robert Scott to cosign with him. The Scotts, perhaps seeing an advantage to themselves therein, agreed to do so. At the end of the period of extension, Myles defaulted and Robert Scott had to pay the debt for him. Banbury the moneylender then returned the phony lease, but gave it to Robert Scott rather than to Myles. Scott, believing that the lease, and thus the inn, now properly belonged to him, entered the premises of the George and tried to evict Myles and Brayne and their families.

Brayne found a remedy in the person of one John Ashburnham of Sussex, esquire, to whom Brayne had lent £190 on an earlier occasion and who had defaulted on the repayment (S.P.12/146, fo. 80). Brayne offered to forgive this debt if Ashburnham would buy the phony lease back from Robert Scott. Ashburnham did so, but then turned the lease over to Myles rather than to Brayne (C.2.Eliz./ B.13/5).

10 November 1581—Brayne a Poor Financial Risk

Meanwhile, still more complications. In 1581, one Christopher Amis of Stepney, gentleman, perhaps an acquaintance of Brayne's from Whitechapel, was in need of cash and had found a scrivener in London named Roger Warde who would deal with him. Amis was either desperately needy or very naive, for Warde's offer was not to lend him fifteen pounds in cash but rather to extend to him merchandise to the reputed value of fifteen pounds, which Amis could then sell on the open market to raise his money. This was a fairly standard, and much remarked on, strategy employed by a certain kind of moneylender: the merchandise so offered was rarely if ever worth the amount claimed. The legal fiction, as written in the bond, would be that Amis was desirous of purchasing certain goods of Warde but wanted an extended term (in this case, six months) to make payment. John Brayne, in his later lawsuit over these matters, for some reason chose to perpetuate the language of this fiction, saying that Amis "had agreed" with Warde "to buy and receive of the saide Warde certaine wares and merchandize valued by the saide Warde at xv^{li}, and for xv^{li} to be paied at daies then to come" (Req.2/181/47).

Amis had persuaded Brayne to stand surety for him in this loan, and on 10 November 1581 Amis and Brayne jointly signed a bond for Warde in the usual double amount, that is, "in the som*m*e of xxx^{li} for the paym^t of fiftene poundes," as Brayne later described it. Warde took the signed bond from the two men but then declined to turn over the merchandise to Amis, expressing doubts about Brayne's "abilitye and sufficiencye" as a surety and asking for a substantiation of Brayne's credit. Brayne acknowledged that he was "of late gretly decayed & indebted by reson of suertishipp for other men" but invited Warde to come to the George Inn and assess Brayne's resources for himself. Warde accordingly "came home to the house of your poore subiecte." Looking about him, he was unimpressed; he told Brayne that he found him inadequate to serve as surety for Amis, even though he had signed the bond but that "if he wolde give vnto him one potte of bere he wolde discharge your saide subiecte of the saide bonde." Brayne agreed, furnished the beer, and they both drank to their new agreement. Warde drew up a new bond for Amis, with one John Clarke named as surety and, happy with this new arrangement, turned the merchandise over to Amis. Brayne neglected to get, from Warde, the old uncanceled bond.

April 1582—The Peckhams and Their Claims

Trouble appeared from an unexpected quarter in the spring of
1582. Giles Allen, Burbage's landlord, had held since 1556 what he
took to be a sound title to the Shoreditch property, having purchased
it jointly with his father in that year from one Christopher Bumpsted, who in turn had purchased it the previous year from a family
named Peckham. The land had come to the Peckhams by way of a
marriage contract in 1554. The arrangement had seemed to cause no
difficulties until 1582, when the Peckhams determined to recover the
property by arguing that the original contract by which they had got
it was for technical reasons void. The corollary of their argument
was to be that, as their own title was now called into question, their
sale of the property to Bumpsted was invalid, as was Bumpsted's
subsequent sale to the Allens, father and son. The Peckhams, setting
their plan in motion, went to law against Giles Allen and concurrently
began an apparently systematic harassment of Burbage and Brayne,
probably hoping thereby to increase the pressure on Allen to settle.

Cuthbert Burbage, at law himself against Giles Allen in 1600,
recalled the troubles his father had had with "one Edmond Peckham
towching^e the title of the *premises*" on which the Theater stood.
Peckham's constant harassment, Cuthbert claimed, had meant that
"James Burbadg^e [his] father was verie muche trowbled and often
Chardged to finde men to keepe the possession of the said *premises*
from the said Edmond Peckham," and as a result his father could
not "enioye the said *premises* according^e to the lease" given them
by Allen (Req.2/87/74, the replication; Wallace, p. 201). Randolph
May, a deponent in Cuthbert's suit, remembered that James Burbage "was once in danger of his owne lyffe by keepinge possession
thereof from Peckham and his servant*es*"; he "knoweth the same to
be true for that he was then there."

Oliver Tilt, another deponent, was also there: James Burbage "did
pay him . . . wages for keepinge the possession of the Theater from the
said m^r Peckham and his *servantes*," but despite this safeguard "the
players for sooke the said Theater to [Burbage's] great losse." May
concurred that "Burbadge loste muche money by that controu*er*sie and
troble for yt drove manye of the players thence because of the
disturbance of the possession" (Req.2/184/45, *ex parte* Burbage; Wallace,
pp. 240, 242). If these claims are true, the spring and summer of 1582
must have been difficult times financially for Burbage and Brayne.[17]

---

[17] It is not clear from any of the documents how long Peckham's harassment

June 1582—Burbage Arrested

But creditors were not deterred by such considerations. The patient and persistent John Hyde, still pressuring Burbage and Brayne to repay the balance of the   125 they owed him, caused "James burbage to be arrested by proces out of her ma^{tes} Benche about June as he rem*embereth* 1582." As with the earlier arrest in June 1579, this arrest produced momentary results: Burbage came to Hyde's house "wth the officer or bailif that had hym arrest^{d}" and paid twenty pounds toward the debt. On receipt of the money, Hyde—or perhaps Hyde's wife; Hyde could not recall—thereupon "discharged" Burbage "from the bailif" on condition that Burbage "geue vnto hym . . . new boundes wth a surety" for further compliance (C.24/218/93, *ex parte* Burbage; Wallace, p. 54).

John Brayne was having further troubles of his own that year as well, though he seemed to be more successful than Burbage at eluding arrest. William James, the man who had been bailiff of the manor of Stepney in 1579, was still bailiff in 1582 when "ther was Dyrected vnto him at the Sute of one Anne Wilbram wydowe" an "Execucion of an C^{li} debt against the body of the said Jo. Braynes." But Brayne had managed to become invisible; despite "long travell and serche" neither James nor his deputies "could fynde him," and James "was dryven to make his Reto^{r}ne of non est inventus" (C.24/226/10, *ex parte* Burbage; Wallace, p. 91). And in the following year, James still being bailiff, "ther was another Execucion Directed vnto him" against both Brayne and Robert Myles, at the suit of "one Jo. Banberye gentlema*n*" for a debt of eighty pounds. This execution directed James "not only to extend ther goodes but also to attache ther bodyes," but shrewdly "they both absented them sel*fes*" so that he had to return once again a *non est inventus*. James professed not to know what other debts Brayne and Myles might have had, "but he thought them to be gretly in debt" because Brayne had later told him "that they [i.e., he and Myles] had a proteccion vnder Sr Water Waler knight" (C.24/226/10, *ex parte* Burbage; Wallace, pp. 91-92). This last allusion is teasingly unclear.[18]

---

continued. Giles Allen succeeded in retaining possession of the ground until his death in 1608, but his widow seems to have capitulated to the Peckhams by 1612.

[18] Waller was knighted in 1572; little else is known of him.

24 June 1584—John Robson's Lease to the George Garden

Brayne and Myles had borrowed twenty-seven pounds from one
Alice Herne of London, widow, presumably through the agency of
her natural brother, one "John Robson Cittizen and Writer of the
Courte *Lettre* of London." As the due date for the debt drew near,
they cast about for means of renewing it. Robson explained that his
sister needed cash, being herself in debt, and thus was unwilling to
extend their bond; he offered, however, to pay the debt for them
himself, in exchange for a favorable lease to the garden plot behind
the George. They agreed, and in return for Robson's clearing them
of this indebtedness they gave him a ten-year lease to the garden
(which Robson described as being 107½ feet long and 34½ feet in
breadth) at an annual rental of four pence, payable quarterly at
the rate of one penny per quarter. The lease, though dated 22 July
1584, was to run from the previous month's feast of the nativity of
St. John the Baptist, 24 June, one of the traditional quarter days and
locally better known as Midsummer Day. Four years later, in 1588,
Robson would take them to court for their breach of this lease
(Req.2/262/42).

During this period they had other creditors as well, one of whom
was a widow seeking to collect a debt owed to her late husband:
Brayne and Myles had owed some twenty pounds on a bond to
Anthony Noble, a carpenter, the debt growing due "for Carpentrye
woᵏke at the In wᵗout Allgate called the George." Noble had died in
the autumn of 1580, so the work in question must have been done in
the early months of Brayne's lease. His widow Ellen had then
married one White, her second husband, and White at one point
"caused the said Brayne to be arested" for the debt. He was released
when two friends, John Gardener and James Burbage, stood surety
for him for the payment of the debt "and of more money wᵗ all." The
arrangement was that Brayne would pay five pounds a year until the
debt was retired; but despite the assurances of his guarantors,
Brayne refused to pay, even though the widow Noble "and her said
husband Whyte made many Joᵣneys from ther housse in Sᵗ Johnes
street to the place called the Theater beyond Shordiche to the said
Brayne for the said money but had it not." White, in anger, finally
sued Burbage and Gardener, an action that produced results in the
form of yet another agreement to pay the debt (C.24/226/10, *ex parte*
Burbage; Wallace, pp. 88-89). It is not clear what impelled Burbage
to stand surety for Brayne at this juncture, in the midst of their own
quarrel about the playhouse.

9 November 1584—Brayne and Warde at Law

Roger Warde, the London scrivener and moneylender who three years earlier had found Brayne insufficient to serve as surety for a loan and had "forgiven" him in exchange for a pot of beer, surprised Brayne at this juncture by suing him in the Court of King's Bench for the debt. Brayne brought a countersuit in the Court of Requests (Reg. 2/181/47), rehearsing the circumstances of the signing of the bond, of Warde's rejection of him as surety, and of his understanding that the debt had been made null and void by the pot of beer.

Winter of 1584/85—Brayne Rejoins the Grocers

For some reason, John Brayne was moved in 1584/85 to renew his membership in the Worshipful Company of Grocers. The accounts for this year include an entry for "John Brayne—ij^s" as payment of the annual assessment of brotherhood money. Brayne had last paid this assessment in the accounting year 1577/78, some seven years earlier. Perhaps his intention was to renew his association with his company, perhaps even to return to the trade of grocer in some fashion, though likely from the fringe of Whitechapel rather than from his former central location in Bucklersbury. But such an ambition, if it existed, was not to be realized: Brayne appears no further in the Grocers' accounts after this last entry of two shillings.

15 June 1586—Brayne's Death and Burial

The registers of St. Mary Matfellon, the Whitechapel parish church, record the burial of "John Braines" on this date (GLRO, P.93/MRY/4). Henry Bett, an attorney of Lincoln's Inn, remembered in 1592 having heard stories of a physical struggle between Brayne and Myles, that Brayne had "charged Miles wth his deathe" because of "certaine stripes geven him by Miles," and that Brayne's widow had had Myles called "befor an enquest held by the Crowner for the Countie of Middlesex, for the enquirie thereof" (C.24/226/10, *ex parte* Burbage; Wallace, p. 86). None of the other deponents or litigants recollected these matters; Bett, however, was the only lawyer among them.

10 August 1586—Brayne's Will Proved

John Brayne's will was proved on this date in the Commissary Court (GHL, ms. 9171/17, fo. 29ᵛ). For guildsmen active in their companies, some notice of death usually appears in the accounts— some legacy left to the company in the case of prosperous members, alms given to widows in the case of less fortunate brothers, sometimes funeral obsequies or memorials. No such entries occur in the Grocers' records to mark the passing of John Brayne; indeed, there is no evidence that his company was even aware of his death.

Two years after Brayne's death, James Burbage spoke of his deceased brother-in-law as "Late of White Chappell" and noted that "he had no children" (C.3/222/83; Wallace, p. 42). A year before that, in 1587, Brayne's widow had described her circumstances at the George Inn in 1580, affirming that in that year Brayne "had not any childrene or any other greate charge save only hym selfe and . . . his wief" (C.2.Eliz./B.13/ 5). But Brayne and his wife had not always been childless: the registers of St. Stephen's Walbrook record the christening of three sons and a daughter over the course of eight years. By the time of Brayne's leasing of the George in 1579, however, all of these children had died.[19] The problem does not end there, however; a provision in the will of Brayne's widow, Margaret, further complicates the matter. Margaret Brayne made her will in April 1593, a few days before her death, and in it she requested that Robert Myles "keepe, educate & bringe vpp Katherine Brayne my husband*es* daughter of whome I hoape he wilbee good vnto and haue an honest care for her p*referment*" (GHL, ms. 9171/18, fo. 26ᵛ; ms. 9172/16A, no. 96). The wording implies that the child was her husband's but not hers. The girl must have been at least seven years old in 1593, given the date of Brayne's own death; and as she still needed bringing up, she was probably not over sixteen. Had there been an illicit liaison in his last years which Brayne manfully acknowledged? The record is silent.[20]

---

[19] Robert, christened 18 October 1565, buried 16 January 1566; Roger, christened 23 December 1566, buried 13 August 1568; John, christened 4 March 1573, buried 2 April 1573; Rebecca, christened 2 November 1568, no record of her burial at St. Stephen's, though the widow Brayne's testimony suggests that she was dead before her tenth year.

[20] In a forthcoming essay Herbert Berry takes a different view, proposing that Katherine was indeed Margaret's daughter; the wording of the will, he suggests, was designed to counter a painful rumor that the child was hers but not her husband's.

II

This [the notion of language as mediation] will not be news to literary theorists, but it has not yet reached the historians buried in the archives hoping, by what they call a "sifting of the facts" or "the manipulation of the data," to *find* the form of the reality that will serve as the object of representation in the account that they will write when "all the facts are known" and they have finally "got the story straight."

—Hayden White

Brayne's death in 1586 provides a convenient stopping point for this synoptic view of the documentary history of the early years of the Theater. The chapter, already overlong, has not yet exhausted even the materials available for those first ten years. I stop well short of achieving the goals ascribed by Hayden White to those imagined archival drudges intent on knowing "all the facts." I have not reached that point, nor have I "got the story straight"; indeed, I have tried to resist constructing a story, preferring instead to explore the gaps and discontinuities in the evidence itself.

The Theater had another decade and more of its life still to endure at the Shoreditch site; and its major timbers, after a brief trip up the river, were to stand for an even longer period on the Bankside. As the building's active life continued, so did the disputes that surrounded it. Brayne having died, Robert Myles finally came into his own, launching a series of claims and counterclaims that would finally exhaust the patience of the courts. Myles held a shaky but exploitable title to the George Inn, both in a legitimate lease to a moiety of the holding and in a phony lease to the whole of it. On the strength of these documents he proceeded, in April 1587, to have the widow Brayne evicted from the premises (C.2.Eliz./B.13/5). He also began a steady stream of litigation against the Burbages, on behalf, so he argued, of the widow Brayne's rights in the Theater and Curtain.

But that is a further story, and 1587—the year of Jerome Savage's death and of Henslowe's groundbreaking for the Rose playhouse—is far enough to come for my present purposes. Setting the materials

---

The epigraph is from Hayden White, *Tropics of Discourse: Essays in Cultural Criticism* (Baltimore: Johns Hopkins University Press, 1978), p. 126.

for an account of the Theater against the materials available for an account of the playhouse at Newington Butts, one is struck not only by the far greater quantity of information available for the former but by the different kinds of issues each set of documents raises. The complexities of financing the Theater, and the antagonisms between its two principal entrepreneurs, must make us wonder if Jerome Savage did not face similar problems with money and with partners. The surviving Newington documents, concerned with other issues, are silent on these matters. In constructing an account of Savage's enterprise, we too are made silent by lack of evidence, and we omit consideration of matters that the Theater records teach us must have been as important to Savage as to Burbage. *Pas de documents, pas d'histoire.*

CHAPTER EIGHT

Another Playhouse at Shoreditch: The Curtain, 1576

I

I will do what I can for them all three, for so I have promised, and
I'll be as good as my word.

— *Merry Wives of Windsor*, III. iv

Surviving accounts of the Curtain playhouse are even more
sketchy and unsatisfactory than those of the playhouse at Newington Butts, though the Curtain's location in Shoreditch has enabled it
to ride along on the coattails of our interest in the Theater and thus
to remain better situated in our common consciousness. Chambers
was able to devote four pages to it (as against only one for the Butts
playhouse), but he had to acknowledge that his account of it was
"little more than a pendant" to his narrative of its better-known
neighbor (*ES* 2:402). We have also had a name, that of one Henry
Laneman, available to us since 1913, when Wallace published his
transcriptions of the lawsuits involving the Theater, though we have
not been entirely certain how to understand Laneman's description
of himself in his Chancery deposition as "having the profit*t*es of the
playes Done at the housse called the Curten."[1] Wallace took these
words to mean that Laneman was the "proprietor of the Curtain," a
reasonably safe if unhelpful reformulation.

At the time of his deposition in 1592, Laneman had presented
himself to the court as "Henry Laneman of london gentlema*n*" and

---

[1] PRO, C.24/226/11; C. W. Wallace, "The First London Theatre: Materials for a
History," *Nebraska University Studies* 13 (1913), 149.

was so spoken of by Burbage and others during the course of the lawsuit. It may be that none of them knew Laneman in any other capacity. Such titles were easily adopted in the later sixteenth century and often had little to do with lineage or breeding; we have seen that the stage player John Garland became a "gentleman" in Old Ford, though we cannot say exactly how. Something similar probably occurred with Henry Laneman; his status was likely adopted by force of will, abetted by a perceived financial standing, rather than conferred by birth. Like Richard Hickes, the first landlord of the Butts playhouse, Henry Laneman had begun his adult life as a yeoman of the queen's guard (though not, it seems, by way of an apprenticeship in the Company of Grocers). In their capacity as guardsmen, Hickes and Laneman would likely have known one another—the queen's guard seldom numbered above twelve dozen men—and thus would have been aware of their correlative roles as the titular holders of land on which playhouses stood.

Laneman was born about 1538, by his own testimony, and may have been somewhat younger than Hickes; certainly he was later in beginning his career in the royal household. Hickes's name appears in a list of yeomen of the guard as early as 1559, while Laneman's first appearance was in 1576. Lists have not survived for each year, so there is at present no way to be more precise about these relative events than to say that Hickes was a guardsman in 1559 and Laneman (who would have just entered his twenties in that year) was not. Hickes died some two decades before Laneman, but little about their respective ages can be concluded from this datum.

By 1576, the date of his first appearance in a list of yeomen, Laneman had already assumed the status of gentleman; perhaps it seemed a reasonable accoutrement for one of the queen's guard. The registers of the parish church of St. Andrew's in Holborn (GHL, ms. 6667/1) record the christenings of "Mary landman doughter of henry landman gent" in 1577, of "Christiver Laneman sone of henry laneman gent" in 1580, of "Richard lanman sone of henry lanman gen" in 1581, of "Elsabeth laneman dought^r of henry lanesman . . . in B of Ely Chappell" in 1584, of "Alexsander lanman sone of henry laneman gen" in 1588, and of "William Landman sone of henry landman gent" in 1590. These entries indicate a continued residence in the same parish for at least fifteen years.

Laneman also appears with some regularity among the various documents in the Public Record Office, where the name is invariably spelled "Lanman." His first appearance, as "Henrie Lanman" in

1576, is in the lay subsidy roll that identifies him as a yeoman of her majesty's chamber in ordinary. He continues to appear among the yeomen of the chamber in subsequent lay subsidy rolls for the royal household through 1602. "Henrie Lanman one of the yeomen of her Maiesties Chamber in Ordinarie" appears also in several certificates of residence issued in connection with the subsidies, from 1590 through 1604. The certificate for 1592 has him living in the ward of Farringdon Without (the ward in which St. Andrew's parish lay), while those of 1601 and 1604 describe him as living at Greenwich.[2]

The move to Greenwich was one of the steps in Laneman's attempt to better his station. His first recorded effort in that cause was in 1580, when "yor faythfull servaunte Henrye Laneman one of the ordynarye yeomen of yor Maties Chamber" petitioned the queen for the grant of a lease in reversion of "so muche of yor Highnes landes ... as shall amount to the cleere yerelye valew of xx^{tie} markes [i.e., £13 6^s 8^d] . . . wthowte fyne." The request was not unusual,[3] and the grant was awarded within the month, to the parsonage of Kingsbury, at the northern edge of Warwickshire, some thirty miles north of Stratford. In 1583, in response to another petition, the queen granted to "henr*icum* lanman unu*m* ordinar*iorum* valect*orum* cam*ere* n*ostre*" a reversion to the rectory and precincts of Broad-hempston, near Totnes in Devon.

Such grants were in essence gifts of income, requiring only a proper degree of stewardship. But in 1593 Laneman was awarded the keepership of the royal park at Greenwich ("Custodiam & offic*ium* Custodie Parci n*ost*ri de Grenewiche"), a grant apparently entailing residence—hence the move, as noted above. He was there by 1597, for in that year Henry Laneman of Greenwich, yeoman, was one of the defendants in a Chancery suit regarding the

---

[2] The terms "yeoman of the chamber" and "yeoman of the guard" were used interchangeably in the records to describe this group of functionaries. The relevant rolls are PRO, E.179/69/93, /69/95, /69/100A, /70/107, /70/115, /266/13; the certificates are E.115/242/162 (Farringdon Extra), /243/22 (Greenwich), /243/31, /243/145, /248/127, /250/36,/251/56 (Greenwich).

[3] Wallace T. MacCaffrey describes the granting of such petitions as "royal favour of a more or less routine character," of which a common form was "a lease of royal land on special terms: among grantees of such leases are to be found not only the great ones of the court but such humble royal servants as cooks, yeomen, or porters. The lease (sometimes in possession but more commonly in reversion) was granted without payment of a fine, enabling the recipient to sublet, probably to the sitting tenant, collecting the fine himself and reaping a handsome profit" ("Place and Patronage in Elizabethan Politics," in *Elizabethan Government and Society: Essays Presented to Sir John Neale*, ed. S. T. Bindoff, J. Hurstfield, and C. H. Williams [London: Athlone Press, 1961], p. 114).

nondelivery of certain obligations. In 1605, after a dozen years in the post, Henry Laneman, the keeper at Greenwich, surrendered his grant to the king for confirmation; it may not have been returned to him, for he is soon found back in the City. His name disappears from the lay subsidy rolls and from the certificates of residence at this point, and on 17 February 1606 "Mr Henrie Lanman" was buried in the chancel of St. Mary Woolchurch Haw, a parish in whose registers other Lanemans, including his son Christopher (then twenty-six), may be found.[4] Laneman apparently never made a will: two weeks after his burial the Prerogative Court of Canterbury issued letters of administration to "*Christo*fero Lanman filio *natu*rali et *legi*timo Henrici Lanman . . . def*uncti*" authorizing him to dispose of the estate.[5]

The bulk of these documents (the lay subsidies, certificates, petition and grant, privy seal warrant, and surrender) clearly refer to one person, the queen's yeoman; the remainder (the Chancery suit, burial, and administration, along with the baptismal records from St. Andrew's) quite probably refer to the same person, in his alternative role as gentleman. I would not, like Wallace, claim to have made an exhaustive search, but, as with Jerome Savage earlier, I have found no evidence of anyone named Henry Lanman or Laneman in any contexts other than the yeomanly and gentlemanly ones I here adduce. Unfortunately, none of these documents, not even the petition, bears the signature of Laneman the yeoman. The proprietor of the Curtain playhouse, who described himself in 1592 as "Henry Laneman of london gentlema*n*," age fifty-four or thereabouts, signed his deposition twice, once on each page, and each time as "henry lanman*n*." We need some way of demonstrating that all these instances involve the same person. A conventional means of making such an identification is to find a signature of Laneman of

---

[4] Peter Hunningborne and Margaret Hickes, two of the participants in the Newington Butts narrative, were married in this parish, a fact suggesting that the Hickes family may have been parishioners as well, though there is no subsequent record either of Richard Hickes's burial or of any Hunningborne baptisms. The Laneman family probably settled there late in the 1590s.

[5] The petition is Cecil Petitions no. 1599 (Hatfield House), abstracted in Historical Manuscripts Commission, *Salisbury* (1892), 4:76, and the burial is recorded in the parish register (GHL, ms. 7644). All the other documents are in the PRO: the Kingsbury ("Kynesbury") grant is C.66/1376, memb. 10; the Broadhempston grant is C.66/1225, memb. 15; the privy seal warrant for the Greenwich grant is C.82/1558, memb. 4, and the corresponding enrollment is C.66/1397, memb. 44; the Chancery suit is C.2.Eliz./L.11/46; the surrender is C.54/1780; the letters of administration are Prob.6/7, fo. 30.

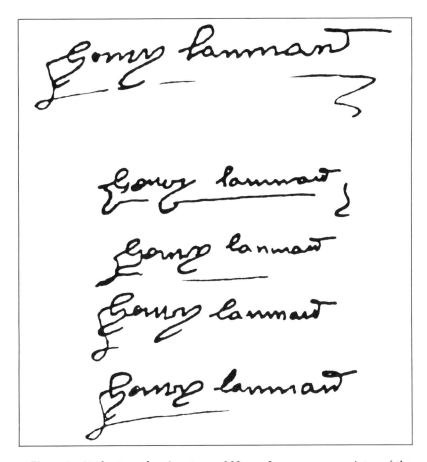

Figure 8. At the top, the signature of Henry Laneman, proprietor of the Curtain playhouse, in 1592 [PRO, C.24/226/11]; below that, four signatures of Henry Laneman, yeoman of the queen's guard, from 1582 [BL, ms. Harl. 1644]

the queen's guard for comparison with the two surviving signatures of Laneman of the Curtain. Fortunately a dozen such signatures survive, in the account book for 1581 of Sir Thomas Heneage, the treasurer of the queen's chamber: Laneman the guardsman signed his name in this book each month when he received his pay (see Figure 8). Heneage's clerk noted against each of Laneman's payments that the money was "paid to his owne hand*es*," so the signatures are his own. These match the signatures on the deposition, thus confirming the identification of the gentleman with the yeoman.[6]

With these several links in place, then, we have the beginnings of a rudimentary biographical frame for the "proprietor of the Curtain." We may note, first, that Laneman seems to have felt no greater need to live near his playhouse in Shoreditch than Richard Hickes felt about living at Newington. From 1576 and possibly earlier until 1593 or so, Laneman lived in Holborn, in the northwestern quadrant of the City; then he moved to Greenwich for about ten years, then back to the City, to St. Mary Woolchurch Haw, perhaps to live with his son, retaining all this while his connection to the royal household and his status as a yeoman of the guard. One is tempted to speculate, on the grounds of this similarity, that Laneman was no more involved in the actual construction or management of his playhouse than was Hickes but that he stood, like Hickes, in an intermediary position between the primary landlord and the actual entrepreneur, whoever that latter person may have been in the case of the Curtain.

We have a fair sense of who the primary landlord was. Maurice Long and his son William, citizens and clothworkers of London, had purchased the property in 1567 from James Blount, Baron Mountjoy. Maurice Long mortgaged the lease to one William Allen in 1571 but apparently redeemed it and later passed his interest to his son; whether before or after 1576 is not known.[7] The most circumstantial description of the property is contained in a deed of sale, dated 18 March 1581—four years and more after the Curtain playhouse had been built—by which William Long of London, clothworker, promised to transfer his title and interest in the premises "before the laste daie of Aprill nexte com*m*yng" to Thomas Harbert of Cheapside, London, girdler. The property that was to change hands at that time was described therein as "All that the house ten*eme*nte or lodge com*m*onlie called the Curtayne And also all that parcell of grounde and close walled and inclosed with a bricke Wall on the West and Northe part*es* and in part With a mudde Wall at the West side or

[6] BL, ms. Harl. 1644, ff. 110^v, 118^v, 126^v, 134^v, 143, 150^v, 160^v, 169^v, 177^v, 185^v, 193^v, 201^v.

[7] These details are in *ES* 2:401. Maurice Long was master of his company in 1567; he died in 1577 and was buried in his parish, St. Peter's Westcheap; administration of his estate was granted to his widow, Jane, in accordance with the terms of his will, in which he left bequests to his son William and eleven other living children.

ende towardes the southe called also the Curtayne close. . . . And also all and singuler other mesuages tentes edifices and buildinges With all and singuler their appurten^ances erected and builded vppon the saide close called the Curtayne or vppon any parte or parcell thereof or to the same nere adioyninge." The various buildings so imprecisely described in this passage were further said to be "nowe or late in the seuerall tenures or occupacions of Thomas Wilkinson Thomas Wilkins Roberte medley Richard hickes henrie lanman and Roberte manne or any of them."[8]

Wilkinson and Manne, who had also been named in the earlier deed transferring the property from Mountjoy to the Longs in 1567, would seem to have been tenants in some part of the property for nearly fifteen years by the time of the sale to Harbert. The other names are presumably of people who had taken up tenancy since that date. "Tenancy" as described in such documents means little more than the holding of a lease; these people may have lived on the premises, or held their parcel for some other purpose, or sublet it to others. Of the six men so named (or the five, if "Thomas Wilkinson Thomas Wilkins" is a scribal error), only two, Richard Hickes and Henry Laneman, hold out hope of further identification.

Fleay had come upon this document in the 1870s and, recognizing none of the names, took the six to be players in "the Curtain Company, 1581."[9] Some of them may have been, but if so they are otherwise lost to us. But since Wallace published his transcriptions in 1913, the name "henrie lanman" has evoked other associations. It seems likely that the "henrie lanman" named here is the guardsman of our inquiry and that his name appears in this list not because he lived here—we know that he lived in Holborn during these years— but because he was the leaseholder of "the house tenemente or lodge commonlie called the Curtayne."[10]

Even more intriguing, the name immediately preceding Laneman's in the list is that of "Richard hickes"; one is sorely tempted to imagine that this is our man as well, Laneman's fellow guardsman. The Hickes of our earlier narrative lived in the City, presumably in

---

[8] PRO, C.54/1098.

[9] F. G. Fleay, *A Shakespeare Manual* (London, 1876), p. 120. Fleay also names Isaac Dowle, Thomas Stoddard, and Richard Bent as players in this company, though without comment; these names are untraceable to the best of my knowledge.

[10] The phrasing may seem to suggest a structure other than a playhouse, but in a deed of 1611 (PRO, C.54/2075, memb. 17) the building is described as "that large messuage or tenemente built of Timber & thatched now in decay called the Curtaine . . . wherein they vse to keepe Stage Playes."

the parish of St. Mary Woolchurch Haw, from which his daughter Margaret was married in 1572. We know that he did not live at Newington, even though the dean and chapter of Christ Church, Canterbury, regarded him as their tenant there. In similar fashion, the Richard Hickes of the present document need not have lived at Shoreditch. If he is our man, then his name may appear beside Laneman's because he, like Laneman, held tenancy rights to property in Curtain close while living elsewhere.

In sum, then, we have an identifiable landlord in the Longs (or perhaps, by 1576, only in William Long), and five or six identifiable lessees or tenants of whom one, Laneman, apparently held the ground rights to the playhouse site. We still lack any information about the person or persons who might actually have erected the playhouse. If there is to be a Curtain narrative, someone is needed for the role played in our other narratives by Jerome Savage and James Burbage; if we had a name to fit that role at the Curtain it would probably tell us something as well about the playhouse's first occupants. Conjecture on this latter head has been curiously muted. Fleay proposed that the first occupants were the players of the earl of Sussex, who was lord chamberlain from 1572 to 1583. The leader of the Sussex group in 1576 was John Adams, later (like John Singer and John Garland) one of the charter members of the queen's players. This is a quite reasonable guess and worth further consideration. Chambers, for whom such free speculation was uncongenial, maintained that the companies that occupied the Curtain "can for the most part only be guessed at" (*ES* 2:402) and declined to entertain Fleay's proposal. The question has proved intractable (or perhaps merely unchallenging) for later scholars as well.

Adams is a possible candidate, but the historian who elects to pursue him soon finds difficulties. Unlike James Burbage or Jerome Savage (or Henry Laneman or Richard Hickes for that matter), John Adams has a name that is ubiquitous in documents of the period. Any researcher bent on finding instances of someone with that name will quickly be inundated with references, virtually all of which will turn out (sometimes after laborious reading) not to be the stage player. Life being too short, I have not pressed this investigation as exhaustively as I might have; but the prospect of an Adams-Sussex link with the erection and first use of the Curtain continues to strike me as worth entertaining.

An alternative construction is, of course, that Laneman himself was the motivating force behind the erection of the playhouse. Nothing in his life (the little that we know of it) suggests such an interest on his part, but the absence of evidence is not in itself evidence for anything other than its absence. A corollary for this position is that we know very little about the life of Aaron Holland, the builder in 1605 of the Red Bull playhouse, and the little that we do know suggests no greater interest in the stage than we seem to have with Laneman. In Holland's case we have suggestions of an ongoing business relationship with the player Thomas Swinnerton but no evidence that the Red Bull was Swinnerton's initiative. We know rather more than that about Laneman, in that we have his own testimony about his role in 1585 as "having the profit*tes* of the playes Done at the housse called the Curten," whatever we may finally take this to mean.

II

Thou shalt have a share in our purchase, as I am a true man.
—*1 Henry IV*, II. i

Laneman's description of the profit-sharing arrangement into which he had entered with Brayne and Burbage in 1585 remains the principal piece of information we have had about the Curtain since Wallace published his documents. We may recall that Burbage, when he signed the twenty-one-year lease for Giles Allen's Holywell property in 1576, had committed himself to spending two hundred pounds to improve the existing buildings on the premises within the first ten years and that Allen, for his part, had agreed to respond to the improvements by renegotiating the lease, again for a twenty-one-year period, at any time within those first ten years. The ten-year period would conclude on 12 April 1586; in the ninth year, in 1585, Burbage went to Giles Allen for his extension.

All had not gone smoothly for Burbage during those nine years, as we have seen. True, he had spent two hundred pounds and more, or so he claimed, and had erected a playhouse; but he had overextended himself, entered into a clumsy arrangement with Brayne which led to arbitration and then to litigation, even pawned the lease for £125 to John Hyde. Burbage seems to have been in no hurry to redeem it from Hyde: the lease was still in Hyde's possession in 1585, with thirty pounds or more yet owing, when Burbage began to treat with Giles Allen for its redrawing. Allen, for reasons of his own, kept putting Burbage off: 1585 turned into 1586 with no new lease agreed on, and shortly thereafter the ten years were concluded and the option was void (*ES* 2:387; Wallace, pp. 151, 167).

Burbage's need for money in 1585 was perhaps no more acute than it had been earlier, but his efforts to improve his position were becoming more imaginative. As we saw in the previous chapter, he seems to have found it easier to be unscrupulous in his dealings and to be unmoved by the claims of the Brayne faction that he filched money from the common box, or stuffed it down his shirt, or otherwise attempted to deceive his fellows. If Burbage was growing more reprehensible in his behavior, he was also growing more secure about being in debt. By 1585 he had managed to keep his and Brayne's creditor Hyde at bay for six years; if the negotiations with Giles Allen for the new lease, had been successful, Burbage might have been tempted to default on the remainder of that debt by arguing that Hyde's lease was now a worthless piece of parchment. Fortunately, Burbage and Brayne were spared the hazards of such a course, for Allen's intransigence supervened; Burbage and Brayne ultimately failed to get their new lease and were forced to redeem the old one from Hyde and to prepare for its expiration in 1597.

I take it as part of Burbage's growing ambition that he opened negotiations in the summer of 1585 with Laneman about the business prospects of their two playhouses. The Curtain, having been in existence almost as long as the Theater, was probably twinned with it in the popular consciousness and may well have been meeting with equivalent success as a financial enterprise. The outward tenor of the proposal made by Burbage and Brayne to Laneman was that they pool their profits for a term of seven years, each party taking half the revenue from each playhouse. We learn from the depositions that Laneman agreed to these terms, from which we must conclude that they all saw the arrangement as somehow advantageous; but Laneman was also properly chary of Burbage's good faith, perhaps from firsthand observation, and would not agree to the arrangement without binding Burbage and Brayne more securely for their faithful performance.

Burbage recalled his own side of this agreement in a deposition taken some six years later, on 16 February 1591, in which he spoke of his payments to Laneman as a "graunt." He deposed that he and John Brayne did "Joyne in A graunt to one Henry Laynmann gent / of the one Moytie of the said Theater & of the proffittes and comodities growing therby for certain yeres yet enduring / as by the

Dede *therof* maye appere / and bound them self in g^t bond*es* for the performa*n*ce thereof."[11] Burbage's statement in this deposition complicates an otherwise simple issue. In his answer to this interrogatory (no. 2), he tried to explain why he could not, in 1590, surrender a moiety of the Theater to the widow Brayne by her agent, Robert Myles, in accordance with the agreement between Brayne and Burbage made in 1578. Burbage argued that the agreement to share the playhouse was voided by Brayne himself when he joined with Burbage in 1585 in awarding a moiety of the Theater to Laneman. Burbage deposed that in 1590 Myles came to him demanding "the moytie of the said Theatre and the Rent therof" for the widow Brayne, claiming that by the terms of Burbage's agreement with Brayne "the moytie of the Theater & the Rent therof are to be had & receyved by [her]." "So it was indede," replied Burbage; but that was "before Jo. Brayne himself and [Burbage] Did . . . Joyne in A graunt to one Henry Laynman*n*," etc. This claim by Burbage is the only suggestion on record of Laneman's receiving any interest in the property itself. The other deponents, and the framers of the interrogatories as well, speak of the arrangement with Laneman as an agreement to share profits only. Laneman himself described the agreement in those terms. I see the weight of the evidence as favoring the latter view, discounting Burbage's perhaps opportunistic claim to have surrendered half the playhouse.

Laneman's own deposition, taken in the following year, describes both sides of the agreement, and is even more circumstantial: "about vij yeres now shalbe this next Wynter [i.e., Michaelmas] they the said Burbage & Braynes having the profitt*es* of Playes made at the Theater / and this Depo^t having the profitt*es* of the playes Done at the housse called the Curten / nere to the same / the said Burbage and Braynes taking the Curten as an Esore to their playe housse / did of ther own moci*o*n move this Depo^t that he wold agree that the proffitt*es* of the said ij° Playe howses might for vij yeres space be in Dyvydent betwene them / Wherunto this Deponent vpon reosonable condici*o*ns & bondes agreed & consented and so co*n*tynueth to this Daie."[12]

Edward Alleyn's older brother, John, one of the admiral's men, recalled the externals of this agreement. He knew that "one Henrye Laynman*n* had . . . part of the proffitt*es* of the . . . [Theater] & so must till Mych^es now next coming" [i.e., 29 September 1592]. Alleyn

[11] PRO, C.24/221/12, *ex parte* Brayne; Wallace, p. 62.
[12] PRO, C.24/226/11, *ex parte* Brayne, 30 July 1592; Wallace, p. 149.

also recalled having seen Burbage make some of the payments to Laneman, "wch profittes (as this depo^t hath heard the said James Burbage saye) were due vnto the said Lenmann / and that he & the said Brayne were both bounde by wryting to paye the same vnto him / in consideracion that the said lenmann did graunt vnto them the one half of the proffittes of the other play house there by / called the Curten."[13]

Since 1913, when Wallace published the documents from which these citations are drawn, historians of the theater have been in the awkward position of having to note the existence of this arrangement without being able to say much about it. Chambers tried his best to make sense of it; to his mind, the arrangement must have had something to do with the companies of players occupying the two houses. He had not, in *The Elizabethan Stage*, suggested the queen's own players as possible occupants of the Curtain in 1585, but he later began to entertain this possibility, and though he could not bring himself to state it outright, he hinted at it in his *William Shakespeare*, conjecturing there that "the Queen's men proved strong enough to occupy more than one playhouse" in 1584 and further proposing that this hypothesis "may explain an arrangement by which the Curtain was taken for a term of seven years from Michaelmas 1585 as an 'easer' to the Theatre."[14] Chambers's rhetorical reticence prevented him both from formulating a proposal any more concrete than this and from engaging in intelligent speculation; as a result, the combined intimations of his claim are studiously nebulous.

Further, in their very terseness the intimations are misleading. The "strength" of the queen's players in occupying more than one playhouse seems to have been primarily a skill in proliferation, to judge from contemporary comment. The Court of Aldermen observed that in 1584, when the queen's players had been the only company licensed to play within the City, "all the places of playeing were filled with men calling themselues the Quenes players"; the aldermen believed that the players should be constrained "not to diuide themselues into seueral companies." No doubt the queen's men were guilty as charged, but their practice may have been confined to the City innyards, for against the evidence of the aldermen we have William Fleetwood's observation of the same

---

[13] PRO, C.24/228/10, *ex parte* Burbage, 6 May 1592; Wallace, pp. 125–26.
[14] E. K. Chambers, *William Shakespeare* (Oxford, 1930), 1:31.

summer that though the queen's men were playing in the suburbs at the Theater, the company in the Curtain was Lord Arundel's.[15]

In any event, the queen's men presumably managed their own affairs. Had they desired in 1585 to divide themselves and engage a second playhouse, they might have done so on their own initiative, also deciding among themselves how they might share their profits. In his 1591 deposition, James Burbage, Lord Hunsdon's man by Burbage's own admission, claimed that he was not serving as their manager and would not feel called upon to bind himself "in g^t bonds" to Laneman on their behalf or, for that matter, to enter into any arrangement with Laneman at all. The 1585 agreement between Burbage and Laneman was most probably an arrangement between two playhouse owners, quite unrelated to the possible needs of prospective tenants. Such a position may in fact simplify the problem, for, as Chambers observed, "the relations between companies and playhouses during this period are very obscure."[16]

Somewhat less obscure, but nevertheless puzzling, is Laneman's comment about Burbage and Brayne "taking the Curten as an Esore." We are not certain what an Esore is; "easer" seems to have become the popular interpretation, but the meaning of the statement is sharpened only slightly by this change. The substitution of "easer" invites the inference that Burbage wanted the Curtain to provide relief from some strain or pressure on the Theater. Laneman may possibly have seen the agreement in that light, but the nature of the pressure is not clear. It cannot have been governmental, for the Curtain would have been equally subject to any such restraints. It cannot have been economic, for while an excess of spectators is proof of success, overflow crowds would seem to require a larger playhouse, not a second one. It cannot have been an excess of actors or of play scripts, for supernumerary players do not need an additional stage unless they intend to perform an additional play, and though an excess of plays might suggest to Burbage a useful possibility for expansion it could hardly have been a pressure on his existing facilities in other than a metaphorical sense. Nor is there help in the standard references. The examples listed in the *Oxford English Dictionary* under "easer" are all medicinal or curative in import rather than mercantile. The nearest potential equivalent, "easement," seems more appropriate as a contractual term but is

---

[15] *ES* 4:302, 298. Perhaps Chambers had forgotten these materials by the time he came to write his biography.

[16] Chambers, *William Shakespeare*, 1:31.

equally perplexing, for it is not clear in what technical sense (e.g., as a right of way) the Curtain might serve as an easement to the Theater.

Further, the very syntax of Laneman's comment is ambiguous. Burbage and Brayne, "taking the Curten as an Esore to their playe housse" (so run his words), urged Laneman "of ther own mocion . . . that he wold agree" to their proposal to share profits. The construction suggests that the Curtain was already an Esore during their negotiations. From Wallace onward, students have taken Laneman's comment to mean "desiring to take (i.e., engage) the Curtain as an Esore," but it may equally be construed "taking (i.e., perceiving) the Curtain to be an Esore," a perhaps undesirable condition to be alleviated by the terms of the agreement. The matter is very slippery, I am aware, but the question must be posed.

It may seem disingenuous on my part to look for reasons underlying the arrangement between Laneman and the Burbage-Brayne partnership when we cannot even be certain what the arrangement itself was; nonetheless, I intend to propose a narrative, which I think is independent of the Esore problem. Let me begin by reviewing the relation, described in Chapter 6, between Richard Hickes and the playhouse at Newington Butts. Having leased his playhouse lot to the player Jerome Savage, Hickes soon turned over to his son-in-law Peter Hunningborne the responsibility for managing the property and collecting Savage's rents. Hickes seems never to have lived at Newington himself. Laneman seems never to have lived in Shoreditch, either, unlike the Burbages, who settled there in 1576 and never left. Laneman's steady residence in Holborn, his resettlement at Greenwich, and his return to the City in his final year would seem to argue an ordering of priorities similar to Hickes's. Laneman may have known by 1585 that he had lost interest in the Curtain. He may have been ready, after the example of Hickes, to agree that someone else, perhaps his son Christopher, should manage the details of his playhouse for him, only remitting the appropriate revenue from time to time.

The surviving evidence does not suggest that Christopher Laneman undertook such duties. His name nowhere appears in connection with the playhouse, or in any context that would allow us to make a presumptive link. My own assumption is that Henry Laneman, having determined in 1585 to find someone to act as his agent for the playhouse, found James Burbage ready at hand on his own doorstep. But why did Burbage make his offer, and Laneman accept it, in 1585 rather than earlier or later? In pondering this question I realize that I have material for some anterior assumptions as well. By bearing in mind that Hickes might have been a tenant with Laneman in Shoreditch and by recalling that Hickes died early in 1585, I find a possible context for Laneman's agreement with Burbage in the late summer of 1585. I can imagine a scenario in which the guardsmen Laneman and Hickes, jointly holding a lease to some ground in Curtain close in the mid-1570s, found themselves after 1576 the joint proprietors of a playhouse called the Curtain, in a curious mirroring of the Brayne-Burbage association next door. My scenario presumes that Hickes, like Brayne, was the better business head in the partnership and that his death in 1585 left Laneman as sole proprietor of the playhouse, a role he did not wish to play. If there is any likelihood at all in this interpretation, it will make Richard Hickes—ground holder in 1576 for two of London's three new playhouses—a figure about whom we will wish to learn much more.

The initial agreement between Laneman and Burbage was for seven years. If the arrangement was indeed of a managerial nature, and if the relationship was satisfactory—and there is no indication that it was not—it is perhaps odd that the arrangement was not continued. The deponents quoted above all speak of a fixed term for the payments, two of them specifying the termination at Michaelmas 1592. No one suggested that the arrangement was to continue. A somewhat more radical scenario would posit that Laneman, who may have been ready in 1585 to lease his playhouse, was persuaded instead to sell it, and to sell it for the equivalent of seven years' income—the latter figure to be arrived at by averaging the earnings from both houses. Among Burbage's reasons for wanting the building may have been simple security: the absence of any record of litigation involving the Curtain playhouse suggests that Laneman's landlord, Thomas Harbert, was more tractable than Giles Allen, and this casualness may have appealed to Burbage. In his deposition, Laneman recalled that he was urged by Burbage and Brayne by "ther own mocion" to accept the proposal, and the bonds he required of them for their good performance further support such a notion. With a comfortable income from this arrangement, Laneman could turn his attention to matters of greater interest to him. If my conjectural Hickes scenario has any validity, Laneman may have preferred all along to have someone else manage the playhouse for him, leaving him free to be known as "Mr Henry Lanman of London gentleman," like his younger contemporary Francis Langley of the Swan, rather than as the "fellow" who was "the owner of the [playhouse]," as Fleetwood, a City official, had spoken of Burbage (*ES* 4:298).

One objection to the proposal that Laneman's agreement with Burbage was an agreement to sell might be that seven years' purchase is a low figure, the norm in such matters being fifteen. Evidence for this longer term comes readily to hand. Francis Langley, who held the Manor of Paris Garden, estimated its yearly value in 1594, in rents and revenues payable to him, at two hundred pounds. Ten years later his widow would complain of its low sale price: "the said manour being better woorth then two hundred poundes by the yere . . . was sould . . . for little more then twelue yeres purchase namely for the somme of five & twentie hundred poundes."[17]

But a playhouse was another matter. Its income was not fixed, and good entrepreneurship might increase it significantly. Henslowe's *Diary* shows receipts at the Rose of some £450 for the 1594/95 season, and of some £340 in the following season. Fifteen years' purchase at these figures would price the Rose at £6,000, an absurd amount when one recalls that a new playhouse could be built (as the Rose indeed was) for less than £1,000. But Burbage was no doubt aiming at just such profits. It might not be amiss to speculate from Henslowe's figures that the Theater or the Curtain was capable, in 1585, of £175 to £200 a season for the housekeepers. Seven years' purchase at these latter figures would bring us in the neighborhood of £1,300 or £1,400, a more credible sum, comprising (as it must) the purchase of both the building and the lease.

One might then construct a narrative in which Henry Laneman was receiving, between 1585 and 1592, an annuity of perhaps two hundred pounds, while Burbage and Brayne—soon Burbage alone— were operating two playhouses on the income from one. These would almost of necessity have been years of straitened circumstances. Burbage would have completed his purchase of the Curtain in 1592 and would have had one winter season of full profits from both playhouses before the plague closed him down in the spring of 1593. The plague of 1593/94 was a major watershed in the history of the playing companies, and a near disaster for playhouse owners, as Henslowe's surviving papers indicate. When playing resumed in

---

[17] PRO, C.2.Jas. I/L.13/62, the bill.

1594/95, however, business was better than ever. The Swan went up in 1595, and in 1596 James Burbage, with the expiration of Giles Allen's lease drawing ever nearer, purchased the building in Black-friars which he did not live to occupy. It is possible that he raised the capital for this purchase—some six hundred pounds for the lease alone—by carefully husbanding the profits of a successful 1595/96 season; it is equally likely, however, that a second source of funds for him came from the sale to his fellows of shares in the Curtain playhouse, for from this point onward the Curtain is to be found only in the hands of players. Thomas Pope held shares in both the Globe and the Curtain at his death in 1604. In 1611 the Curtain playhouse itself, "now in decay" but "wherin they use to keepe stage playes," was held by Thomas Greene of Queen Anne's men. John Underwood of the king's players held shares in the Curtain, the Globe, and Blackfriars at his death in 1624; as he did not join the company until about 1608 he must have acquired his share of the Curtain at that time.[18]

It is difficult, however, to ascertain when the letting-out of shares began. Burbage may have sold shares almost immediately in 1585, as a way of capitalizing the operation of two playhouses. There is no mention of this in the litigation of 1591/92, so it may be unlikely; but there is little mention of the Curtain at all in those voluminous records, so it is not out of the question. Alternatively, and more likely, Burbage may have offered shares to his fellows at some point between 1592 and 1596. If it was in 1595 or 1596, the general theatrical enthusiasm may have spurred their purchase, but by that time such shares may have been of limited value; the building was twenty years old, presumably somewhat the worse for wear, and of no certain future. A few years later, once the Globe was completed, prudence might well have dictated the selling of such holdings. This divestiture may explain why so few players are found on their deathbeds still seized of a piece of the Curtain.

One would wish to know a great deal more about the first ten years of the Curtain's life and more about the possible Laneman-Hickes partnership, if such there was—more, too, about James Burbage's expansion into the Curtain in 1585, and how it affected his operation from that point on. My own sense is that Laneman's action was tantamount to a withdrawal from the Curtain and that Burbage, who had had his hands full managing one playhouse from

---

[18] The descriptions of the Curtain in 1611 are from PRO, C.54/2075, no. 17.

1576 to 1585, found himself (on his own initiative, to be sure) from 1585 until perhaps 1596 the owner and manager of two playhouses.

III

> What players are they?
>
> —*Hamlet*, II. ii

A playhouse is a firmer and more substantial organization of the environment than is a playing company. It stands like the fix'd foot of Donne's compass, marking its steady presence on the ground even as its succession of occupants comes and goes. The historian of playhouses benefits from the general propensity of such structures to attract notice in a variety of records, from maps and plans through deeds and leases to assessments and lawsuits. Even a playhouse as underreported as the Curtain has left enough traces for us to hazard some guesses about its ownership and management. Companies of players, by contrast, are often quite invisible; the players of the earl of Sussex, for example, whom I earlier commended as reasonable candidates for the initial occupancy of the Curtain, are all but nonexistent in City records.

And yet the erection of the three playhouses we have just been considering—the Newington Butts playhouse, the Theater, and the Curtain—will have provided us with little more than the materials for an entrepreneurial history of land use if we make no effort to populate them with the assemblages of stage players for whom they were principally built. There seems to be some credible evidence for locating Warwick's players at the Butts from its first opening until 1580, and Oxford's thereafter; and Leicester's men ought reasonably to have been the first occupants of the Theater, even though we have no evidence to support such a presumption. But once past these assertions we are on swampier ground; the linking up of playhouses with playing companies is no less risky and uncertain now than it was in Chambers's day.

Chambers readily acknowledged the difficulties. "Before 1576," he wrote, "the Earl of Leicester's men and the Duttons were alone conspicuous" (*ES* 2:4); nor did he see matters improving in the years immediately following that date. More assiduous digging in the records, perhaps the chief contribution of our own age to the advancement of theater history, has altered our sense of what "conspicuous" might mean in this context; for example, in the decade between the Common Council's proclamation of 1574 and the formation of the queen's players in 1583, we have managed to accumulate, over the course of the last half century, evidence from various official documents of more than thirty-five companies of players with recognizable patrons.[19] Some of the companies identifiable during this ten-year span are mentioned only in provincial records, and are therefore sometimes described by modern scholars as "provincial" companies, a term that seems principally to mean that we have no evidence of the company's seeking a foothold in London. John Stockwood, in 1578, spoke of "eighte ordinarie places" in the City as occupied by players, a statement theater historians often take as an invitation to determine which eight playing companies were based in London in that year. But we need not restrict ourselves in that fashion; my own sense is that any company with an accredited patron and with business in London would have tried to secure its presence there and that the eight playing places might well have been host during that first decade to any number of companies seeking an audience and a reputation.

We know that "visibility" in London—which means, for us, survival in City records in some fashion—requires that a company had a brush with the law, a summons to court, or a fortuitous mention in some other document. We know of the existence of the players of Lord Vaux, for example, a group Chambers described as "extremely obscure" (*ES* 2:103), only because they were mentioned in a letter Gabriel Harvey wrote to Edmund Spenser in 1579; but Harvey spoke of Vaux's players in the same breath in which he named Leicester's, Warwick's, and Lord Rich's players. Such a context hardly implies that Vaux's players were fresh from the provinces or otherwise unknown in London; however, but for the chance survival of Harvey's letter we would not have known about

---

[19] The volumes of record transcriptions published by the Records of Early English Drama project have greatly augmented our awareness of the existence of playing companies. Added to our information from such other sources as the Malone Society *Collections*, these volumes furnish evidence of companies during the period 1574–1583 belonging to the earls of Arundel, Bath, Derby, Essex, Leicester, Lincoln, Oxford, Pembroke, Sussex (the lord chamberlain), Warwick, and Worcester; to the countess of Essex; to the lords Abergavenny, Bartholomew, Berkeley, Chandos, Clinton, Compton, Hertford, Charles Howard, Hunsdon, Morley, Mounteagle, Mountjoy, Rich, Seymour, Sheffield, Stafford, Stourton, Strange, Vaux, de la Warr, and Windsor; to Sir James FitzJames, Sir George Hastings, and Sir Thomas Lucy.

them at all. The probability remains strong that in the late 1570s and early 1580s there were other companies of players in London as familiar to playgoers as was Lord Vaux's, and with equally prominent patrons, even though they have left no trace in the records.

If I am right, then the task of identifying playing places with playing companies becomes well nigh impossible. The temptation to beg the question is therefore strong, especially as any proposal will be open to challenge. The venues open to playing companies after 1576 would have included, in addition to the three playhouses just discussed, the four "playing" inns where plays were known to have been performed in this period (the Bell, the Bull, the Cross Keys, and the Bel Savage), perhaps additional inns not known for playing in this period but known to have accommodated plays earlier (such as the Saracen's Head in Islington) or both earlier and later (the Boar's Head in Aldgate); and perhaps one or more private playing places such as Trinity Hall or Carpenters' Hall, both the sites of plays before 1576. Blackfriars, too, was active at this time, but with a company of children under Richard Farrant's direction, and so cannot properly be counted in our list. Stockwood's eight ordinary places may have comprised any combination of the above or included others unknown to us.

The picture that emerges from our discussion so far is of a City reasonably furnished with a variety of places where companies of players might ply their trade; furnished as well, so it would seem, with a population sufficiently interested in seeing plays to support the activity in those places, and perhaps even in others. The picture also suggests a fairly large number of playing groups that might have been present, on and off, in the City, and a City governing body that was intermittently, but not constantly, concerned about such presence and about the frequency and ubiquity of such public playing. Pieces of this picture might have appeared in their own day to be auspicious and might well have encouraged some companies of players to presume that it was not impossible to succeed in the City, and further that a degree of prosperity would attend their success. This presumption may be one way of explaining the presence in the City, in the decade after 1576, of companies such as Lord Vaux's, ready to try their hands at making a living. The paucity of evidence in this case suggests that Vaux's men failed in the attempt, but this should not be construed to mean that they were not there, or were not trying.

Playing Places, Players, Play Texts

I don't know whether I like it or not, but it's what I meant.
—Ralph Vaughan Williams, speaking of his Fourth Symphony

Any narrative centered on "1576" will inevitably find itself principally concerned with the erection and operation of playhouses. My own intention, professed at the outset, had been to learn more about the players and entrepreneurs involved with those playhouses; but their very involvement has forced my discussion reflexively back to the objects of their own attentions. As a consequence, the buildings themselves, as subjects of controversy and objects of litigation, have loomed larger in the book than I had initially intended. I have, at the least, tried to avoid any discussion of them as artifacts; my account pays no attention to the details of their construction, their size or shape or seating capacity, or even their outward physical appearance. While these matters would have been proper concerns of the entrepreneurs and players themselves, they are today principally the concern of the historian of playhouse architecture. My own interests lie elsewhere, inside and outside the buildings rather than with the buildings themselves, and the narratives I have been entertaining are not dependent on these features for their viability. Nonetheless, the building as notion, the building as locus, cannot be erased from any such account.

Indeed, after 1576 the existence of playhouses marks perhaps the most striking difference between playing "in London" and playing in the provinces. Before that date—with the possible exception of

The epigraph, Vaughan Williams's comment, was made during a BBC interview.

idiosyncrasies such as the Red Lion—players in both the City and the countryside played their plays and passed their hats in spaces not principally designed or intended for their occupancy. With the building of three playhouses in the environs of the City in 1576, a new kind of legitimacy arrived, social and economic rather than governmental or civic, psychological rather than legal. After 1576 there were, for playing companies with the right access to their proprietors, three proper places available for playing. A decade later a fourth appeared, then a fifth and sixth.[1] The presence of these buildings must have altered the mental landscape for players and playwrights alike; though one would be hard pressed to anchor such a notion in the relevant texts, it bears contemplation.

The relevant texts, or rather their absence, constitute the chief burden for the theater historian concerned with this issue. I speak not so much of documents, whose paucity has already been amply demonstrated in the foregoing chapters, but, more important, of the literary and theatrical texts that would add flesh to the bones of historical evidence. At least thirty-five identifiable playing companies with named patrons have been found in the records in the years immediately following 1576, and John Stockwood's reference to "eighte ordinarie places" of playing in the City in 1578 suggests that at any given moment eight of these companies were likely to be playing in those places. If, for the sake of argument, we were to take this number as a maximum, assuming that no more than eight companies played in or about London in this period, and if for these eight companies we were to guess conservatively that they played for only nine months in the year and only four days each week, then those eight companies alone would have provided over twelve hundred performances each year for London playgoers. How many different play texts would twelve hundred performances require? If we assume a generous average of a dozen performances for each text—Henslowe's average at the Rose was less than two-thirds that number—the playing companies in these eight favored locations

---

[1] I have not speculated in these pages on the reason for an eleven-year delay after 1576 before a fourth public playhouse, the Rose, made its appearance. If the three playhouses of 1576 were financially successful, or perceived to be so, one would expect other entrepreneurs to have followed their lead sooner. If, on the other hand, the three 1576 playhouses were only indifferently successful, Henslowe's project in 1587 may have been more rash than we assume. After the erection of the Rose, one waits another nine years, until after the disappearance of the structure at Newington Butts, before the next playhouse, the Swan, is built.

would have required a hundred or so different play scripts each year to satisfy the demands of their spectators. The twenty-odd companies not playing in London would have had a different set of constraints on their performing, but they too would have required play books. Even if they required only a third as many as the London players, our estimate would still need to rise to something like two hundred plays a year.

I mentioned earlier (in Chapter 5) how the Dutton brothers and Thomas Gough, all stage players, had contracted with one Rowland Broughton in 1572 to supply them with eighteen plays over the course of thirty months (whether Broughton was to write the plays or merely procure them is unclear). Such an arrangement strongly bespeaks a need for play books in goodly numbers, and there may well have been other such arrangements now lost to us. Broughton's failure to hold up his end of the bargain was sufficient grounds for the Duttons and Gough to take him to law, a move suggesting that what was at stake was not negligible. After 1576, with three additional playing places available, the demand for play books may have been even greater.

Yet for no single year in the ten years between 1576 and 1586 have more than five or six play texts survived, and the bulk of these are courtly or university plays. Scarcely a dozen in that whole decade may be classed as intended for the public playhouse or innyard; included in that dozen are a few of John Lyly's plays for children's companies and—surely the best known of the lot—the anonymous *Famous Victories of Henry V*, in which Richard Tarlton played to great acclaim at the Bull Inn. These few plays can hardly be representative, yet they are all we have. There is, in short, virtually no literary evidence to document what must have been an astonishingly active period in the life of the secular professional English drama.

So long as our focus is on dramatic texts, we are likely to view this early period as a desert and to remark on the sudden and gratifying appearance, in 1586 and 1587, of plays by the group collectively known as the University Wits, as though theatrical activity in London were waiting to be invented by graduates of Oxford and Cambridge. The appearance of their plays is, however, a key to the debt we do owe them: they seemed to understand, better than the commercial playwrights who were their contemporaries, the importance of publication. The sudden increase in the number of surviving play texts from the late 1580s onward is surely in part a consequence of the commercial playwright's introduction to new notions about the printworthiness of plays.

Robert Wilson and Richard Tarlton, playwrights whose apprenticeship had been on the stage rather than in the study, were among the beneficiaries of this new attitude, as their colleague Thomas Atchelow apparently was not. Certainly these men were nearer to the center of the adult professional playing tradition than were Lyly and George Peele and the other university men. We are fortunate that a few plays by Wilson and Tarlton have survived; had they not, we would have had virtually no access to this strand in the development of the commercial play text.

Much work remains to be done before a full history of the early adult professional theater can be written. Some of that work can be done in the archives, but not all of it; finding the pieces is not the same as fitting them together. The former activity is essential because it allows us to anchor our claims in evidence and thus to make what Hayden White calls "truths of correspondence," in contrast to the truths of coherence which may result from our adeptness at connecting these claims to one another. The hazard attending the latter task is that any resultant coherence will likelier be more characteristic of our account of reality than of reality itself. In this same vein, Richard Rorty warns us against believing "that the world splits itself up, on its own initiative, into sentence-shaped chunks called 'facts,' " and White himself observes that "any given linguistic protocol will obscure as much as it reveals about the reality it seeks to capture in an order of words."[2] The other part of the task facing theater historians, then, is to construct a viable set of premises within which their narratives may safely and effectively function.

---

[2]Richard Rorty, *Contingency, Irony, and Solidarity* (Cambridge: Cambridge University Press, 1989), p. 5; Hayden White, *Tropics of Discourse* (Baltimore: Johns Hopkins University Press, 1978), p. 130.

Did Richard Hickes Build the
Playhouse at Newington Butts?

An entry in one of the Act and Minute Books of "the deane and Chapter of the Cathedral and metropoliticall Churche of Christe in Canterbury" indicates that the subject of Hickes and his lease formed one of the topics of discussion at a meeting in the autumn or winter of 1566. The volume is heavily damaged, and each folio has lost about half its area; the bound portions nearest the spine are the best preserved, but tops, bottoms, and outward edges have all perished. The minutes of this meeting were recorded on the recto of folio 68 (the number survives), beginning about halfway down the sheet; in the heading, the name of the month has perished, though the day (the 27th) and year (1566) remain. The previous meeting of the dean and chapter had been in May 1566, and the subsequent one was in March 1567. As the days leading up to Michaelmas would be a convenient time to discuss the renewal of leases, I conjecture the unknown month to have been September, though nothing hinges on this guess. Hickes's 1566 lease was dated 26 November, though like most of the other leases to this property it probably recognized his interest as running "from Michaelmas last past." On the twenty-seventh of some month between May 1566 and March 1567, then, the chapter clerk made an entry in the minute book, of which the following text is all that remains (the bracket denotes destroyed material):

> Itm̃ where Rychard hickes h[
> the churches Landes at Ne[
> for terme of yeres yet to comme [
> Richard hyckes hath built [
> vppon one parcell of the sail[

243

> Lurkelane which with A [
> thereunto Laide conteyni[
> highwaye leading from [
> newyngton xliiij yard*es* [
> in lyke length in the sy[
> xliiij yard*es* and vppon th[
> South xiiij yard*es* yt ys ag[
> Rychard shall haue a leas[
> and garden as yt is now [
> for lx yeres to begynne at [
> payeng therefore yerely aft[
> fully to be determyned at [
> shilling*es* and bearing [
> howse and inclosures the [
> Hyckes or his assignes when [
> A new lease of the foresai[
> w^t hym in A former leas[
> his assignes shall not [
> dymyse [
> [

One's eye will be caught immediately by the fourth line of this entry: "Richard hyck*es* hath built"—then a teasing lacuna. Farther down in the document, another line begins "howse and inclosures," tempting one to speculate that "howse" is the second half of a hyphenated word carried over from the preceding line.

Could these entries refer to a playhouse? Could Richard Hickes have built a playhouse at Newington Butts in 1566, thereby dislodging even the Red Lion from its newly won primacy? My argument in the foregoing pages has not taken account of this possibility, but as the mutilated document cited above may invite such speculation, I ought, in the interest of completeness, to explain why I believe such a hypothesis is weak.

The earliest surviving volumes of chapter minutes, covering the period from 1561 to 1607, each have at their back an index, written in an early-seventeenth-century hand. In this, the earliest volume, the index portion has suffered its share of damage, but the segment under "Newington," on a part of the folio near the spine, has survived intact. The entire index entry, referring the user to folio 68 and thus to the text cited above, reads "Newington new Buildings— 68."

There are other entries in later, undamaged minute books relating to the Newington property and dating from before 1576. None of them mentions a playhouse, either in the index or in the body of the text. Conversely, minute entries after 1576, and their index references, make a point of using the word "playhouse." This practice is consonant with the practice we have seen in the leases and is congruent with the evidence from the sewer records, where there is no mention of a playhouse before 1576. Had Richard Hickes built such a structure in 1566, its very oddity would surely have invited some comment, either from the dean and chapter or from the sewer commissioners, as it did from both bodies after 1576.

What, then, did he build? A clue can be found in the minutes of a chapter meeting of 15 June 1603 (fo. 231ᵛ), from which we learn that Paul Buck's tenancy continued into the seventeenth century. The full text follows.

> Yt is agreed that vppon the surrender of a Lease of a Messuage or tenement in Newington late builded by one Richard Hickes one a peece of lande there called Lurcklane together with a garden there late made and graunted to Paule Buck gent shalbe graunted to him for the terme therein to comme vnder the present covenᵃntes and condicioons. And also that an other Lease made to him of certaine landes inclosed in the garden aforesaid shall vppon his surrender thereof be renewed to him for xxj yeres from the anunciacion last

The text makes clear that Buck had the lease to a structure built by Hickes on the parcel called Lurklane, a structure still standing in 1603, though we know that the playhouse was down by 1595. It seems likeliest, given this collocation of evidence, that the "house" built by Hickes in 1566 was just that and no more—a house of some sort. It was probably where Savage lived, and it must have been the dwelling that Hunningborne claimed to need in 1576 for his own family. The playhouse, built later and demolished earlier than this other building, was a different structure.

Index

Some names are mentioned so frequently in this book that full reference to them would be counterproductive. In such cases—the City of London, the Court of Aldermen, the Privy Council, E. K. Chambers, C. W. Wallace, to name a few examples—indexing has been highly selective.

Library of Congress Cataloging-in-Publication Data

Ingram, William, 1930–
   The business of playing: the beginnings of the adult professional theater in
   Elizabethan London/William Ingram.
      p. cm
   Includes bibliographical references and index.
   ISBN 0-8014-2671-5
   1. Theater—England—London—History—16th century. 2. Theater—Economic
aspects—England—London. 3. Theater and society—England—London.   I. Title.
PN2596.L6I54   1992
792'.09421'09031—dc20   92-52760